Clear Heart

Clear Heart

Joe Cottonwood

2008

David Minard, graphic wizard, designed the book cover. Tom Dodd and Terry Allen, good builders and good men, improved many of the construction details. David LeCount and Taruno Vega improved my Spanish, especially the cussing. Connie Mariottini, a fine decorator, was my tour guide to bad taste in the Silicon Valley. Doctors John Rosenberg and Leah Malhotra were my medical advisory team. Jiab Sopitsuda Tongsopit helped me with Thailand. Thank you, all.

Tools are special and individual. Each of us has a different size of hand, strength of muscle, sense of grace. When I name a particular tool in this story, it's neither placement nor endorsement. It's just how tradesmen talk. My own hammer (a Vaughan California Framer, hickory handle), which balances so nimbly in my hand, might feel in your fingers like a Chevy rear axle.

One more thing: I made up the characters. Carpenters, clients-from-Hell, everybody is fiction. What exists in real life are the tools, the sawdust, and one particular toy chest—plus a few of the houses, each one a miracle.

Visit www.booksurge.com to order additional copies.

Clear Heart

ALSO BY JOE COTTONWOOD

For Grown-Ups

The Naked Computer

Famous Potatoes

Frank City (Goodbye)

Poetry

Son of a Poet

For Children and Grown-Ups

The Adventures of Boone Barnaby

Danny Ain't

Babcock

Quake!

One

Somehow, each new day, year after year, the plywood seemed heavier while the quality seemed crappier—*just like my body*, Wally was thinking. Awkwardly balanced on the ladder, Wally pushed a raggedy four-by-eight-foot panel up toward the roof. Sweat trickled along the hairs of Wally's armpits and dripped to the second-story subfloor fourteen feet below. He supported the plywood with the top of his belly, a splinter digging into his flesh, as he shifted his grip.

Standing above Wally, straddling two roof trusses, Juke was ready. While Juke took hold of the top of the panel and lifted from above, Wally pushed the plywood from below.

Wally's arms trembled.

They both saw it.

"Fork it, Boss," Juke said. "You're too old for this."

"Respect—" Wally said, panting, "—your elders." Wally was fifty-five. He was wearing a faded black T-shirt with the sleeves ripped off, his gray hair tied back in a ponytail.

Juke, less formal, wore no shirt at all, just cutoff shorts, steel-toed boots, and a living mural of tattoos. Laying the plywood over the trusses, squinting a practiced eye, Juke lined up the edge and set to work with the nailgun. *Phap phap phap.*

"No bounce-nailing," Wally said as he climbed down the ladder.

"Yes, sir, fork you, sir," Juke said indifferently as he concentrated on the nailing. *Phap phap phap phap phap.* "And fork your mother too, sir."

"Bounce-nail, go to jail," Wally said, equally without passion.

"And I tender my forkin' resignation." Juke shifted his weight over the nailer. *Phap phap phap phap phap phap phap.*

It was a well-polished conversation, abbreviated from years of practice.

In bounce-nailing, a skilled operator—and Juke was as nimble as they came—could bounce the pneumatic nailer down a sheet of plywood, driving a nail each time the tip of the gun made contact with the surface of the wood. It was like precision dribbling of a basketball. In fact, watching Juke on a roof reminded Wally of a Harlem Globetrotters warm-up routine. Instead of a ball, Juke bounced a Duo-Fast nailer they'd named Debbie Doofus, a venerable tool, indestructible like a block of concrete, too heavy for most carpenters—but not for Juke.

Wally hated bounce-nailing, though it was common practice in the industry. Since the trigger was permanently on, the nailgun would fire on contact with anything. Besides the danger, in the hands of an amateur it left a sloppy line of nails. Wally had tried to ban it years ago, but Juke threw a legendary shit-fit that ended with Juke shouting, "I tender my forkin' resignation." So Wally gave in—*if* Juke agreed to wear safety glasses. Juke hated the "goggles," but that was the deal.

Wally had a head for business, caution, and social skills. Juke had a head for craft, speed, and trashy women.

Phap phap phap. "Who you gonna hire?" Juke called down from the roof. *Phap phap.*

"Had a guy," Wally said, sliding the next sheet of 19/32 CDX ply up the ladder. "Maybe you saw him. Showed up yesterday morning, supposed to start—"

"Yeah, saw him." Juke reached down for the plywood, which was still below his grasp. "Blue forkin' Dodge with side boxes."

"—and he's holding a beer can in one hand and a joint in the other. At eight in the morning." Wally, now at the top of the ladder, raised the sheet above the angle of the truss.

"So I guess you fired his ass." Juke was no stranger to alcohol—or marijuana—or just about any method of impairing one's brain—but he knew Wally's Laws, plain and simple. Wally's Law #14: Get wasted *after* work. Juke could abide. He liked working for Wally.

Still leaning down, Juke grasped the top of the plywood with his fingers and pulled.

And at that moment on that hillside where the frame of a house was rising among live oaks and wild oats with a red-tailed hawk soaring above, the world stirred. On this calm day, with neither Juke nor Wally noticing, clouds had formed. The oak branches bent. The oats flattened. The hawk shot out of sight.

Juke was just turning sideways when the wind hit. Suddenly, from out of nowhere a bolt of air was pulling the plywood—and Juke along with it—like a big, stiff kite.

Down below, meanwhile, Wally still had a hand on the plywood in addition to supporting it with his belly and, for one brief moment, no grip on the ladder. The updraft whipped the plywood out of his fingers and knocked his body off balance. Instinctively, Wally shifted his weight.

The ladder shifted, reacting to Wally's sudden move.

Up above, Juke realized that if he didn't let go he would be lifted to hang-glide into the sky under a four-by-eight panel of plywood. So he let go. The rough edge of the sheet ripped the tips of his fingers and sailed away. Juke fell back against Debbie the Duo-Fast, which started to slide down the slope of the roof decking. Juke, with raw, bleeding fingertips, reached for the nailgun and at the same time saw that Wally had lost his balance on the ladder just below.

Their eyes locked.

Wally was fourteen feet up a ladder that was moving to the right while his body was twisting to the left. Juke lunged for Wally's hand just as Wally, whose body had now spiraled a hundred and eighty degrees, was desperately reaching over and behind his head to grab the king post of the truss. Juke had the nailer in his grip. All three—nailgun, Wally's hand, king post—met at the same moment.

Phap.

For Wally, it was a moment of absolute clarity. He felt—and even smelled—the puff of compressed air, stale from a hundred feet of hose, that had driven the nail through his wrist. He felt Juke's hand grabbing his own free left hand, the one that wasn't nailed to the post. He heard the sliding of the ladder and then the clatter as it hit the floor below. He heard a mighty thud and a splintering of wood as the nailgun, dropped by Juke, struck the floor a moment later, and he even had time for the passing thought that the damage had been to the subfloor, not to Debbie Doofus. He kicked his feet in a broad arc searching for support even though he knew that nothing was there.

"Jesus fuck!" Juke shouted from above.

And there was a woman. Where she had come from Wally had no idea. Already she was lifting the fallen ladder, but she wasn't strong and the ladder was heavy.

Inside the nailed wrist, Wally felt two separate bones grinding against the nail. Or maybe the nail had shot right through one bone, splitting it in two. He couldn't tell. All he knew was that inside his body, bone was in contact with steel, that the bone and nail and flesh were supporting the weight of his body, that the flesh was ripping as he wriggled, that the nail felt solid and unforgiving, that the bone felt as if it was bending and would be torn from its little sockets and pop like a broken spring out of his skin. Weird explosive shock waves were racing up the nerves of his arm to overload and confuse his brain. Even more urgent, rising into Wally's awareness above the flood of pain: He couldn't breathe. The weight of his body was stretching the muscles across his chest so that only with a supreme effort could he exhale, making quick ineffective puffs. With rapidly de-oxygenating air in his lungs, he was suffocating.

Juke, still holding Wally's left hand in one of his own, lay down flat on the roof decking and placed his free hand under Wally's armpit. When he had a solid grip he moved his other hand to Wally's other armpit, supporting all of Wally's weight.

With an explosion of fusty air Wally exhaled, coughing, and then sucked a deep gasp of breath.

Juke's face was now pressed up against Wally's, cheek to cheek, stubble to stubble, sweat to sweat.

Wally was panting, catching up on oxygen.

Meanwhile, down below, the woman couldn't lift the ladder. Whoever she was, she'd never before dealt with the unwieldy heft of an OSHA Type A Louisville fiberglass extension ladder.

Juke called down to the woman: "You—uh—you—"

Wally could feel Juke's jaw moving against his own.

"You gotta—" Juke was trying to tell the woman how to raise the ladder but he was handicapped by his speech impediment—an inability to open his mouth without cursing. Juke's personal law of carpenter etiquette wouldn't allow him to swear in the presence of a lady. He might be rough but he was gallant. Or if not gallant, at least fearful: Juke still had nightmares starring angry nuns.

"Walk it up," Wally said in a voice that sounded strangely high-pitched to his own ears.

The woman, confused, raised her face toward Wally. "What?"

For an instant, Wally stared. Her eyes, even at this distance, the eyes of a puppy, luminous and brown.

Juke, meanwhile, stared as well. He could see right down the front of her jersey. Nice rack.

"Grab one end," Wally squeaked, trying not to screech, to remain calm, to ignore the electric buzz that was running up his arm. "Place the tip against the wall, and then walk under the ladder, lifting it higher as you go, keeping one end against the wall. Can you do that, please?"

The *please* came out a little higher than Wally had intended. Screechy high.

The woman tried. She raised the ladder half way, sliding it up the studs. A moment of extended arms, trembling. As she tried to shift her grip, she lost it. The side of the ladder bounced against her shoulder and then rattled to the floor.

"I'm sorry," she said. Briefly she laid a hand on her shoulder, wincing.

"You all right?" Wally said.

"My God. What a thing for you to ask right now." Already she was trying again. This time she seemed to get a better angle on it, walking the ladder up the frame of two-by-fours without overextending her arms.

With something like a ballet move, Wally was able to arch his potbellied body and swing his legs sideways while the woman slid the ladder until his foot, and then two feet, once again supported his weight.

Juke could now let go of Wally. There were bloody fingerprints on Wally's arm. Wally's body was blocking Juke's access to the ladder. Juke whispered, "Now what, Boss?"

Wally spoke to the woman below. "See that saw? No, behind you. The Milwaukee. There. Yes, that. Can you bring it up the ladder and give it to my partner here? You'll have to reach around my body—no— better idea—I've got a free hand—you hand it to me and I'll hand it to him. Carry it by the handle so you don't touch the trigger." Always Mr. Safety. "Make sure it stays plugged in to the extension cord. Okay?"

Oops. His voice had squeaked again on the *okay*.

Juke whispered, "No, Boss. I ain't cuttin' your hand off."

"Cut the post," Wally said.

And that's exactly what Juke did.

Wally walked on his own two feet out of the house and straight to his truck, his hair powdered with fresh sawdust, his left hand cradling an eighteen-inch piece of two-by-four Douglas fir that was still nailed to his right wrist, trailing blood. But then as Wally reached for the door handle his knees buckled.

Juke grabbed him by the belt.

"How about my car?" the woman said. "He could lie down."

And so it came to pass that Wally lay in the rear of an old Subaru wagon on a blanket smelling of dog, driven to the emergency room by a woman he'd never seen before, a woman with thick, rich chestnut hair gathered loosely in a blue ribbon. Juke was riding shotgun, silent, stiff, nervously beating his knee with his fist and glancing to the rear where two golden retrievers were wagging their tails and taking turns licking Wally's face.

"By the way, I'm Wally," Wally said from beneath the slobber of a dog. "And this is my partner Juke."

"I'm Opal." The woman flashed a smile. "Pleased to meet you. Well. You know what I mean."

"Nice to meet you," Wally said. He was glad that his voice was no longer screeching, though the pain that had moved temporarily to the background while he was arranging his rescue was now coming full blast. There were two separate tortures: one from the specific point where the head of the nail was embedded in his flesh up against the bone, the other a more general agony that made his brain throb.

Juke said nothing.

Wally wished he could have another look at Opal's face, into those puppy eyes. He said, "If you don't mind my asking, what are you—"

"I'm a photographer," Opal replied without turning around. "For the belt sanding? At lunch time? Guess I was late. Sorry."

On Fridays they raced belt sanders. Word had spread, and lately every Friday at lunch a small but rowdy crowd would gather at the construction site. Some came to watch, some to bet, and some came to match their own belt sanders against Wally and Juke and anyone else who happened to be on the construction crew that day. This particular Friday a newspaper reporter came too, but his photographer never showed up, so he didn't think the editor would run the article.

"Maybe," Wally said, "you were just in time."

Juke relaxed slightly. This was no lady. This was a photographer. He turned to face Wally: "Hey, Boss, I am so forkin' sorry—"

"At least you missed my heart," Wally said.

"Yeah, Boss, missed your brain too," Juke said. "Speaking of brains, you hear about that forkhead who was unjamming his nailgun, had it cradled in his forkin' *lap*, still had the forkin' *air* hose connected, and—"

"*Agggh*," Wally gargled, instinctively crossing his legs.

At the sound of Wally's *agggh*, the golden retrievers intensified their licking.

"Leary! Timothy!" Opal turned to the dogs. "Leave the poor man alone."

Wow. Those eyes. Combined with that chestnut hair she reminded Wally of a dog he once had, high-strung and high-joy, a nervous, playful mostly-Irish-setter pup. "Too bad," Wally said, "you didn't get your picture."

Opal faced the road again. "Got *one*," she said.

Two

Opal gave Juke a ride back to the construction site. She'd pitied him in the hospital waiting room, flopping about like a fish in a bucket. Clearly he was not a man to be confined. Or to make small talk. He was lanky, awkward like an overgrown kid, tongue-tied in the presence of unfamiliar women, nearly indecent wearing boots and cutoff shorts, no shirt, with red chest hair and vibrant tattoos. Not cute, but she knew plenty of women who would find Juke irresistibly sexy: strong, wild with a hint of danger, a stallion in need of a bridle.

In the Subaru they rode in silence, side by side, up the long, winding road from the flatlands into the hills overlooking the Silicon Valley. Juke fidgeted. The dogs panted in the rear. She wanted to ask Juke about Wally, an odd mixture of a man, this fellow with the face of a scholar who wore a tool belt patched with duct tape, a man who while hanging nailed to a board asked her if she was all right.

Finally she said, "Should we call somebody? His family?"

Juke shook his head.

"He has no family?"

"Kids gone. Just the wife."

"He has a wife?"

"Uh-huh."

"Then shouldn't somebody call her?"

"No, ma'am."

"They're divorced?"

"Uh, no. No, ma'am."

"Separated?"

Juke stopped fidgeting for a moment and looked her straight in the eye. He seemed angry. "She ain't forkin' *there*, ma'am. Okay?"

"Okay, gotcha," Opal said, blushing. She hated being transparent. Even this roughneck carpenter could see what she was up to, probably better than she knew herself. What *was* she up to, anyway? And why did she have the feeling that Juke was trying to protect Wally from something? From her? "I mean," she said, "I figured, like, with a man you never know, but since he wasn't wearing a wedding ring—"

"He's still married," Juke said. "Can't wear a ring in construction. Catches on shit. Rip your finger off. Writes a letter to her. Every forkin' day."

She discerned an almost imperceptible pause, a slight pursing of lip, a tiny tension before the word "forkin'." A filter, she realized. It reassured her to find a hint of civility in this man who—face it—had probably never, ever, flossed his teeth.

"A letter?" Opal said. "That's sweet. Where is she?"

"She's gone."

"She left him? Is that it?"

"No, ma'am."

Opal tried to drop it. She told herself, Please, just once in your life, leave somebody's relationships unexplained. But about a minute later she said, "Couldn't he call her sometimes? Send e-mail?"

"You don't get it."

"My God. Is she in jail?"

"No, ma'am."

"Then why can't she—? I mean where would—? Antarctica?"

Juke sighed. "She's dead, ma'am."

"Oh, how awful." And yet somehow, Opal was relieved.

"He's still married, ma'am. Writes her a letter, every forkin' day."

"Does he mail it?"

"No, ma'am. He ain't psycho."

Three

The sun was setting as Juke stepped out of the Subaru. Alert for movement—thieves, vandals—he crossed the construction site. In the panic they'd left their tools out, unguarded. The rest of the crew had gone home after the belt sander races, something Wally let them do every Friday. Only Juke had stayed with Wally to help finish off the roof decking.

Some coals were still glowing in the barbecue. One of the crew, a big man named Steamboat, always brought a barbecue to the site and cooked himself some lunch. Fridays, he made ribs for everybody. Finger-sucking good ribs.

Twice before, the site had been vandalized. Snotty-ass kids. Somebody had spray-painted THIS HOUSE SUCKS on the foundation wall, and another time somebody had slashed twenty-two sacks of ready-mix concrete and then pissed over them, spelling out what looked like a raggedy "Beelze," which had hardened over a weekend into concrete graffiti. And then there was the uphill neighbor, a guy named Pilpont, big-shot stockbroker who kept filing bullshit lawsuits trying to stop the construction, keep the view, preserve the land as open space. Everybody suspected Pilpont had something to do with the spray paint, not that the man would do it himself in any way that could be traced to him.

Right now, though, the site was calm. There was a smell of fresh-cut wood borne on gusts of wind. The sky was orange, visible through the skeleton of the house. To Juke a fully framed house was a thing of beauty, lovely like a woman, sensual, strong and yet vulnerable, naked to the weather, the vandals.

Gotta button up fast now, roof and siding, before she gets hurt. THIS HOUSE SUCKS? Plumb and true, each and every stick, and solid as granite. No gaps in these joints, no bow in these boards.

"Forkin' tight, Boss," Juke said to himself.

A rustle.

The sound of his voice had flushed some creature—or some person. Where? Juke, a born hunter, stood absolutely still, listening. Shadows, a slight motion behind a stack of insulation batts. Juke crept closer. He dove. Tackled. Legs, blue jeans. Got 'im.

A scream. Kicking. "Let me go, let me go!" It was a girl. Teenager. Zit face.

Surprised, Juke let go.

And immediately something solid like a steel pipe smashed him on the neck.

"Hey!"

She was running.

Juke leaped to his feet and chased. The first floor was a maze of two-by-fours, the bones of walls you could pass right through or dodge around. The girl scrambled between studs and leaped to the ground. Juke hurtled through the six-foot frame of a window and raced after her.

She was quick.

He was quicker. Caught her arm. Held on. "You," Juke said. "You—"

"Let me go!"

"No. You ..."

She gave up struggling. She was panting. A big girl. Stocky. Clouds of breath in the evening air. In her hand a long black Maglite, switched off.

Juke tried again. "You—uh—you ..."

She looked scared. Juke still had a hand clamped over her parka. She said, "Please don't hurt me."

"I ain't."

"Please."

"You. Uh. Look. You. Hey. Uh."

Juke had the feeling she was studying him, sizing him up. He tried again: "You ..."

Pause.

"You. Hey."

Suddenly she looked defiant. "What's the matter, can't you talk?"

"Yeah. You ..."

"Would you please let go of my arm?"

"No."

Her eyes narrowed. "So what am I supposed to do—suck your dick?"

Juke drew a deep breath. "Forkin' little bitch. I oughta call the cops."

Again she looked scared. "Please don't."

"I oughta."

"I didn't do anything."

"Then what in holy horseshit are you doing here?"

"Nothing."

"Yeah? You ran."

"Because you scared me."

"You *bashed* me. With the forkin' flashlight."

"Because you tackled me."

"You were *hiding*."

"Because you look like a creep."

"I *work* here. You're trespassing."

"You assaulted me."

It stopped him. He held on, silent, glaring.

She glared back. "What do you want?"

"Somebody's been jacking this place. Spray paint. Tore open the ready-mix and pissed on—"

"I didn't do that. Jeezo. You think I—? Jeezo. I chased them away."

"You *chased* them?"

"Yes."

"You know them?"

"No."

"Kids?"

"Yes."

"So you been here before?"

"Yes."

"You live around here?"

"Sort of."

"Sort of?"

"Yes. I live around here."

Juke let go of her arm.

She didn't bolt. She shivered, shaking from head to foot like a dog shaking off water. But she stayed.

He should talk to her parents. *Yeah, right. And say what?* Juke knew how he'd appear to the people in this neighborhood of electric gates and security cameras. He could build a house on their street but he'd better not knock on their doors. Around here twenty acres was considered a small plot and guys like Pilpont, if they didn't like how you landscaped your estate, they'd file a lawsuit. Juke came from a place where nobody had landscape, just parking space, and if you had a dispute with your neighbor you shot out his windows.

"What's your name?"

"FrogGirl."

"What?"

"Frog. Girl."

"What kind of a name is that?"

"Mine. It's my name." She ran a hand through her hair, which was red, curly, short.

"Hey," Juke said. "I get it. You're French?"

"No."

"So then. What?"

"Look. I don't have to explain my name."

Juke squinted, studying her. "You don't look that much like a frog."

"Thank you."

"No. I mean."

"I know what you mean. It's all right. We can't all be cute."

"Yeah. I mean."

"Yes."

Two uncute people. Their eyes met briefly. Hers were dark green and at the same time bright. An angry teenager from a rich neighborhood. And Juke was a convicted felon. Not to mention what he wasn't convicted of, what he wasn't even suspected of, what the law didn't know and Juke wasn't telling. He could see who had the power here. Big danger. *Assaulted her. Shit.* And yet something about her seemed okay. Like he knew her. Like she was a kid sister, a troublemaker, but kin.

"Okay, hey," Juke said, looking away. "Just don't come messing around here again."

"Nobody took your tools. I made sure."

"Uh, hey. Thanks."

"No problem." She started to walk away. It was almost dark now. "Cool house," she called, looking back. "Forkin' tight, Boss." She flashed a smile that lit up the twilight. Then she turned away.

Juke noted her walking: like a man. No waddle to her butt.

She never turned on the Maglite. She simply disappeared into the deepening shadows.

Four

Wally, from a sound sleep, heard a ringing phone, sat up, tried to grasp the handset with the bandaged hand. Why wouldn't his fingers close? He beat at the handset with his bandage, sending explosions of pain through his arm. Which woke him up. Using the left hand he picked up the phone. The room was black, lit only by the glow of the clock radio dial.

"You all right?" It was his daughter's voice. Sally.

"I'm fine. Are you? Sally, what's wrong?"

"I'm fine." Sally was a Peace Corps volunteer in Kenya. "It's about you, Dad. You sure you're okay?"

"Sally, it's five in the morning here. What's wrong? Where are you?"

"I'm standing at the edge of a corn field. A bunch of little kids are staring up at me. I borrowed this satellite phone and there's only about thirty seconds left on the battery. Dad, I saw the picture. You really okay?"

"What picture?"

"On the Internet. The picture of you nailed to the house."

"There's a picture?"

"You didn't see it?"

"Sally, I was in the emergency room until midnight. I've had about three hours of sleep. My arm feels like—like a bullet went through it. My God, Sally. I'm your dad. You call a dad at five in the morning and do you have any idea what kind of horror runs through my head? But I love hearing your voice ...Are we still connected?"

Silence.

Apparently, the battery had died.

Kids. You gotta love 'em. Sally kept in touch with the home town news whenever she could find an Internet cafe.

How do they build in Kenya? Mud? Grass? Or stick-frame construction? Would they use two-by-fours or some weird metric crap? Wally lay back, imagining. It scared him having her in Africa—terrorists and AIDS and all the evils of the world out there, and he could do nothing to protect her.

Remembering the warm sound of her voice, for a few minutes he could forget the cold pain in his body.

The next call came at eight in the morning.

"You okay?" It was Leo, Wally's youngest.

"Yeah, sure, I'm okay." Wally was in the kitchen, pouring Grape-Nuts into a bowl. "How'd you know?"

"I saw a picture in the *Post-Dispatch*." Leo lived in St. Louis.

"So," Wally said, "a construction accident in California is news in St. Louis?"

"It was just a great photo. You're in a work of art, Dad. Didn't even give your name, but I knew as soon as I saw it. Man, that must have hurt."

"No big deal."

"Dad, it had to hurt."

"Okay, it hurt. It's over."

"Break anything?"

"Nicked a bone. Nothing broke. Stretched something—tendon or ligament or whatever—hanging there with all my weight on it. Missed the artery. Coulda been worse."

"Anything I can do, Dad?"

"Just keep calling. Just let me hear your voice."

"I'll do that. You sure you're all right?"

"I'm fine," Wally lied.

After saying good-bye, Wally lay down on the kitchen floor. A wave of nausea was rising as, under the bandage, tramping elephants were crushing his arm. He was wearing the same clothes as yesterday—after sleeping in them, including his boots—because with one useful hand he couldn't figure out how to button the pants or retie the shoelaces if he took them off. Likewise he hadn't changed his bandage in spite of the nurse's instructions and it was soggy with yellow ooze. The floor was gritty with sand and smelled of rot. Turning his head to the side Wally could see a fruit, shrunken, fuzzy with fungus, in the toe space under the sink cabinet. Months ago, he vaguely recalled, he'd dropped an avocado and never bothered.

Maybe the nausea was something serious like a heart attack. Maybe he would just die right now and remain lying on the floor until he too was shrunken and fuzzy with fungus. Bummer.

He was still lying there when the doorbell rang.

Five

In the hierarchy of real estate values on the San Francisco Peninsula, altitude means wealth. Other than a few pockets of comfort such as the leafy estates of Atherton, the least desirable property is located in the flatlands east of the railroad tracks, which is where Opal found Wally's neighborhood, a low-rent section of Redwood City where clunker cars were parked three-deep on front lawns and half the houses had iron gratings over the windows. Wally's yard had no cars on the lawn, but then it had no grass either, just an old water heater lying on its side, some plastic buckets, and a mound of bare dirt. There were no iron grates, but one window was broken, covered with cardboard. Paint was peeling; gutters drooped; a screen door had no screen.

Blurt, she told herself. *Don't be frightened. Just blurt. It's what you do best.*

Opal rapped her knuckles on the door.

For a minute nothing stirred.

She rapped again.

Now you can go, she told herself. *Nobody could blame you.*

She heard a shuffling sound from within the house. A bump, a crash. More shuffling.

The door opened.

He looked like the house: unmaintained. It wasn't just the dirt-smeared bandage around his hand and arm. It was the hair, uncombed; the face, unshaved; the clothes, same as yesterday. Had he slept in them? Had he slept at all? He smelled of sweat and sawdust and something more—something both putrid and medicinal wafting from the gauze that was taped around his wrist.

Blurt, girl.

"Hi!" Opal said with as big a smile as she could muster. "I brought you some extra copies of the paper. I suppose you've seen it already?"

"Yeah."

"Lucky shot, right? Didn't it come out great?"

A moment of silence. Staring blankly, Wally said, "Congratulations."

"I can't brag," Opal said, "because *you're* the star. The way your arms are spread out, that expression on your face where you look resigned and—and, you know, angry and—so woeful all at the same time. Even your toes point down. And the track of blood, the way the clouds light up in the background, the angle of the shot from down below ..." Suddenly Opal got it. "Are you in pain?"

"Some."

"Oh! I'm so sorry. You want to sit down?"

"Yes."

She reached for his elbow. "You need help?"

"I can walk."

"I'm so stupid." Opal followed Wally across a cluttered living room and into a grimy kitchen. "Here I am babbling about my wonderful photo without even asking how *are* you and all the while you're standing there in agony and naturally you hate that picture. It humiliates you. Right?"

"Sort of."

"You've been building houses for thirty years or something and you're probably a superb craftsman and when do you get your picture in the paper? When you get nailed."

Wally sat down. On the table in front of him was the front page, the photo, the caption: "A bad day at the office." For a moment he stared at her through wire-rim spectacles while Opal tried not to be repulsed by the greasy gray ponytail, unbrushed and flecked with sawdust. She tried not to look at the ceiling, cobwebs hanging tattered with dust and dead flies. She said, "Didn't they give you something? For the pain?"

"Doesn't work."

"And you don't want to take something stronger, right? You probably hate drugs?"

"Yeah." Wally looked at her curiously.

"I think I know how you feel. Because pain is lonely. Nobody can see, nobody can feel, I mean people can know you've got pain but nobody can do anything about it and it's such a lonely thing. It puts you on the other side of something. It alienates you."

"Yeah." Wally was watching her with open wonder.

"And here I am intellectualizing," Opal continued, "which doesn't help you one bit. I'm sorry. But I think I know how you feel. Lonely."

"Sounds like you've been there."

"You bet."

"You want to talk about it?"

"No!"

"Good." Wally smiled. "Because I'm a lousy therapist."

"I don't need a therapist. I'm sorry I gave you that impression." Sometimes when she was in blurt mode, she felt herself slipping out of control. This was one of those times. "Can I come back and start over? Here I barge into your house and start talking about pain and loneliness. You must think I'm toxic."

"At least you got me off the floor."

"Omigod. You were lying on that filthy floor?"

"A little nausea."

"That bandage looks oozy."

"It's supposed to drain."

"Do they always smell like that?"

"I don't know. I've never been nailed before."

"I'd better take you back to the emergency room."

"No!"

"Oops. Sorry."

Wally was studying her again, as if she were a puzzling photo in a gallery. "You like some tea?"

"Yes, please. You? Let me fix it."

"I know how to cook water."

"But you're hurt. I didn't mean anything. Can't we be friends?"

"Yes." Wally's eyes widened. "I'd like that."

"Me too."

Silently, digesting those last words, Opal filled a sauce pan with water, lit the gas, found mugs and tea bags without having to ask. Not coffee. Tea. Who was this man?

Seating herself at the opposite side of the table from Wally, dabbing the Lipton's bag up and down in the mug, Opal said, "I feel like I know your wife."

Arched eyebrows. "How so?"

"I know where to find things. It's like I've known this kitchen all my life, like I organized it myself. Except I'd clean it."

Wally smiled. "So would she."

"Juke told me. He didn't want to, but I pried it out of him. That your wife had died. Am I being intrusive?"

"Not yet."

"Did you make this table? And the chairs? They're so lovely! What kind of wood is this? I'll bet it glows. That is, it would if it was ..."

"Clean."

"Yes. Cared for."

Wally shrugged. "I'm a little behind in the housework. A couple years."

Next to Wally was half a wall with ragged edges of torn-out drywall and exposed wiring covered in a layer of dust and grease. Clearly the kitchen had once had a breakfast nook, and he'd stopped in the middle of tearing it out.

On the table was a full bowl of cereal, dry Grape-Nuts. By the bowl was a newspaper and a sheet of paper, the letter half written, the penmanship abominable. Opal tried not to look, tried to keep it from creeping into the corner of her eye. But Wally caught her anyway.

"I admit," Opal said, "Juke told me you write letters."

"You want to analyze that?"

"No. I think it's sweet."

Wally reached for his tea. "No more letters. For a while."

"Why?"

"Using my left hand—I get this feeling she won't be able to read my handwriting." He laughed, softly.

"Want to dictate the letter to me? I have good handwriting. And don't worry, I'll attach a note to explain that I'm your temporary secretary and assure your wife that our relationship is purely platonic."

"Is it?"

Their eyes met. His were a deep, warm brown.

Wally laughed nervously.

Opal pushed back her chair. "I'd better go."

"Please. Don't."

She stood with her side against the stove. "Honest to God, I'm not like that."

"Me neither."

"And that's not why I came here."

"Why *did* you come here?"

"Something stupid. Never mind. And it wasn't to brag about my picture, either."

There was an electric clock built into the backboard of the stove, humming, the clock face covered with old brown spatters of grease.

"The last time I made a pass," Wally said, "it must have been thirty-five years ago."

"And she ended up marrying you?"

"Yes."

"Must have been one heck of a pass."

"Better than that one I just made."

"Next time you want to hit on somebody, change your bandage first."

"I'll remember that."

"And you might wash your hair and change your clothes."

"I'll remember that too."

"Not that I should be giving advice. And not that you should make another pass at me."

"I'll definitely remember that."

Opal placed thumb and index finger over her eyelids, breathing in, breathing out. When she opened her eyes she saw Wally sitting patiently, hopefully, at the table gazing up at her. Like a friendly dog. She said, "I'm sorry if I was seeming flirtatious."

"You weren't. I leaped to a conclusion."

"I think I give out the wrong—I mix my signals a lot. Somebody used to call me the Queen of Mixed Signals. What you should know is, I sing in the Presbyterian choir."

"I see." Wally nodded his head. "Yes." He smiled. "If I'd known you were Presbyterian, I never would have made a pass."

"Okay. I must sound like a complete idiot."

She was still standing. Wally gazed up at her from the table and said, "I want you to know I'm not normally the kind of guy who hits on women. Once every thirty-five years. That's my limit. So who called you the Queen of Mixed Signals?"

"Some guy." Her ex-husband, actually. He'd also defined her, somewhat fondly, as Ms. Blurt-and-Backpedal.

An empty dog food bowl lay in the corner next to the back door. Opal asked, "Where's your dog?"

"It died."

"Omigod. I'm sorry."

"No letters."

"I wasn't even thinking—"

"Look, I appreciate you being here. Being so perky. I could use perk. Won't you please sit down?"

She'd come on a mission. So far, it had been a disaster. Could she possibly pull it off now? She thought of two dogs meeting for the first time, approaching on tiptoe, fur erect, going through all those funky dog-greeting rituals before they could relax and play. Eventually she and Wally would be ready to relax, to move on. Beyond butt-sniffing. Already she knew some things about him. It was in his choice of words, his gentle manner. And in spite of his hair and his housekeeping she knew without asking that he flossed. Every night.

Retaking her seat, Opal gulped a slug of tea without tasting it. "Just so you know, I have two children."

"How old?"

"Abe's eighteen. Ronny's two." And she thought: *This man hasn't wiped his stove during Ronny's entire lifetime.*

Wally leaned forward. "Big gap."

"I had a big gap between marriages. Different fathers. I mean, just so you know. Two husbands, two children, two exes." She watched to see if Wally flinched. She'd just told him in a continuation of butt-sniffing that she was damaged goods. Twice failed.

Wally was nodding. "Me, three kids. One wife." An ironic smile. "Just so you know."

"It's okay, the age gap thing. Matter of fact at this very moment Abe's watching Ronny. An in-house babysitter. But I'll lose him in September. He starts college. Princeton."

"Ooh la la." Wally ran a finger around the rim of his mug. "So Abe's a good kid?"

"Oh yes. Except when he gets in a mood. Then he goes out and sits on the roof. In the rain, even. For hours."

"How often does that happen?"

"About twice a day." She laughed. "He's got some things to sort out. It's hard. He never had a father figure. Actually, he had a couple of anti–father figures. My fault of course. So out of guilt I've probably been too soft on him. I don't want to make him sound like a spoiled brat because he's not, but he needs a little focus. A little discipline. This is mother talk. I'm sorry. I must be boring you."

"I like mother talk. Does Abe have a girlfriend?"

"Sort of." Without thinking, Opal had picked up Wally's pen from the tabletop and was doodling in the margins around her photograph. "With all the usual issues."

"What issues?"

"Hormonal." Opal shifted in her seat. "The icky stuff."

"Ick?" Wally looked amused. "*Ick* happens."

"It *is* happening. And I know I can't stop it. But must I approve? And if I don't approve but I don't want them sneaking around should I, like, enable it?" Opal sat up straight. "You've been there. What did you do?"

"Enabled," Wally said.

"In the house?"

"Sleepovers. Sure."

"But I don't want to walk in on—I don't even want to hear—I mean didn't it ever get, like, icky?"

"They had to be discreet. That was the deal. Discretion is advised. Like the example I hope we set ourselves."

"Discretion is advised. I'll needlepoint that and hang it on the wall."

"You can bet those kids don't want you walking in on them, either. Or hearing them. They'll be careful. Because to them—" he smiled "—you're the *ick*."

"I am not," Opal said. Then she laughed, hearing herself. "Of course I can't even talk to him about it."

Wally's finger moved faster around the rim of the mug. "This summer. Abe got a job?"

"No." The pen, without Opal's awareness, advanced up the page to begin doodling around the weather report.

"He doesn't want a job?"

"Not if I find it for him." The pen was obliterating the entire forecast: Today, utter blackness. "But he's shy. Doesn't like to—to present himself."

Wally's finger slowed, still circling the rim of the mug. "Any work experience?"

"None whatsoever. Other than babysitting."

"Skills?"

Opal looked up, pen poised. "He's very smart."

Wally's finger stopped, rested on the rim of the mug. "Is he physical?"

"As opposed to mental? No. I'd have to say mostly he's a thinker. Loves astrophysics. And pure math."

"Is he strong? Athletic?"

"No. Used to play soccer—badly. And baseball was a disaster. Your basic skinny kid with eyeglasses. Not totally spastic but ...He just never seemed to be paying attention in sports. He's into music. Mandolin. Good with his fingers."

"Hmm."

"What?"

"Nothing."

"Oh."

Wally stared at his finger on the rim of the mug.

Opal set down the pen, crossed her legs, and folded her hands on her lap. She forced herself to be silent for five seconds. Ten. Twenty.

Finally Wally looked up. "Can he swing a hammer?"

"I thought you'd never ask."

Wally heaved back in his chair. "Far out!" He was grinning, shaking his head. "Is that why you came here?"

Opal nodded. "You hire a lot of teenagers?"

"One or two every summer. I seem to get the misfits. Pissed off, punk, picked-on, maybe just plain weird—but they come around. Not always. But mostly. You build something, you see the results, you feel good. Teamwork. Discipline. Pride."

"You sound like the Marines."

"We only shoot nails." Wally was still grinning. "Why didn't you just ask about the job?"

"I'm sorry. I'm not usually a devious person."

She was checking me out, Wally realized. *And I almost flunked the secret test.* All right, so he shouldn't have made a pass at her. A perky Presbyterian, for Christ's sake. With two children and some mystery baggage, because beneath the poise she was frightened of him—he'd picked up the vibe. She'd manipulated him, found the kid a job. What was she so scared of? And yet here she was, sitting in his broken-down breakfast nook: a woman who understood the loneliness of pain. A woman who came to him in a moment of clarity as a nail blasted through his body, as he looked down into those puppy eyes, as he saw what a pathetic piece of crap his life had become. Writing letters to a dead woman. In a kitchen full of crud.

With those thoughts, all Wally said was, "Isn't this a case of what Abe hates—of you finding him a job?"

"You're a father. A real one. You've been there. You'll think of something."

And Wally knew he would. Not because he was keen on hiring this klutzy kid but because for the first time in ages, he'd felt that electric thing. That attraction to the scent and quiver and explosive emotions of a living, breathing woman. A dog person, the best kind. Freckled like bird's-eye maple. A lush, casual head of hair. Earrings, little white doves. He wanted to see her again. He wanted more than that. He wanted to overcome her fright. He wanted to play. To share food. To watch old movies and drink lemonade from sweaty glasses and cuddle on the sofa while dogs scratch on the rug. He wanted someone, perhaps, to love. And ick.

Six

Ground fog covered the job site. It was one of those California mornings where everything is wet, the trees are dripping, and no rain has fallen. In the parking area in front of the power shed and Steamboat's barbecue, Wally stopped his old yellow truck next to a brand new gleaming black beemer.

Patience, Wally commanded himself. *Maintain calm and peacefulness. Ommm ...*

The BMW belonged to Anton Krainer, boy wonder, who had owned it less than two weeks. A rack on top of the car held a couple of Litespeed bicycles—likewise owned less than two weeks—each titanium frame worth more than Wally's entire Toyota long-bed, which he'd owned for over two decades.

"There's a hole in that roof truss," Krainer shouted cheerily as a greeting. He was standing on tiptoe, holding the string of a plumb bob against the top plate of the wall between master bedroom and master bath. The bottom of the plumb bob, at floor level, was swinging like a pendulum.

"Little accident," Wally said, joining him. "Fix it today."

"My friends are asking me why I'd hire a contractor who nails himself to houses."

"I'm sure you'd rather nail me yourself."

"Ho ho," Krainer said sarcastically.

Won that one, Wally was thinking. *Neutralized him with the truth.* Wally tried to avoid jock humor—the kind that was competitive and aggressive without being particularly humorous—but it was the only way to spar with this kid. Krainer had blond hair and dimpled cheeks. Life came easy to the golden god. He'd dropped out of Stanford to found an Internet startup company that in less than a year had an IPO that spiraled into a bidding frenzy. Krainer bought an old ranch on a hillside overlooking Silicon Valley. He hired an architect who in turn recommended Wally for the construction because the architect had dealt with Wally before and they'd worked well together.

The original plan was to preserve most of the acreage in its natural state as a private, personal wildlife refuge where deer could browse and coyote could roam. Overlooking the meadow, and with a view of the entire Silicon Valley plus the San Francisco Bay and the mountains beyond, would be a house that was modest in scale but perfect in detail. The gig appealed to Wally, whose standards of workmanship could be summed up as "Slow down and do right." Also, it was a wonderful piece of land. He wanted to be paid for working among the spirit of hawk and wild oats, the rush of wind through a lone Bishop pine, the rough and craggy arms of oak trees, the ghosts of ancient redwoods cleared and gone. There was even a plan for a butterfly garden, an area stocked with native flowering plants that would bloom in sequence through the seasons attracting a timely progression of butterflies including the migrating Monarchs.

Then, as the construction began, stock in Krainer's company soared. Krainer had gone from merely wealthy to obscenely rich. And the prospective house began growing in size, from modest to mansion, from ten rooms to thirty-three. The goal of perfection in detail remained, but the details had grown in scale.

Wally had signed up to catch a marlin and now he was chasing Moby Dick. He would never accept such a large project if it were presented in advance. He had to sub out work he'd normally handle with his own crew, which made it harder to maintain the quality. Also, Krainer could throw the occasional tantrum. Wally found himself checking the stock market about once a week and, oddly, he was hoping Krainer's wealth kept growing—not so Wally could add more rooms but so Krainer might reach the magic billion. In Wally's limited observation, once you have a billion dollars, it tends to sober you up. Not always—not one particular software mogul, for example, suave, satyric, sue-happy, of whom tradespeople told stories that would, um, never mind—but sometimes it helped.

Krainer seemed to believe that his wealth validated his sense of taste even as it became increasingly apparent that he had, as Wally would put it, aesthetic impairment combined with wretched excess. There was, of course, the mirrored ceiling to be installed in the master bedroom with video cameras hidden in all four walls and Wally didn't want to ask why. There was the master bath with hot tub, fireplace, built-in wine cooler, and big-screen television, plus mirrors on every possible surface including one mirror etched with the sandblasted image of a life-size couple who were, well, coupling. There was the media room with purple velvet–upholstered chairs and strip lights down the aisles. Every room would have remote-controlled curtains; all lights would be controlled by a central computer; heating and cooling would be a state-of-the-art geothermal system involving underground pipes for heat exchangers whose cost could never be justified in this mild California climate.

And then there was the grotto. Next to the outdoor pool, Krainer wanted a fountain of his own design—a winged and very naked angel with water spouting from her breasts—at the top of a waterfall running over rocks. The fountain was bad enough, but Krainer wanted the "rocks" to be built by a group of "artisans" from southern California who had built the faux rock "hardscapes" of Disneyland. Both Wally and the architect had taken a stand on that one, conceding the fountain—you have to choose your battles—but arguing that the mini-Disneyland hardscape would be tacky, tasteless, ugly, and stupid, that it would look like something the highway department had installed. Still, they would have lost the battle if Wally's landscaper, Little Landscaper Lucy, hadn't come up with an alternate plan. Lucy had only signed on because she loved the idea of the butterfly garden, which remained as an afterthought but was now in the background of larger schemes. Lucy proposed a grotto using real dirt growing real moss and real ferns combined with real rocks placed by cranes. Her rocks would cost half as much as the Disneyland ones and, as she pitched it, "look just as authentic as the fake ones." Further, she said, there was a quarry near Santa Cruz that had "the perfect rocks."

Bingo. The perfect rocks. Anton was sold.

What bugged Wally the most was that Krainer believed he'd *earned* that money. Otherwise, the guy was likable enough. You just had to remember the main thing: Krainer was a kid. Half Wally's age and would never grow up. Would never have to.

Wally knelt at Krainer's feet, steadying the plumb bob so it wouldn't swing.

Krainer's female friend was wandering among the stud walls with a camcorder. Her name was Lenora. Willowy, wearing a bulky fisherman's knit sweater with the sleeves pushed up, long dark hair gathered in a tight knot on top of her head with a few loose strands dangling carelessly, Lenora from the waist up looked casual, East Coast, old money, sophisticate, ballerina, anorexic. Waist down, she wore tight stretch pants with the cameltoe clearly visible at the crotch, glittery ankle bracelet, bright red toenails, high platform shoes—like a Las Vegas prostitute. Krainer had first introduced her to Wally as "Lenora from Gomorra," which Lenora had tolerated with an icy smile.

Peering through the camcorder, Lenora seemed to be filming every wall, board by board.

Krainer called, "Lenora, you get that truss on tape?"

Lenora didn't bother to answer. She too treated Krainer as a child—though, in physical age, she was younger. She made Wally nervous. Once when Krainer was out of sight she'd flirted—blatantly—with Wally, fixing him in a steady gaze and casually lifting her own shirt and tracing her long red fingernails over her concave belly as she spoke. There was a line of black hair like a fuzzy caterpillar starting just below her navel, crawling over the lower tummy, then widening at the bottom as it disappeared into the top of her pants. In a husky voice with a vaguely British accent she said she used to be a student at Stanford, psych major. She told Wally, who hadn't asked, that she was forced to leave Stanford after a compromising situation involving the chairman of the psychology department that was his fault, but she got the blame. Also without being asked she said she was born and raised in Boston but would never go back, not even in a coffin. Smiling, momentarily looking vulnerable, she said, "It's so cool you know what you're doing. You're strong and you can build things. I envy that." Wally wasn't remotely attracted.

What you hope for with somebody like Krainer, somebody who grows too rich too fast, is that he finds a woman who brings everything he lacks—a woman with taste and values and social skills—a woman who can fill the gaps. Lenora, in Wally's opinion, only widened the gaps. She broadcast a general vibe of kinkiness, though vague and undefined. He'd never seen anything resembling a look of affection between her and Krainer and could only assume that it was a relationship of convenience: frequent and probably outlandish sex for Krainer, money and security for Lenora. Plus she looked magnificent in a convertible. A trophy mistress. The whole world of uncommitted sex was a mystery to Wally, though he enjoyed puzzling over it. All he'd really wanted in life was a good and steady woman, preferably well-padded, cheerful, and smart.

Juke was leaning against a window frame, silent, alternately glowering at Krainer and studying Lenora—below the waist. *Juke,* Wally thought, *is somebody who could understand what makes her motor run.*

Lenora started filming Juke.

Juke, glaring into the camera, methodically picked his nose.

Lenora, giggling, filmed the entire nose-reaming.

"Isn't the bathroom supposed to be bigger?" Krainer said.

Here we go again. Aloud, Wally said, "Juke, would you go to the trailer and bring out the plans?"

With a nod, Juke walked down the rough stairs to the first floor, then down the gangplank and across the mud.

Lenora followed with the camcorder, filming every step.

"What are we doing with this plumb bob?" Wally asked, still kneeling.

"Is the wall straight?" Krainer asked. "It looked off."

"It's within a sixteenth," Wally said, standing.

Krainer pocketed the plumb bob. "Meaning it's off by a sixteenth of an inch. It's a fact."

"Sixteenth is tight," Wally said. "Most contractors settle for a quarter inch. Three-eighths in the tracts." Talking to Krainer, Wally often felt like a high school teacher lecturing a bored but dangerous student. "Over time, those walls move. Moisture changes. Wood expands and contracts."

"Shouldn't we at least start with plumb? Give the walls a fighting chance?"

"A variation of one-sixteenth of an inch over eight feet of span is plumb, Anton. With the lumber you get today, that's great construction."

"What you're saying is, 'That's great enough construction.' I don't want great enough. Remember the goal here? We're building the perfect house."

Wally had seen plenty of grandiose mansions where they'd built the fireplace out of Italian marble but undersized the floor joists, where below expensive crown molding you could bump your shoulder against a wall and feel the entire house shake from end to end, where condensation formed because of sloppy insulation, where builders cut corners and buyers bought glitz. Wally called it Hollywood construction, and Krainer—in spite of his efforts with the plumb bob—was a Hollywood buyer. What saved Krainer from himself was the fact that he'd hired a good architect and an honest contractor, though he sometimes seemed bent on alienating them both.

"What I'm wondering, Anton, is why you came here today bringing a plumb bob. It's not something most men carry around in their pockets—unless you're trying to make up for a deficiency."

"Ho ho."

Got him again. "Really, Anton, I have to think you came here today looking for a fight."

"Why would I do that?"

"That's what I'm trying to find out. Could it have something to do with the fact that you owe me two progress payments?"

Wordlessly, Krainer handed Wally an envelope. Sealed.

Rudely, Wally tore the envelope open right then and there and examined the check. "That's one payment. Half what you owe."

"The next payment is contingent on completion of the wall framing. If a wall's out of plumb, it isn't completely framed."

"Crap, Anton."

"Hey, I'm easy." The dimpled smile. "I'll settle for a sixty-fourth of an inch."

Wally was uncharmed. "Tomorrow morning. The check. Or I stop work. And Pilpont will be ever so happy."

Krainer scowled. Any mention of his uphill neighbor put him in a cold fury. So far, Pilpont had filed lawsuits demanding a zoning revision, a geotech study, an endangered species review, an anthropological history investigation, and an environmental impact report. The odd thing was, Pilpont's property was set back on a natural terrace making it barely visible from Krainer's. Nobody was blocking anybody's view. Pilpont hadn't even objected to the original plans. Only when Krainer's stock ballooned in worth while the project doubled, then tripled, then quadrupled in size did Pilpont become a born-again environmentalist claiming the land was a "heritage site" where Ohlone Native Americans had camped and buried their ancestors, a land that was teeming with endangered red-legged frogs and San Francisco garter snakes, a land where a historic ranch had once stood, a land that was "our last, best chance to preserve all we hold dear." A land, he failed to add, from which he had carved his own property and grand estate.

Wally actually sympathized with the environmental arguments. So did Krainer. It was the hypocrisy that pissed them both off. And the fact remained that on a thirty-five-acre parcel, Krainer's sprawling castle with all its associated pieces—the parking area, the pool and grotto, the tennis court, even the butterfly garden—would cover only three of those acres. The rest would remain meadow and oak and seasonal creek, a home to the frog, the snake, the wandering deer and coyote. Krainer wanted a natural preserve. All he asked was to live at its edge—and live there in luxury.

"You'll have the check," Anton said. "If I have a sixty-fourth."

"I'll do my best," Wally said, purposely vague. Then quickly he changed the subject before Anton could quibble—and before Wally might blow up. "Hey, you got any triathlons coming?"

"Killer. Switzerland." Anton described the uphill and downhill challenges of the coming event. Wally listened, idly wondering what would happen if all the energy expended in triathlons were applied to, say, building houses for the poor. Then Anton started bragging about the winery he was building in Sonoma County. This was news to Wally. Anton had bought the land for a pittance, he said, because the hillside was too steep for normal production methods, but he was planting a vine he'd found in Croatia that could thrive there—a rugged, ancient variety that could blend into a sensational pinot noir. It would sell for a thousand dollars a bottle, it's a fact. Again, Wally wondered about energy expended—and cash. Was his progress payment going to a Croatian grape?

And if this is to be a perfect house, do you want to make me grovel for every dollar? Do you know about karma, Mr. Krainer?

At last, Juke returned from the trailer with the rolled-up plans. Wally couldn't blame Juke for avoiding Krainer as long as possible and in fact was glad that he had, given Juke's visible contempt. Lenora wandered behind Juke, swinging the camcorder from her wrist. She'd untied her hair so it tumbled over her shoulders and down to her waist, still looking cool and composed. Juke, by comparison, looked flushed.

Wally and Anton examined the plans until Anton conceded that the bathroom was framed exactly as drawn. But, he said, the drawings were a mistake; he wanted the toilet in a separate alcove.

Stock must have gone up, Wally was thinking. Every time the stock went up a point, Krainer added another room. "That'll be a change order," Wally said.

"Just do it."

"I'll write it up."

"Meanwhile, get started."

"Not until you sign for it."

Krainer sighed.

Wally folded his arms. He knew what happened to contractors who made changes without written agreements.

Krainer brightened: "Hey, I'm buying a belt sander. When's the next race?"

"Every Friday," Wally said. "Noon."

"Please, let's go," Lenora said, grasping Anton by the arm.

"See you Friday," Anton said as Lenora pulled him away. "Prepare to eat dust. And that goes for you too, Juke."

At those words, Lenora and Juke exchanged a glance. Immediately, they each looked elsewhere. Lenora was tugging Krainer toward the BMW. But Wally had seen enough.

As the beemer drove away, Juke leaned out the rough window. The glassless frame held a commanding view of the Silicon Valley and beyond: the sprawl of San Jose, the giant blimp hangars of Moffett Field, the cool waters of the bay stitched by silver bridges, the crawling cars glinting sunlight, lovely Mt. Hamilton and the white dome of the Lick Observatory to the south, massive Mt. Diablo behind the hulking brown hills of the East Bay. With binoculars one could see the crowded skyscrapers of San Francisco, the great ship-loading cranes of the Port of Oakland and Alameda, the dozen or so freighters packed high with containers that had crossed the Pacific Ocean and slipped under the Golden Gate Bridge to idle in blue water awaiting a berth like toys in a giant bathtub. Just twenty feet away one could see wild roses tumbling over an old grapestake fence as hummingbirds hovered and darted.

Juke squinted, still leaning out the window frame, and spat toward the valley.

Wally said, "I can't believe you did that."

"Did what, Boss?"

"You know how much money that guy owes me?"

Juke turned to face Wally. "So?"

"So. In the trailer."

Juke shifted uneasily. "What about the trailer?"

Wally said nothing as he folded his arms across his chest and shook his head slowly from side to side.

Juke broke: "Hey. She started it. She was steamin'."

"Are you aware of Wally's Law number thirteen?"

"No. What's Wally's Law number thirteen?"

"No mortise-and-tenon with the clientele."

"Hey. She mortised me."

"Just because she comes on to you, Juke, you don't have to ...Like that housewife in Los Altos Hills? And then she expected a *discount*. Or that au pair in Atherton? How old was she—fifteen? Just because they love the tools doesn't mean you can go around boinking every—"

"You want me to tender my boinkin' resignation?"

"Don't bother. If Krainer doesn't send me a check first thing tomorrow, the whole gig is boinked, anyway. And so are we."

"Sorry, Boss."

"Just go clean your dick. Then we gotta check out a prospect."

Seven

Abraham Jupiter Rainbow Fromberg, better known as Abe, was sitting with his back against the chimney, downhill side—his crow's nest. A broad suburban valley spread before him. The distant roar of freeway traffic blended with the more local blast of a leaf-blower. It was hot, the sun baking down after the morning fog had burned off. Abe, though, wasn't aware of the heat or the noise. Just one hour ago, his girlfriend Rachel had left in a huff, and he wasn't sure she would ever come back— or if he wanted her back.

The subject of their disagreement was oral sex. He was *pro*, she was *con*. Or, actually, to be more fair to her position, she was *pro* too in a reluctant sort of way but not every time they got together no matter how briefly and not three times a day and not when it meant ducking into broom closets at school or the dressing room at Target and especially not the bathroom at McDonald's. And when he'd pointed out that they'd only done the McDonald's thing twice—once, really, if you didn't count the time the manager kicked them out before they'd barely gotten started—and the broom closet thing wouldn't happen anymore because they were finished with classes, and besides it wasn't really a broom closet but more of a utility room with that giant hot water heater that always smelled like seeping sulfur—when he pointed these things out in what he thought was a reasonable, calm manner, Rachel went ballistic.

What made it even more of a bummer was that just this morning Abe's mother had let it be known—in the world's most excruciatingly awkward conversation—that "it would be okay if sometimes Rachel, um, spent time alone. In the house, that is. In your room, that is. Not alone, that is, but with you, that is. Just so you know. And don't you dare hurt her—ever—but beyond that as long as you can be respectful. Discreet, that is. Not that it's shameful for you to want to be alone together but you need to be respectful of other people's feelings. Mine, that is. Discretion is advised. And I'm not trying to push you into anything and in fact would prefer the opposite, and beyond that I don't really want to know. But if you must. That is, just so you're aware, um, I expect you've already heard this but goddammit you have to use a condom all right?" Yet just when Abe passed this wonderful news on to Rachel, she'd decided it was time to Discuss the Relationship.

In the street below, a little yellow pickup truck pulled to a stop. Two men stepped out and unstrapped a ladder from the rack. The golden retrievers in the yard ran to the fence, barking and wagging their tails at the same time. The older-looking man, gray hair in a ponytail, kneeled at the fence, greeting the dogs. Then while Leary and Timothy danced with joy, totally useless as guard dogs, the two men carried the ladder through the gate, tilted it against the side of the house, and climbed to the roof.

Scarcely glancing at Abe, nodding a greeting as if it were perfectly normal to find somebody sitting against the chimney, they set to work at the far end of the roof. The younger guy, a redhead, manned the tape measure while the older guy—with a bandage on one arm from elbow to fingertip—wrote figures on a clipboard with his one usable hand.

"Ain't too bad," the redhead said.

"I'm gonna recommend a ridge vent," the old guy said.

They paused, crouching, at the dormer that was Abe's bedroom window.

"Flashing's forked," the redhead said.

"Shingles too," the old guy said. "It's like a path."

For the first time, Abe saw what he'd done to the roof: shingle edges mashed and rounded or split entirely off. He'd worn a trail from the window to the crow's nest. Practically plowed a furrow.

Now the two men were standing by the chimney, talking as if Abe weren't there. "It just needs a repair job," the old guy said. "Good for another ten years. You wanna take it, Juke?"

"Need an Alfredo," Juke said.

"Just pick one at the corner."

"You oughta hire a full-time Alfredo as long as your hand's forked. She-yit, Boss, hire some kid for a summer gig."

"Kids today, I dunno. You got any prospects, Juke?"

"Hey. You. Hey. Forkface. Roof-wrecker. Yeah, you. I'm talkin' to you. You know anybody needs a job? Good forkin' pay? Hard forkin' work?"

"Maybe," Abe said, turning sideways so he could see them. He had to squint in the sunlight. They seemed gigantic standing above him leaning against the top of the chimney. "I need a job."

Wally and Juke exchanged a glance. Wally stepped back and folded his arms. Juke leaned forward, right into Abe's face, and said, "You? We're lookin' for somebody with hair on his balls."

"Uh, excuse me? I have—uh—that."

"How old are you?"

"Eighteen."

"Eighteen? College guy?"

"I, uh, start college in September."

"Pretty smart, huh?"

"Uh, good enough, I guess."

"Where?"

"Uh, Princeton."

"Princetown? Where's Princetown?"

"Princeton. It's in New Jersey."

"Now if you're so smart, why in the name of donkeyshit would you want go to New Jersey?"

"It's not that I want to go to New Jersey. It's where the college—"

"Listen, Forkface, can you lift a house?"

"Uh, no."

Juke leaned even closer. His eyeballs seemed lit by wild red veins. "Then why would we hire you?"

"Uh, maybe I misunderstood. What exactly do you mean by lifting a house?"

"I mean forkin' lift it."

"Do, uh, do you lift houses?"

"Hundreds. Board by forkin' board. Nail by forkin' nail."

"Oh. I think I get it. Okay."

"Because that's what you're gonna do, Forkface. Lift houses. Haul trash. Dig holes. Slop poison. Breathe fiberglass. Sweat your balls off. Pull splinters, eat dirt, and shit concrete."

"Uh, okay."

"Okay what?"

"Okay," Abe grinned, "I'll forking do it."

"Hey! Don't you *ever* cuss on the job site. *Never!* Got that, Forkface?"

"All I said was—"

"Shut the fork up! You want to embarrass your forkin' crew? We're a *team* here. You *never* swear. I don't care if we drop a forkin' *wall* on your toe, before you even say 'gosh darn'—before you even *think* it—you say, 'Request permission to swear, *sir!*' Got that?"

"Uh, okay."

"Okay *what?*"

"Okay, uh, sir." It was the first time in his life that Abe had ever addressed anybody as "sir." To cap it off he saluted, hoping it didn't seem like mockery.

It did. Juke glared.

"Uh, sorry, sir. I salute you with all due respect. I won't do it again. Sir."

"Wally, hire this kid's ass."

And Abe, heart pounding, felt as happy hearing those words as he'd felt when he opened the big envelope from Princeton, though he couldn't say why.

Eight

Mornings, Juke liked to arrive early. Sitting in the El Camino, he'd pour a cup of coffee from the Thermos and stare out over the job site at stacks of boards waiting to be given life once again, boards still bleeding the wetness of the forest. Juke's brain worked in images, not words, but the images went something like this:

> Wood lives twice.
> Tree becomes house.
> House breathes air
> in and out,
> drinks water,
> comes to life.
>
> A house has a personality.
> A house grows.
> A house has a soul.

It was all part of Wally's Law #12: Each house is a miracle.

Or, in Juke's words, a forkin' miracle.

And those thoughts in the form of vague mysterious images passed through Juke every morning while sitting in the cab of his El Camino before anybody else had arrived. It was the one reliable moment of calm in his life.

This morning, though, as he was just settling in, he noticed something blue on the second floor. Blue and baggy. Peering through the windshield, he squinted ... *Well, fork a dork.*

Gently Juke let himself out of the El Camino and, still carrying mug and thermos, walked softly across the dirt, up the gangplank, across the first floor and up the rough stairs. On the plywood subfloor of the master bedroom, in a sky-blue sleeping bag next to a sky-blue backpack, FrogGirl lay sound asleep. Next to her lay the big black Maglite, a blunt weapon within easy reach.

Juke sat himself down cross-legged on a box of nails.

FrogGirl, lying on her back, seemed to be dreaming. Her eyeballs moved beneath the lids. She sucked deep gulps of air, held for what seemed like minutes, then blew out and sucked again. Suddenly she rolled to her side, took another gulp of air—and opened her eyes.

"Coffee?" Juke said.

With a start, she sat up straight. Almost immediately, she placed a hand to her forehead, winced, and lay back down.

"That," Juke said, "is just how I feel in the mornin'."

Flat on her back, alert and at the same time calm, with furrowed eyebrows, she gazed back at Juke. The top flap of the sleeping bag lay open. She was wearing a sweatshirt and sweatpants, both gray.

Juke held out the mug. "You take it black?"

Without a word she rolled to her side, took the mug, and sipped.

"Thought you said you lived around here," Juke said.

"I do." She tried to hand the mug back to Juke, but he waved her off and poured a cup for himself in the cap of the thermos. She said, "I live here."

"This house?"

"Night, yeah. Overslept today."

"Runaway?"

"No." She studied Juke, considering her next words. "Well. Technically, yes. Except I bet they're glad I'm gone. So, technically, you might say I'm homeless. If you don't count this place." She scratched her scalp through the short red hair. "I don't hurt anything. Always straighten up. Leave it like I found it. I'm kind of a neatness freak." Again, she was studying him. "You gonna tell?"

The way she studied him, Juke wanted to squirm. Like all women, even this teenager seemed to read him better than he read himself.

"*I* ran away," Juke said.

"Really? Jeezo."

"Long time ago." Juke winked. "Saved my ass."

"Why?"

"I was runnin' from a bad situation. You tell me your story, I'll tell you mine."

"Can't right now." FrogGirl slid out of the sleeping bag. "Gotta go."

"Where?"

She stuffed the sleeping bag into a sky-blue sack. "Gotta barf. Then I go to work."

"You sick?"

She slung the backpack over one arm. "Sometimes coffee makes me barf."

"Then why—?"

"I dunno."

"Where do you work?"

"Starbucks."

She rushed from the house to the porta-potty. Juke heard the sound of retching, and it made him sad. *She coulda used the ground,* he thought. *Nobody should have to hurl into the hole of an outhouse.*

Nine

Phone rang. Left-handed, Wally answered. "Hello?"

"Hi, Dad." Jaspar's voice. Wally's oldest son. Living in Boston. Biotech research.

"Hey, Jas. How are ya?"

"How are *you*, Dad? I just heard about your accident."

"How'd you hear?"

"Saw the photo. You know, the one in *Time*."

"*Time* the magazine?"

"You didn't know?"

"I'm gonna kill that photographer."

"No! It's a great shot. Didn't give your name. Just said 'a carpenter in California.' But I knew. So will this finally make you slow down a little bit? Relax and take some time off?"

"I can work. It's just sort of like going through the day wearing a boxing glove."

"Does it hurt?"

"Nah."

"Ennnh!" Jaspar made a sound like a game-show buzzer. "Lying! Dad."

"All right. Maybe a little."

"That's why I'm cloning spiders. Pain stuff. Can't say more than that. You know."

"Yeah. I know."

Not only was his son more educated, but even if Wally could understand the science Jaspar couldn't talk about work in progress. Contracts and patents and confidentiality agreements. Botheration. But Wally was proud of him. *My son the scientist. Look what I built.*

Ten

Wally, running a little late, arrived at the job site just as a pink Miata was backing out. In the passenger seat were two tennis rackets. Like Krainer's bicycles, those rackets were probably worth more than Wally's entire truck.

Wally's pickup, a five-speed Toyota long-bed, had clocked 337,000 miles so far and still, as Wally said, purred like a kitten (a kitten that burned a little oil and tended to pop out of reverse). He'd bought it brand new in 1984 and it reflected his values: Don't overdo it. You buy a good tool and you take care of it. That 22R engine was practically bulletproof. He'd kept it maintained and sharp until about two years ago when everything—truck, business, life—had started to fall apart.

Lenora, wearing pink sunglasses, pink ribbon in her hair, pink lipstick, pink low-cut and very tight shirt with pink aureola half moons rising, shouted from the little sports car: "I left the check with Juke."

Wally waved at her, smiling, while thinking *cunt*. So Krainer came through. Wally now realized that he'd been half hoping that Krainer would try to stiff him, that he'd be able to take the day off. His wrist—in fact his whole arm all the way to his fingertips—was hurting more, not less, with each passing day, and a nasty smell was wafting out from under the bandage. He'd made a doctor's appointment for the afternoon.

Abe was sitting on a stack of two-by-fours.

"Where's Juke?" Wally asked. "He was supposed to get you started."

"He was, uh, busy," Abe said.

Just then Juke came around a corner of the house carrying two sacks of Quikrete, one under each arm.

Wally suppressed a smile, knowing what was coming. Those sacks weighed eighty pounds each, but Juke made it look effortless as he walked up to Abe and said, "Here, Forkface. Take one, okay?"

Abe reached out. Juke casually unwrapped his arm from around one bag and let it fall into Abe's hands.

Abe staggered backwards. He lurched sideways. The sack was slipping from his grasp—and both Abe and the concrete collapsed to the ground. Juke, meanwhile, had turned his back and was walking away singing "If you ain't got the dough re mi, boys ..."

Wally held out his left hand. "Hello, Abe. Welcome to the trade."

Abe stared up from the ground at the outstretched hand. The sack had split open. His face and hair and eyeglasses, even his lips, were gray with the dust of Portland cement as he said, "Request permission to swear, sir."

"Permission granted."

But Abe found that he no longer wanted to say anything. An oil drum of a man, looking as if he could sub at left tackle for the '49ers, was crouching over Abe and studying him, hands on knees, head slightly cocked, as he might study a new tool—skeptically, judging heft and worth and durability. "I'm Steamboat," the man said. "You'll be working with me. I always break in the Alfredo."

"I just got broken," Abe said, getting to his feet.

"Good start," Steamboat said, and he handed Abe a new sack of Quikrete. This time Abe was ready and didn't drop it, though he didn't think he could possibly carry it with one hand the way Juke had. Fortunately, Steamboat didn't try to give him another sack. Unfortunately, he didn't tell Abe what to do with the concrete either, so Abe stood there cradling an eighty-pound bag in his arms while Steamboat buckled on a tool belt and engaged in some minor housekeeping: shifting a screwdriver from one loop to another, sorting out two different sizes of nails that had ended up in the same leather pouch, then cinching the belt a little tighter.

"You got a belt? Tools? Anything?"

"No, sir."

Steamboat shook his head.

Abe heard the unspoken *You just can't hire good help these days.*

"I'll see what I can scrounge." And Steamboat walked away, leaving Abe and his eighty pounds of dry concrete mix, which seemed to gain a few pounds with each ...

...passing ...

...minute. A kind of pain that Abe had never experienced was flaming in his shoulders, his arms, even his hips, and he started shifting his weight from one leg to the other. His fingers were trembling. He was dripping sweat mixed with the gritty gray powder that had coated his body.

At last, Steamboat returned carrying a raggedy tool belt made out of cloth. It was just a couple of nail pouches with a loop for a hammer. "Best I could find," he said. "Hey, you coulda put down that bag. What do you think this is, a test?"

"I guess I did," Abe said.

"Look, man, the second thing you need to know on this gig is to work smarter, not harder. And it's still plenty hard. We don't need to test you. Half the Alfredos don't make it past the first day. We don't fire them. They just disappear." Steamboat paused, scratching his jaw. "Of course, we reserve the right to jack you around some."

"I got that," Abe said. He shifted the concrete in his arms. "So what's the first thing I need to know?"

"Work safe. A lot of guys in this trade, by the time they're sixty, they can't count to ten no more. They're lucky if they can count to nine and a half. If you get what I'm saying."

"I get it." Abe looked down at his fingers, still trembling under the load of the concrete. Counting didn't worry him. Playing the mandolin did.

Abe's first task was to help Steamboat move some lumber and then build a landing for some stairs that would descend from a deck that a couple of carpenters—who seemed to speak only Spanish—were framing at the rear of the house.

Steamboat could carry twenty-foot two-by-sixes three at a time, over his shoulder. Abe could barely lift one. The wood was heavy with water, treacherous with splinters—rasty wood, Steamboat called it. And those rasty boards were so long that Abe couldn't seem to keep both ends off the ground at the same time. While Abe was still hauling his first, Steamboat went back for three more, whistling.

Then there was nailing. Steamboat could drive a three-and-a-half-inch nail with just a tap to start and then two swings of the hammer. Abe couldn't even keep track of how many blows he needed to drive a nail, especially since most of the time the shaft bent and had to be straightened.

"You play baseball?" Steamboat asked.

"Used to."

"Then you know what happens when you try to kill the ball?"

"I strike out."

"Same with hammering."

Abe had always struck out whether he tried to kill the ball or not, but he knew what Steamboat was talking about. He eased up and tried a new nail.

Same result: bent shaft.

"Third thing you need to know," Steamboat said. "What looks simple, ain't."

And what could look simpler than building a rectangle out of two-by-sixes, then filling it with concrete? Abe noted the care Steamboat gave to all the details: He shoveled the ground flat, a little deeper around the perimeter, and then tamped it firm with his flat-soled boots. He made sure the form was square and exactly the right distance from the edge of the deck, measuring twice. He leveled the boards with his fingers by pushing dirt under one corner, scooping some away from another, eye to the earth, butt to the air. With an electric saw in a shower of sparks Steamboat chopped a piece of rebar into four pieces and laid them like a tic-tac-toe puzzle on top of some little concrete biscuits that he called dobies. He pounded in the stakes, wetted the ground, showed Abe how to use the noisy, smelly gas-powered mixer, slowly adding water to the ready-mix until they had just the right consistency.

"Like oatmeal," Steamboat said. "That's how you want it. Now we pour. Hey. No. Don't just dump it. Watch. See this board? Call it a splash board. See how I'm doing? You use the splash board to direct the flow. Now, take that square shovel and spread the concrete tight against the corners and edges. Kinda shake it, vibrate it—yeah, like that—so none of them boogers leave bubbles."

Next he showed Abe how to strike off the top with a screed board, which was just a regular old two-by-four, pulling it back and forth along the top of the form in a sawing motion, cutting off the high spots, backing and filling the low spots. With a running commentary all the while, Steamboat seemed quite happy to be slopping concrete in dirt, practicing a skill that until this moment Abe had never given a thought, much less any respect.

Abe's one moment of glory came when it was time to mix the concrete. Steamboat told him they'd need about a dozen bags of Quikrete, and Abe in spite of himself said, "Ten and three-fourths."

"Says you?"

"Yes, sir."

Steamboat seemed amused.

Blew it, Abe thought. *Now I get jacked.* It wasn't that he was wrong—Abe knew for sure he'd calculated the volume perfectly, two-thirds of a bag equals one cubic foot, slight irregular ellipticity of the bottom calling for some simple calculus ...Abe had always tried to conceal the fact that he was a little strange about math. And astrophysics, which is basically math as it applies to the deepest questions of the universe. He had just finished reading an entire book about Fermat's Last Theorem. Just for fun he had spent entire evenings constructing fractals. Somehow, in social situations, talking about fractals never seemed to advance his popularity. It had thrilled him—actually sent chills down his spine—when he saw Steamboat checking the squareness of the form by measuring diagonally across the corners to see if they matched. *The diagonals of a four-sided figure are only equal when each angle is exactly ninety degrees.* What could be more real—more actual math—than a big, sweaty guy on his hands and knees in the mud with a tape measure employing an abstract geometric concept before pouring concrete?

Instead of teasing, all Steamboat said was, "You want to put money on that?"

"Yes, sir."

They mixed eleven bags. After screeding they had just a little clod of concrete left over, about enough to fill a large paper cup. Wally, Juke, and the two other carpenters had gathered to watch. And as Steamboat passed Abe a ten dollar bill, money changed hands among the rest of the crew. Abe was surprised: *Look where the money's going. Wally bet on me. And—amazing!—so did that maniac.*

"Good work, Forkface," said the maniac.

"Thank you, sir."

The onlookers drifted off, but the job wasn't finished. Steamboat showed Abe how to swing a wooden floater in circles, working all the stone ("boogers") in the mix so they dropped below the surface, holding the leading edge of the tool up slightly to keep it from plowing. The wet concrete had an odd quality under Abe's hands, feeling both solid in its mass and grudgingly liquid on its surface, sort of bouncy, as the tool swept over. There was magic the way the pebbles disappeared, as if the floater was sucking smoothness from the mix. Lastly, Steamboat showed Abe how to run a steel edger along the forms, pulling the concrete away from the two-by-sixes and leaving a curved corner.

"Now hose out that mixer," Steamboat said. "I don't want one grain of cement left inside that drum—or anywhere else on that machine. Got that?"

"Yes, sir."

Steamboat nodded toward the landing. "Lookin' good," he said.

"Yes, sir."

Abe liked saying sir. He knew he didn't have to, it was a joke, but he didn't want to stop. He liked the ache in his muscles that would grow into strength. He liked the smell of wet concrete. He liked this work—so solid, so basic, so real. It would be a good summer.

Eleven

At the end of the noisy day, Wally and Juke carried the heavy table saw into the Wells Cargo trailer, swung the big door shut with a final boom of metal, snapped the padlock, and then stood for a minute. Wally was taking in the splendor of it all. The live oaks dropped long rippling shadows over the wild oats. Fog gathered on the ridge of the California coastal range above them. Such a beautiful spot for a house. A house that made peace with the landscape. Not this house.

Eventually Wally said, "So, this morning, you and Lenora—you cool it?"

Juke suddenly needed to rearrange some dirt with the toe of his boot. "Uh, it weren't so easy."

"Juke ...Hey."

"You got the check, Boss."

"She's the client's girlfriend. This is dynamite. You can't play."

"She ain't his girlfriend. Just his ...thing."

"She's Krainer's thing."

"It ain't so good. She don't tingle."

"Tingle?"

"She kinda likes me."

"Do you have any idea what she sees in you?"

Juke spat. "Must be my charmin' personality."

"That, and your impeccable manners. You know she's just slumming, don't you?"

"You think I'm slum?"

"Figure of speech. But she's high class. Money. Power. Spoiled rotten. She can be dangerous."

"She says *I'm* forkin' dangerous, Boss. That's her turn-on. Man, she just creams when I—" Juke's grin faded. "Money's his. Krainer's. She don't have none. Just acts like she does. Family disowned her."

"Disowned her?"

"She says it was her father's fault but she got the blame."

"Blame for what?"

"She don't wanna talk about it. All I know is she came here from Boston bringing nothing but a three-leg cat."

"She told you all this in ten minutes in the trailer?"

"Last night. Sorry, Boss. I know what you said but we sorta got together. Drove around."

"In the Miata?"

"My Camino. Little extra, uh, elbow room. And then at my place."

Juke lived in an unheated garage in East Palo Alto. The decor was early machine shop. "How'd she like your place?" Wally asked.

"Musta seemed okay. She stayed."

"All night? Is that why you dropped that glue-lam today? No sleep?"

"We mighta dozed off once. But you don't get it."

"Get what?"

"She's more'n pussy. Great pussy. More'n that. We kinda ...tingle."

"What in the world do you—Juke, excuse me if this is a rude question but I'm—uh—what do you like about her?"

Juke gazed toward the fog that was creeping down the hill. "It's sorta. Appreciation." Juke spoke slowly, thinking between each word. "She ...appreciates me. Who I am. What I do. Don't do. She says once you rub the dirt away, there's silver just needing some polish. Me—*silver*. You know what it's like when a lady appreciates you?"

Wally nodded. "So what don't you do?"

"It's kinda personal."

"Okay. Sorry."

"Hurt her." Juke rubbed the back of his neck.

"Krainer hurts her?"

"Dunno what he does. The pain thing. It's yes. It's no. It's now. It's not now. She says I'm the only guy who gets that. The not-hurt part."

"So she asks to be hurt?"

"You gotta know where to stop."

"And you like that?"

"No. So I stop. It's easy."

"Then I still don't get what you like about her."

"Appreciation, Boss. I told you. There's that. And the stuff."

"What stuff?"

"Uh. You know."

"I *don't* know. What stuff?"

"Hair."

"Hair?"

"You seen her pits?"

"No. Saw the belly."

"Yeah! Exactly! She don't shave her pits. Just trims 'em a little. And you wouldn't believe the inside of her thighs. Like bangin' a deer. You think I'm pervert?"

"Only the deer part."

"I ain't even told about her furbelow."

"Her what?"

"Furbelow. Forkin' jungle. But I ain't talkin'. Some things are private."

Opal sat at the computer retouching a photo of a man who had just rescued seven kittens from a burning house. Somehow, no matter how she adjusted, this heroic and happy man looked slightly haunted, driven by demons. Her editor had remarked: "Opal, your pictures always bring out the inner warmth in women and the inner evil in men."

Unfortunately, so do my relationships.

Except the picture of Wally. It was a lucky shot, a providential accident, but possibly a new departure for her. If she took Wally's photo again she'd reveal no hidden evil. She saw it in his face, the eyes of a big old friendly dog, a working dog, a Saint Bernard, wet and warm and totally without guile, a dog who flossed. Not a psychiatrist or a professor or any kind of a brilliant authority. If only it was as easy to keep a man around the house as it was to keep a dog.

The door flew open and Abe burst into the house. Smeared with mud, splashed by concrete, sprinkled in sawdust, he looked triumphantly happy.

"How'd it go?" Opal asked.

"Fine," Abe said, going blank.

"Oh, Abe. If only Rachel could see you now."

"We broke up."

"I know, but if she saw, she might change her mind."

"Because I'm dirty?"

"Because you're on the way to becoming a man who knows how to do things. Build things. Fix things. Let me tell you, there's nothing more seductive than a man who comes into your house and starts fixing things."

Abe considered a moment, then broke into a laugh. "You're talking about old people."

Opal felt herself blushing.

"I mean," Abe continued, "no disrespect or anything."

"You must think I'm totally ignorant, right? I was just offering a little advice. It might apply to someone you meet sometime."

"Mom." Abe rolled his eyes. "Can you imagine me going into some girl's house and, like, fixing her faucet or something? It might impress her mother—or her grandmother."

"All right, Abe. You can drop it."

"No, wait. Not that I know how to fix faucets or anything. The way it might apply to me—like, if I want to score with some girl from my high school—that is, based on my skill set—such as it is so far—I need to find some cute cheerleader who just wishes more than *anything* that she had a concrete stair landing."

Twelve

"Slight change of plans," said Anton Krainer as he unrolled a fresh set of blueprints across the hood of Wally's truck. "That front entry? The boring little box? I changed it to a tower."

Wally leaned over the prints. "Am I reading that right? You want a tower that's thirty feet high? A round tower on a house of squares?"

"I just woke up the other morning and realized I've always wanted a tower."

"What did the architect say?"

"Gone." Krainer adjusted the sunglasses on the bridge of his nose. Ray-Bans. He was wearing a pink shirt and white shorts, clean and crisp.

Wally, without shades, squinted against the sunshine. He was dressed in cruddies—work clothes. "Fired?"

"Resigned," Krainer said. "Draftsman drew these up."

"So the architect wasn't exactly enthusiastic about the tower?"

Krainer frowned. Even frowning, he had dimples. "We've had some ...disagreements."

"Like the California modern style mixed with the Greek columns? Or does he maybe disagree about designing separate rooms for a home theater, a den, an office, a library, an exercise room, a family room, a great room, and a living room plus three walk-in closets, two guest rooms, three bedrooms, and six bathrooms including two bidets for an unmarried man without children? Not to mention the wine cellar, the seven-car garage, the indoor spa with fireplace, the swimming pool and grotto, the fountain, the tennis court, the—"

"So you don't like my house?"

"I love your house, Anton. It's my job to build it, so I love it. I'm just speculating about what the architect might not agree with."

Krainer stared out at his view of the valley, which today was a brown puddle of smog ringed by golden mountains. "He never got it. The mission."

"To create the Perfect House?"

Krainer smiled. "You got it."

"That's my job."

Krainer seemed satisfied.

Wait'll Pilpont sees this tower going up, Wally thought. *Can you sue for aesthetic distress?*

After Krainer departed, Juke and Steamboat reappeared (they tended to remember urgent work in distant corners of the job site when Krainer came around). Wally showed them the plans. Abe stood behind them, eavesdropping.

"Is he kidding?" Steamboat said.

"Looks like the house has a hard-on," Juke said.

"This is gonna be the ugliest house I ever worked on," Wally said. "But at least it'll be a well-built ugly house." He thumped his good hand on the drawing. "Do we actually know how to build a round tower?"

"Double the sticks," Juke said. "Eight inches on center."

Wally nodded. "How do we round the sill and the plates?"

"Plywood," Steamboat said. "Make our own glue-lams."

"You done this before?" Wally said.

"All the time," Steamboat said.

"Okay, Steamie, you're in charge."

"Hey," Juke said. "I can do this."

"So can Steamie." Wally walked away. Juke followed, arguing that he should be in charge.

Alone with Steamboat, Abe asked, "Where did you build towers?"

"Never done it." Steamboat smiled. "Neither has Juke. Wally just needed to hear, so he could tell the client we got an experienced, crackerjack team." Steamboat rolled up the plans. "C'mon, Princeton. You're gonna help me tear out these walls. Then we're gonna frame the perfect erection."

Possibly by telepathy, the entire crew suddenly seemed to decide that Abe's name was no longer Alfredo (or Forkface) but Princeton. And that everything was his fault. If a board split while Steamboat was nailing he'd say, "Dammit, Princeton, you got some *rasty* old wood." If a bolt wouldn't fit when Wally tried to install it, he'd say, "Princeton, your bolt's too short." If an air hose tangled while Juke was yanking on it, he'd say, "Princeton tied the forkin' air hose." Even Pancho, wiping sweat from his face, was muttering, "*...esta pinche caliente ...pendejo* Preenceton."

At the end of the day, Wally asked Abe to stay a few minutes after the others had departed. "Little help, Princeton," Wally said.

"Yes, sir."

Together they pulled a blue tarp to expose a stack of lumber. Empty acorn shells and a few shiny bits of insulation foil were scattered over the wood—plus a silver-colored piece of jewelry. A small animal scrambled away from the sudden daylight.

"Pack rat," Wally said, picking up the sparkly jewelry. From a wire clip, a small green stone hung by a delicate chain. The clip was shaped like the outline of a tiny pair of scissors. "Is this an ear ring?"

"Uh, no, sir."

"A nose ring?"

"No, it's a clip." Abe knew what it was for—Rachel had worn something similar in a special location for special occasions. And Abe knew he'd better keep his mind away from that location and those occasions or else he might start missing her badly—except he already missed her excruciatingly, painfully, mournfully. When he'd had her, he'd thought the attraction was all about sex. Now he knew it was about a whole lot more. He longed for the more. And he wouldn't mind the sex again, either. "Not for a nose," Abe said after a moment's pause. "Would you want a stone dangling from your nose?"

"When something dangles from my nose, I get a Kleenex." Wally twisted the chain between his fingers. "Dumbest thing I ever saw." He dropped the clip, chain, and stone into the pocket of his cutoff blue jeans.

The boards were partly black and partly silver with age, gouged, badly split, dotted with nail holes, spattered with stains. The old wood smelled of something familiar that Abe couldn't identify at first. What was that scent? Something basic, deeply alive.

"I'm doing a little salvage," Wally said, and he explained how when Krainer bought this ranch they'd found a funky pile of boards partly overgrown with blue forget-me-nots and scarlet columbine that flowered through the cracks. Some gold-rush guy, after he couldn't find any, had come to this hill and started a farm, cut some trees, and built a barn. Wally tried to convince Krainer to use the wood, but Krainer's stock was already flying and he had no interest in salvage, which, though noble in intent, would be imperfect. So the wood was Wally's. "The real gold in these hills," Wally said. "Feel that." Wally ran his fingers over one of the boards.

Abe did the same. A hundred fifty years of sun and rain had sculpted the pattern of the grain into valleys and ridges like a relief map of an endless, writhing chain of mountains.

"Redwood," Wally said. "Old growth. Heart. Some of these one-by-twelves are actually clear. You couldn't buy this today. And they used it for siding on a barn. Can you imagine?"

"Uh, imagine what?"

"You know what I'm talking about?"

"Not entirely."

"Clear wood has no knots. Nicer grain. Straight and true. It's from the center of the tree. The heart." Wally covered the basics: Grain is tree rings. When a tree grows fast, the rings are farther apart. When it grows slowly, the grain is tight. The inside rings get squashed—compressed—as the outside adds more. Tight grain is stronger. A redwood grows fast for a hundred years, then slowly for another five hundred, sometimes two thousand years. The outer part of a redwood tree is sapwood. It's white, rots easily, soft as Velveeta cheese. The inner part is red from the tannin, the same stuff that makes wine red. The tannin protects the wood from insects and rot. For a while, anyway. Redwood *will* rot, but it takes longer. Few carpenter bees got in," Wally said, pointing to some insect holes the size of pinpricks. "Anyway, the red part is called heartwood. All you see is silver and black because the surface gets burned by the sun, but inside—watch this."

From his pocket Wally pulled out a Leatherman and unfolded a blade that had saw teeth. With a few strokes in the soft wood, he cut a notch revealing the deep brownish red inside. "This could have started growing when Jesus walked the Earth."

"Yes, sir," Abe said. "Amen."

"You mocking me?"

"No, sir."

"More likely the trees here were younger, probably just one thousand years. Ten *centuries*. Some of that sawdust that fell on your boots might be from, oh, the eleventh century."

"Ninth. Actually. Ninth century, sir."

Wally paused, considering. If the tree was cut down a hundred and fifty years ago, and it was a thousand years old ..."You're right. Ninth century. No wonder we call you Princeton."

Abe leaned forward until his nose was against the notch Wally had cut. Breathing deeply, he now recognized the scent, so rich and familiar: It was blood.

Wally was gazing out from the hillside toward the late afternoon haze of the Silicon Valley. "You know what was happening in the ninth century?"

"Bunch of dumb wars?"

Wally looked startled, as if he'd expected a more thoughtful answer. Then he frowned. "Arabs were kicking butt. Discovered coffee, invented algebra, studied astronomy, made an astrolabe—"

Abe grinned. "Amazing what a little caffeine will do."

"So anyway, every day I load a few boards on my truck and take them home."

"For what, sir?"

"Dunno yet. Gotta communicate with these boards, figure out what they want."

"You a wood whisperer, sir?"

"Not out loud." Wally laughed. "And no, they don't talk back. Grab that end, okay?"

As they walked the old planks to the truck, Wally said, "You're catching on pretty fast. Think this'll give you a head start in the Ivy League?"

"Oh, yes," Abe said. "I'll probably place out of the lecture class, you know, Construction 101. They'll let me register for the graduate seminar."

"Which is?"

"Existential Issues in the Art and Philosophy of Banging Nails."

"Oh yeah," Wally said. "I remember that class."

"You went to college, sir?"

"Not exactly Princeton."

Abe laughed nervously. He sensed he'd touched on a sore point. Trying to make light of it, he said, "You know what, sir? This work—this summer—might improve my social life."

"How?"

"Stuff I care about—astrophysics, math—girls don't want to hear. But now ...Girls like it when guys know how to build things. Fix things. That's what my mom says. She says the sexiest thing a guy can do is come into a woman's house and start, you know, repairing faucets and patching walls."

"She said that?"

"Actually, she didn't say 'sexy.' She couldn't say that word."

"So what did she say?"

"Most seductive."

"Seductive, huh? She really thinks that?"

"Yeah." Abe shrugged. "Not that she has a clue."

Thirteen

Buried in beaver, lying on his back, Juke was approaching a decision.
Lenora's thighs, warm hairy carpets, squeezed his hips. Juke's hands
slapped her butt once, twice, and then spread the cheeks while his
fingers reached into the crack. Lenora squirmed, urging him deeper.
Unlike any other woman Juke had known, she kept her eyes open,
pupils dilating wildly as she grew more and more excited, mouth ajar,
lips forming an oval as a low humming sound escaped in rhythm with
their thrusts.

It was Juke's first time in Lenora's bed, first view of her Saratoga
condo with a balcony over the swimming pool. Beyond Lenora's
humming Juke heard the shriek and splash of children along with the
fwop of tennis games billowing through the wind-blown curtains into
this spacious, sunny room. A room, she had told him, paid for and
maintained by Anton Krainer, the golden chump. *Wally's my boss and
Krainer's the client and I'm forkin' the goose who laid the golden gig. And I
gotta quit. In a minute. Maybe.*

Lenora, eyes still wide but now entirely white, groaned as her belly
fluttered, and Juke felt warm slick pulsating pussy enveloping him,
devouring him.

Gasping, shivering one last time, Lenora lay like liquid on top of
Juke. Her irises descended from inside her head. After a minute, raising
herself on her elbows, staring into Juke's eyes, she said, "Good job,
Carpenter."

"Yeah?" Juke felt the muscles around her puss making little nibbling
motions on his joint. He appreciated the attention.

Dreamily she said, "That's what we want."

"We?"

"I'm not talking to you." Stretching her arms above her head while
arching her back, she pushed her bantam breasts against Juke's chest.
"I'm answering the question, 'What do women want?'"

"To get laid?"

"To get *nailed*." She wiggled slightly side to side, scraping pointy nipples across Juke's tattoos.

Juke was looking at the headboard, hand-carved in Mexico, flowers and angels and a Virgin Mary with a halo. He said, "Who asked?"

"Sigmund Freud."

"I got a saw blade named Freud."

Lenora giggled. They were still joined. The giggling belly bounced her up and down on top of him.

"You are really something, Carpenter."

"Plumb and true."

Lenora squeezed. "Very plumb," Lenora said. "Very true."

Lenora's three-legged cat, an ancient animal with bare spots in its fur and a permanent odor of mothballs, jumped onto the bed and started rubbing her side against the top of Juke's head, purring.

Reaching for the cat, Lenora stroked the splotchy pelt. At the same time Lenora began languorously weaving her hips, bringing more response from Juke.

"Build it," she whispered. "More plumb. More true."

"That ain't what I mean."

Frowning, Lenora stopped moving and studied Juke, their faces just inches apart.

Juke was looking at the gold-framed mirror, the closet full of clothes, all bills covered by Anton Krainer. "Anything I make," he said, "I got to have pride. I build a foundation, I make it plumb and true. That's what's strong. That's what's right. Door frame. Forkin' flower box. I do it plumb and true."

Lenora propped her head on her hands, elbows to each side of Juke's neck. "I've seen you work, Juke. I adore that. Your fingers, the look in your eye. You hold a piece of wood like you're handling a woman. Like it's worth something." She giggled. "And then you nail it."

"You're worth something," Juke said. "More'n some old board." He licked his lips. It was going to be hard to say these words. "But what you're worth, Lenora, it ain't my money."

Her body tensed. "If I know what you're thinking," she said, "you'd better not."

"I think I gotta."

"You're *inside* me and you say that." Lenora pulled off, rolled over on her back. "You're jealous."

"Of Krainer? No. But you're bought and paid for. You ain't true and I ain't plumb. That's all."

"Could you pay for this place?"

Juke snorted. "No, ma'am. But I could build it better."

"Not without money you couldn't."

"Yeah. *His* money."

"I don't believe it. You sound like Boston. I could've stayed there if I wanted to hear this."

"I never been to Boston, but I bet plumb is plumb everywhere."

"It wasn't plumb in my house, you stupid shit."

"Hey. Don't call me stupid."

"You'll be so sorry."

"I'm already sorry, Lenora. But we can't. No more."

"You don't know how sorry you'll be."

Fourteen

Abe was starting to see the big picture: Building a house was just a string of separate projects, a long labyrinth, like a video game made physical and sweaty. Each little phase of construction seemed like a mini-adventure with its own small goal and its own mysteries of craftsmanship. Advancing to a new level required special sets of skills as if you were gaining magical powers. And each step, Abe saw, presented its own puzzles calling for a wizard to make the crucial decisions.

For building the round tower, the crucial decision came right at the beginning: Could they use the existing foundation? It would be like trying to balance a round peg on top of a square hole. Juke wanted to keep the existing foundation walls and just double or triple some of the joists in a cantilever arrangement that could bear the weight of the circular erection. Steamboat said it would look like crap unless they tore it all out and started over. Wally listened to both arguments, then came up with a plan that was basically a compromise: They'd tear out the front half of the foundation where it would show beneath the tower. They'd replace it with a deep-drilled cylindrical pier and a rounded block wall which would later be faced with stone.

"Abe," Wally said, "I've got a little job for you." These were words that Abe soon learned to dread. "Sorry about this," Wally said.

Abe had the ball-buster job of removing the old foundation wall. He quickly found out why nobody else wanted to do it. His tool for the day was a rented demolition hammer, Hitachi Model H65. It looked like a rifle on steroids and weighed in his hands like a block of concrete. Two blocks of concrete. Abe had to hold the tool Rambo-style in front of his body while the chisel point struck the vertical wall fourteen hundred times per minute with twenty pounds of force in each blow. There was a recoil of those same twenty pounds of force absorbed by Abe's hands, arms, shoulders, and ribs—fourteen hundred times per minute. Chips of concrete flew out like little bullets striking any exposed skin and finding their way up his sleeves and down his shirt collar and even down his pants.

Abe spent the entire day pummeling the concrete wall into manageable pieces, cutting rebar with a Sawzall, and wrestling with a wheelbarrow—loading the chunks, rolling, losing balance, tipping, picking up, and refilling, and then finally lifting the chunks and throwing them onto a pile of other debris that, Abe assumed, resulted from a previous change of plans. Mostly, though, he rattled with the demolition hammer. In spite of work gloves he grew blisters on both hands. Behind stifling hot safety goggles his eyeglasses steamed over and sweat ran like raindrops down the lenses. His arms and straining back quickly tired of holding a forty-pound tool in a horizontal position. His cheeks jiggled. Even his eyeballs trembled. His shoulders went numb from the shaking and for a while—as he was taking a break—his fingers stopped working altogether as quick needle points of pain danced up from his fingertips to his armpits and back down. Steamboat mentioned the time he'd worked on an extension to the perimeter wall at Folsom Prison—the extra thickness, extra-strength concrete, extra rebar were all similar to how they'd built this "perfect foundation."

Back at work after the break, the safety earmuffs isolated Abe from the normal sounds of the rest of the crew, leaving him in a bubble where all he could hear was the thumping and grinding of the chisel point, the gurgle of his saliva, the roar of blood in his veins, and the clattering of his own teeth. Concrete dust clogged the inside of his nose like mud. Drops of perspiration striking the hot metal of the tool sizzled—and then vanished. For a while he fantasized that he was tearing down the Folsom wall—the rebar like a steel cage—through which he and all the other lowly workers of the world would escape and pour into the streets to seize the yachts, the vacation estates, the private jets and vaults filled with gold. Anger created energy but, like all the other strength in his body, it faded. Abe was vaguely aware that Folsom Prison was not populated by the noblest workers of the world and that he in fact would not want to be circulating among them. Eventually the vibration drove fantasy and all sensation from his carcass and any thoughts but one from his brain: *Get it done. Just get the forking job done*.

At last, at the end of the day, the wall was gone. As feeling slowly returned to his flesh, Abe twitched all over. He blew the gray sludge out of his nose. An ache of cold pain began pulsing, deeply embedded in his shoulders.

Switching on the radio, Abe drove home in his dual–air bag Honda Civic hatchback, the car selected by his mother for its safety. At this moment, though, Abe felt like he'd been in a non–air bag accident. Grime coated Abe's body; sore muscles fluttered randomly. Brain a blank, radio blasting bluegrass, he had made his prison break, he was drained, he'd earned his pay—and he felt insanely happy, at peace with the world.

On Steamboat's advice, Abe bought a tool belt, speed square, hammer, cat's paw, utility knife, twenty-five-foot tape, carpenter's pencil, and a torpedo level—the framer's starter kit. In the first week, though, the only tools he was allowed to put to use were the hammer and the cat's paw. The cat's paw was mainly for undoing the damage he'd done with the hammer.

In frustration Abe demanded of Steamboat: "Would you just let me use a nailgun? I mean, hammers are so obsolete. Like, why don't you let me—Is there any good reason why I can't—I mean, what's the *deal* anyway?"

"No," Steamboat explained.

Steamboat didn't talk much. He cut wood, drove nails, and tended his barbecue. Abe found him easy to work with. As a side benefit, Abe was learning how to cook ribs.

Sometimes Juke joined Abe and Steamboat for a few hours, broadcasting that he could do whatever Steamboat was doing, only better. Abe hoped the rivalry between them stayed under control.

Friday morning they were framing a gazebo, something Krainer had added on a whim to overlook the pool grotto. The drawing they were working from was more of a wish than a plan, an open-sided octagon with a roof, so Steamboat and Juke were basically making it up as they went along. Abe found himself in the middle. Steamboat would hold a board over whatever gap he next needed to fill, copy the angle and then mark the wood with a pencil. "Save the line," he might say, and Abe would carry the board to Juke and repeat, "Save the line." Juke would cut the board so that not one speck of wood showed beyond the penciled line. Abe would carry it back to Steamboat, hold it in place, and Steamie would nail it. Then Abe would pick up the next board that Steamie had marked, and this time Steamie might say, "Save the line big." Juke would then cut the board with a slight sliver of wood showing beyond the penciled line.

"Split the line."

"Gimme a hair."

"Kill the line."

"Shave it a bright red pussy hair."

Abe kneeled, carried, held in place, lifted, watched, learned. The flow of work, the hot breath of the power saw and the whine of the blade, the heft of the wood in his hands, scratches on Abe's elbow where he collided with a four-by-four, drops of blood sprinkling in powdery sawdust, the sharp fresh-cut scent of fir, the nails whacking true, the prickling heat of the sun, the outline of the gazebo forming and then filling, board after board, joist to beam to rafter, the skillful and yet spiritual rhythm of it all was like a song. Or a prayer. The frame came out tight as a drum.

Fifteen

Friday at noon Juke gave the cry: "Gentlemen, start your forkin' engines!"
Beer, bets, and belt sanders received equal attention. Steamboat served
succulent ribs. A couple dozen pickups and vans parked haphazardly in
the dirt of the construction area—plus one shiny BMW. Even Lenora's
pink Miata showed up, though she only seemed to want a word with
Krainer before departing.

Wally drank an Odwalla smoothie. He'd just handed out the weekly
paychecks to the crew, so everybody was in a happy mood. Fingers
sticky with barbecue sauce, they'd race their sanders, then they'd race
to the bank.

"Hey! Princeton!" Juke was calling. "C'm'ere and meet somebody."

Next to Juke stood a muscular man with a thick silver mustache
who was carrying two belt sanders, one in each hand.

"This is Alfredo," Juke said. "The forkin' original."

Alfredo smiled amiably at Abe. "*Como le va?*"

"*Muy bien,*" Abe said. "*Y usted?*" After four years of high school
Spanish, Abe had a lousy accent but could understand what was spoken
pretty well.

Juke slapped Alfredo on the shoulder. "Started with us, he didn't
know shit. Right, Alfredo?"

Alfredo nodded, smiling.

"Now he's got his own company. This pisshead underforkinbids
us. And you know what? Wally loaned him the money to buy his first
truck."

Again Alfredo nodded, smiling.

"And," Juke said, "I taught him everything. Right, Alfredo?"

"*Si, cabron,*" Alfredo said, still smiling. Turning to Abe, Alfredo
shook his head. "*Wally ya me dijo: No te juntes con Juke Jacobs! Fue un buen
consejo, y ahora te lo paso a ti. Oye bien. Quedate lejos de ese hijo de la chingada
forking Juke Jacobs!*"

Alfredo winked—and laughed. Juke, who had only understood the
words "forking Juke Jacobs," laughed too. Abe joined in the laughter

but was pretty sure that Alfredo was warning him not to follow in Juke's footsteps.

"And over here," Juke said, guiding Abe by the arm, "is Larry Ludowski. Larry, Abe."

"How do you do?" Abe said, meeting the handshake of a large unsmiling bald man. The touch was quick but nearly crushed Abe's fingers.

Juke said, "What's shakin', Larry? You cheated any widows 'n' orphans lately?"

"Not today," Larry said, frowning. "I was too busy cornholing your mother."

Quickly Juke steered Abe away, but not before Abe saw the vein start throbbing in Juke's eyeball.

"What was that all about?" Abe asked.

"Just want you to know the enemy," Juke said.

"What does cornholing mean?"

For a moment Juke chewed his lower lip while studying Abe as if he didn't know what to make of such appalling innocence. "Butt-forkin'," Juke said. "Brags about it. With a lady, pork 'n' blab, all the details, guy's got no class. Porks a client, don't tell, but we see the results. He can build good as anybody but he ain't happy unless he can sleaze it. Undersize the bolts where nobody can see. Lower grade of lumber. Gives us all a bad name."

"So he's a cheapskate?"

"Ain't the money. Pennies, man. Butt-forker."

"Don't some women—I mean, I don't know, probably not your mother of course—don't some women like that stuff?"

"Not how he does. Nothin' wrong if you do it right. You gotta know what a lady likes."

"What does a lady like?"

Again Juke studied Abe, as if gauging his readiness for such important information. "Givin'."

Abe had been expecting some secret technique from the master craftsman, some special stroke or touch. "Giving?"

"Hey. Sex is givin'. Not gettin'. And the better you give, the better you get. Now don't tell nobody I said that." Juke looked slightly embarrassed, as if he'd shown a weakness.

"Is that one of Wally's Laws?"

"Oughta be."

Abe felt the awkwardness too. *Juke's Law. Did all these guys have Laws?* Abe changed the subject: "Was Ludowski an Alfredo with you guys?"

"Nope. If Wally'd trained him, he couldn't cheat nobody."

"Why not?"

Juke frowned. "Cuz you don't."

"Uh. Yes, sir."

"And when we call you an Alfredo, understand, it ain't no disrespect. It means we hope you do as good."

Abe watched Alfredo with his Latino workers. Just as Wally was king of his crew, respected and obeyed, so was Alfredo with his men. Abe wondered if he could ever succeed like Alfredo, make Wally proud, be king of a crew. What makes some people leaders? And what makes some go to Princeton?

First up were the stock races, meaning belt sanders that ran pretty much the way they came out of the factory: no changes of gear ratio allowed, no extra capacitors, no motor modifications.

Krainer had bought a rice burner: a top-of-the-line Makita with a belt speed of 1,640 feet per minute, the fastest—theoretically, by the numbers—of the stock competition that day. It was a sleek-looking machine, teal-colored like all Makitas, running as quiet as a snake in grass. And it lost. In spite of major horsepower, slick engineering, top belt speed, Krainer was eliminated in two quick rounds. He lost to Steamboat's workmanlike boxy red Milwaukee, and then he lost to Pancho's beat-up, piece-of-crap little black Craftsman that Pancho had bought at a flea market after haggling it down to a dollar and five cents and a couple of Lucky Strikes.

Juke, in a show of generosity, tried to explain to Krainer: "It ain't about the price you pay for a tool. It's the worth."

"You mean," Krainer said, "this sander isn't worth what I paid for it?"

"She's a forkin' good sander," Juke said. "Good for sandin'. But she ain't got the heart of a racer."

"So it's got worth as a sander. I get it. And this would apply to any kind of tool?" Krainer looked around. "What's worth the most—what tool?"

"See that nailer?" Juke pointed at Debbie the Duo-Fast, lying in dust where he'd dropped her after making an emergency repair to the race track. "Ain't worth crap as a resale, but to me she's priceless."

"That?" Krainer squinted. Then he broke into his boyish, dimply smile. "To each his own. Like a scruffy old cat. Nothing can replace it."

"If you like cats," Juke said.

"Exactly," Krainer said.

Alfredo won the stock class, as he often did, with his old bulldog of a Porter Cable 504, a machine whose design hadn't changed since the days when an airplane was a DC7 and a truck ran on a flat-head V-8—which happened to be the motor in Alfredo's 1948 Mercury pickup, powder blue, lovingly restored. The 504 looked like a locomotive and wouldn't surprise anyone if it could pull a small freight train. It was dull gray, ridiculously heavy, stubborn, powerful. You could sit on it and it would carry you across a room. Alfredo with fanatical attention to detail kept it tuned, balanced, and clean—just like his truck.

After the stock class came the modified. In these races, you could do just about anything to your sander as long as it still ran on a sanding belt and drew on electricity as the power source (like, no rocket boosters). Amid the smell of beer and scorched plywood, through double elimination rounds a winner emerged: Juke, driving a weird-looking Black and Decker with a motor substituted from an angle grinder, extra capacitors held on with duct tape, custom gears from an outboard boat engine, and Juke's home-brewed lubrication that he called pussy grease.

For a final round, there was a run-off between the winners of the stock and modified classes. One would expect Juke's blazing-fast modified to be the favorite with its belt speed of about three thousand feet per minute, but a lot of money was siding on Alfredo's stodgy old Porter Cable clocking at fifteen hundred fpm. Partly it was the two-to-one odds, but mostly it was the knowledge that a modified sander, especially one in the hands of Juke, was an unreliable beast. A Juke-built sander was likely to jump screaming off the track into the spectators—it had happened before—or simply burn out in a quiet *pfft* with a plume of curly black smoke.

This time, the mechanical demons did not appear. The gods of garage tinkering smiled on Juke. He won. He buried Alfredo in a rooster tail of sawdust.

Now all eyes were on Wally.

"As you know," Wally said, "we have a little tradition here. Yes, sir, we have a special prize for the winner. We have a prize that reflects the importance and solemn value of the belt sander races. Something worthy of all you good people who joined us here today. In other words, we have something ugly. Useless. Something *stupid*. I'd like to thank Pancho once again for contributing last week's prize. I'm sure you all remember that paw of road-kill possum. Such a good-luck charm. This week's prize was donated by a pack rat. Juke, would you step forward, please? By the powers invested in me as Grand Master of the Belt Sander Races I present you—*ta da!*"

From his pocket Wally pulled a shiny piece of jewelry.

Everyone leaned forward, squinting.

Juke turned pale white.

A small green stone dangled by a silver chain from a wire clip that was shaped like the outline of a tiny pair of scissors.

Juke grabbed Wally and pulled him away—far away to the other side of the house. "What the suckin' asshole you doin', Boss? You know what that is?"

"All I know, it's not a nose ring."

"It's a pussy clip."

"A what?"

"A lady wears it—down there. Don't you know who lost it?"

"Who?"

"In the power shed, Boss. Where I took it off her. Where the pack rat found it."

"Oh, my God."

Wally looked around. Pancho and Steamboat were dismantling the race track so they could store it in sections. The electrician was rolling up cords. Abe was picking up beer cans. Gathered at the tailgate of a pickup, a knot of men were laughing about some joke. And in the street a BMW was roaring out of sight.

Sixteen

Wally stopped at Opal's house in the foothills just above Palo Alto. She didn't have the Krainer/Pilpont altitude—and acreage—of extreme wealth, but her lot was comfortably higher than the flatlands, near Stanford, and in realtor parlance she was *prime*. From the lawn came the scent of fresh fertilizer. Next door at somebody's sprawling ranch house, laborers were digging trenches, installing sprinkler pipe. Across the street at a Spanish colonial was the truck of an air-conditioner repairman. In front of a McMansion with an insanely complicated roof, two installers were lifting a heavy roll of carpet from the back of a van. Scattered along the block were the trucks and vans of a pool cleaner, a gardener, a maid service. The street had the quiet, buffered feel of big money at rest, tended by small money at work.

On his previous visit when he and Juke had checked out Abe while pretending to check out the roof, they'd never gone inside Opal's house. Still, Wally had already formed an impression of the place: basic, adequate construction (assuming no crooks were involved) limited by the standards of when it was built. Rim foundation and pier blocks. You could bet on shallow footings. No shear-wall bracing, no hold-downs whatsoever. Probably no bolts in the mudsills. She'd better have earthquake insurance. Part of the kitchen looked like an addition. The tip-off was a change in the sizing of the exposed rafter-ends, about an eighth of an inch, which jumped out at Wally but would pass unnoticed by most people. Cracks in the stucco, nothing serious. Single garage, door rotting at the bottom. Aluminum windows aging badly. A low-end house in a high-end neighborhood, ripe for an upgrade, good profit potential.

To Wally's surprise, a little boy just able to reach the doorknob answered the chimes and stared up without saying a word. In the air wafted the wet scent of lavender shampoo.

"You must be Ronny." As Wally spoke, two golden retrievers dashed between his legs, knocking him against the jamb. The dogs raced down the driveway and into the street.

Opal walked barefoot into the room wearing a blue bathrobe, hair wrapped in a blue towel. With a frown at Wally, she said, "Why'd you let the dogs out?"

Running, Wally caught up with the first dog about a block away. "Come!" Wally called, hoping the animal was trained. Apparently it wasn't or else it was choosing to forget, and also it didn't fall for the make-a-fist-as-if-I've-got-a-treat-for-you trick, either. Not even the kneel-down-and-scratch-the-ground-as-if-there's-something-interesting-and-you'd-better-check-it-out trick. But when Wally threw an empty 7UP can, the dog cheerfully retrieved it, prancing to Wally with can between teeth. Wally grabbed the collar as Opal drove up in the Subaru with Ronny buckled into the front seat. Barefoot, she had shed the towel wrap but was still wearing the blue bathrobe, which gaped open as she leaned forward. Wally tried, unsuccessfully, not to look at her breasts.

"Leary!" Opal called. "Good boy. Get in."

Timothy was a tougher case. He loved pursuit. They finally caught up with the dog at a playground where he had stopped to help two boys who were digging tunnels in a sandbox.

Once again, Wally found himself on a blanket in the rear of a Subaru with two golden retrievers who were wagging their tails and taking turns dispensing excess saliva—this time mixed with sand—over his face while Opal drove the mile back to her house. "We have to stop meeting like this," Opal said.

Wally laughed, a mistake in that it seemed to signal the dogs to increase their lathering—though just about everything seemed a signal to slobber. It was the laughter that comes not from the head but from playing with dogs and children, the kind that wells up from the belly, a joy Wally hadn't felt in what seemed like years. In a cloud of lavender plus another more pungent odor, he made no effort to hold off the dogs as the sandy slime thickened over his cheeks and nose and lips and chin.

Opal's eyes met Wally's in the rear view mirror. She said, "I hope Timothy didn't find any cat poop in that sandbox. Because, you know, he eats it."

Back in the house, Opal excused herself so she could get dressed. Glancing at the framed photos on the walls—hey, she was pretty good—and noting the quality furniture—was that an actual Eames chair?—Wally found his way to the kitchen where he washed his face with the sprayer in the sink. Ronny and the two dogs followed his every step, three faces gazing up at him.

Dabbing his cheeks with a paper towel, Wally crouched down to the level of the three faces and said, "Hi, my name is Wally." He held out his unbandaged left hand. The two dogs each lifted a paw for a handshake. Ronny just looked puzzled.

"You know how to shake hands?" Wally asked. "The dogs can. See?" Wally shook hands with Timothy, then Leary. Timothy was smaller with white tips on his ears.

Solemnly, without a word, Ronny held out his left hand. Just as solemnly, Wally shook it.

"You know why people shake hands? To show trust. Because if you touch somebody, and they touch you, it means you trust each other enough to do that. You have any idea what I'm talking about? You know what trust is, Ronny?"

Ronny said nothing. If Opal had puppy eyes, Ronny's were like a puppy cartoon. Same dense hair only softer, a lighter shade, tawny brindled with chestnut.

"What's that on your face?" Wally placed his hand in front of Ronny, pinched the nose, and then withdrew his hand in the shape of a fist with the tip of a thumb protruding between two fingers. "Oh, it's your nose," Wally said. "I've got your nose in my hand."

Ronny said nothing, but his eyes grew wide.

"Here, let me put it back," Wally said. He ended the move with a tweak of Ronny's real nose, and the boy giggled.

"Gotcha," Wally said.

Ronny said nothing, but he was grinning.

"That's how you teach trust?" Opal said. She'd thrown on a turtleneck and blue jeans. Earrings and a bracelet, each of turquoise. She was leaning against the doorway to the kitchen, arms folded. To Wally she looked arty, casual, approachable, with freckles, honest wrinkles, unfussy hair, decent padding—not a model's body, but a human one.

"Guy bonding thing, you know, stealing noses," Wally said as he stood up in front of the sink. "Trust was the subtext. Noses were the metaphor."

"You tricked him."

"You're angry?"

"I might be." Opal opened a heavy, clunky, sliding glass door—leaning, heaving with her entire body—and shooed the dogs into the yard. A fenced yard.

"But he liked it. And that's what games are all about. To learn the hard stuff without being cruel."

"You a teacher?"

"Was. High school."

"Shop?"

"No. English."

"Ooh la la."

"That's French."

"You know what I meant."

"Yes." Wally smiled. "English to construction. How far the mighty have fallen."

"So that's why you don't talk like a contractor."

"How do contractors talk?"

"They don't say 'subtext.' Or 'metaphor.' Why'd you quit? The money?"

"Didn't quit. I loved teaching. They fired me because I tried to talk one of my students out of joining the Army." Wally shook his head. "And you know what? He's career Army. We still keep in touch."

"You've got that thing. That good teacher thing. With kids. I like the way you don't talk down to Ronny. What about teenagers? Do they talk to you?"

"Of course they talk to me."

"Well, they don't talk to me. Not even my own son most of the time. And is that what brings you to my house? Has Abe screwed up already?"

"Abe's doing fine."

"Really? Something physical? He's doing 'fine'?"

"I like his hustle. Good attitude. As for skills, well, not yet. But I'm here about the estimate. For the roof? I've got some numbers."

"You're kidding."

"You really do need some work on that roof. Just as you need to tighten the hinge on the front door—that's why it doesn't latch right—and you need some blocking under that soft spot in the entry floor—or else it's termites. You've got nail pops on that wall. The wheels are broken on that sliding glass door, which is why you had to put your whole body into opening it, and you might consider updating it with something more—"

"Would you shut up?"

"Huh?"

"What are you thinking? You walk in here and start criticizing everything?"

"I walk in a house, I look around. Second nature."

"Well then, don't you dare go into my bathroom. I couldn't afford it."

"Guess I started off on the wrong foot here."

"And which foot would that be?"

"The one in my mouth. I was just trying to help. Let me fix that hinge. No charge. Okay?" Without waiting for an answer, Wally hustled— almost ran—to the front entry, checked to make sure the dogs were still in the yard, then opened the door. From his pocket Wally removed a Leatherman tool, unfolded the Phillips-head screwdriver, and started tightening the top hinge. Ronny had followed, silently observing. When the top hinge was tight, Wally crouched and loosened the bottom hinge enough to allow him to slip a few business cards behind it as spacers, then retighten. "Okay Ronny, see if you can close the door now."

Without a word, Ronny pushed the door closed.

With a solid click, the latch popped into place.

"We fixed it, Ronny. Gimme five."

Confused, Ronny held out his hand for a handshake. Smiling, Wally shook it.

Coming up from behind, Opal tousled Ronny's hair. "Good job, Ron."

There was an awkward silence. Wally knew he should leave now, but he didn't want to.

Opal squeezed Ronny's shoulder. "So what do you think, Ronny? Do we need a new roof? Should we let this nose-stealer state his case? And invite him to stay for hamburgers and salad?"

Big-eyed, Ronny said nothing.

"That's a yes," Opal interpreted. "You a carnivore?"

"Omnivore. Can I help? Is Abe here? Is he coming?"

"Abe left me a message about going out with somebody in your crew. Actually, I assumed it was you."

"Nope." Wally searched his memory for an image of who Abe had been hanging with after the belt sander races, but he drew a blank. *Steamboat,* he hoped. *Not Juke.* Abe wasn't ready for Juke.

Opal was pulling vegetables out of the bottom drawer of the refrigerator, passing them to Wally. "You want a beer?"

"No."

Opal placed thumb and index finger over her eyelids, breathing in, breathing out. Going inward. Wally had noticed that tendency— she'd done it in his kitchen. Opening her eyes, she handed Wally a few radishes and said, "Abe's graduation is tomorrow. Did he tell you he's the valedictorian? I'm so proud."

Please, Lord, don't let it be Juke. Out loud, Wally said, "Wouldn't it be better with the door opening on the left?"

"The fridge? It came this way."

"You know it's reversible?"

"Would you *stop?*"

"No charge."

While Opal cooked, Wally reversed the hinges on the refrigerator door. He also tightened the handle on the kitchen faucet, replaced a light bulb that had broken off and become stuck in its socket, mounted an over-the-stove spice rack that Opal had bought but never installed, and adjusted the latch of the door to the under-sink cabinet so it would close all the way. Without a word, Ronny followed his every step, carrying Wally's Leatherman and, when asked, helping Wally select the smallest screw from a box of assorted sizes.

Finally as they sat eating hamburgers, Ronny spoke to Wally: "Big band-aid."

"Yeah, I got, uh, hurt by a nail," Wally said.

Ronny looked blank.

"You don't know what a nail is?"

Ronny shook his head.

"Mom," Wally said, "every boy should know what a nail is."

"Go ahead."

So for a demonstration Wally fetched from his truck a few eight-penny nails, scraps of one-by-four pine, and a hammer—just the little sixteen-ounce finish nailer, the Estwing with a steel handle, blue rubber grip, nice balance, always felt good in his hand. Since the accident, Wally hadn't used his favorite, a twenty-four-ounce Vaughn California Framer with a wooden handle, comfortable and intuitive as if an extension of his arm—but only his right arm. Hammering with his left hand, Wally felt like a clumsy amateur, but it was good enough for show and tell. Ronny then tried a few taps, grabbing the Estwing with both of his little hands plus guidance from Wally who never for a moment let go, not even when in the middle of steering Ronny's swing Wally glanced up at Opal and saw an expression on her face that spoke of soft thoughts, long term.

Seventeen

Abe was a little worried about Juke. Only a little. It was hard to worry about anything after six shots of tequila, which was six more than he'd ever had in his life before this night. The waitress, who had clearly been sampling the merchandise, had asked to see Abe's ID and after staring at it blearily served whatever he ordered just as Juke had said she would. Two senoritas in thongs were dancing on the bar. Their headlights were small but the tailfins were ample. Juke was tossing dollars on the bar and pointing at Abe. One of the dancers, crouching, backing up, wiggling, still backing up, picking up the dollars from the bar and still backing up—backed right into Abe's face and buried it between golden, quivering thighs.

Juke whooped. "You see this guy? His name is Forkface. And you know what? He just got his face forked!"

From a table in the corner, a man with a smile like steel was waving two women toward where Abe and Juke were sitting. One was short and round in a low-cut blouse with plenty of jiggle. She gave Abe a smile as she sat down beside him. "You order me dreenk?"

"Coming up. Uh, *si. Que bonita.*"

"*Te gusta?*"

"*Si. Muy gusta.*"

She laughed at his bad grammar. More jiggles.

Another thing Abe had never done in his life before this night: talk to a whore. And he was wondering: If sex is giving, what besides money can you give to a prostitute?

The other woman was sitting cross-legged next to Juke. She was pouty-lipped, angry-eyed, and skinny except for the outline of a pair of amazing mounds with the clear outline of nipple like the nose of twin Buicks defying gravity within her halter top. No jiggling there. "We wanna make a forkin' donation," Juke said as he folded some paper money, "to the forkin' Community Chest!"

Somewhere in the depths of Abe's brain was the thought that he might be better off leaving this place and pulling Juke along too. But tequila number seven was clouding the thought even more and, besides, Miss Jiggling Bonita with her fingertip was drawing circles up and down his thigh.

Eighteen

Opal could see that once they had shared the hammering, Ronny and Wally were bonded for life. Or at least Ronny was. She wondered if carpenters who had hammered together were like soldiers who had fought in battle together, where men of wildly different backgrounds became lifetime brothers. Probably not. Anyway, there was no stopping it when after dinner Ronny insisted that Wally see his wooden building blocks and help him make a house. Ronny's idea, it turned out, was to nail the blocks together, but Wally was successful in nudging the project into a more conventional piling of blocks one on top of another, embellishing the structure with an arbor, deck, hot tub, and—why not?—a backyard race track where matchbox cars could *vroom vroom vroom!* and *crash crash crash!*

"He's so wound up, I'll never get him to bed without a good long bath," Opal said.

Ronny hugged Wally's knee. "You baff!" he screamed.

"I'd like to help," Wally said, "but you see, Ronny, I'm not allowed in your bathroom."

"Oh all right," Opal said. "Just don't notice anything."

Opal drew the water and helped Ronny out of his clothes. Wally sat on the toilet lid.

Standing in the water, bubbles up to his thighs, Ronny said, "You go."

"He likes to bathe alone," Opal explained.

"Wally stay."

Opal froze. Brainlock.

Wally was waiting.

"Wally stay!"

Opal's body was trembling. "I hate this," she said. "I hate that I even think these thoughts. What a world we've come to live in."

"I'll leave," Wally said.

"No. You can stay. I'll wash the dishes."

"We'll, uh, leave the door open."

"Thank you," Opal said. "I'm sorry. It's not about you."

"It's okay."

Loading the dishwasher, she could hear giggles and splashing and occasional raucous laughter, both high and low voices. When she returned to the bath, Wally discreetly stepped out.

"Wally stay!"

"I'm going to dry you," Opal said.

"I'd better go," Wally said.

"It's fine for you to hang around," Opal said. "We still haven't talked about the, you know, the estimate. If you can just wait a few minutes."

"Sure. I'd like to ...go over the estimate."

A few minutes became a half hour of dressing in footie pajamas and reading a story and tucking Ronny under covers. She was feeling guilty about keeping Wally waiting when she returned to the living room.

Wally was sanding a rough spot on the stair rail. "Hope you don't mind," he said. "And I ran a knife blade around the edge of that window? The one that was painted shut?"

"Thank you. So what about the bathroom?"

"I didn't notice."

"Yes, you did. Why is the paint crumpling up in that corner by the tub?"

"Rot. Wall's rotten. So's the floor. That's why it's bouncy and soft. You'll have to pull the tub."

Opal kicked the wainscoting below the stairs. There were thousands of dollars expressed in that kick. "God damn you," she said.

"Sorry." Wally continued sanding.

"You're probably wondering about his father. How they get along."

"Actually, I wasn't." Wally squatted on the stair so he could see where he was rubbing on the underside of the rail.

From above, Opal could see that the hair gathered into Wally's gray ponytail was covering a bald spot. Or at least, a thin spot. She said, "I have full custody. But it's not what you think."

"I wasn't thinking anything."

"He's a brilliant man. He never hurt Ronny in any way."

Wally stood again, moved up a step, continued sanding. "Ronny seems like a healthy all-American boy."

"A little slow in speech development. I try not to worry about it."

"But you do."

"He's been evaluated. Within normal range. That is, low end of normal. We just have to wait. But this isn't about Ron. We need to talk."

"Okay." Wally stopped sanding. "I really did bring an estimate."

"Not that. We need to, like, talk."

"Okay."

She took a breath, turning inward.

Wally waited.

After a moment, she launched: "I feel safe with you. Like I can open up to you. You interest me. And you wouldn't still be here sanding my stair rail if you weren't, you know, interested too. We're grown-ups. We can admit these things. And it's such a bonus that Ronny likes you. You're such a departure from ...where I've always put myself. I have a history of being attracted to brilliant men. Difficult men. Dazzling intellects, social defects. I always thought I could fix them. My own little rehab projects. Sort of like what you do, only with people." A quick smile. "Are you dangerously attracted to brilliant houses?"

"No."

"I don't know how to say this." Opal searched for the words.

"That I'm not brilliant?"

"You're not difficult. And your social defects are mostly within the normal range."

"Mostly?"

"Low end of normal. Okay? Don't distract me. I'm trying to, you know, talk."

Wally waited, sanded a small spot, waited again.

Opal grabbed a baluster, one in each hand. She was staring down at her feet. "I just don't know how to say this."

"That sentence never comes before good—"

"I don't do sex."

"Huh?"

Now she could look at him. "I just don't. Won't. Anymore."

Wally sighed. "Did I make another pass? I'm sorry if I—"

"No. It's nothing you said. Although, let's face it, this whole evening has been one giant pass. By both of us. I mean if you look at everything people do as either pass or not-pass. Which I don't. But it's nothing you did, exactly. I mean it's not your fault. This is new policy. Experimental. And I know I'm jumping ahead but I just wanted to warn you. Obviously it's not like I've never done sex. And not just regular, you know, but all the, you know, icky stuff. Maybe I should say I don't do sex well. Maybe I'm giving you some insight about why I'm divorced. Twice. Anyway I wanted to warn you even if it means standing here humiliating myself. And no, I'm not HIV positive. This isn't about that. Or any disease.

And I'm not incapable of the big O. Just so you know. I must sound totally bizarre."

"Not totally." Wally shook his head. "Low end of bizarre." He sat down on the stairs. "Wow." The balusters separated them. "I'm sorry." He started sanding a knob of wood without looking at it. "I wish I could say something. To make you feel better."

"I feel okay. Really I do."

"I was attracted to you from the moment—honest to God—when I was still hanging from that nail. I wish—" He stopped sanding. "Should I go now?"

"Do you want to go?"

"No."

"Then stay."

They were face to face, balusters between, Wally with sandpaper in the left hand, fingertips—she noticed—twitching from the tip of the bandage on the right. Impulsively Opal reached through the balusters for the bandaged hand and held it, softly, between both of hers, feeling fingertips twitching between her palms as if she'd caught a butterfly.

For a moment, they were quiet. Cradling, she thought. What I'm doing is the *meaning* of cradling.

Wally broke the silence: "When you hold it like that, the pain goes away."

"You mean it hurts all the time? It's been hurting ever since the accident?"

"Well, yeah."

"How do you stand it?"

"Hey, I'm in construction."

"So?"

"Pain is like noise. Comes with the job."

"That's sad."

"Not sad. Like dust and stinky porta-johns. You get used to it."

"That's awful. You're so much better than that. Couldn't you go back to teaching?"

"It's been thirty years."

"But you shouldn't be doing this."

"Hey." He withdrew his hand. "It's not like I'm wasting my life."

"You said, 'How far the mighty have fallen.'"

"I was joking."

"But you're a natural teacher. You can actually talk to teens. That's magic. And you said you loved it."

"I'm also a good builder. Why don't people honor labor? What's so bad about working with your hands?"

"You didn't say you love it."

"I like the craft. The business, well, it's business. And what do you mean I'm 'better than that'? Better than a construction worker? What's wrong with construction workers? Are they bad people?"

"Yes!" Immediately Opal put her hand to her mouth.

Wally gaped.

"Only one," Opal said. "Sorry. I guess I generalized."

"Which one?"

"Nothing. Nobody. Never mind." Opal brightened. "Is this our first fight? Wow, we move fast. I mean we've barely met, and already we've not had sex."

Wally snorted.

"I mean," she said, "I couldn't have made myself more vulnerable. And you handled it pretty well."

Wally smiled. "Low end of pretty well."

"Were you a drug addict?"

Wally's smile vanished. "You keep surprising me."

"Were you?"

The fingertips were twitching again. "*Addict* is pretty strong," Wally said. "I never hit absolute bottom. Dependent, let's say, if I may draw that distinction. Amphetamines. Clean for years."

"So that would be after teaching, before construction."

"During construction. Unfortunately."

"Which is why—now—you won't take painkillers. You don't even drink beer. You didn't say, 'No, thank you.' It was just, 'No.' And no bottles in that junkyard of a kitchen, either."

"You were checking?"

"I walk in a house, I look around. Second nature." She smiled. Got him. "And the letters to your wife. They help. With that."

"Yes."

"She got you through it. And kept you straight. And stayed with you even in the hardest part."

"Yes."

Taking his fingertips into her hand again, she said, "God, I admire her."

"Me too."

The conversation moved to easier topics. About her photos, a series she seemed to be accumulating, pictures she'd taken of people at their barbecues. She liked the smoke, the casual dress, the folks at ease.

"Barbecues of California," Wally said, "The fearless, ground-breaking exhibition. What's your goal here, Opal? You want to put them in a gallery? Publish a book?"

"No goal," Opal answered. "It's just a hobby. I'm not ambitious. I don't define myself through my work."

"How do you define yourself?"

Opal shrugged. "A lot of women, I guess they define themselves through their men. I guess I tried that a couple times." Opal thought a moment. "I define myself through my children. My brilliant, wonderful children."

"Indeed they are."

At 11:45 Wally was still there. He'd explained his concept of the poetry of everyday life. He said there'd probably been a poem in that conversation they had at the stairs. It's when you explain the simple things, the basic stuff, that you make poetry. Especially when you talk to children:

This is a nail.
One end is sharp
and is called the point.
Be careful or it will poke you.
The flat part on top
is called the head.
When you strike it with
a hammer the nail goes
into the wood
like this.

"That's not poetry," Opal said. "That's just stuff."

"Get used to it," Wally said. "I'm not brilliant, remember? Here, try this one. Something I heard myself saying to my son, long time ago." He scribbled with awkward left-hand penmanship on a sheet of paper:

Wind is air that is moving.
It shakes the leaves in the trees.
It bends the grass in the field.
Wind pushes the clouds across the sky
and blows the hair
that tickles your face.

They never got around to the estimate for the roof repair. They did talk about the perfect house, how it wouldn't be anything Wally built for somebody else, especially not for somebody like Krainer, who believed that a perfect house could be created by perfect construction. Wally knew compromise. Lumber is imperfect. So is paint. So, even, are concrete, glass, and steel. Different egos—and different finances—demand different levels of compromise. But in the end, through imperfect materials installed by imperfect tradesmen you may create the perfect home. Perfect for somebody, somewhere. Like the one Wally had always been planning to build for himself if he ever got the time and the money and, lately, the motivation.

"What would motivate you now?"

"Somebody to share it with."

Wally wondered if they would kiss goodnight, or kiss at all. Is kissing "doing sex"? And what about hugging? She'd held his hand, so touching was okay. Or was it only okay if she initiated it? What were the rules? Who in her life had been through a twelve-step program? Had she been raped? Molested? Was she simply bored with sex? Could they actually be lovers without sex? Did he want that? Would it be weird? Could they ever live together? Sleep together? Get used to each other naked?

So much for seduction. And she was wrong, Wally decided, in what she'd told Abe. A guy who fixes things isn't seductive to her. A guy who has rapport with her children, a guy who gives one kid a job and the other a bath, that's the guy.

Opal, meanwhile, wasn't worrying about seductions or sex. She too had felt an instant attraction for Wally when he was still hanging from a nail. Fortunately she'd already snapped the photo, because from the first moment of eye-to-eye contact her mind had been altered. She had fallen into another adventure. Not love, she hoped, but something: fondness, maybe. She only knew one way to love somebody—fully and without reserve. Twice, it had ended horribly. There was something wrong with her, some blind spot to what should be obvious or some craving for what she should not have. Not this time. She wouldn't let it happen. And anyway, Wally's wife had set the bar so high, no one could possibly compete. They could be friends. Possibly he could love her, but it would be love with an asterisk, a love that for Opal wasn't enough. She could never be the love of his life. The role was taken.

They were watching a DVD of *Sullivan's Travels*, Opal's all-time favorite movie. Wally had never seen it. They needed a break from talking. Opal was on the sofa with a dog on each side of her, a glass of Chablis on the Corbusier coffee table, Wally in the Eames dozing off even though the chair was less comfortable than it appeared. And then the phone rang.

It was the police. About Abe.

Nineteen

On stage under bright afternoon sun, Abe tried not to slouch in the folding chair. Rachel, his co-valedictorian and ex-girlfriend, stood at the podium giving her speech. Sitting on top of the podium was a big green watermelon, a playful gift to a normally unplayful young woman. Rachel was being honored for organizing a watermelon-smashing contest that had raised $5,862 for charity (and cost the school $200 in overtime cleanup expenses).

Among the two thousand victims of broiling sunshine and predictable rhetoric were Abe's mother and father. Ex-father. They would be sitting separately. Also out there somewhere, at Abe's last-minute invitation, would be Wally and possibly other members of Wally's crew, maybe even Juke. Ah, Juke. Abe had some pressing questions for that maniac.

From where Abe was placed, the angle of the sun made it impossible to determine who was who in the audience but very possible to see a silhouette of Rachel's body backlit through the fabric of her dress. Abe did not at this moment want to be reminded of the perfect shape of Rachel's ass. He wondered if Dr. Schwartz, the principal seated two chairs away, could also see it. Hard to say, since Schwartzie was hiding behind dark sunglasses and an expressionless face like some South American general. He might even be asleep. Or dead.

Which was where Abe wished himself to be. Asleep, that is. He already felt half dead. The pulsating pain in his head might be coming from the tequila of last night or it might be coming from the dozens of stainless-steel surgical staples that the hospital's emergency-room doctor had shot from a white staple gun into Abe's scalp after Abe had walked headfirst through a motel window. Or had he been thrown? The jury was still out on that one.

Rachel was thanking the usual suspects for inspiration and guidance: her parents, her grandparents, her favorite teachers, her old calico cat. Not among the thanked was Dr. Schwartz. Abe and Rachel had shared a passion for imagining macabre deaths for old Schwartzie, such as slipping on a watermelon rind and flying airborne to land anus-first on Rachel's violin bow, which would penetrate his body and come out his mouth with little pieces of gut hanging from it. This was Rachel's favorite. Frida Kahlo reprise, she called it. She had a nicely bent sense of humor, that wench, as well as a perfect ass. Abe's loss would be Amherst's gain.

It was Wally who'd come to fetch Abe from the emergency room, Wally who'd spoken with the cop, Wally whom his mother sent as a substitute because she needed to stay home with Ronny.

"So she called you at midnight?"

"She asked me, yeah."

A soft bandage, growing damper by the minute, covered the right side of Abe's head. Part of the dampness was sweat caused by the brutal sun but most was from "leakage," as Wally had called it, quoting the doctor. The bandage would need to be changed a few times for the first couple of days. After that, he'd look a little "orange peely" and need to be "delicate" in brushing his hair. At least they hadn't shaved him, though he'd lost a few divots as they dug out the shards of motel window. The Novocain they'd used had long since worn off, at least on the outside. Could it still be numbing the inside, the part that was supposed to be thinking? Competing with the scalp, aching more by the minute was Abe's neck. He'd suffered whiplash when his head struck the window. Basically, Abe knew he had no business being up on that stage—much less trying to give a speech—when he was nauseous, shaky, in deep pain, and profoundly in need of sleep.

When Wally had entered the emergency cubicle where Abe had been left alone lying on a gurney with his head in bandages, Wally's first words weren't "How are you?" or "What happened?" but rather "Were you with Juke?"

"Yes."

"Where is he?"

"Dunno."

"Do the police know?"

"Know what?"

"That you were with Juke."

"No."

"Good. Don't tell them. Please. Okay?"

"Uh. Okay."

"What have you told them?"

"I told them my head hurt and I was going to throw up."

"That's all?"

"Then I threw up. Forever. It just kept coming."

"Do you know what happened?"

"No."

"You went through a motel window. From the inside to the outside. Do you know why?"

"No."

"Your blood alcohol was point two five. What were you drinking?"

"Tequila."

"Was there a woman?"

"Two."

"What did they tell the police?"

"Nothing. They disappeared. Like Juke."

"Good."

"I got my face forked."

"At a bar?"

"Yeah."

"Let me guess. Juke took you to the Papaya. Right?"

"Yeah."

"You like it?"

"I dunno."

Schwartzie had already scrutinized and approved the words that were written on the sheet of paper in Abe's hands, as he had also approved the speech of Rachel. In addition Dr. Schwartz had taken Abe aside and warned him in no uncertain terms that he must not make any changes to the text, and in particular there would be no mention of the stinking mound of that, uh, that animal excrement that unknown person or persons had placed on the middle of Schwartzie's office desk just minutes before a visit by the superintendent of schools. And should the identity of the perpetrator or perpetrators of that prank become known—and Dr. Schwartz had a definite hunch of who it might be—word would be sent to the admissions office at Princeton, which still had the option of rescinding Abe's acceptance.

Abe wondered if Princeton might be more amused than shocked by the incident, especially if they learned the details, the exquisite execution of the plan of attack. But you never know. It surprised Abe that Dr. Schwartz had never identified the "animal excrement" as bat guano, ten gallons' worth. Abe was certain of the exact volume because he had carried it in two five-gallon plastic buckets. Amazing how heavy it was, ten gallons of turds.

Regardless of Schwartzie's warning, in the small section of brain that was still functioning Abe was composing a new speech:

Friends, parents, faculty, and fellow graduates: Greetings. It is an honor to stand before you. I would like to thank my mother for her inspiration and guidance, and I would like to thank my estranged (and very strange) father for finding the time to show up today.

Nah. Would they listen to some science dork settling grudges? They'd be thinking, Shut up you lucky shit.

Polite applause. Rachel, watermelon tucked under one arm, was taking her seat. Schwartzie made the introduction.

Abe rose unsteadily from the chair. One step, two, three, to the podium. Look at all those faces.

Abe unfolded the paper and smoothed the crease. There were words down there, but he couldn't see them. And he didn't care. He felt dizzy, overheated, almost out of his body, observing from above.

Abe placed his hands on the podium for balance, leaned toward the microphone, clearing his throat.

Good afternoon.

Now what? Drilling into the back of his head, Abe felt the cold stare of Dr. Schwartz. In front of him were a couple of thousand restless bodies, overdressed, hot, praying for brevity.

After twelve years in a classroom, I took a job last week on a construction crew. I found that my grade point average didn't make a lot of difference. Some of the men I work with never even finished high school, and yet they know so much more than me. Now I'm learning a whole new body of knowledge. Physical, practical knowledge. Like the Zen of swinging a hammer. The more you force it the worse the result. Your role is to guide the hammer's own internal force, not to push it. If any of those carpenters are in the audience right now, they're laughing at me because they would never call it Zen. They'd call it banging nails.

I'm learning a new set of laws. They're intended for construction, but they might apply to life in general.

Work safe.

Work smarter, not harder.

What looks simple, isn't.

Measure twice, cut once.

Honor thy tools.

Respect the tree.

You have to get dirty.

Don't leave a mess.
Help your crew.
Slow down and do right.
Build it tight.
Each house is a miracle.

If you've ever built a wall—framed it, sheathed and insulated—and a week ago, I couldn't have told you what sheathing was—if you've ever built a wall and with the help of five other workers tilted it, lifted and nailed it into place with muscle and brain and heart, then you've had a chance to practice each of those laws.

Abe was getting dizzy. Splotches of vibrant color were floating before his eyes. He'd better wrap it up. Stay focused. Maybe one more thing.

> I'm learning new units of measurement. I always knew that a hair was a unit of measure—like, 'That board is too long by a hair'—but did you know that a pussy hair is a smaller unit? And a red pussy hair is the smallest unit of all?
> And there are other laws, stuff about how to work, like Get wasted *after* work, not that you have to get wasted, but when you do, and I just learned something about that ...

Suddenly Abe was no longer in front of the microphone. Dr. Schwartz had shoved him aside. Which was just as well, really. If he stood there one more minute, he was going to faint. Abe turned and staggered back to his folding chair. There was no applause. *Blew it, made a complete ass of myself, Schwartzie's mad, and I don't care.* With his sleeve, Abe wiped sweat from his forehead. Colored splotches continued to dance. Placing hands in lap, he tried to stay conscious and tried not to slouch.

Dr. Schwartz returned to his seat, scowling at Abe. The commencement speaker, a graduate of Silicon High just fifteen years ago, now a venture capitalist and a billionaire and thus a very wise man, began his speech.

Warm fingers touched the back of Abe's hand. It was Rachel, sitting beside him, watermelon on lap. "What do you mean," she whispered, "about respecting the tree? Don't you destroy trees to make lumber?"

"Not now," Abe whispered. "Please."

"What happened to you?"

"Went through a window."

"Head first?"

"I think so."

"Why?"

"I'm not sure."

"Where?"

"The Pirate."

"The motel? Isn't that a dump?"

"I didn't notice."

"What were you doing at the Pirate?"

"I'm not sure."

Strands of Rachel's black hair had caught in the sweat of her face, clinging to her brow and temples. She was studying Abe with an expression he knew well, a look of total focus and absolute sincerity. She whispered: "I used to think you had secret virtues."

"Sorry."

"Schwartzie's pissed."

"Yeah."

Rachel leaned closer. "Too bad he didn't get electrocuted by the microphone. Lightning strikes the PA system. I liked your speech, actually."

"You're the only one."

"It started better than it finished."

"Rachel, I miss you so much." At that moment Abe couldn't look at her. He looked out over the audience wondering how many people had been watching him and Rachel whispering to each other instead of paying attention to the speaker, who at least had the sense to tell self-deprecating jokes.

Now Abe could look at her. She was staring at him, wide-eyed. He leaned toward her—and her eyes widened even farther—and he whispered, "That's what I should've done in my speech: tell self-deprecating jokes."

Rachel nodded, blinking. "There's a lot you could deprecate." She swiped hair from the side of her face and tucked it behind her ear. Then she smiled. "Really, Abe, the beginning of your speech was not ungood."

He smiled back. "I am not unthankful to you for saying that. Something else I learned—left out of the speech—and I think maybe I'm starting to understand it now: The better you give, the better you get."

Shifting her position, sitting up straight, catching the watermelon just before it rolled off her lap, Rachel looked out over the audience and whispered, "What are you doing after the ceremony?"

"Sleeping."

"I've got family stuff," Rachel whispered. "Grandparents taking us out to dinner. But later tonight? Can I see you?"

"What for? So you can deprecate me?"

"Well if you don't want to see me ..."

"Please. Rachel. You want to come over to my house?"

"Okay."

"I could show you how to frame a round tower."

Rachel tucked another sweaty strand of hair behind her ear. Still gazing out over the audience, frowning, she whispered, "I think I already know how to do that."

Twenty

Degrees bestowed, speeches speechified, ceremony ended, Wally approached—and stood just outside—the conversational group in front of the stage: Dr. Schwartz, Opal, Ronny, Abe, and a wild man. The wild man had long stringy hair hanging down his back and an equally long stringy beard hanging down his front with what appeared to be bits of bread crumbs stuck in his mustache. Abe's father, no doubt. The first ex. A brilliant man. He was wearing a suit and tie, pants that were too short, one black sock and one navy blue, and good leather shoes with one knot unraveled. He was resting a hand familiarly on Abe's shoulder, though Abe looked as if he wished he could sidle away and hide. Opal looked tense but determinedly friendly. Ronny was shielding himself behind Opal's legs.

Dr. Schwartz was apparently at the end of an explanation for why he had cut Abe's speech short, to which the parents were both agreeing that he had done the appropriate thing.

"I should add," the wild man was saying, "the lessons Abe has drawn from construction are not without merit. And Abe has already shown a proclivity for certain manual labor. In my garage he—"

"Uh," Abe began, "let's not—"

"Just a minute, Abe. In the loft over my garage Abe worked an entire weekend—"

"I really don't think Dr. Schwartz wants to hear—"

"He worked an entire weekend removing bat droppings that had accumulated over a period of neglect. The sheer volume—and the wretched stench—of several years of bat droppings is truly remarkable."

"That's very interesting," said Dr. Schwartz. "When was this?"

"Years ago," Abe said.

"About two months ago," the wild man said.

"And," Dr. Schwartz asked, "how did you dispose of this fetid pile?"

Abe glared into Schwartzie's sunglasses as he said, "I found a place that was worthy."

"A pleasure to meet you all," Dr. Schwartz said coldly. "And Abe, we'll be in touch." Abruptly, Dr. Schwartz moved on.

"Hello, everybody," Wally said, stepping forward. "How you doing, Ronny? Congratulations, Abe."

"I'm so glad you could come," Opal said. At the sight of him, Opal visibly brightened. Ronny came half way out from behind Opal, smiling, and held out his hand.

Wally bent low as if bowing and shook Ronny's hand.

The wild man frowned. "And who is this?"

"I'm Wally," Wally said, straightening. "I'm the one Abe is working for this summer. And you must be Abe's father. Congratulations, sir. Abe is a fine young man."

The wild man's frown deepened. "I'm the one *for whom* Abe is working this summer."

"No," Wally said, grinning. "Actually, I am." He winked.

The wild man turned to Opal and said, "This is him? This idiot? Our son is in the hospital and instead of his father you call a *carpenter*?"

Opal folded her arms across her chest. "It was easier," she said, and she turned to Wally. "Wally, this is Aaron. Abe's father. As I guess you can tell."

"Pleased to meet you," Wally said.

Ignoring Wally, Aaron said to Opal: "Easier? One phone call. Either you dial his number or you dial mine. It's the same area code. What is it—do you have him on speed dial?"

"I didn't have to dial," Opal said, arms firmly folded.

"He was there? At—what time was it? Midnight? He was in our house at midnight? You were in bed?"

"No no. In a chair."

"You were doing it in a chair?"

"*Separate* chairs. It's not what you think—"

"And Ronny was there?"

"Yes. Of course. Ronny was there—in his bedroom—sleeping. That's why I couldn't go to the hospital."

Without another word, Aaron turned and walked away.

"He was there at midnight?" Abe said.

"We were watching a movie," Opal said, blushing, flustered. "*Sullivan's Travels*. And I repeat: in *separate* chairs. I'll never lie to you, Abe."

"Yeah. Okay. Whatever. I guess it's none of my business."

"In a way it is your business," Opal said. "That's part of being a family. I'm sorry, Abe. I wanted to ease into this gradually."

"Ease into what?"

"This—um—relationship. Wally and me."

Abe scowled. "So you have a *relationship*?"

"A friendship. Yes."

Abe glared at his mother. Wally smiled.

"Could we please go home?" Abe said. "I'm about to collapse."

"You need a hand?" Wally asked, slipping an arm under Abe's shoulders.

"Get away!" Abe shook him off. "Don't touch me. Or her."

"Sorry."

Opal looked sickened. "Come over later," she said.

"Don't," Abe said.

"Wally, please come over later," Opal said. "I'm going to need some help."

"Would you permit that, Abe?" Wally asked.

Abe looked grim. "Request permission to swear, sir."

"Granted."

"Fork you, sir."

"Acknowledged. Now would you allow me to visit your mother this evening?"

"Whatever."

"How about you, Ronny? Is it okay if I come over and visit this evening?"

Ronny said nothing. His nose twitched.

"That's a yes," Opal interpreted.

At that moment, Abe's eyes rolled heavenward. His knees buckled. Before Abe hit the ground, Wally caught him under the armpits bringing a stab of pain that shot up Wally's right arm. Wally dropped to his knees, holding Abe from behind, arms wrapped around Abe's chest.

Abe opened his eyes. "What happened?"

"You blacked out," Wally said.

"We're not fighting? That's not why you're holding me?"

"No."

"Then let go."

Wally withdrew his hands and arms.

Still on his knees, Abe swayed to one side, then straightened himself. Cautiously, he rose to a standing position.

Wally remained on his knees. The pain in his wrist was asserting itself. Looking up at Abe, feeling momentarily and strangely like a supplicant, Wally said, "Can you walk to your car?"

"Yes."

Wally stood. "I'll follow you."

"Whatever." Abe started shambling toward the parking lot.

Wally trailed him just a step behind.

Suddenly Abe stopped and turned. Wally was so close that he bumped into Abe, almost knocking him over.

"Sorry," Wally said.

"Actually, I'm sorry," Abe said. He placed a hand over the bandage on the side of his head. "I don't know why they call it blacking out. Everything turned red. Then yellow. Splotches. Sort of paisley. I'll probably be less of a jerk tomorrow. Sir. And as for you and my mother and your quote relationship unquote—all I ask is—like—don't you dare hurt her and beyond that, I just really don't want to know about it. A little—you know—discretion is advised."

Twenty-One

Juke felt something hard digging into his hip. Like a nail. Why was there a nail in his bed? Eyes still closed, he rolled onto his back. A puff of breeze lifted a lock of hair from his forehead. Somewhere, a blue jay was squawking. There was a smell of damp sawdust. Slowly, cautiously, Juke opened his eyes.

Sitting cross-legged on a five-gallon bucket, FrogGirl held out a paper cup. "Coffee?" she said.

Juke sat up with a start. Just as quickly, he lay back down on the plywood floor. The pain was directly behind his eyeballs.

"Forkin' shit," Juke said.

"Yeah," FrogGirl said. "Exactly that."

"How did I get here?"

"You drove. Wasted. Asshole. You shouldn't—"

"Was anybody, uh, following me?"

"No. And you were howling."

"Yeah. That happens." Cautiously, Juke stretched first one arm, then the other. "Friend of mine went through a motel window." One at a time, Juke stretched his legs. "You say I drove here?"

"Yes."

"My El Camino—that's what I drove, right? I mean, I didn't take nobody's car, did I?"

"It's a Camino."

"Did I bang it up any? Comin' here?"

"How could anyone tell?"

"Smart ass." Juke smiled. He sat up slowly. "You watchin' me all this time?"

"No. I went to work this morning. It's afternoon now, in case you don't know. You want this coffee? Cappuccino, actually. Cold. Still foamy. But cold."

"Thought you hated coffee."

"It's what I was making when they fired me. It was still in my hand—I noticed it when I got here. Hitchhiked ten miles holding a cup and didn't even know it."

"Forkin' fired?"

"I have 'attitude'."

"No shit."

Now FrogGirl smiled. Quickly, it faded. She said, "Your friend okay?"

"That's what I gotta find out."

FrogGirl frowned. "Let me get this straight. Your friend went through a window? You don't know if he's okay? And you ran away? Note to self: Don't count on this guy."

"Hey. You heard of three strikes?"

"Jeezo. Like, felonies?"

"Yeah. Forkin' jeezo." Juke rubbed the back of his neck. "Don't worry. I ain't violent. Burglary. No handguns. Just tools. And shut up with cops."

"You didn't, huh?"

"Never woulda convicted if I kept my mouth shut. Even if you're innocent. Even if you're framed. Just shut the fork up."

"Noted. So. Speaking of burglary. You know about the trailer?"

Juke jerked to attention. "What about the trailer?"

"I thought you knew. I thought that was why you were howling."

Juke sprang to his feet. In seconds he was down by the open rear door of the trailer. Every tool was gone. Table saw, chop saw, air compressor—gone. Framing guns, shop vac, grinder, even the shovels—all gone. The padlock hung open, undamaged.

"When did this happen?"

"Last night. Before midnight."

"You *watched* them?"

"I was out."

"Out? You said you were watchin' this place."

"I can go out."

"Where?"

"Out. *Daddy*. I don't have to tell you."

"We let you forkin' sleep here and you said you were watchin'—"

"It's cold. It's dark. I go out sometimes. I was at a bookstore. They let you hang out. You don't have to buy anything. I was reading."

"*Reading*? Why?"

"No disrespect, but can you read?"

"They even took the extension cords. Forkin' bastard son of a lesbo dyke bitch."

"What's the matter with lesbians?"

"Every forkin' tool. Son of a—"

"Don't say that again."

"What's your problem?"

"I'm a lesbian."

"Why?"

"What do you mean? There's no why."

"Well I'm a carpenter, and we got a house to build, and some son of a, uh, forkin' asshole just walked away with every—"

"Probably drove away."

"I don't care if he rode off on a forkin' *horse*. Horseforkin' son of a—" Juke squinted. "You want a job?"

"Doing what?"

"Laborer. Carpenter's helper."

"I don't know how."

"Scared?"

"No."

"You start, you're an Alfredo. You carry shit. Dig shit. Clean up shit. Run out and buy shit."

"I can do that."

"You lose the attitude."

"Okay."

"You take orders."

"Okay."

"You call me *sir*."

"Okay. Uh, sir."

"You get dirty."

"Yes, sir."

"You get splinters."

"Yes, sir."

"You hear bad language."

"No shit, sir?"

Suddenly they both smiled.

"Sometimes," Juke said, "I just howl. Don't mean nothin'."

"Coyote was answering you."

"Really? What'd it say?"

"I think it was calling somebody. Raoul! Raoul! You know somebody named Raoul?"

"Useta. And he'd slit your throat if you give him a chance."

"Jeezo. Where'd you meet him?"

"Prison." Juke spat, cleared his throat, spat again as if something was caught in there—like a bad memory. "Now on, you want to swear, you gotta ask permission first."

"Yes, sir."

Juke started walking toward his El Camino. "Gotta call the boss," he said. "Wally's gonna brick a shit."

Twenty-Two

A man's got to carve out a little private space in his life, a little time when the public, especially the business public, can't reach him. Wally had a long-standing policy of ignoring the cell phone on weekends—of not handling any business on weekends. Friends and family knew they had to call his home phone where he had an unlisted number.

Yet he kept the phone in his pocket, switched off.

In the afterglow of graduation, Wally stood by his truck in the parking lot of the high school. Opal, Abe, and Ronny had already departed. Now Wally watched the stream of young men and women, faces he wished he had known, minds he wished he had taught, personalities he wished he had befriended. Such a pleasure lost. Yet he felt happy, just witnessing them. Painstakingly, using the roof of the truck as backing, Wally wrote some thoughts on a sheet of paper. He had a smaller bandage now, so at least he could hold the pen in his right hand, though it was like torture to grip anything.

Words written, Wally flipped open the phone. He was planning to call his son Jaspar and then maybe his younger son, Leo. He wished he could call Sally in Africa too. Just to share his happy feeling. But as soon as the phone powered up, he saw he had fifteen new messages. Fifteen! And immediately it was vibrating with a fresh incoming call from a number he didn't recognize. Against his better judgment, he answered.

"I'm in a great mood," Wally said. "Please don't spoil it."

"Boss?"

Wally sighed. "Yeah, Juke."

"You better come over to the job site. And call the forkin' cops."

"You in trouble?"

"No. Some dipshit got in the trailer. Cleaned us out."

What Wally liked about Juke, among other things, was the "us." The business belonged to Wally—sole proprietor. Juke was just an employee—a lead carpenter, yes, and a partner in the buddy sense but not in the business sense. As long as Wally remained in his right mind, he would never enter into a business with Juke. Not that Wally was doing so well on his own.

"I'm on my way," Wally said.

First, though, Wally stopped at Wells Fargo. Already he was thinking ahead. He'd give some cash to Juke. They'd split up and hit the flea markets on Sunday afternoon. Who knows, he might find his very own tools for sale. More likely, they could pick up a few things so the crew could get started first thing Monday morning. Nothing would be brand new or the latest edition, but good tools stay good. You just have to look for the classics: the Porter Cable 504 belt sander, the Hitachi NR 83A nailer, the Skilsaw 77—or, heck, any wormgear Skil—the Milwaukee Sawzall. Somewhere there ought to be a tool Hall of Fame.

The ATM refused to give him any cash. Questions? Call this number. (A fee will be charged.)

Wally paid the fee and phoned the number where despite it being a weekend a surprisingly pleasant and efficient woman quickly got to the core of the problem. Two checks that Wally had deposited had been returned: Krainer's progress payments.

Abandoning all hope of a private weekend, Wally called in to his voicemail box and listened to pissed-off messages from people who had tried to cash their paychecks late Friday afternoon, including Pancho's: "*Que te la mame tu madre!*" There was also a civil but cool message from the lumberyard asking him to please call back "so we can discuss your account."

Wally called Krainer. To Wally's surprise, Anton answered.

"Your checks bounced."

"Both of them?"

"Yes."

"Oh. I'm sorry."

"You don't sound sorry. And sorry doesn't cut it."

"There's a bit of a cash flow problem."

"You put a stop on those checks, didn't you?"

"Only one."

"I'm pulling my crew. Immediately. And let me remind you, I've got a mechanic's lien on your property."

"Well if you're going to be nasty, let me remind you that you have not met a single deadline that was spelled out in our contract."

"How can I meet deadlines when you keep changing the plans? Since we started, the house has quadrupled in size, you've added a grotto and a gazebo and a tennis court and a wine cellar and four more cars in the garage and now a tower that's gonna take a couple of extra weeks plus the—"

"The contract is quite clear."

"The contract means that when you make changes in design or scope, the deadlines change."

"Contracts don't *mean*. Contracts state the terms. The terms include deadlines. You haven't met a single—"

"Is this personal?"

"What do you mean?"

"How's Lenora?"

"I wouldn't know. Maybe you should ask Juke."

Driving to the job site, Wally reflected on the idea that imminent bankruptcy could be a lot like jumping off a tall building—on your way down, your entire foolish financial history passes before your eyes. Of some twenty-odd loans he'd made to tradesmen who had either once been employed by him or else found some other way to exploit his guilt, only one had ever repaid: Alfredo.

After the heat of the day, as the sun was setting and fingers of fog began creeping down the hillsides, Wally gazed into the empty trailer. He frowned at the padlock hanging open in its slot. Turning to the cop, whose name was Diefendorf, Wally said, "Maybe one of these boot prints in the mud would tell you something?"

Diefendorf the cop shook his head, smiling. They knew each other, sort of. Sometimes Diefendorf stopped by during the belt sander races. One time he even placed a bet. Problem was, whenever Diefendorf showed up, some of the Latinos—the street-corner hires—hightailed it for cover, never to be seen again. After losing two good day workers, Wally asked Diefendorf to stop coming around—and Dief agreed. He had no interest in busting those guys.

"You want to dust the box for fingerprints?"

Diefendorf rolled his eyes.

"You gonna do anything?"

"File a report."

Snatching the padlock from its slot, Wally flung it to the ground and stomped, driving it into the mud.

"You tried your key in that thing?" Diefendorf asked.

Prying the lock from the dirt, Wally inserted his key. It fit, but it wouldn't turn.

"Broke it," Wally said.

"Switched it," Diefendorf said. "You leave the trailer open all day, right? With the padlock dangling? Like everybody else? Somebody who was here yesterday—delivery guy, sub, maybe just somebody walking by—happens, right? People coming in and out all day? He can't walk off with all your tools, but he switches the locks. When you leave, you lock it—looks just like your regular lock. But your key won't open it. His will. Night, he comes back when nobody's around. Heard about a guy working this scheme. Races yesterday. Who was there?"

"The usual suspects," Wally said.

"Make a list of what you lost," Diefendorf said. "I'll file a report."

Diefendorf walked toward his squad car.

"Forkin' Ludowski," Juke said, spitting. He hadn't said a word while Diefendorf was present.

"Doubt it," Wally said. "Wrong psychology."

"Wrong?" Juke spat again. Juke had the well-honed skill of forcing a narrow spray of spit through the gap between his two front teeth. "He's a rip-off artist."

"Ludowski rips clients. He knows if they catch him, worst that can happen is he loses money. But if he steals from the trades, likely what happens, we all take turns crushing him into a stinking pile of bones and eyeballs."

Juke brightened. "Can I go first?"

"I heard that," Diefendorf called from his car. "Don't be vigilantes." Then he drove away.

"Wasn't Ludowski," Wally said. He watched as a pair of coyotes, tongues lolling, came loping through the meadow and up the hill toward the Pilpont property. A pair of coyote pups, eyes bright, came bounding after them. Suddenly Wally missed his old dog, missed him bad.

For a moment Wally considered the possibility that Pilpont had something to do with this rip-off. The man played a rough game, but he played it with paper. With lawsuits. And Pilpont's beef was against Krainer, not Wally. Stealing Wally's tools wouldn't make the house go away. Attacking Krainer's cash would be the way to go. And, come to think of it, something of that nature seemed to have just happened.

"Can you front me a few dollars?" Juke asked. "Until Monday?"

Wally sighed. "Krainer bounced two checks. The money was coming so easy, I took my eye off the ball."

"Big bucks?"

"Enough to buy, say, four brand-new pickup trucks."

"Forkin' shit. Big ones? With racks and winches?"

"Loaded."

"The pussy clip?"

"Maybe. Didn't help, anyway."

Juke spat a hard stream. "I broke it off with her, Boss. Just like you wanted."

"How'd she take it?"

"Not so good. Forkin' shame. My heart is broke."

"You're joking, right?"

"Dunno. Honest. Never appreciated no lady before. Dunno what it's like. Had no idea until after. I think I'm loyal to her. Maybe a hundred? Just until Monday?"

Wally found four twenties in his wallet and gave three of them to Juke.

"Thanks, Boss." Juke tucked the money in his jeans. "Gonna miss the old girl."

"Lenora?"

"No. Deb."

Debbie Doofus. Purchased thirty years ago after severe haggling at a garage sale, Wally's first nailgun was ancient even when he bought it—bulky, cantankerous, beat-up—like an old carpenter, and just as hardworking. Later, when Wally decided to throw out the old Duo-Fast, Juke took it home for "a few changes." And that's when Wally discovered Juke's genius with tools—erratic, lacking in the aesthetic, but genius nonetheless. Juke replaced the nose piece, modified the magazine, redesigned the trigger, and swapped out half the internal parts (kids, don't try this at home). He created a mongrel, not pretty but a tool with animus—heavy with power, indestructible, one of a kind.

Juke was shaking his head, remembering. "Only gun we ever had could shoot a three an' a half nail flush into a Parallam."

"Yep, she had balls," Wally said. "Of course nobody in his right mind would modify a nailgun. I always expected her to blow up on you."

"Yeah, me too."

"Really?" Wally studied Juke. "Then why'd you keep using her?"

"Hey. I'm loyal." Juke spat. "I met somebody wants a gig."

"Juke, we don't have a gig. Nothing. *Nada*. We're pulling off this job."

"Nickel and dimers?"

"Yeah, I'll be making some calls." Wally always kept up a small-job home repair operation as a sideline to the one big job he'd be working on at any given time. The small jobs provided work for crew members who weren't needed on any particular day, plus they kept his name in circulation in the community. Often, the little jobs led to big ones down the line. Otherwise, they were barely profitable. "But I really can't hire any new—"

"Just check her out."

"*Her?*"

"Hey! FrogGirl! Cop's gone. You can come out now."

From inside the shell of the house, a stocky girl emerged. A girl who hid from cops. Wally didn't know what her secret was but only that she had one. She was dermatologically challenged but strong in her bearing, square in her approach. Wally didn't know how he could possibly provide work for his existing crew. Yet with one glance—from the set of her jaw to the green flame of her eyes, before the obligatory questions, the pawing of dirt with the toe of his shoe—already Wally had decided to hire her. Animus. And possibly explosive. She reminded him of Deb.

Twenty-Three

Rachel followed Abe up the stairs, sensing the eyes of Abe's mother on her back. As Abe closed the door of the bedroom behind them—there was no lock, she noticed—Rachel felt momentarily awkward. There were only two places to sit—on the bed or at the desk—so Rachel chose the wooden chair. On the wall behind the desktop was a poster of stars, galaxies, cosmic dust, labeled at the bottom "The Universe." For a moment she wondered if it was amusing—or simply appalling—that somebody thought the universe could be reduced to a poster. Or not. *There you go,* she thought to herself. *Why do you find it necessary to have a moral position about somebody's poster?* On the desktop, a fish tank hummed and bubbled, smelling faintly of seaweed.

Abe sat on the unmade bed. On the ceiling above him was a poster of Einstein sticking out his tongue.

Rachel smiled, a look of mischief in her eyes. "You really thought you should tell several thousand people about how to measure with pussy hairs?"

"I'm a little embarrassed."

"Actually, honestly, I'm not here to deprecate you."

"It wasn't what I meant to say. Somehow it changed before it came out my mouth."

"What was it, Abe, before it came out your mouth?"

"Something like this: 'I'm learning there's a different kind of genius. Not mental like we're taught in school. I'm learning from some people who think with their bodies. I'm learning a person can be a physical genius.'" Abe sighed. "Which I'm definitely not."

Rachel's tongue came out as if to lick her lips and then froze for a moment, just slightly exposed.

"What?" Abe said.

Rachel withdrew the tongue. "Nothing," she said.

Abe was wearing blue jeans and a T-shirt with the sleeves ripped off. He was not the Abe that Rachel had known, the math nerd. Already his shoulders looked broader; his hands, rougher, his skin, a rich tan.

She doubted he could ever become a physical genius, but she liked the changes so far.

Abe leaned forward. "I missed you, Rachel."

Rachel crossed her legs. "What, exactly, did you miss?"

"Your sharp mind. Your little curly sideburns. The way you stick your tongue out of your mouth just before you tell me I did something stupid. I missed *you*. Mostly. I mean I can't deny that I liked, uh, you know. The stuff. But I just want to be with you again."

"No more stuff, Abe. It's kid stuff. I want to be a grown-up now. Are you okay with that?"

"Grown-ups don't have sex?"

"Grown-ups don't do blow jobs in the McDonald's bathroom."

Abe bowed his head and spread his hands as if conceding the point, but then with a frown he said, "I could dispute that. But whatever you want. I'm okay with it."

"I could argue too, Abe. I could argue that what we did wasn't sex. What we did was rebellion. What we did was just a giant fuck-you to the rest of the world. I could argue that I'm still a virgin right now."

"I wouldn't dispute that point."

"Good." She studied his face. "Do you have an erection right now?"

"Rachel, I always have an erection. That's the big problem."

"Big? You really think it's extra large? You honestly believe—?"

"Rachel. Please stop."

"Damn." Rachel studied her fingers. "There I go again. The combat queen. I'm sorry."

"No, my fault. I'm sorry."

"Can't have it, Abe. This one's mine. My fault. My assumption. My ...debate instinct."

They fell silent. Rachel leaned back in the chair. She admired his restraint. He hadn't pointed out that she had misrepresented their actions as blow jobs in the McDonald's bathroom, that it wasn't just him exploiting her. It was two-way. And yes, she had enjoyed it. When it was private. When they were safely alone. When it was an expression of affection. He was patient and yet playful. He was inquisitive, almost maddeningly so. There was never penetration. And the sensation, she had told him more than once, was not unfantastic.

Abe pressed a hand gingerly against the bandage above his ear. When he pulled the hand away, Rachel could see that it was damp.

"How's your head feel?"

"Not unpainful."

Rachel studied the fish tank. A couple of tetras darted about mindlessly while a catfish snuffled the bottom with his whiskers—to those fish, an entire universe. "I'm trying to see what happened in a good light," Rachel said, "but I'm having trouble coming up with a good-light scenario that puts you at the Pirate Motel going headfirst through a window."

"It's mostly bad-light," Abe said, leaning back on the bed. He reached for his mandolin, held it on top of his stomach, and began to pluck strings while staring at the ceiling. "I mean, I guess I wasn't unwilling. " Abe sat up. His fingers stopped moving over the strings of the mandolin. "Okay, we started at this bar. The Papaya Dulce. Over on Fifth Avenue? There were a couple of ...sort of ...prostitutes. Which probably explains the motel, though I really don't remember. What's coming back to me—and I think I've got this right—is I remember all of a sudden needing to get away. Wanting to get out. Like a panic. I just had to get out of there. And I don't think the window was intentional. I just wasn't thinking too clearly. But here's the good light, if there is any: I didn't do anything. With the women. Maybe because of my high moral standards—which I'm sure would surprise both of us—or maybe because of that movie we had to watch in Health Ed. Or maybe because I had to throw up. So you could argue that I'm still a virgin too."

Abe resumed playing the mandolin.

Rachel was studying some papers on Abe's desktop. Sheets with a Princeton letterhead. Abe had run a yellow highlighter over certain phrases: "Princeton has an honor code that we take seriously ...We expect every applicant to abide by our honor code ..."

"Schwartzie found out?"

"My father. Inadvertently."

"That's terrible. You must be worried. Still, I don't think Princeton would ...Let's see." She studied the papers. "'Integrity, principle, and intellectual honesty.' Nope. Nothing about bat droppings."

"They have 'the highest expectations'."

"So do I. I think you'll be good for Princeton. You'll walk in Einstein's footsteps. Except when you act like a total jackass. Which you will sometimes. What did that old hippie give you?"

"You mean Wally?"

"Your boss. That guy downstairs who gave Ronny a big plastic tugboat bath toy that toots when you squeeze it. He handed you an envelope. Is it money?"

"No."

"Is it better than money?"

"Yes."

"Is it better than a big plastic tugboat?"

"I dunno. That's a pretty high standard."

"Won't you let me see it?"

Abe removed the envelope from his shirt pocket and handed it to Rachel. Inside, she found an awkwardly handwritten page:

Abe,
I thank whatever playful
twist of fate brought me
as a last-minute invitation
to your graduation.
Excuse me if I sound sappy but
I became a delirious
drooling optimist as I witnessed
those joyful groups: exuberant
grads surrounded by
dazed but proud parents
and family. I too am
somewhat dazed but oh
so proud of you and all these
suddenly adult,
beautiful,
smart,
wildly energetic,
soberly idealistic beings.
The planet is in good hands.

"I don't think I'm quite ready to run the planet," Rachel said, folding the paper and handing it back to Abe. "Do you think we're suddenly adult?"

"I think you're beautiful and smart. Not so suddenly." Abe smiled—a tentative flicker of a smile that Rachel could quickly snuff, as she had snuffed it many times with one look, one word. After all, she was Rachel the English nerd, the bookworm-with-a-body, the captain of the debate team, the girl it was like combat to talk to—she knew what people said about her. But right now she wanted Abe's cautious smile to blossom for all the reasons that had brought her to this desk chair in this bedroom. By morning—if they could just shut up long enough—and if Abe's mother didn't change her mind and come blasting into the bedroom—by morning, they would no longer be virgins. They might not be grown-ups, but they would not be children.

Twenty-Four

Downstairs, Wally had watched Opal as Rachel and Abe headed up the stairs.

"Omigod," Opal said softly. Even in her worry, she had a shine to her face, and Wally knew it shone for him. For the hot evening she was wearing sandals, shorts, and a sleeveless top revealing a pudge of midriff. Her toenails and fingernails were painted blue. On her face, as far as Wally could detect, she wore no make-up whatsoever. The colored nails seemed playful to Wally; the lack of other cosmetics put him at ease. Women who slathered creams and colors on their faces made Wally nervous—he always thought of war paint.

"They're good kids," Wally said.

"Still," Opal said. "Omigod."

"Baff!" Ronny said, tugging at Wally's pants. In one arm he held the big plastic tugboat.

"In a minute, Ronny," Wally said. "Opal, is this a good moment— well, it's never a good moment—but later tonight I need to ask you about something that's kind of awkward to bring up but—"

"Is it spelled s-e-x?"

"No. It's spelled m-o-n-e-y. L-o-a-n."

The shine disappeared from Opal's face.

"Baff!" Ronny said.

Wally realized he'd made a bad move. The worst move. *Idiot.* Opal wasn't saying anything, but in her face he saw his new status: l-o-s-e-r.

"Give him a bath," Opal said wearily. "Then we'll talk."

"I'm sorry, Opal."

"Don't apologize. Just don't say *anything.*"

"Baff!" Ronny said.

"Yes, sir," Wally said.

After the bath, after Opal had tucked Ronny into bed, she found Wally back in the bathroom again with his hand reaching into the water tank of the toilet.

"The flush valve," Wally said. "Just needs a little adjustment."

Sitting on the edge of the bathtub, Opal crossed her legs and folded her hands in her lap, back straight, the picture of poise. "Abe was such a dear little baby," she said. "So pink and wiggly. He made these little clucking noises while he was nursing. Even his poop smelled sweet. Now he and Rachel ... They're still up in his room."

"You're not supposed to think about it."

"How can I not think about it? And why did he put a sock on his doorknob? Is that some secret code?"

"It means you shouldn't let it enter your mind," Wally smiled, "that right now they're probably screwing their brains out." Wally flushed the toilet, studying the water as it circled the bowl.

"What if Rachel's parents call? What do I say to them?"

Once again, Wally reached into the water tank. "Say, 'Yes, Rachel's here.'"

"What if they want to speak to her?"

"Then you go up and knock gently on the door."

"What if I *hear* them?"

Wally pulled his hand out of the toilet and dried himself with a towel. "You want to tell me what happened?"

"You mean the trauma of my youth?" Opal braced her hands, blue fingertips on the edge of the bathtub. "No. I don't want to talk about it. No, thank you very much. And you shouldn't be driving a pickup."

"What does that mean?"

"It means, what's the matter with you? You're getting old, Wally. It's time to grow up."

"Grow up how?"

"Get a real job."

"What's the matter with driving a pickup truck?"

"It's so. I don't know. Working class."

"Working class? Did you actually say working class? You live in this house—in this neighborhood? You couldn't possibly buy it on the salary of a newspaper photographer. And your kid's going to Princeton? Is it alimony? Trust fund? Inheritance? *Working class?* I can't believe you said that."

"This is humiliating. How much money do you need?"

"Never mind. Forget I ever asked."

"But you did. You asked. 1 won't forget." Tears were brimming in her eyes.

"It's not like I used you, Opal."

"How so?"

"We never even had sex."

Now the tears were streaming down her cheeks as she said, "I thought if we didn't, it would be easier. I was wrong."

"What would be easier?"

"Not getting hurt."

"Opal, this is killing me."

They fell silent. *So it's really this simple: I'm a man of low property value. She's a woman with prime.* Wally made one final adjustment, then flushed. After studying the water—the satisfying gurgle of a complete washout—he placed the lid back on the water tank.

"Fixed?" Opal said.

"Seems to work," Wally said.

Opal wiped her cheeks with her fingers. Even while crying, she'd never lost her poise. "How much money do you need?"

"I don't want any." Wally handed her some sheets of toilet paper.

"You need money." She was dabbing her face. "How much?"

"I withdraw my application."

"You never even kissed me."

"You said no sex."

"You never even tried."

"If I kissed you right now, would you forget about the money?"

"No. I can't."

Grasping her upper arms, Wally lifted Opal to a standing position from her seat on the edge of the tub. Opal whispered, "I may giggle. Just warning you."

Wally replied in a whisper: "Why would you giggle?"

"It just might happen."

"Okay." Wally leaned forward. This close, he could see the downy fuzz of her cheeks. He could smell the mild musk of her perspiration, the sunshine and dust caught in her hair, the faint and fading aroma of lavender shampoo. "Giggle if you want."

As their lips almost met, Opal jerked backwards. "Are you going to use your tongue?"

Wally froze. He whispered, "No."

Opal closed her eyes.

Wally leaned forward and kissed her gently on the lips. Hers were warm, welcoming, and slightly wet from the tears. Salty.

Opal giggled. "Sorry," she said, pulling away.

"Nervous?" Wally said.

Opal started to say something, checked herself, stared for a moment into Wally's eyes, then lunged forward and kissed him hard on the mouth.

After a few moments, or minutes—Wally wasn't keeping track of the time—Opal broke off the kiss. Silently, seriously, she studied his face, running one index finger over his cheeks, his eyebrows, down his nose.

Then she ran out of the room.

Wally followed. In the fantasy section of his brain, she was in the bedroom stripping off her clothes. In reality, he found her in the kitchen removing the checkbook from her purse.

"You know what?" she said. "Kissing is overrated."

"Uh, sorry."

"How much money do you need?"

"None."

"Please, Wally. How much?"

"I'm not taking any."

"Why won't you take any money?"

"Because I love you, Opal."

"Omigod."

Silence. Wally checked his watch. With her fingers Opal fanned the checks, which made a slurping sound. From the butcher block counter, the lingering scent of lemon oil.

"Less than ...?"

"What?"

"Never mind." Opal stared hard at her hands.

Wally stepped forward. "Will I love you less than I loved my wife?"

"I withdraw the question." Opal was still fanning the checks. "I blurt. You'll have to get used to—I never meant. Out loud."

"But you're wondering," Wally said. "So am I."

"Stupid to ask. I'm sorry."

Wally ran a finger over the butcher block counter. A little rough, there. Next visit, he'd sand it. "There's no answer, Opal."

"You barely know me, Wally. How could you say you love me?"

"Sorry. I got confused. Must be the drugs."

"What drugs?"

"Just kidding."

"See? If we really knew each other, I'd know you were joking. And you'd know it's not funny to me. We need to ...explore each other. Uncover the ...issues. What we need to know."

"Okay." Wally stood with his hands in his pockets, saying nothing, available for knowing.

"This is my mother's house, Wally. I grew up here and now I'm the parent and my mother's in an institution. She has Alzheimer's. She's endowed—a lot of savings. From my father's life insurance. And I'm the conservator. Just so you know. Since you asked."

There was a *thump* from upstairs, Abe's bedroom. They both heard it.

Opal glanced upwards, grimaced, then went on: "There's no trust fund but I'm comfortable and some day I'll inherit what's left, and I hope that's a long time away. Aaron—Abe's father, the rude man you met today—will pay for half of Princeton. My mother will pay for my share of Princeton. That's a decision I'm making on her behalf and it's somewhat awkward because it's in my self-interest but there it is. It's what she'd want. And I hate—I *despise* talking about my finances. Okay? I'd rather stand here naked than talk about my money."

"I'd rather that too." Wally grinned.

Opal felt a chill. She placed her hands over her chest, one hand still holding the checkbook.

"Oops," Wally said. "Sorry. Another bad joke. I get stupid this time of night. I should go now. Good luck with Rachel and Abe. Good night, Opal."

"Good night."

Opal stood in the kitchen, hands over chest, staring after Wally as he walked out of the house. He stumbled once on the edge of the carpet, bumping into the side of the Eames chair. Then he was gone. Like a man who wasn't quite sure where he was going.

Okay, he wasn't Sir Lancelot. And the ponytail—omigod. And he wanted to borrow money—at this stage in their relationship? What was he *thinking*?

She wished he hadn't made that remark about her standing naked. At least he'd had the sense to realize, instantly, that the jest had gone sour. Or did he mean himself—he'd rather stand naked than talk about his own finances? Or did he mean they should both stand naked, metaphorically speaking, face to face, and discover who they really were? Wasn't she trying to do just that?

He could fix toilets. He could fix entire houses. He was nonthreatening. She'd had to ask him to kiss her. If only she'd known him when she was thirteen. He could have protected her. He would have stopped that evil stranger who ripped a hole in her soul.

Opal heard soft footsteps. Barefoot, Abe and Rachel were coming down the stairs.

"That is so-o-o different," Rachel was saying just before they spotted Opal in the kitchen. Immediately their faces went neutral.

"Uh, we were planning to make some popcorn," Abe said.

"I'll get out of your way," Opal said, stuffing the checkbook back into her purse. Abe and Rachel sparkled: so vivid, so natural and young. In spite of trying to notice nothing, Opal couldn't help but be aware that Rachel was wearing Abe's T-shirt, the one with the sleeves ripped off, the one Abe had been wearing when they went to his room. The arm holes were much too large.

What happened to discretion?

Retreating, Opal fled from murmuring voices punctuated by the beeps of the microwave oven, laughter, tickles—Abe was tickling Rachel.

Tickles!

If only she could fly away to the shelter of the man who fixed houses. Imagine tickles bringing pleasure instead of panic.

Opal drew herself a bubble bath and, masked by the sound of running water, she sobbed aloud.

Stupid, stupid, stupid. Why the comment that kissing was overrated? It wasn't even true.

Later, calming down, spent, in the warm water amid the tiny chinkling sounds of the bubbles, as she watched drops of condensation running down the mirror, she decided to examine—with ruthless detachment, if possible—her life. Her feelings. The ick. Beginning with her reaction to the combination of Rachel and Abe, two lovely souls fresh as peaches in July. Why did she feel so awkward with them? Embarrassment? Prudery? Fear?

Yes, all three. But why?

How could she be scared of Rachel and Abe? If she felt any fear it should be of Wally, a man the same age as the cold-handed cretin stinking of cologne who stepped out of a pickup and dragged her behind a fence and brought pain, utter helplessness, shame, revulsion, and stole from her what was most precious: her youth.

And there it was. The ick.

It was in the way Rachel and Abe could take such delight simply making popcorn together, sharing secrets, tickles, bumbling blundering passion that shone in their eyes.

The ick was not embarrassment. Not prudery. Not fear.

It was envy.

It was regret.

It was her adolescence: the discovery, the wonder she'd never had.

Twenty-Five

Opal bathed, unaware of the world outside. Wally drove halfway home in his truck and then, reaching a decision, took a U-turn and headed back toward the hills. He passed the turn for Opal's house, continuing higher, unaware that on top of Opal's house Abe and Rachel with their bowl of popcorn had climbed out Abe's window. They cuddled on the roof with their backs against the chimney, listening to the passing night, unaware that Wally was driving up the mountain and unaware that south of them in Saratoga Juke sat in the cab of his El Camino. In fact, nobody in the world was aware of Juke, who had been sitting for hours. He was sucking on his fourth bottle of Corona. Across the street, Lenora's windows were dark. Her Miata was missing from its spot in the parking lot. Juke had no particular expectation that she would come home at all tonight, and if she did he had no particular plan about what he would do. He was simply sitting, drinking, waiting for something. Or nothing. Whatever.

Idly, he was gazing at the roof over Lenora's unit. It was something he did, study a roof. Looked like a six-in-twelve slope, three-tab shingles. Condo quality, he could bet, meaning bad stapling and botched detail. In cheapo roofing, it's the flashing where they screw up. Along the edges of the skylight, that's where the first leaks will show up.

Lenora had two skylights, one over the bathroom and another over the bed. It had made Juke nervous. He'd told her, "I ain't no exhibitioner. What if some big old 747 is coming in for a landing, coming right over the forkin' bedroom, and suddenly there's five hundred people looking down at what we're doing on this bed?"

Lenora had laughed. She'd said, "You've never been in an airplane, have you?"

Juke had installed that kind of skylight before. Velux. You just drop them over the curb and screw them to the frame from the outside. And if somebody wanted to enter Lenora's condo, somebody could just climb onto the roof, remove a few screws, and be waiting in her bedroom when she came home. Now who'd want to do such a thing?

Traffic approached on the quiet street. Two pairs of headlights. A pickup came to a stop at the curb while Lenora's Miata pulled into the lot. A man got out of the truck and met Lenora at her Miata. They seemed mighty friendly toward each other as they walked to the entry. Lights came on in the windows, a glow from the skylight over the bedroom.

Juke set down the now-empty bottle. He stepped out of the El Camino and wandered nonchalantly across the street. The truck was a blue Dodge with side boxes. He remembered seeing it before. Couldn't remember faces, but he never forgot a truck. There was a black lumber rack, sloppy welding, looked homemade. Cheapo side boxes. The usual crap in the bed: yellow electric cords, a five-gallon bucket of joint compound, scraps of two-by-fours, a bundle of shims, a scattering of framing clips, a couple of sawhorses on their sides, a shovel, a raggedy old broom, some empty tubes of caulk. The side boxes had the old kind of lock, the simple kind you could open with a wrench and a screwdriver if you didn't mind doing a little damage. Not that Juke would do such a thing. He would never steal another man's tools, not even from this guy who was up there with Lenora under that skylight at this very moment and who couldn't possibly appreciate her the way she ought to be appreciated. No, sir, he wouldn't mess with the man's tools. But he did need to pee. And the window on the driver's side was open just a crack at the top. Just enough to get a grip with fingertips and push down and—there—nobody else on the street—stand on the step and open his fly and—ahh, like a firehose—flush four bottles of Corona out of his bladder and into the cab.

Twenty-Six

Slightly after midnight, Wally pulled his truck into the construction site. Leaving the headlights on, he stepped into the gray cloud of fog and called out: "FrogGirl! Are you here?"

She appeared from behind a stack of empty cardboard boxes, a big black Maglite in her hand shining back at Wally.

"You sleeping?" Wally asked.

"No." She was dressed in sweat pants and sweatshirt.

"About you sleeping here ..." Wally's voice echoed harshly in the acoustics of an unfinished house.

"You kicking me out?"

"I'm inviting you to sleep at my house." As he spoke he was monitoring the echo, trying to soften the tone. "I've got two empty bedrooms—that is, still looking the way my kids left them. You'd have sheets. A roof. Four walls. You can take down the posters. Or put up your own."

"You got a basketball net?"

"Rim. Backstop. We could get a new net. You play?"

"Some." Warily, she studied him. "Any conditions?"

"Be tidy. No drugs. Music negotiable. And what kind of a name is FrogGirl, anyway?"

"It's who I am. It means *cute people suck*."

"Do I suck?"

"Well, you're not cute."

Wally laughed. "Are you coming? What have you got here?"

"Just a backpack."

In the cab of the truck, down twisty, narrow Page Mill Road, windshield wipers flapping intermittently, FrogGirl asked, "You divorced? What happened to your kids?"

"My wife died. The kids grew up. So I've got this house."

"How long ago? Your wife."

"About two years."

"And you weren't divorced?"

"No."

"But she died."

"Yes. What's your point?"

"Not a happy family."

The tires hit the ditch. Wally in momentary rage had closed his eyes. He steadied the steering, swung back to pavement. If he'd swerved to the other side, they'd be rolling down a cliff. FrogGirl looked frightened. Wally forced himself to speak in measured tones: "Somebody who runs away and lives homeless and calls herself FrogGirl and hates cute people—I think that person may not be an expert on happy families. Maybe you shouldn't sit in judgment of what I constructed, what I had, something you know nothing about."

"I don't hate them. Not all cute people. I mean, I'm not a bigot."

They were silent. Wally tried to stifle his anger. She was just a child. The fog thickened to a steady mist. As they drove farther downhill, the road grew wider, less twisty, and the acreage of the estates became smaller, though many of the houses were just as large. As wealth had washed up the hillsides from Palo Alto it had surrounded but not eliminated many older, modest homes like Opal's. Also remaining—though an embarrassment to the neighbors—were one or two old hardscrabble farmhouses and even remnants of a couple of hippie communes, one of which Wally had briefly joined until Aimee, his wife, became pregnant and they had decided that group living was no way to raise a child, at least not for them. Getting pregnant, Aimee had said, was when they grew up.

"Sorry." FrogGirl broke the silence. "Your wife. How'd she die?"

"Ovarian cancer."

"That sucks."

They drove on, quiet again, but the space in the cab felt warmer. They shared a bench seat that Wally had covered with sheepskin after the original vinyl had worn through.

Wally nodded his head at a Thermos on the seat between them. "Want some hot chocolate? Probably still warm."

"I better not."

"Is it like coffee? Makes you puke?"

"Juke *told* you? Jeezo. Then I suppose he also told you I'm a lesbian?"

"Uh-huh. Smart move. Good way to keep Juke from hitting on you."

"He wouldn't. I thought he might at first. But he wouldn't."

"Yes." Wally spoke with certainty. "He would."

"Juke's not dangerous. I woulda thought you knew him better than that."

"I *do* know Juke better than that."

"Ooh—sore point," FrogGirl teased.

She had him. He knew the damage Juke could cause and it wasn't only with clients—Wally remembered it every day. For certain. Not that he would talk about it.

FrogGirl was shifting in her seat. "What makes you think I'm not a lesbian?"

"Are you?"

"I might start. How'd you know I wasn't?"

"I just knew."

"See? Same with Juke. I just know he's not dangerous."

"Be careful what you know."

They came to the overpass of Interstate 280, where Page Mill widened from a country lane to a divided highway. Traffic was scarce. The rolling landscape of dry golden grass and deep green pockets of trees reminded Wally of photos he'd seen of the African savanna. There should be zebras, elephants, giraffes. Instead, after a traffic light, they drove past the west coast office of *The Wall Street Journal* and the sprawling parklike campus of Hewlett-Packard. The road was lined by companies that were no more than meaningless names to Wally: Accenture, CV Therapeutics, Beckman Coulter, Genecor, Wilson Sonsoni, Agilent. Wally could remember when none of these enterprises existed, when there were horse pastures and plum orchards. The buildings gave no clue as to what happened within—there were no smokestacks, no loading docks, no cranes, no mounds of ore. The architecture was low-key; the signs denoting each company were modest and sometimes hard to find. It wasn't cool to look flashy on Page Mill Road.

FrogGirl reached for the Thermos. "Want me to pour you a cup?"

"Please. Thank you."

As she handed him the mug, FrogGirl said, "Why'd you have kids?"

"Huh?"

"They cover you with snot. They—they shoplift. You turn into something weird. You turn into a *parent*. They grow up and hate you."

"They don't hate me."

"Please? I promise I won't smirk."

"I guess it's about love." Wally took a sip of hot chocolate. Lukewarm.

"I'm not smirking, but that was really lame."

Wally took a bigger sip. Swallowed. He tried again: "We wanted to change the world. And we did. We created love. It's the only accomplishment that matters—the love I pass on to my children. Not the houses I've built. Not the money I've blown. It's the love."

"Still sappy."

"The big things in life are all sappy. And if you have to ask why have children, you can't understand the answer. It's beyond explanation. It's a matter of faith, like religion."

FrogGirl was shaking her head. "People with faith get run over by trains. You think faith can stop a train?"

"Uh, no. But I'm not sure I see the connection."

"You don't know! How could you say that?"

"Say what?"

"About *trains*."

"What did I say about trains?"

"*Nothing*!" FrogGirl glared at him, then turned her back.

Wally turned left on Middlefield Road. Finishing the chocolate, he wondered if FrogGirl had dozed off. Her face was turned toward her window.

Suddenly he could feel those burning green eyes on his face.

"Sorry I bugged you," she said.

Saying nothing, Wally drove by the ivied, cedar-shingled houses of Professorville.

FrogGirl fidgeted. "I'm not as dumb as you think."

"I don't think you're dumb," Wally said.

"Naive. Innocent. You think I'm a teenager."

"You're not?"

"I am. That's the problem."

"What's the problem?"

"Teenagers suck."

Another mile passed in silence. They drove by a high school with low-slung rows of classrooms, a factory of education. In daylight hours when Wally used to drive past, he used to smile and wave at the students gathered on street corners and often they smiled and waved back. Wally had abandoned the practice after a security guard came after him. There was something suspicious about a man being friendly to teens.

"You can ask your question," FrogGirl said.

"Huh?"

"Your turn. It's only fair."

Wally considered.

They had passed the genteel overgrown hedges of Atherton and suddenly, as if emerging from a tunnel, had entered the polar opposite — Wally's neighborhood — the scuffling, bustling Fifth Avenue section of Redwood City: Donut Depot, Hometown Noodle Viet & Chinese, Roberto's Shoe Repair, Maldonado's Auto Body, El Paisano Food Market, Muebleria Uruapan, Discoteca El Indito, All American Muffler. There were shops for small motor repair, furniture reupholstering, laminate fabrication, metal plating. Despite the late hour and clinging mist, one lone woman in high platform heels paced under the streetlight near One Stop Liquors, waiting for business.

Feeling comfortable, nearly at home, Wally turned to FrogGirl and asked, "When I came to the construction site, how come you weren't sleeping?"

"You mean, like, what was I doing sitting there in the dark?"

"Well, yeah."

"I was waiting. Don't laugh."

"Okay."

"For the ghost. I don't go to sleep until after the ghost goes through."

Wally jammed on the brakes and pulled to the side of the road in front of Bay Area Super Smog. The engine idled. The wipers squeaked. Wally gaped.

"There's a ghost," FrogGirl said. "You promised you wouldn't laugh."

"I'm not laughing. I just ...First of all, I don't believe in ghosts. Second, it's a brand new house. It isn't even built yet. Ghosts don't live in brand new unfinished houses."

"How do you know what ghosts do if you don't even believe in them?"

"What does the ghost look like?"

"I'm sorry I told you."

"No, I really want to hear."

"Never mind."

"Is it tiny?"

"I don't want to talk about it."

"When are you due?"

"I—jeezo—what?"

"You're pregnant. Right?"

She had retreated in the cab, wedging herself with her back in the space where the seat meets the door. For a moment she studied him. She looked like a cornered animal. "Does it show?"

"No." Wally paused, told himself to soften his tone. Gently, he said, "How far along?"

"Ten weeks."

Feeling brutal but needing to go there, he said as softly as possible: "And ...keeping it. Have you made up your mind?"

She hugged herself as if she were cold. Then with eyes closed, just a whisper: "No."

"FrogGirl, I—will you—I just want to say ..." Wally checked himself. He didn't believe in ghosts, but he definitely believed in spirits, and Wally could feel the spirit of the unborn child not in FrogGirl's womb but hovering somewhere nearby, possibly inside the cab of the truck, uncommitted, unanchored but definitely present, listening, anxious to learn if it would live or die. "On second thought, I'm not going to say anything to you. And I'm not going to tell anybody. It's still your secret. That's a promise. You can trust me. But if you ever want to talk, just say so. I'm here. I'll listen. I won't judge. Okay?"

FrogGirl's face, lit in the glow of the instrument panel, was soft but inscrutable. "I appreciate it," she said.

At Wally's house FrogGirl selected Sally's bedroom, which was a time capsule of how Sally had left it: overflowing with dozens of plush stuffed animals spilling out of shelves and burying the bed.

"I'll clear out some of this garbage," Wally said.

"Why?" FrogGirl said.

So he let it be.

In the morning as Wally passed Sally's room on the way to the bathroom, her door had swung open because the latch wasn't quite lined up with the strike—*Somebody really oughta fix up this place,* Wally told himself—and he saw his houseguest curled up on the bed, sound asleep, cuddled among a velvet dog, a hairy bear, and a quilted goose, her arms wrapped around a big, green, fuzzy bullfrog.

Twenty-Seven

A long time ago when Wally had been contracting for only a couple of years, when he had one child and his wife was pregnant with the second, they were living over a garage as caretakers for an estate in Atherton. Coming home early one day, Wally spied a man on the roof of the main house nailing cedar shakes. The man moved rapidly, almost at a frantic pace, but from ground level Wally judged that the work was of decent quality. Lines straight, spacing good. Oddly, though, the cedar shakes he was installing so professionally looked just as mossy and weather-worn as the rest of the roof, as if he had removed and was now putting back the original shakes of a house built thirty-five years ago. Normally, once you pull such an old shake, it's busted. Wally picked up one that had fallen to the ground. It was soft gray on the surface but brittle in the grooves, cracked, with expanded nail-holes where the wood had worn and blackened.

From the foot of the ladder Wally shouted up to the man: "Problem with the underlayment? Rotten rafter? What's up?"

"Fuckin' piece of shit." The man's nailing, already fast, became even faster.

"You work for a roofing company?"

"Fuck no."

"Handyman?"

No answer.

"So what are you doing?"

"Fuckin' fixin' the fuckin' roof."

"What's the problem?"

"Fuckin' leak."

"Why aren't you replacing the shakes?"

No answer. Still nailing.

"Who hired you?"

"Fuckin' owner."

"That's interesting. Because I'm the person who's supposed to repair things like that."

"So I took your fuckin' job. Fuckin' sorry, man."

"Why aren't you using new cedar shakes?"

"None of your fuckin' business."

"Actually, it is my business. I'm the caretaker here. The owner is in Bermuda. If you're not going to do the job right, she should know about it."

One of Wally's pet peeves was fly-by-night carpenters who overcharged, underperformed, and gave everybody else a bad name. Without thinking what his next move would be, Wally pulled the ladder away from the roof and laid it on the ground.

Now the man stopped nailing. "Put the fuckin' ladder back."

"Not yet."

"You lost the fuckin' job, man. Now put that fuckin' ladder back."

"I'm going to make a phone call."

"Fuckin' asshole."

Wally turned to walk away, which was a mistake as he learned seconds later. Two boots, leading the force of one hundred and eighty pounds of body mass, landed on the back of Wally's shoulders after leaping from the edge of the roof twelve feet above. Wally crashed onto the grass in a shower of nails. The roofer fell to the side, rolled over once, sprang to his feet, and took off running with the hammer in one hand, a chisel in the other.

For a moment Wally was stunned. Sharp, intense pain shot from his shoulders where the boots had hit. Quickly, though, a red ball of rage took control. Thinking ceased. There was no pain, no logic, no plan—nothing but wrath. Wally was running hard.

The roofer had already sprinted across the lawn and was opening the door of an old primer-gray Plymouth station wagon with a shattered taillight. The car needed a few cranks to get started but took off in a belch of black smoke just as Wally ran up to it.

The streets of Atherton were narrow and winding. Most of the intersections had no street signs on the theory, Wally supposed, that if you didn't have directions from one of the wealthy homeowners then you didn't belong there. As the Plymouth spun away, Wally vaulted over a low rock wall. He raced across the neighbor's lawn and around the swimming pool, through the rose garden and over another rock wall. He landed on the road just as the station wagon was approaching out of a hairpin turn. At the sight of Wally the roofer accelerated—veering directly toward Wally's body. Purely on adrenaline, Wally grabbed a stone the size of a bowling ball from the top of the rock wall and heaved it at the oncoming car.

Wally leaped to the side.

The stone smashed into the windshield and lodged itself in the web of shattered glass. The Plymouth swerved wildly and plowed into an old oak tree that, Atherton-like, lived in the center of the roadway with asphalt circling it. Steam shot from the station wagon's hood.

Wally stared at the smoking Plymouth and then at his own hands as the muscle memory of his body caused him to wonder why he had thrown the rock with his left hand. Suddenly it dawned on him that he couldn't lift his right hand higher than his waist. Before he could think any further, the rolling cloud of Plymouth was backing up and, still in reverse, coming right at him.

Again without thought Wally ran away from the oncoming Plymouth, ran down the road with one arm hanging at his side, ran never once realizing that he could avoid the car by simply jumping over the rock wall from which he had come or perhaps realizing subconsciously that with one arm useless it wasn't safe to attempt any vaulting.

He ran back to his driveway just steps ahead of the Plymouth, which was making a racket like pebbles shaking in a tin can. Turning into the driveway, Wally's feet slipped on the loose gravel and he fell again, this time rolling over after he hit the driveway and just avoiding the wheels of the Plymouth, which clattered past him and plowed its rear end into the side of Aimee's blue Volkswagen beetle. Aimee, eight months pregnant, balancing one-and-a-half-year-old Jaspar in one arm and a bag of groceries in the other, had just stepped away from the beetle when the Plymouth crushed it against the brick wall of the garage. In the near-silence that followed, as Aimee gaped at the wreckage, with the smell of gasoline and the trickling sound of coolant dribbling from the Plymouth's radiator into a green puddle on the driveway, Jaspar leaned forward in Aimee's arm, pointed toward the Plymouth and shouted: "Car!"

It was Jaspar's favorite word.

The roofer was banging around inside the station wagon. The door seemed to be jammed shut.

Wally pulled a pry bar from the back of his truck.

The roofer sprawled over the front seat into the rear deck of the Plymouth and, still lying on his belly, opened the rear door. As he slithered into daylight, Wally with his left hand swung the black steel of the pry bar down on the back of the roofer's head. Slumping, the man slid headfirst out of the car and onto the gravel of the driveway, face down in a small but spreading pool of blood.

For a moment, nobody moved.

"Is he dead?" Aimee said.

"I hope so," Wally said.

"No, you don't," Aimee said.

"Ain't fuckin' dead," the roofer said, rolling over. He blinked his eyes once, twice, three times. "Somebody got a fuckin' aspirin?"

Wally raised the pry bar.

"Fuckin' don't!" The roofer held out his hands. "Fuckin' sorry, man."

"You nearly killed me and my kid and my wife," Wally said. "And she's *pregnant*."

"Didn't fuckin' mean to," the roofer said.

"What's this all about?" Aimee said.

The roofer glanced toward Aimee. "Beg your pardon, ma'am."

"Why'd you smash my car?"

"Didn't fuc ...—uh—didn't mean to, ma'am."

"So what's this all about?"

"I—uh—begging your pardon, ma'am, but he stole my fuckin' ladder."

"I didn't steal it," Wally said. "I just took it away."

"I see," Aimee said, nodding.

"He was pissed," the roofer said, "because, uh, again begging your pardon, ma'am, but I took his fuckin' job."

"It's not that," Wally said. "You *jumped* on me. You were trying to run me over. You were trying to *kill* me."

"Not to make you fuckin' *dead*. Just fuckin', you know, run you over a little."

"Wally, put down the pry bar," Aimee said. "You're scaring me."

"Me too," the roofer said.

Wally lowered the pry bar but still held it at his side.

"Wally," Aimee said, "your shoulder's weird. On your right side? There's a drop in it. Like a stair step."

"You separated the fuckin' shoulder," the roofer said. "I seen it once before."

"*I* separated? *You* separated my shoulder." Wally raised the pry bar.

"Put it down," Aimee said.

"Fuckin' *please*," the roofer said. "I fuckin' told you I was fuckin' sorry. I'll fix your fuckin' car."

"Fix it? It's *squashed*."

"I'll make it up to you. That's a fuckin' promise. Uh. Beg your fuckin' pardon, ma'am. I mean, uh, beg, uh, you know. Without the fuckin'. I mean. Shit."

"Wally," Aimee said. "He's out of his mind. He's bleeding badly. I bet you cracked his skull. Can you drive?"

"Shifting might be difficult."

"I'll fuckin' drive," the roofer said.

"I'll drive," Aimee said. "Get in the truck. Everybody. Now!"

Wally sat in the center holding Jaspar on his lap. The roofer sat by the door, acting twitchy, touching his pocket, opening the glove box and closing it again.

Aimee was a kindergarten teacher before taking her current job in human resources at Hewlett-Packard. She'd often said that handling five-year-olds was perfect job-training for dealing with squabbling high-tech engineers. And Wally was aware that she often used those same skills at home, on him.

From behind the seat Wally pulled out a red bandanna he used as a flag when hauling long pieces of lumber. "Hold it against your head, man. You're bleeding all over my seat."

"That rag? It's fuckin' dirty, man."

"You better put pressure," Wally said, "or you won't make it to the emergency room."

"Fuckin' fuck," the roofer said, but he folded the bandanna and pressed the cleanest section against his wound. "I fell off the roof. Okay? I hurt my head when I fuckin' fell off the roof. You gotta help me here. Or I'm fuckin' dead."

"I don't exactly owe you a favor."

"We'll do it," Aimee said.

Wally stared at her. "This a friend of yours?"

"No. But you nearly killed him."

"He tried to kill *me*."

"Not fuckin' tryin'."

"Could've fooled me."

"I don't fuckin' kill people."

"You almost killed my wife and my kid and my unborn—"

"Shut up, both of you. Honestly. My God."

The roofer's eyes closed. He slumped to the side toward Wally and Jaspar. Splattering blood all along the way, his head struck Wally's limp right arm, slid downwards and came to rest on Jaspar's thighs.

Jaspar screamed.

"Hold the rag on his head," Aimee said.

"I can't," Wally said. "I'm holding Jaspar, and I've only got one arm I can use."

"He's gonna die."

Running a red light and barreling down the Alameda at sixty in a thirty-miles-per-hour zone, Aimee grabbed Jaspar and pulled him onto her lap in the narrow gap between her immense pregnant belly and the steering wheel, never taking her eyes off the road.

"You're gonna kill us all," Wally said.

"Hold the rag on his head."

Wally loved her so much at that moment. She was a force of nature. Mother nature.

At the Stanford Hospital emergency room, Aimee took charge: "They fell off a roof. Head injury here. Separated shoulder there."

The nurse looked puzzled. "They landed upside down?"

"Freak accident," Aimee said.

"Very freaky," Wally said.

Early the next morning, with his arm in a sling, Wally awkwardly climbed the ladder and inspected the roof. Not bad. The guy should've used new shakes, but he'd managed to make a decent job of it. In fact, if Wally hadn't seen him up there, he might never have noticed that any repair had taken place. Which, Wally was forced to admit, was the mark of excellent craft.

From the rooftop, Wally saw a man walking up the driveway wearing a turban. No, they were bandages. The roofer.

Wally scrambled clumsily down to the ground before the roofer could get any ideas about pulling the ladder away from the roof.

"They discharged you already?" Wally said.

"Didn't fuckin' de-charge me. I put on my pants and left."

"I was just looking at the work you did up there, and I think I owe you an apology. Nice job. Very neat. I don't think I could've saved those shakes."

"Well. Uh. Thanks."

"But I'm still pissed."

"Hey. Next time you'll probably get the fuckin' job."

"Not that."

"The car thing? Told you I wasn't fuckin' tryin'. And I told you I'll fuckin' make it up to you."

"How?"

"Sign on your truck says you're a fuckin' contractor."

"That's right."

"I'll fuckin' work. For fuckin' free. You said I do good fuckin' work."

"I don't think so."

"Gimme a fuckin' break, man."

"It's not about skill. It's about character."

"You sayin' you don't fuckin' like me?"

"Something like that."

"You don't fuckin' trust me?"

"Something like that too."

"I came back. I'm fuckin' here. I coulda fuckin' disappeared, you know. I want to fuckin' make it up to you. I gave my word to your wife. My fuckin' word, man."

"You really serious?"

"I just need a fuckin' break, man."

"If I don't pay you, how would you get by?"

"Sleep in the fuckin' car."

"That car's not going anywhere. Not without a lot of work."

"Perfuckinfecto. Don't need to go nowhere for sleepin'."

"That would be almost like moving in with us."

"If you say so."

"I don't say so."

"I just need a fuckin' break, man."

"Wally." It was Aimee. "Do it."

"Why?"

"Like he said. He needs a break."

"You want a guy sleeping in the driveway?"

"For a while. Until Mrs. Politzer comes back, anyway." Mrs. Politzer was the owner of the estate, now summering in Bermuda. "If he works for free," Aimee added, "you might actually make a profit for a change." Aimee was the primary breadwinner. It was a sore point with Wally, though not with her.

"The problem," Wally said, "is about character."

"Character?" Aimee laughed. "You guys are perfect for each other. Don't you get it?"

"Get what?"

"You'll see. By the way," Aimee said, turning to the roofer, "you left something in the truck."

"A gallon of blood," Wally said.

"You found it?" the roofer said.

Looking the roofer directly in the eye, Aimee said, "I'll see it gets back where it belongs."

The roofer frowned.

Wally didn't ask what they were talking about. But he saw the spark in Aimee, had seen it from the very beginning when the roofer was still lying in the driveway in a spreading puddle of blood.

"Still a problem," Wally said. "The cussing. I work for high-end clients. I can't have somebody saying fuck all the time. You know what I mean?"

"Fuck yeah," the roofer said. "Uh, I mean ..."

"You know the riddle?" Aimee asked. "What begins with *f* and ends with *k*, and sometimes instead of the real thing people use their fingers?"

The roofer grinned. "Name's Juke," he said. "You won't regret this. That's a forkin' promise."

A promise that for the most part he kept. Three weeks later, after Wally told Aimee how delighted he was with how Juke was working out, she told Wally what she'd found in the glove box of the truck: a pair of diamond earrings and a ring with a giant ruby cluster. The ring was one-of-a-kind. Aimee and Wally had seen it several times—on the hand of Mrs. Politzer.

"Yeah," Juke admitted when Wally asked, "I was the Hidden-Key Burglar. Forkin' famous, wasn't I?"

According to the police reports, a rash of burglaries in the Atherton area had been committed by somebody who seemed to know the location of everybody's hidden key. There was never a sign of forced entry.

"Sometimes I took out a window. Section of siding. Attic vent. Whatever. Doors? Who needs doors? People put twenty forkin' locks on the door, but a house is just a buncha stuff nailed together. Carpenter built it. Carpenter can crack it. Good carpenter can make it look like nothin' happened."

"Can I really trust you?"

"I just needed a job, man. Prison's the shits. I ain't goin' back. Your wife is a saint."

Actually, Wally knew that Aimee wasn't always saintly. And from the get-go Juke had known it too. But Wally wasn't going to dredge up bad memories now that she was dead. As Wally was becoming interested in another woman and feeling guilty to the memory of Aimee to whom he wanted to be everlastingly loyal—and who had ultimately proved her loyalty to Wally—he had to be careful not to let his mind play tricks on him. Not to make comparisons. Not to remember fights and betrayals. Especially betrayals. Never a sign of forced entry. It really did seem as if Juke had a hidden key. But Wally wasn't thinking about his wife, naked, her belly wet with sweat and her throat making little pleading sounds as she throbbed in the heat of passion with his best friend and business companion. No, not one little neuron would think about what he wasn't thinking about.

Aimee would approve of giving FrogGirl shelter. In fact, Wally suspected it was Aimee's spirit totally imprinted in his own that had made him offer to take FrogGirl to the house, bringing her, on this Sunday morning, to be sleeping on his daughter's bed among a zoo of old stuffed animals.

As Wally was looking in on her, FrogGirl stirred and opened her eyes. "What're you staring at?"

"Good morning," Wally said. "Glad you're here."

Wally's good mood vanished when he sat down with his Grape-Nuts and read yesterday's newspaper. In the business section was a photo of Anton Krainer. "Hubris Humbled: History of an Accounting Scandal." The reporter got at least one detail wrong: Krainer's "partially completed palatial estate in Los Altos Hills" was actually in the upper Palo Alto hills. One detail Wally hadn't known: A week ago a landslide had wiped out Krainer's vineyard in Sonoma County, the natural result of trying to cultivate such steep terrain. Croatian grapes. Hubris, indeed. No mention of the contractors and tradesmen and farm workers and all the little people who would be humbled—*stiffed* was more like it.

Another detail that caught Wally's eye: A certain hedge fund had made a killing by spreading rumors and shorting Krainer's stock. The fund was named Pilpont Associates.

What followed was a crazy day. When it was over, Wally took a tally from his day planner. He'd made forty-two phone calls and visited eight prospective clients. In addition, he'd withdrawn cash against his credit card and cruised two flea markets. Wally had insurance—with a big deductible—on the tools. In a month or two, with luck, he'd get a check worth half of what he lost. Meantime, he needed some basics to keep his crew going. In the mail this week, almost as if they'd known he would be needing them, he'd received offers of three different credit cards. America, it's wonderful. It meets needs. He decided to use all three.

At the flea market Wally's first buy was a rusty old Delta chop saw with bearings that screamed like a fire siren. He couldn't get sentimental about chop saws—either they worked or they didn't. At the price, this one would do the task until the bearings croaked, and then he'd get another. A disposable tool. Next he found a banged-up Senco nailer with a hundred feet of hose, going cheap because the piston was frozen—a job for Juke. The old 325 was a decent gun, strong and durable.

Steamboat in particular had used one for years and years and still often wondered aloud why Senco stopped making them. Now Steamboat could be happy again. The thought warmed Wally's soul.

There were no bargains in compressors, though, only a sweet-running dual-tank Emglo that brought lust to Wally's guts but was simply out of his reach until the insurance settled. At the end of the day as everybody was packing up—on an impulse, and because it was dirt cheap—Wally considered buying a semioperable Hitachi H65 forty-pound demolition hammer. He hadn't lost a demo hammer to the thief. He'd never owned one. It simply seemed too good to pass. Maybe the seller would take fifty dollars. Maybe Juke could hot-rod it, or at least make it work right. The seller said he'd bought the new Makita forty-pounder, which was so much better that nobody was buying the Hitachi anymore, though he wouldn't have made the switch except for an eight-story building collapsing on the old tool.

Wally asked, "Anybody hurt?"

"Nope. Killed a Mexican."

"That's disgusting."

"It's a joke. From a book."

"Not funny. Not even close. And I know the book. I used to teach it."

"Sorry. You a professor?"

"Heh. No. Contractor. Taught high school a long time ago."

"Blew it, huh? So now you have to actually work for a living."

"Hey. Teaching's work."

"Tell that to your shoulder—and your back and your knees. And mine. Anyway, nobody was hurt. Don't worry. The tool ain't haunted."

Wally shook his head. "I don't want it any more. Best worker I ever had was from Mexico. He was so good I couldn't keep him. Started his own business. I loaned him the money for his first truck."

"I said I was sorry. Take it. Fifty bucks."

Wally turned his back. "You put bad karma on it."

"Look, you can have it for thirty bucks."

"No." Wally was walking away.

"Twenty-five?"

"Sold."

It came with bull and chisel points, a clay spade, a digging chisel, and even a tamper—attachments worth a couple hundred dollars even if the body couldn't be salvaged. It worried Wally, though, the bad karma. That awful racist joke was like a curse placed on this tool. Something bad would come of it.

When Wally finally arrived at home he found a clean kitchen. The stovetop gleamed; the floor sparkled. On the table two places were set with matching plates, silver, napkins.

FrogGirl stepped out of the bathroom in Sally's old bathrobe, hair wrapped in a towel. "Something you should know," she said. "I'm kind of a neatness freak."

"This is great," Wally said.

"But I don't know shit about cooking."

"I'll make spaghetti."

She looked uneasy. "Something else you should know? I hope you don't mind but I cleaned up your bathroom."

"Fabulous! But you shouldn't."

"Yes. I should. That big old orange fungus growing behind the toilet? I really had to."

Twenty-Eight

"Who's the chica?" Pancho asked.

"This is FrogGirl," Wally said. "She's the new Alfredo."

"*Alfreda*," Pancho said.

Casually, Juke sauntered out from behind the empty trailer lugging two sacks of concrete, one under each arm, as he sang at the top of his voice: "Oh I wish I was in Dixie, away, away ..." Showing no sign of strain as if he were carrying two sacks full of Styrofoam, he came to a halt in front of FrogGirl. "Hey. You. Gimme a hand."

Wally, Abe, Steamboat, Pancho—everybody watched, nobody said a word. Pokerfaced.

Looking somewhat wary—but then, FrogGirl always looked wary—she reached out.

"In Dixie land I'll take my stand ..." Juke unwrapped his arm from one bag and let it fall.

FrogGirl was ready. She caught the Quikrete with back straight, elbows against her body. Curling the bag against her chest, she glared a challenge at Juke. "The other one?"

Juke scowled.

"Lay it on me," FrogGirl said.

Juke raised the bag and then let go, dropping it—a fall of about twelve inches—on top of the one FrogGirl was already holding.

It was, Wally thought, like trying to catch a falling piano.

FrogGirl staggered as the bag hit. Bending down to her knees, she was losing the top bag as it was slipping off center but just in time she wrenched the angle of her body, curling to the side and then straightening, still holding on.

Wally felt a stab of pain in his own back simply from watching her. Holding that much weight, you don't twist your body like that. You just don't. He couldn't stop what was happening because he couldn't reveal that FrogGirl was pregnant—he'd promised—and he couldn't show favoritism or the men would never respect her.

Biting her lip, legs trembling, slowly FrogGirl began to rise—and raised herself to a standing position. Tilting her head to the sky, she shouted, "Away down *south* in Dixie!" missing half the notes.

Pancho muttered, "*Madre de Dios!*"

FrogGirl leveled her gaze at Juke. "Where do you want these?"

Wally broke in: "In the back of my truck. Just one bag at a time. Better yet—use the wheelbarrow. Please. I don't need a worker's comp claim on your first day." Wally turned to the other workers. "That's our job for this morning. Load up everything that isn't nailed down—lumber, concrete, insulation, adhesive, screws, joist hangers, rafter clips, rebar, scraps of plywood, drops of snot, everything—load up the trailer and fill up all your trucks and bring them to my house. Pile them in my back yard. I haven't been paid. And until I get paid, all these supplies are mine."

"Then what?" Steamboat said. "Any more jobs?"

"Nickel and dimers," Wally said. "Brush up on your manners."

After lunch, Wally drove off in Abe's Honda to start the crew on their various jobs, leaving Abe and FrogGirl to finish the hauling with Wally's truck, which everybody called Old Yeller. Standing in the dust at the building site as Abe followed the Civic with his gaze, FrogGirl said, "That's so typical."

"What is?" Abe asked absently.

"He gave you the keys to the truck. Because you're the *guy*."

"I have seniority."

FrogGirl snorted.

Abe twirled the key ring on the end of his finger. "You don't like me, do you?"

"I hear you're going to Princeton."

"Something wrong with that?"

"It's where cute people go."

Abe dropped the key in his pocket. "I'm cute?"

"I never said."

They started walking to the rear of the job site. Abe said, "Cute or not, Princeton happens to be a great school."

"It happens to be a great *privilege*."

"I had to work real hard for that privilege."

FrogGirl sighed wearily. "Lots of people work hard, sonny boy. All their lives they work hard. But I guess they aren't as deserving as you."

Abe and FrogGirl began to load boards from the stack of old barn wood into the back of Old Yeller. The silence of the job site surprised and slightly unnerved Abe. He'd grown used to the clatter and percussion of construction, the obnoxious buzz of the air compressor, the tapping of nails, clomping of boots, the tinny salsa music on Pancho's cheap radio, the bullshit bravado of carpenters bragging. But then FrogGirl began to fill the void.

"Why doesn't Wally have a real truck?" she demanded. "Steamboat has a bigger one than the boss. What's with that?"

"Maybe Wally lets other people do the heavy hauling."

"*We're* hauling. Maybe he's *cheap*."

"Maybe it's who he is," Abe said, and then he hoped FrogGirl wouldn't ask what he'd meant by that. It was something he'd been thinking about lately, how the workers and their trucks were so unified. Steamboat had a nearly-new Ford F350, big enough to haul just about anything, powerful, hardworking—and he'd already banged up the paint tossing pipes and nail-embedded boards around. It was Steamboat: a big guy, not too worried about his looks but solid and strong. Pancho had a ten-year-old full-size F150, waxed and polished, better-looking after ten years than Steamie's at less than one. That was Pancho: meticulous attention to detail. Juke's hoodless El Camino was all motor and tires and hubcaps. Instead of a muffler, it seemed to have an amplifier. It was all about performance. The body shell was a hodgepodge of color, salvaged parts, swaths of gray primer. And Wally's yellow Toyota was like a good old tool, one he'd used so long and so thoroughly that it had molded itself to the shape of his body.

FrogGirl was talking: "Look at this wood. This stuff is *garbage*." She slapped a hand on a board. "It's full of *cracks*. Nail holes and *rat* shit. He should just *burn* it."

"Old growth," Abe said. "That's what you call this stuff."

"Old? This wood is *dead*."

"Feel the grain," Abe said, running a finger over a plank.

Skeptically, FrogGirl did the same.

"Tight grain," Abe said. "Clear. All heart. The real gold in these hills. You know why the grain's so tight?" Against his better judgment, aware that he was probably walking into an ambush of attitude, Abe launched into a little lecture to FrogGirl on everything that Wally had told him about the difference between heart and sapwood, about knots versus clear wood, about tannin and rot resistance, about the life cycle of the tree. To his surprise, she listened without comment.

When the lumber was loaded, they climbed into the cab. Abe clicked his seat belt, turned the key ...

And the truck lurched forward into a stack of wooden pallets.

"What are you *doing?*" FrogGirl shouted. Pallets leaned on the fenders with one resting on the hood.

"I thought it was in park."

"It's a stick shift."

Abe stared at the floor pedals. "I can't drive a clutch."

"Jeezo, Princeton."

They pulled the pallets off the hood and fenders, then traded places. Abe couldn't tell whether any of the dents were new. Some of those paint scratches, though, were definitely fresh.

FrogGirl eased Old Yeller with its heavy load over the bumps of the building site. Turning onto the pavement, she kept the speed slow. The frame was shaky with the weight of lumber. "Maybe we overloaded this thing."

Abe said nothing.

Picking up a little speed, FrogGirl said, "I bet you think you look really cool cruising around in your *automatic* Honda Civic."

Abe sighed. He watched her, saying nothing. She was chewing her lip.

Staying in low gear, leaning forward slightly, squinting, FrogGirl steered the truck slowly down the narrow winding road toward the valley. Without taking her eyes off the road she said, "At least you have a car. It's not like I'm doing so great myself. At least you have parents you can live with."

"One parent. I can live with."

"One is so much more than none."

"You an orphan?"

"I wish."

Abe said nothing. He appreciated how cautiously she was driving. He wouldn't have expected it.

"I had an uncle I liked," FrogGirl said. "Only person in my entire family who was worth a shit."

Abe couldn't resist: "That is, plus yourself? Being worth a shit? I mean let's show a little self-esteem here."

"Well, yeah," FrogGirl said. "Of course plus myself. Self-esteem, that's me."

Abe made chiseling motions with his hands. "That's probably what they'll carve on your headstone, right? *FrogGirl. She was worth a shit.*"

FrogGirl grinned.

She had one of those high smiles that exposes the entire upper gum but covers the lower teeth as if the lips and jaw aren't in alignment.

The top teeth were bunched together with a gap next to the molar. It wasn't bad-looking or anything; in fact, it was kind of endearing in an uncute sort of way. Abe wondered if you have to be careful with an off-center mouth like that, if you might stick a spoon in there and hit your front teeth. Probably not. One thing Abe knew: You get used to the body you're born with. You might not like it, but you learn to live with it, as he had learned to live with being tall, skinny, and a total sucko at sports.

"Anyway, he was a storyteller, my uncle," FrogGirl said. She was still hunched slightly forward, never glancing at Abe. "Uncle Ellis. His parents named him Elvis. Isn't that an evil thing to do to your kid? So he told everybody his name was Ellis. He couldn't sing. He loved frogs."

"Hmm."

"Yeah. Hmm." FrogGirl glanced at Abe, then turned back to the road. "Me and him, we used to go down by the railroad tracks to this smelly old pond near his house and watch frogs. He could watch all day. Frogs would hop up on the tracks, and he'd run around shooing them off so they wouldn't get squashed. He was that kind of guy."

"Sounds like a good uncle."

"Good. Yeah. Not right in the head. So one day Uncle Ellis sits down on the railroad tracks. And stays there. Big old freight train cut him in half."

Abe flinched. "That's awful. I'm sorry."

"Next day I'm gone." FrogGirl fell silent, tapping her fingers on the steering wheel. "He came to me. After he died. To say good-bye. He came to my bedroom and sat on my bed and said he was going. And I should go too."

"He told you to *die?*"

"No. To leave home. So I did."

"Where you from?"

"Pasadena. I came to Palo Alto to see my other uncle but then I changed my mind because it turns out he's a total turd. So I'm walking around downtown Palo Alto on University Avenue and everything's so upscale—the stores are upscale and the restaurants are upscale and there's La Strada for God's sake—I mean, even I've heard of La Strada—and everybody's so rich and cute or else they're Stanford students which means they're even richer only they don't know it yet. I'm feeling like total alienation and I walk into this little club called Saint Michael's Asshole or something like that and meet a couple of musicians. Sort of jazzy bluegrass guys. Mandolin and a fiddle."

They're not rich, Abe thought. *They're just normal. Or what passes for normal around here.* And, it occurred to Abe, he was part of that normal. But he wished he wasn't. "I play mandolin."

"So you're not a complete waste of a human being after all. Did Wally tell you I'm a runaway?"

"No."

"I wasn't abused or anything."

Abe said nothing.

"Unless you count emotional torture," FrogGirl added. "But then maybe that's typical. Deranged family, cute sister, bitch mother, bizarre high school, the typical teenage experience, right? Wrong? I mean, what do I know? I'm only a *teenager.*"

Abe laughed.

"And so are you, Princeton. Mister Big Shot. You're only a teenager too. The difference between you and me is you know what you want. All I know is what I don't want."

"And what is it that you don't want?"

"Emotional torture."

"So how long have you been in Palo Alto?"

"Ten weeks."

FrogGirl went silent, chewing her lip. She seemed to have gone inward.

Abe kept sneaking glances at her—and every time she caught him. *What is it with girls—they always know when you look at them.* He was, he had to admit, slightly attracted to her. All right, more than slightly. She had spunk.

"So where do you want to go to college?" Abe asked.

"Don't you get it? I just ran away from high school."

"You could finish here."

"I was flunking."

"Why? You're not stupid."

FrogGirl seemed surprised. "You flatter me."

"Not really. But you're obviously bright."

"My Uncle Ellis said I've got some problems with authority."

"No kidding."

FrogGirl chewed her lip again. "As a matter of fact, so did he. And look what happened...He was a good man ...Anyway, I'm not planning to lie down in front of a freight train."

"Whew." Abe pretended to wipe sweat from his forehead.

"You care?"

"Of course I care."

"You don't even know me."

"I'd like to."

"I'm a lesbian."

"Whatever."

"You don't believe me, do you?"

"Not really. But it's okay if you are."

"Just because I played basketball. Just because I was good at it. One time my elbow—it was an accident—knocked somebody's tooth out. The wrong tooth on the most wrong girl possible. Ever after, I was a dyke."

"But you're not."

"I could start. How did you know I'm not?"

"I didn't know," Abe said. "How could I? I'm just a *teenager*."

She grinned.

Abe found that he liked making her grin. She was pretty when she smiled, off center and all. Totally real, Abe noted. Acne and everything— just like him.

"It's not so much cute," Abe said. "Palo Alto. It's that they're soft."

"Soft." FrogGirl chewed on the word, considering. "Squishy squashy."

Abe knew he was talking about his friends, neighbors, classmates. Until he started working with Juke and Wally and everybody, he was one of the soft ones too. Now he felt as if he were on the outside, looking back.

When they reached Wally's house, Abe hopped out and guided FrogGirl using hand signals while she backed the truck into Wally's yard, which already looked like a junkyard.

As they were unloading the lumber, FrogGirl asked, "Did they do that concrete bag thing to you?"

"Yes," Abe said.

"How'd you do?"

"I collapsed," Abe said. "First bag. Squishy squashy."

FrogGirl hesitated. They were holding opposite ends of a sixteen-foot plank, so when FrogGirl stopped, Abe stopped moving too. "Notice I'm not laughing at you," FrogGirl said. "You must've toughened up some since then."

"Thank you."

"Not the concrete exactly, but I was kind of expecting some hazing."

Without any signal, they both started moving again with the old board. *How'd we do that?* Abe wondered. *How'd we get in sync?*

"I didn't just collapse," Abe said as they laid the plank on top of the pile. "The bag broke and dumped all over me. Inside my clothes. In my mouth. My nose."

"Did it get in your eyes? Did it sting?"

"I must've shut my eyes. Reflex."

"Good thing. I gotta watch it, actually. With cement and stuff. Chemicals."

"What for?"

"Just—you know—they're not good for you." A shiver ran down FrogGirl's spine.

"You okay?" Abe was studying her. "Something scare you? You looked—"

"Come on, Princeton. There's more work to do."

FrogGirl returned to the cab of the truck. Her heart seemed to have made a choice without bothering to inform her brain until this moment. *Hello, brain. We have created another soul inside this body, and you will protect it from harm. Always. Forever.*

Her heart had already made one very bad decision: the few minutes she had spent with a fuzzy-faced fiddle player in his Palo Alto basement bedroom. Was she making another? Was it an act of faith? Uncle Ellis had faith in the beauty of frogs. Was it really about love? What did she know about love? *What do I know about anything? I'm seventeen years old and I made the most idiotic mistake a girl can make. But I'm not stupid. Abe said so.*

Twenty-Nine

People and their homes. Wally loved it. And no contracts—strictly handshake deals, Wally's favored method of business. He set up Steamboat at a comfy old ranch house in Menlo Park where the elderly couple wanted a platform built in the garage above where they parked their Lexus so they could store suitcases and Christmas decorations. Steamboat climbed up a ladder to look around. The old woman, who was wearing a flour-dusted apron over a calico dress, said to her husband, "Eugene, you'd better move the cat dish from under the ladder. We wouldn't want the carpenter to fall on it and hurt himself."

Not budging and in no hurry, white-haired Eugene stared first at the loft area and then slowly lowered his eyes to the floor. "If he falls," the old man said, "he'll hit the beam up there and break his neck. He'll be dead long before he reaches the cat dish."

"Oh," his wife said. "All right then."

"Work safe, Steamie," Wally said.

"Gotcha," Steamboat said.

Steamboat was easy-going, a good match for these old folks. He worked slowly but meticulously and would build a storage loft that was solid and strong, just like himself, no great beauty but something you could always depend on. And that's why Wally had chosen him for this job.

Next Wally set Juke to work at a handsomely designed house of redwood and glass in Portola Valley where an underground leak had dug a gully under a concrete patio, sending a stream of water cascading down an embankment and into the street. A neighbor wandered over and said he'd told the homeowners about the problem a couple of months ago. All that the owners had done was shut off the main valve to the house except for a half hour or so in the morning and evening—living mostly without water for the last two months. "When did they call you?" the neighbor asked.

"Last week," Wally said.

"Amazing," the neighbor said.

"People procrastinate," Wally said.

The neighbor shook his head. "Either they're cheap or they're idiots."

Wally, Juke, and the neighbor all studied the house. It was probably worth several million. The husband was a surgeon, the wife an attorney.

"Don't underestimate inertia," Wally said.

"Or tightwads," the neighbor said, and he wandered off.

Wally pulled the flea-market demolition hammer from the back of his truck. "Your assignment, Juke, should you choose to accept it, is to make this hammer work. Then open the patio, find the leak, fix it, and patch up the concrete."

Juke studied the hammer. "Was there a train wreck?" Juke asked.

"Eight-story building fell on it."

"And you think I can fix that thing? Couldn't we just rent a real jackhammer? Wanna talk about tightwads?"

"Honor thy tools, Juke."

"That's about good tools."

Juke was Wally's best man for creative solutions. Whatever problem lurked beneath that concrete, Wally was confident that Juke could solve it just as he could solve the repair of the Hitachi hammer. Juke's weakness was in exposure to women. Wally couldn't put Juke in a situation where he'd be alone with a female, be she the client's wife, nanny, daughter, architect, or housecleaner. Disaster was likely to follow. This project— alone on a backyard patio with no human contact—seemed a perfect fit.

At Wally's next stop, he and Pancho examined a shelf unit that a homeowner had built out of pine. The unit was eight feet long. When the man tried to move it from his back yard, where'd he'd built it, to the bedroom where he wanted it, he discovered that it wouldn't fit around a corner in the hallway. Then he'd had a heart attack. Now his wife wanted Wally to take the unit apart, move it into the bedroom, and reassemble it for her husband who would be returning from the hospital tomorrow.

Wally ran his finger over the pine.

Pancho frowned. To Wally he whispered: "Eet look like sheet, mon."

Speaking in bad Spanish (and only knowing the present tense), illustrating with hand gestures, Wally told Pancho: Make smooth the marks of the hammer. And make square the ends. Run a—how to say—this thing *(pointing to a router)* of the edges to make round a little bit. The nails to the garbage. Use screws. Make hole for screw. How to say? Then, in English: "Countersink the screws." Back to Spanish: "*Comprende?*"

"*Claro*, Boss."

It embarrassed Wally that his Spanish was so bad. He could learn the words, but he couldn't assemble them into a finished product. Somehow he and Pancho always understood each other. Pancho was an artist, something inborn, the best man for finish work combining craftsmanship with a sense of color, proportion, and just the right detail.

Wally told the woman that Pancho would have to bang up the shelf unit taking it apart, but he'd make it look like new.

Actually, of course, the unit would come apart without damage. After Pancho sanded, routed, squared, and assembled everything, the sum of small improvements would look much better but not so professional as to shame the heart-attack husband who built it. Hubby could be proud of it and claim it as his own, which mostly it was.

Wally liked to think that he didn't just repair houses. He fixed homes.

Wally's truck was his office. With folding aluminum clipboard, pads of graphing paper, cell phone, change order forms, an ashtray full of pens and pencils, a Thermos of tea and another of hot chocolate, yellow Post-Its stuck to the windshield and rear-view mirror, Wally juggled schedules and generated business.

Lastly, Wally set up Abe and FrogGirl to help him hang drywall in a garage that was being converted into a children's playroom. He showed them how to score and snap drywall and how to space the nails. It was a simple project, a good one for beginners where Wally could teach basic skills and work habits.

Abe's hammering sucked. He just wasn't getting any better. The bent nail would rip the face-paper open, or else Abe wouldn't drive hard enough to dimple the surface, or he'd drive too hard and punch a hole. The more he tried, the more frustrated he became, especially since FrogGirl got the knack of tapping drywall nails right away. It seemed to Wally that Abe was trying to look good in front of FrogGirl, as if they were in a competition, and the harder Abe pressed, the worse he performed. To prevent further damage, Wally put Abe in charge of measuring and cutting—he could be the math guy. Wally hoped Abe wouldn't slice himself with the utility knife. He wanted Abe to succeed—more important, he wanted Abe to *feel* success—and, oddly, Wally had observed Abe's confidence growing daily even though Abe's skills weren't improving at all. Wally suspected that Abe was so taken with the idea of being a carpenter—and of not being his father, not following his father's intellectual and social footsteps—that he was blind to the actual results. The one time Abe had shown a real talent was the day he'd demolished the foundation wall using, come to think of it, a tool exactly like the one Juke was now repairing. Abe had attacked that wall with such zest, it was almost spooky. Abe the demo master.

As he had placed Steamboat, Juke, and Pancho in the jobs best matching their skills and personalities, likewise Wally believed he had placed himself in the right place: teaching two teenagers the skills, the teamwork. Letting them learn the pleasure of solid results. Instilling hard work and quiet pride.

FrogGirl, at one point, catching Wally alone outside fetching a rasp from his truck, asked, "Is this stuff, the dust and all, like, toxic or anything?"

"No."

Their eyes met.

Wally understood full well what he'd just been told. To his surprise, his heart began pounding. He said, "I'll warn you about anything you, uh, might need to avoid."

"Thanks."

"And I just want to say, I'm so happy you made this choice."

"Were you gonna show me pictures of dead fetuses?"

"No. I would've taken you to the clinic. Not said a word as you walked into the back room. And then I would've sat in the lobby and cried."

"Will you be honorary grandfather?"

"Am I that old?"

"Yeah."

"Who's the father?"

"Nobody." Her eyes were defiant.

Wally considered his options. Basically, none. If she wouldn't tell, she wouldn't tell. He moved on: "After work, I want to stop at a house on the way home. Somebody I want you to meet."

FrogGirl narrowed her eyes. "Who?"

"Friend of mine. Female. Name's Opal. I think you'll like her."

"Don't you dare tell her."

"FrogGirl, I, you, uh, we need help. She'll take you to a doctor. You need a checkup. You need—"

"You take me."

"I don't like—that is, I don't especially want to go there."

"You said you wouldn't tell anybody. You promised."

"Sooner or later, it will be obvious."

"Later."

At her age, Wally suspected, a few months in the future probably seemed like a few centuries.

"All right," Wally said. "I'll take you."

He really, really, *really* didn't want to see an ob/gyn. A feeling of near-panic was clutching his chest. But he could suck it up if he had to. *This is about FrogGirl, not you,* he told himself. She was just a child. She had little idea what she was launching for herself. Somehow suddenly he was responsible for her. By offering shelter, he'd volunteered. *Of course you have to take her to the doctor. You're the designated grown-up in her life.*

Thirty

We might live ninety years on this planet, and yet it is just a few small moments that define our lives. Wally called them moments of clarity. A couple years before FrogGirl dropped into Wally's house, he had been driving home after a pleasant job. He'd been working for Gunther, one of his favorite longtime clients, a retired schoolteacher and fountain of dubious facts who had watched and kibitzed and generally entertained as Wally ripped out a rotten old porch and constructed a new one. While working, Wally had complained about the chronic pain in his back. Gunther responded that the most common injury of the pioneers during the westward movement in the United States wasn't arrows from Indians or gunshots from outlaws but was back injury. Plain old back injury. And here we are in the Silicon Valley of California a hundred and fifty years later and nothing, really, has changed. Which was not a defining moment in Wally's life, mind you, but it was interesting.

Reflecting on Gunther and his amiable company, Wally was driving along Portola Road in the manicured town of Portola Valley, a notorious speed trap where the law was enforced selectively: A Mercedes would get a free pass, a pickup would get a ticket. It was a speed limit for nonresidents. Wally in his pickup took note of six boys in the bike lane ahead, single file, pedaling furiously, apparently racing. Age eleven or so, from a glance. Just as Wally caught up with the trailing bicycle, one of the boys lost control. The front bike wheel wobbled.

Suddenly the boy and his bike swerved. They shot into the road directly in front of Wally's truck—and collapsed. Boy and bike toppled onto the asphalt and scraped a semicircular path.

Wally hit the brakes.

The wheels froze.

The truck went into a skid; the tires screeched. The boy looked up at Wally with naked terror.

Their eyes locked.

The truck jerked to a stop with its front bumper about six inches shy of the boy's head as the toolboxes in the bed crashed against the back of the cab.

Then there was absolute silence.

Wally could smell the smoke of tires.

The other boys had stopped, staring, jaws dropped.

The kid stood up. He was wearing a helmet. Road burn on one arm.

For a few seconds, Wally and the kid just gazed at each other, separated by a windshield, not a word spoken. The boy had blue eyes, blond hair, a body fair, uncompleted, restless. No apologies and no thanks. In fact the boy seemed angry as if it were all Wally's fault. Hopping onto his bike, the boy joined his companions and hightailed it out of there.

Wally couldn't move.

He was shaking.

Those blue eyes still blazed into Wally's. And—from nowhere—something had crystallized in his soul.

We zip through our days hustling from one petty crisis to another thinking we are doing important things and then—*wham!* Something puts it in perspective. Okay, some of Wally's thoughts were practical: like, he was speeding. Forty in a 35–miles-per-hour zone. If he'd hit Kid Blue-Eyes, little Adonis, little surfer-snot, they would've nailed Wally. He was enough of a workingman to believe the law would never treat him fairly and enough of an intellectual to realize that this line of thinking was trivia. Something far more important had spoken to him in that moment, something powerful, a message from somewhere outside.

Wally drove home. Slowly. Reflecting. He was fifty-three years old. He had raised three children, two college graduates and one nearly so—heartstoppingly beautiful children who would do wonderful works for this planet if nobody killed them first. Wally had been through the midnight barfings, the rampaging toddlers, the schlepping from soccer to birthday party to dance lessons. Aimee was a fantastic mother but they shared it. Wally could take some credit too. Raising children was something he seemed to be pretty good at, perhaps (or so he thought in his darker moments) the only thing he'd done well in his entire life.

Aimee in the kitchen was cutting veggies for soup. She saw trouble in a glance, set down the knife. "What happened?"

"A kid. I came this close."

She studied the space between Wally's hands as if she could see the whole scene. And maybe she could. Wally told her how it all happened. Then he said, "I know you won't want to do this, but I just want you to know how I feel."

"Do? Do what?" Standing at the cutting board, carrot in hand, Aimee waited. Already, Wally suspected, she knew what was coming. You live that long with a person, you get telepathic.

"I want to do it again," Wally said.

"It?"

"A baby. More kids."

"Oh, shit."

"Okay." Wally capitulated. "Never mind." She didn't need to marshal arguments. The *oh, shit* said it all. Running the math. If they conceived one today, Wally would be seventy-two when the kid turned eighteen. Aimee would be sixty-eight. Social Security. Medicare. What a stupid idea. But still to his surprise he felt crushed. And his face undoubtedly showed it.

Gently, Aimee said, "It's too late, you know. Hormone-wise."

"Not entirely."

"I'm on the edge. Who knows what's going on down there?"

"You know, Aimee. You've always known." She could always tell when she was ovulating.

She stepped up to Wally, put her hands on his shoulders with a carrot still in the grip of her fingers while Wally placed hands on her waist as if they were going to dance, but they stood there, and she did not say that he was out of his mind, or that he was upset and should calm down, or that having a kid would ruin them financially (which it would), or that he was trying to deny his age. Instead she said, sadly but wisely, "I'm really looking forward to being a grandparent. I'm really looking forward to helping our kids get established in the world. I want to do that. I want to stay part of their lives. If we had a baby, we'd lose that. We couldn't travel. They aren't coming back to live here, and to see them we'll have to go to Boston or Africa or who knows where. And …you know …we're getting kind of decrepit." She brought the carrot to Wally's neck and rubbed it up and down below his ear. Nothing decrepit about her soul. Her face was deeply freckled, deeply lined, the work of forty-nine years. A sun worshiper, always dark-skinned. To Wally she seemed to soak it up by day and beam it back at night when they were alone. Now she was looking up at Wally as if he were the light. Seeming sad and proud and regretful all at the same time, she said: "We made masks today." She'd gone back to teaching kindergarten. "And Andy— you remember Andy?"

"Of course." She was always telling about Andy. He had no self-control.

"Andy was so happy with his mask, he punched me in the stomach."

"Because he was happy?"

"Yep."

"So did it hurt?"

"Yep."

"You okay?"

"Yep."

From the shed outside they could hear the wail of electric guitar—Leo, their youngest, home for the summer from college and practicing with his band. The thump of the bass. It was a song Leo had written, called "Who Invented God?"

Aimee swayed her hips to the music, bobbing her arms with a carrot in one hand, and said, "There's nothing near as sexy as a good man who wants a baby."

"You know any good men?"

"One." She closed her eyes, touched her forehead to Wally's chest.

He had that tingly feeling. That man-woman feeling where everything quickens, where suddenly you notice the smell of hair, of sweat, where every stupid thing you've been thinking has disappeared and all you feel is warmth coming at you from that other body like a wave.

Her voice, muffled against Wally's chest: "How'd you know?"

"What?"

"You must have known."

"What?"

Slowly she lifted her head, raised her eyes to him. "I'm ovulating right now."

"You sure?"

"And I don't want to waste it."

With the carrot in one hand she led Wally with the other down the hall, a precious egg now floating somewhere in her body, hitchhiker on an empty road. From the shed, another song: Leo's drum and wah-wah guitar version of Pachelbel's "Canon." Wally locked the door. Aimee was unbuckling her jeans. They were eager as teenagers. Making babies was so different, so fantastically superior to plain old making love that Wally believed there ought to be a better word for it. They felt the presence of other souls, an audience of the unborn, tiny spirits hovering in an aura that glowed in that bed, that room, that house that they had lived in—temporarily—for twenty years, waiting until Wally could find the time and money to build the house of their dreams. Together, right here in this same bed that had followed them from house to house, they had framed three wondrous beings. Could they make more? They had shared the child-raising, each working part-time, sacrificing jobs, changing careers while their friends bought better houses, better cars. Gradually they had increased their working hours as the kids grew older until now at last they were both at full-time. At last earning almost as much as they spent. What now? What insanity—their aching muscles, grinding bones—to become rooted again to the demands of a helpless infant. But sanity is overrated.

Afterwards, as the day faded, they lay on the sheets in the heat and dampness, cuddling flesh to flesh, sharing the carrot, chewing noisily, not talking. The aura faded and a vast black unknown opened before them. Aimee whispered: "Don't tell anybody. Let's."

"Yeah."

No expectations. And no ridicule. Again that feeling like teenagers, like they'd sinned but they'd had to.

Voices in the twilight outside the window, boys coming out of the shed. Band practice was finished. Wally and Aimee hustled to get up and be decent but still as they dressed in near darkness they said nothing, a little thoughtful, a little scared.

And so it began.

In case Aimee conceived, she stopped taking medicine. Her cholesterol level shot up, endangering her life, but she was willing to take the risk. Eventually Wally and Aimee revealed to one dear old friend what they were trying to do. The friend responded: *You guys are nuts.* Then they told one other friend, this one the same age as Aimee but childless. This friend said: *You're making me want one too.* They told no one else. They started noticing how young most parents seemed—how energetic and fresh. They met with a lawyer about writing a will. Wally started shopping for a truck with antilock brakes. Aimee missed a period—but nothing came of it. She made an appointment with her ob/gyn and Wally went with her and so they both sat in Dr. Robinson's office together, side by side in semicomfortable chairs, when the news was delivered that Aimee had ovarian cancer. Two months later she was dead.

Life isn't as complicated as we try to make it seem. Ultimately it all boils down to a few things like birth, love, death. Watching FrogGirl, who was learning a trade while on the cusp of motherhood, missing Aimee who still wasn't answering his letters, falling in love with Opal who didn't want sex, Wally felt that he was struggling with a mix of all three. He'd be okay. He was an adaptable guy. If necessary, certain events in his past had taught him how to function with a high degree of hurt. Right now, though, he felt no pain. Just confusion. Some sadness. Some hope. Some need to adjust. Which is why after taking FrogGirl to Dr. Robinson and sitting in those same semicomfortable chairs, after bringing home a dinner of pizza and sparkling water, as FrogGirl tidied up a few dishes while humming "Smells Like Teen Spirit" to herself, Wally stared into the bubbles in his glass and said, "Would you like to help me with a little project?"

In the back yard, Wally stood before the stack of old redwood. "You know what this is?" Wally asked.

"Old growth," FrogGirl said.

Wally arched his eyebrows. "That's right," he said.

"The real gold." FrogGirl ran a finger over a plank. "Tight grain. Some of this lumber probably started growing in the ninth century. Think of that."

"Golly," Wally said. He felt secretly proud.

Wally selected only the ugliest boards, the ones nobody would want if they were looking at the surface. He and FrogGirl carried the old planks into the shed that Wally used as a workshop.

Shining a bright, hand-held light over each board, they inspected for embedded nails and removed them. FrogGirl started to dig at an inset nailhead with the claw of a hammer and Wally had the pleasure of saying, "A hammer is a *vulgar* tool," something an old Swedish carpenter had said to Wally back when he was just learning the trade. He showed her how to remove the nails gently, carefully tapping them back with a nail set and then pulling with pliers or else rocking the hammer on a scrap so as to leave no new blemishes in the wood.

Wearing baseball hats over their hair and bandannas over their noses they belt-sanded each plank with the roughest paper, forty grit, until the sawdust on the floor rose over the tops of their shoes. Free-floating, spicy-smelling powder coated their clothing and their exposed flesh. Behind the safety glasses dust piled on their eyebrows like little drifts of brown snow. Beneath the black and silver surface, a rugged rosy-brown color of good wood emerged along with naked streaks of damage where insects had burrowed, water had soaked, oil had penetrated, tools had mauled, horses had kicked, weight had crushed.

Hesitant at first, FrogGirl was good with her hands and strong enough to keep the heavy Bosch belt sander under control, pointed with the grain, and constantly moving so it wouldn't gouge the wood.

Every evening after work, Wally guided FrogGirl through another step of the task. With the radial arm saw, an ancient DeWalt that groaned as it started and squealed as it braked, they cut off the ragged ends and chopped out the rasty sections.

With finer paper, eighty and then hundred-twenty grit on the whining Bosch, they resanded the remaining planks to a smooth dull sheen. Wally examined each piece for quality, for potential color, for strength, or for a special ripple of grain.

To Wally's exact dimensions they cut the planks again. FrogGirl imitated Wally's crouching eye-to-the-wood, butt-to-the-air aligning of pencil mark to blade. Then rising, pushing the red button, she flinched at the rumble as the motor gained speed. Wally gave her some sound-deadening earmuffs to wear, but she kept removing them so she could hear his quiet instructions. Wally was working slowly, deliberately, enjoying every minute. A great peacefulness of mind came over him whenever he worked in his own little woodshop on his own little projects, no deadlines, no commitments. No actual plans.

"Not to be too nosy," FrogGirl said, "but what are we making?"

"Toy chests," Wally said. "Something I saw once. An old Shaker design."

"Shaker as in salt?"

"Religious sect. They shook all over when they got the spirit."

"Like Elvis?"

"Without the drugs. They used to build beautiful furniture, plain and simple. Very practical people building very practical things. I hear they invented the clothes pin."

FrogGirl looked surprised. "What did people do before they had clothes pins?"

Wally shrugged. "You had to stand around holding the wet clothes until they dried."

"Right." FrogGirl nodded. "Maybe that's why they started shaking. They weren't getting the spirit—they were drying the laundry."

While FrogGirl was cutting the planks Wally marked and cut out a dovetail template. Not a purist, Wally would have been happy to use a router or a saber saw, but the ancient wood was too brittle. Only a cautious touch with hand tools—a fine-toothed backsaw, a coping saw, a sharp chisel gently applied—could prevent chipping or cracking. After some trial and error he created a dovetail pattern that satisfied him, using extra-large pins and tails. The ancient wood was too weak and unpredictable for closely-spaced cuts, and the large joints would, he hoped, show the plain virtue of what they were: handwork.

Laying the template on a plank, Wally demonstrated to FrogGirl. To his surprise she could actually do the marking and backsawing better than he—with sharper eyes and a steadier hand. Clamping planks together she could saw four at a time. It was still softwood, easily sliced. As she completed her cuts she passed the boards to Wally for coping and chiseling. Wally worked the chisel by hand, rarely needing the tap of a mallet. The wood yielded to their touch.

They worked side by side, FrogGirl often humming to herself, a sound as pleasing to Wally as the coughing of the handsaw and the burrowing of the chisel.

After two full evenings they had cut their way through a third of the pile. Wally contemplated the remaining stack.

He felt the first twinges of stress creeping into his chest.

Two evenings of dovetailing had been pleasant. Four more would be drudgery. Somewhere you have to strike a balance between getting things right and getting things done. Wally had a personality suited to building houses, not jewelry boxes—to production, not exquisite detail. Among his peers Wally was considered a slow house-builder, a man who took time for quality—but still he had the housebuilder's drive to keep things moving. You could hang a door in an hour that was ninety-nine percent aligned and true in three dimensions, a door that closed with a solid click and never rattled in the wind, or you could go for a hundred pecent and keep adjusting one thing that would throw another thing out of alignment and spend hours on the project. And then the humidity will change, the wood will swell or shrink, and you're back to ninety-nine percent. Life changes. And wood is alive—even when it's dead. Like the Shakers he admired, Wally came to a practical decision: The rest of the corners would be joined with glue and finish nails. The resulting lines would be smoother, less fussy. He wasn't sure which would look better, actually, with or without dovetails. Each would have integrity. Each would have strength—the glue would be stronger than the wood it was holding.

As they glued and nailed, Wally told FrogGirl of the Swedish carpenter he'd met, a man who built and sold Shaker-style furniture. At one point the carpenter had visited some old folks who were actual Shakers. He was expecting to see marvelous examples of their style, clean lines and solid craft, their reverence for good workmanship put to everyday use. Instead he found them sitting in plastic chairs. Somebody had offered what they considered a foolishly high price for their furniture, and they'd sold. Instead of building replacements they'd found these solid, sturdy items at Montgomery Ward. If the Shakers were still building today, Wally suspected that with their respect for the plain, the durable, the functional, they'd be building with plastic.

"What happened to the Shakers?" FrogGirl asked.

"They died out. Didn't believe in sexual intercourse. Sort of hampered their ability to raise children."

"And you say these people were practical?"

"What I like is, they believed that building something well was an act of prayer."

"Amen," FrogGirl said, applying a bead of glue. "They should've tried building babies well. As a prayer. They might've had more fun at it than I did."

And what a shame, Wally thought, *to make a baby without that amazing moment of spiritual unity.* For himself and Aimee it had been their deepest and most joyous bond. *Maybe that was our form of prayer.*

Wally and FrogGirl created the bases for two dozen toy chests. Each box was rectangular. Eight were dovetailed, an eye-catching but busy detail. FrogGirl loved them. She was proud of her work. Wally was more pleased with the nail-and-glue joints: modest and yet honest.

Covering the top of the toy chests would be an arched lid composed of flat planks, each at a slight angle to the next, and in the final step planed to roundness on the top surface.

There is something deeply satisfying about planing wood. Scarcely speaking, hushed as in a church, and awash in the scent of ancient lumber, Wally and FrogGirl spent an entire evening among the quiet scraping of blade on board and the crinkle of shavings underfoot.

After planing, they hand-sanded the domed lids, then experimented with stain. On test scraps Wally showed how the old redwood would darken with oil to nearly black. By mixing white stain with clear oil and adding a hint of red, through trial and error Wally created a blend that avoided darkening and made the old lumber jump with color, regaining the rosy glow of fresh redwood and highlighting the undulations of grain. For another silent evening amid the sweet smell of linseed oil, Wally and FrogGirl rubbed rags over the toy chests as the boards seemed to quicken at their touch.

At last the boxes were lined up in rows, lids open, brass hinges attached, a lingering aroma of linseed and sawdust wafting in the air. Wally wondered if the old trees—witnesses to history, mighty machines of patience and growth—could possibly be satisfied, perhaps even honored, by the result.

FrogGirl seemed pleased.

"Pick one," Wally said, sweeping his hand toward the open toy chests.

"For me?"

"You and the kid."

Something flickered in FrogGirl. Wally's words had startled and then pleased her. Wally suspected he knew what it was: He'd called that pollywog inside "the kid." Probably the first person to do so. As if he'd made it real.

Seriously, studiously, FrogGirl wandered among the toy boxes, the right hand touching them one by one, the left hand unconsciously held flat against the bottom of her belly.

Each toy chest showed variations in grain and color. Some of the boards had sucked up the oil stain, others had resisted. Some were more weathered, softer, patterned by insect burrowing or ancient nail holes, by sun on the south side or moss on the north or, being barnwood, an animal nuzzling and rubbing for year upon year. FrogGirl selected a dovetailed box, dark, a deep rich reddish brown marbled with veins of pure black.

"May I take it now? To my room?"

"You bet."

She wrapped the chest in an old towel, carried it under one arm, hesitated at the door. "Thank you," she said. "I mean, not just for the toy box. I mean, this was real. This was fresh."

"Uh huh."

She hugged the box. "I'm *happy* with this."

"You bet."

Humming, she walked to the house.

Wally lingered in the workshop, leaning with both hands on a worktable, fingers scrunching on curly feathers from the plane. He closed his eyes, taking a deep breath, washing his lungs in the scent. The pressure had vanished from his chest. Yes, the pleasures—and trials—of life were simple indeed. We build shelter, we raise food, we learn a craft, we pass it on. Birth, love, death. And rebirth.

Thirty-One

In lengthening shadows Wally stepped out of his truck on the placid street in front of Opal's house. Loud thumping reggae music—Bob Marley, "War"—was blasting from the open window of Abe's bedroom dormer. On the roof Abe sat hunched against the chimney, scowling at the obese houses that surrounded him. In the yard, the golden retrievers Leary and Timothy alternately wagged their tails at Wally and made worried glances roofward with tails tucked between legs.

Ronny opened the front door. Solemnly, automatically, he offered his hand—the left hand—for a handshake. Though Wally no longer wore a bandage, he made no effort to switch Ronny to the right hand nor would he tell him that shaking hands was an unusual habit for a two-year-old. It was their bond.

"I brought something for you," Wally said, setting down a toy chest.

Squatting, Ronny opened and closed the lid. He wrinkled his nose. "Smelly," he said.

"That's the oil," Wally said. "It'll go away."

"What do you say, Ronny?" Opal said, striding in from the kitchen.

"Fank you."

"It's a toy box," Wally said. "To keep toys in. Something every boy should have."

Ronny seemed skeptical.

"You made it yourself, didn't you?" Opal said. "That was sweet of you."

"Something every Princeton lad should have too. I brought one for Abe."

Opal frowned. "This may not be the best time." She nodded toward the upstairs. "We're having a crisis. I don't normally allow this kind of racket."

There was the tap of quick footsteps behind Wally, a whine of greeting from the dogs. A young woman, dark-haired and intense, stepped in.

"Is he okay?" Rachel asked.

"Just angry," Opal said. "Go on up. You know how to get on the roof?"

"Been there." Rachel hurried up the stairs.

Opal's eyes widened at the "Been there," and a worried frown crossed her face. Then, turning to Wally, Opal took a deep breath. "Abe won't be needing a toy box at Princeton. They just un-accepted him."

"They can do that?"

"Can and did. 'With regret,' but very firm. And it's too late now to start fall term at any other school. I think. We're just starting to scramble on this. It's about bat droppings." Opal glanced toward Ronny. "Could I explain this later?"

"Uh. Sure." Wally kneeled in front of Ronny. "Want me to take this toy chest to your room for you?"

"Baff," Ronny said.

"It doesn't go in the tub," Wally said. "It shouldn't go in the water."

"Baff," Ronny said.

"You want to keep your bath toys in it? In the bathroom?"

"Yes!"

Wally, still kneeling, and Ronny both looked up questioningly at Opal.

"Then the baffroom it will be," Opal said.

"Yay!" Immediately Ronny started pushing the toy chest across the hardwood floor.

"Let me carry that," Wally said, reaching for the box.

"No!" Ronny hacked Wally's hands away.

"Hey!" Wally said with a touch of anger.

"Let him go," Opal said.

"He's scratching your nice oak floor."

"I choose my priorities," Opal said.

If Wally had fostered any doubts about Opal, he erased them at that moment. Her house was to be lived in, used. As was the toy chest, which in the bathroom would quickly be stained by splashes of soap and water. Next visit, he would bring some polyurethane and apply it.

Wally was aware of shouting on the rooftop, both Abe's and Rachel's voices, in addition to Bob Marley. Opal didn't seem to notice. She was studying the retreating toy box. "How'd you put that horseshoe pattern on the front?"

"Just chose the board and put it there," Wally said, and he explained where the wood had come from: One plank on the south wall over the barn door had apparently had a horseshoe hanging from a nail. The shoe was gone, the nail was gone, but a nail hole with rust stain remained as archeological evidence and so did the pattern of the horseshoe where it had shielded the wood from the sun's rays. When Wally had sanded it, the soft surface of the plank melted away except for where it had been protected by the shadow of the horseshoe, leaving a raised pattern, a ghost. He'd chosen the board specially for the front of Ronny's toy chest.

"I hate to think of what he'll do to that box," Opal said. "Sooner or later, it ends up in the tub. And it's so ...so brilliant."

"Competent," Wally said.

"I disagree." Opal wagged a finger at Wally. "Naively brilliant. Like folk art. I love those oversize dovetails. They have a slightly rough edge to them, a sense of limitations in the material or the tools available and yet a decision was made to enhance them, to go with the limitation and make a statement about craft. It's delightful. I sense your effort, your judgment, your soul shaped into the spirit of the wood. It gives me chills."

"You a critic or something?"

"I do some reviews for the paper. And that one was a rave." Opal studied Wally as if she were framing him. "Could I take some photos of you? At a time when you're not nailed to a house?"

"Uh, sure."

"I want to see if I can capture your inner warmth."

"How?"

"With a camera, of course."

"I meant, what would I be doing?"

"I don't know. Posing. It would take some trial and error."

"Would I be nude?"

"Euw." Opal made a face.

At that moment, Rachel came stomping down the stairs.

"Was he horrible?" Opal asked.

Rachel paused at the foot of the stairs. She seemed to be considering whether to share any information with likely-to-be-clueless adults. After a moment she said, "You might say we had a fight."

"I'm sorry to hear that, Rachel," Opal said. "Whatever idiotic thing he may have said, please bear in mind that he's upset."

"Do you know somebody named FrogGirl?" Rachel asked.

"She works for me," Wally said.

It occurred to Wally that FrogGirl and Abe had spent a lot of time together, mostly without Wally around as he attended to other jobs. He would start them on some simple project in the morning, make sure they could handle the skills involved, then check in at lunch and again at the end of the day. First it was drywall. Next, a painting project. Then, denailing a pile of lumber from a tear-out followed by a miserable day on their backs tacking itchy fiberglass insulation in a crawlspace. Then Wally gave them a plum of a job for several days laying a brick walkway in a lovely garden using sand instead of mortar, something that came out particularly nice—possibly because it didn't involve any hammering or tools in Abe's hands. The job had taken longer than Wally estimated, and he had wondered if they had been goofing off.

"FrogGirl and Abe have been working together," Wally said.

"I see," Rachel said. "That explains a few things." She started to walk out the door.

"What does it explain?" Opal asked.

Rachel stopped again. She seemed to be gathering strength. "As his mother," Rachel said, "you might want to know that Abe no longer plans to go to college. *Any* college. He wants to be a carpenter and work with some guy named Juke who seems to be Abe's hero. And, by the way, he wants to marry this person named FrogGirl though she doesn't *know* it yet, and, oh, also, she's pregnant. As for our relationship—if I have this right—he says he still loves me and doesn't love the FrogGirl person as much though he does love her some. The problem is he says in spite of being too deadly serious I'm also too *cute*. Something about my *teeth* lining up with my *jaw*. It's like I'm supposed to *apologize* for having a good *orthodontist*. So now if you'll *excuse* me I really must be going. For some reason I don't want to cry and maybe that proves I'm too serious a person or maybe I'm just too proud of my orthodontia but I do want to stop at the Safeway and buy a cart-full of watermelons and take them home and then one by one I'm going to *throw them against the fucking wall!*"

With that, Rachel steamed out of the house.

Opal and Wally stared after her.

"Pregnant?" Opal said.

"Not by Abe," Wally said.

"Request permission to swear," Opal said.

"Want me to have a chat with him?" Wally asked.

"Holy fucking God damn asshole," Opal said. "And shit. Oh—and piss and hell."

"You don't swear much, do you?"

"Don't make fun of me."

"Maybe," Wally said, "instead of my having a chat with Abe, we should all throw watermelons at him."

"Nobody can talk to him right now. And he had a good orthodontist too—the same one as Rachel." Opal paused—thinking, frowning. "Could you fire him maybe?"

"Let's not do anything tonight. Let the fires cool."

"And then what? Start planning a wedding? Or a baby shower? Or both at the same time? I'm not going to be the one to tell his father. You want that job? And what can you tell me about this FrogGirl?"

"Let's give Ronny a bath." Wally cocked an ear. "In fact I think I hear water running."

They shared a worried look and began hustling toward the bathroom.

"I'm starting to freak out," Opal said.

They came to the bathroom and found Ronny naked, standing outside the tub, which was filling with cold water.

"Tell me why I shouldn't freak out," Opal said as she turned on the hot faucet. "That's your job now."

Wally pondered the implications of *now*. His status had changed. To what? Leaning over both Opal and the tub and testing the stream of water with his fingers, Wally said, "Abe's a smart boy with a good heart. Which he got from his mother."

"He's also hotheaded," Opal said. "Full of latent anger. And in spite of high IQ, he's a moron. Which he got from his father."

Ronny climbed into the tub. Shutting off the water, Wally noticed that the reggae music had stopped. Ronny started playing with a wind-up plastic shark that cruised through the water and bumped repeatedly against the big plastic tugboat.

"Mr. Shark is trying to eat the tugboat," Wally said. "Better get help from the ducks."

Ronny had two wind-up plastic ducks. Wally placed them in the water, where they started randomly banging into the shark, the tugboat, and Ronny in equal portions.

"Uh oh, now they're attacking you," Wally said. "Quick! Get the submarine!"

Holding the submarine underwater with both hands, Ronny bashed any duck or shark or tugboat that swam too close to his body. Each bash created both a splash and a wave. Water sloshed onto the floor and sprayed over Wally and the nearby toy chest.

Opal placed a towel over the toy chest and draped another over Wally's shoulders and across his front like a bib.

A voice came from the doorway: "Can I say something?"

Sudden silence. Wally, Opal, and Ronny all stopped what they were doing and turned to face Abe.

"First of all, you guys are having way too much fun considering that I'm in the middle of the most traumatic episode of my life."

"Uh, sorry," Wally said.

"What else?" Opal said.

"I may have, like, overstated some stuff to Rachel," Abe said.

"Uh huh," Opal said.

"I need a rewind button," Abe said.

"Uh huh," Opal said again.

"I'm going over to Rachel's house," Abe said. "If she'll see me."

"Bring your watermelon shield," Wally said.

"And some flowers," Opal said.

"Gib her dis," Ronny said, standing in the tub and holding out a plastic duck.

"Hey, thanks, man." Admiringly, Abe cradled the toy in his palm. "I think Rachel's always needed a wind-up plastic duck, and I think I've always needed to give her one. This is excellent." Abe smiled. "Thank you all, and good night."

Opal stared at the doorway where a moment earlier Abe had been standing. Then she turned with a beseeching look to Wally, sat down on the closed seat of the toilet and, smiling, began to cry.

Ronny looked worried.

"It's okay, Ron," Wally said. "Your mom isn't sad. She was worried, and now she's not so worried, and because she's happy now she feels safe to cry. Does that make sense?"

Ronny still looked puzzled.

"It's complicated," Wally said.

"Okay," Ronny said, and he wound up the one remaining duck and dropped it into the water.

"I guess you know I'm not freaking out anymore," Opal said.

"You want to have another kid?" Wally asked. He was on his knees on the bathmat with his back to Opal.

"No! Jeesh."

"Okay."

"Why?"

"Just wondering. Watch out for the shark, Ron."

"Was that a serious question?"

"Just. Like I said. Wondering." Wally still had his back to Opal.

"Wally."

"Here comes the tugboat."

"Wally!"

"What?"

"Turn around. Look at me."

Wally turned.

"Oh, Wally."

"It's okay, really. Whatever you want."

"I'm so sorry. I didn't realize it was a real question. I just. I don't know. I guess we should talk about this. At your age. Do you really want to have a baby?"

"No, I want you to have a baby. I just want to be the father."

"Haven't we skipped a few stations here?"

"You mean the station where we figure out that we're in love and then the station where we want to get married? Not to mention the station where we figure out how to conceive a baby without having, uh—" Wally glanced at Ronny, "ex-say."

"We'll have ex-say."

"We will?"

"Of course we will. But we're not there yet. We're still in Station One."

"Which station is ex-say?"

"I don't know. Three. No. Four."

"In Station Four will I have to keep my clothes on?"

"What? Oh. The *euw*."

"Yes, the euw."

"It was an artistic euw. Nothing personal."

"Is that somehow supposed to make me feel better?"

"Could we discuss this some other time?"

"Okay. Whatever." Wally turned to the tub. "I think the tugboat wants to fly."

"Yes," Ronny said.

"Here she goes!" Wally said.

"I need some time to think," Opal said to Wally's back.

"Fine." A tugboat in Wally's hands was flying over the tub. "Coming in for a landing. Uh oh. I think it's gonna crash ..."

Splash.

Ronny shrieked. "Do it again!"

"Your turn, Ronny," Wally said.

"I'm not that much younger than you," Opal said and immediately wondered why she had said it. The fact was, she was just younger enough. And the clock was ticking ...

A tugboat was flying above the tub in Ronny's hands.

Splash.

The spray carried all the way to where Opal was sitting on the toilet.

"My turn," Wally said.

"No! Mine!"

"I'll leave you guys to your game," Opal said.

Neither boy heard her; neither boy answered. A tugboat was flying in Ronny's hands while Wally was shooting at it with a Super Soaker water gun. Opal walked to the kitchen in a daze.

Thirty-Two

Since the demise of the Krainer gig, the belt sander races had taken a vacation. When you're doing a three-day repair at somebody's little suburban castle, you don't invite a couple dozen tradesmen to gamble, drink beer, eat ribs, and race belt sanders on the front lawn. Well, Juke might, but Wally had better sense.

One of the unspoken purposes of the weekly races was to catch up on gossip with other contractors: who's hiring, who's firing, which building inspector is on a rampage. So it was only by chance that Wally happened to see Larry Ludowski as they both were loading plywood into their trucks at OK Lumber in San Carlos, Larry from a stack of nominal half-inch CDX, Wally from the stack of three-quarter-inch. Both, Wally suspected, for the same purpose—subflooring where five-eighths would be standard—but Ludowski choosing to undersize it, Wally to go one size stronger than code.

"Hey, Wally," Ludowski said, "you know a carpenter name of Benton?"

"First name or last?"

"Whitey Benton."

"Blue Dodge, side boxes?"

"That's him."

Wally remembered. Back at the beginning of the summer, he'd turned the guy down for a job when he showed up at eight in the morning with a beer in one hand and a joint in the other.

Ludowski glanced around the lumberyard, then lowered his voice: "Came by where I was working, he was selling tools out the back of his truck. Showed me a nailer. One unusual nailer."

"Doofus? Modified?"

"Mm-hm."

"You buy it?"

"Hell no."

"Appreciate you telling me this, Larry. I know we don't always see eye to eye."

"Comes to stealing a man's tools, I think we do."

It occurred to Wally that Ludowski was buying plywood when OSB would be cheaper. Good contractors disagreed—and you could always start an argument about it—whether plywood was superior to oriented strand board. One thing for sure, though, was that if you paid the extra money for plywood, you had to believe it was better. And Larry was loading plywood. Maybe, Wally thought, I should cut the guy a little slack.

Grabbing the end of two sheets of plywood that Ludowski was starting to load, helping him lift it onto the truck, Wally asked, "Anything besides the Doofus?"

"Nothing in the truck. Said he had more stuff if I was looking for anything in particular. Said he'd bring it."

"Like what?"

"Compressor. Table saw. Whole buncha shit."

"Mine. My trailer. Cleaned me out."

Ludowski grabbed the ends of two sheets of plywood from the three-quarter-inch pile and helped Wally load. "Benton's gone wild," Larry said. "Reminds me of a dog I used to have. The look in his eye. Good dog, started out. Part wolf. Turned on me."

"What happened?"

"The dog? I shot him. I don't know where Benton lives, but I know where he hangs out—woman I used to know. She likes rough trade."

"Rougher than you?"

"I got limits. Carpenter slut. Her name is Lenora."

On the cell phone Wally spoke to Diefendorf the cop while driving his load of plywood back to the job site. Still talking, he parked, got out of the truck, and was joined by Juke, who came out of the house to start unloading. It was a termite job in Mountain View, a little stucco bungalow where they'd torn out a shower and a bedroom floor. Juke and Wally could handle the job. The rest of the crew were out on other projects. Wally had a big job brewing, a new house in Woodside that would bring all his workers together again and also restore sanity to his scheduling and even perhaps let him pay off the credit-card debt, but the plans were still waiting for approval. And in the politics of Woodside the approval process was slow torture, subject to the viciously whimsical objections of wealthy neighbors.

When Wally turned off the cell phone Juke was standing next to him with a sheet of plywood. He'd overheard Wally talking on the phone. Juke didn't know Whitey Benton by name, but he knew the blue Dodge with side boxes. And on Juke's face was a look of cold fury.

"Ain't in his truck," Juke said. "The tools."

"That's what Ludowski said. How'd you know?"

"I looked. Didn't know he was the shitbag. When I looked. But I looked."

"Might be something in the cab. The side boxes."

"Nope. Looked."

"He leave them open?"

"Nope."

"You broke in? Juke, you can't risk—"

"The side boxes, I sorta one night had to pick the locks and check inside. Mighta heard something ticking. Thought there might be a bomb in there. We all got to do our part, you know. In the war on terror."

"And the cab?"

"Thought it might catch fire. Cigarette butt."

"And did it?"

"I wetted it down."

"Let's back up a minute. Why were you anywhere near Whitey Benton's truck?"

"Just runnin' some errands. Passin' by."

"In Saratoga? That must be twenty miles from where you live."

"I got stuff to do."

"Like checking up on Lenora?"

"Just park outside for a minute."

"It's called stalking."

"She don't even know I'm there."

"Sounds like Whitey knows you're there."

"He don't know it's me."

"Why go at all?"

"Dunno, Boss." Juke rearranged some dust with the toe of his boot. "I might still be in appreciation of her."

"Juke, you need to face up to the fact that she's no longer in, uh, appreciation of you. If she ever was."

"She *was*, Boss. She *tingled*. Hell, I guess I tingled too." Juke stomped his boot on the lines he'd been drawing. "We gotta get those tools back."

"Let the Dorf work on it."

"Then, after, can we beat Benton to a puddle of shit?"

"Uh. Juke. Whitey wasn't alone on this."

"So can we beat both guys to shit?"

"Remember that day? Before the tools were stolen, we had a belt sander race? You remember who stopped by for a minute? Just long enough to change the locks on the trailer?"

With one hand Juke was still holding an upright sheet of plywood, one end balanced on the ground. "This ain't good, Boss."

"It was Lenora. It all adds up. Right?"

Juke didn't answer. The sheet of plywood teetered and then toppled to the earth. Juke was already in the El Camino. With a screech of tires and a roar of big beefy engine, he made a U-turn and sped away.

Wally in his truck and Diefendorf in his squad car talked by phone as they sped down Interstate 280 toward Saratoga. They didn't know Lenora's last name or her address, only that she had a pink Miata. All they could do was cruise the streets, of which Saratoga had a fair number, and search for the Miata, the blue Dodge with side boxes, or Juke's gray-primed El Camino.

Wally tried calling Krainer—who would know where she lived—but got no answer. And after a half hour of fruitless cruising, he remembered to call FrogGirl at his home to say that in spite of his promise to help her repaint the bedroom tonight he was on an urgent mission in Saratoga searching for somebody.

"Who?" FrogGirl asked.

"A woman named Lenora."

"Lenora Saunders?"

"You *know* her?"

"Only of her. If it's who you're talking about. Uncle Anton's girlfriend."

"*Uncle* Anton?"

"Didn't I tell you I have an uncle who's a total turd?"

"No."

"How did you think I found that house way out in the hills? Did you think it was totally random?"

"I never thought about it. Do you know her address?"

"No."

Wally called Diefendorf and told him the last name. The Dorf radioed the name to headquarters. And just as Wally stopped speaking, he spotted the El Camino parked with one wheel over the curb as if it had stopped in a hurry.

"Dief! Found it. Cedar Lane Condos."

"I'm on my way."

Wally stood on the sidewalk. It was a quiet street. In the lot, sure enough, was the pink Miata. The sun was slipping behind the hills as the air began to cool, but it was still warm enough for some children playing in the swimming pool in the courtyard. One side of the building was covered with old ivy, the vines as thick as a man's arm. Ever the contractor, Wally cringed at the damage ivy can do to stucco siding: finding hairline cracks, inserting tiny roots, expanding, digging, hungry, relentless. He hated ivy almost as much as he hated termites.

In less than a minute, Diefendorf arrived. Together he and Wally raced up the stairs and down the second floor deck to an open door. Juke was standing just inside, his arms and face smeared in blood. "Don't need you," Juke said in a daze. "Need a fuckin' medic." Lenora lay sprawled in the middle of the room, naked, motionless, face a wreck and fresh bruises blushing all over her body. Wally ran to her. Diefendorf put cuffs on Juke while asking, "She alive?"

"Sort of," Wally said, pulling a bandanna from his back pocket.

"Called 911," Juke said to Wally.

Already sirens were approaching.

"You have the right to remain silent," Diefendorf said.

Juke stared dully at the cop. He said nothing.

"I'll get you a lawyer," Wally said. He didn't know what to do about the sickening bruises—somebody had kicked the crap out of her and judging by the outline of her skinny ribcage some parts were caved in. Wally held the bandanna against a deep cut just below her left eye. Her jaw was crooked, nose bent, tooth missing. Basically her entire face was broken. A pool of blood was spreading around her bottom. Wally was afraid to move her, afraid to find out where the blood was coming from.

"Find the cat," Juke said.

"What?" Wally said.

"Old gray cat. Three legs. It's gone."

"I'll look."

Lenora groaned, stirring slightly.

"Don't move," Wally said, still pressing the bandanna. He couldn't tell if she heard. Her eyes remained shut. Medics coming up the stairs.

"About what happened," Juke began. "Maybe I—"

"Shut up," Wally said.

Juke gave Wally a worried look but said not one word more.

After midnight, Wally returned to Cedar Lane condos. Police, crowd, medic, all were gone; the street was silent. A quarter moon was rising. Wally kept one eye out for the missing cat, but he was on a different mission. He took the loose items from the bed of Juke's El Camino and moved them to his own truck so they wouldn't get stolen. He peered carefully all around to make sure nobody was watching. Most windows were dark; a few glowed with the flickering light of a television.

Wally moved to the shadow at the side of the building. For several minutes he waited, listening and watching. He heard the rumble and wail of a distant train. He heard sounds of traffic, barking dogs, all far away. He heard the shaking of leaves in the live oak trees. He heard laughter and an ad for Bud Lite.

Grasping a vine, Wally found a foothold and began to climb. The rough vines hurt his hands, and the weight of his body aggravated the pain in his wrist, but he could ascend almost as if hoisting himself up a leafy rope. On the roof he found the cordless Panasonic drill/driver that Juke called the Phaser because it looked like one. Next to it was the old orange-handled Vaco screwdriver that Juke always abused as a chisel and a pry-bar. The brass screws lay in a neat row on the flashing against the head curb of the skylight, which lay unattached but still perfectly in place.

From below, earlier in the evening inside the condo, a quick glance had shown Wally the slight air gap around the interior rim of the skylight. He had forced himself to keep his eyes from returning. Everyone assumed Juke had a key or else that Lenora had let him in. In fact, a key was sitting on a table next to the entry. You might even assume that Juke had known the location of a hidden key.

Quickly, with a soft whirring sound from the Phaser, Wally drove the screws back where they belonged. Ramming the Panasonic inside his belt, the Vaco in his pocket, Wally scrambled down the ivy.

For a moment, he stood at the bottom listening and watching. Mixed with the fresh scent of the oaks was the odor of chlorine from the swimming pool. Nobody there. And no three-legged cat. A quick walk to the Toyota, and then Wally drove away.

Wally couldn't afford high-priced legal talent. Over the years he had employed the services of a man named Berman, Gad Berman, who had an office in a shabby building in Redwood City on Fifth Avenue near Wally's house. Berman's office was about the size of a gas station men's room but less sanitary. Nobody would call Gad Berman a brilliant attorney, but he was easy to talk to, cheap, and he had several decades of hard-won street smarts. He also had a heroin habit, which Wally was aware of, and cautious about, but which didn't seem to interfere with Berman's day work. Nights, he was somewhat less reliable but Wally had called him that night about Juke—another advantage of Berman was that Wally had his home number. Berman had seemed coherent as he took the information about Juke's arrest and then, maddeningly, wanted to talk about the Krainer case: "I think they want to settle. We've got some leverage. He needs cash."

"Gad, he *owes* me. He won't get money out of settling with me. He's gotta *pay* me."

"That's the beauty of it. You're lucky there's no bank with a mortgage on the place. Just your lien. He can't sell the property with your lien on it, so he wants to settle."

"I don't follow."

"You could own that property, Wally. For pennies on the dollar."

"The one I was building on?"

"Yes!"

"How?"

"He'll take the debt as equity. You just need to pay off the balance— at way below the market value."

"How much?"

"Maybe four hundred grand."

Wally burst out laughing.

After Wally quieted down, Gad said, "That would be a no, then?"

"Just get Juke out of jail."

"Depends on if the lady dies."

"He didn't do it, Gad."

"Could be murder, or attempted murder, or just—what the hell— aggravated sexual assault and battery. Can we add rape? Sodomy?"

"He didn't do it."

"Because he said so?"

"Because he didn't. He hasn't said anything. Make sure it stays that way."

"Why shouldn't he say anything?"

"He didn't enter that condo through the front door. But they think he did. You make sure they keep thinking that. He's got two strikes already. You make sure he comes out of this squeaky clean."

"Somebody beat the crap out of the woman. A cop heard Juke say he'd stomp whoever stole the tools. *She* stole the tools. And before that they had a romance, and they broke up, and so they hate each other. Not to mention he's a convicted felon. I love this case."

"She didn't steal the tools. She was an accessory. He doesn't hate her. He ...appreciates her."

"That'll make a great alibi."

"Try for reduced bail."

"Oh yeah. You betcha."

Thirty-Three

Now Wally was having a cell phone morning. He sent Steamboat out to install a garden window at a claustrophobic granny unit in Belmont. Pancho he sent to the Stanford campus where a widower professor wanted to convert a laundry room into a library. FrogGirl he sent with Pancho to hopefully ease the communication with the professor and maybe even help with the craft if Pancho could get over the macho barrier and take the time to discover her rough but natural talent for woodwork. Abe he sent to the high school—Abe's first solo assignment—a simple project where some handyman had botched the installation of a flagpole. Normally Wally would go with each worker to each separate job and make sure they had a successful launch: clear understanding with the owners, no questions about the goals and methods and standard of work to be expected. Today he had no time. The termite job in Mountain View still had to be finished. In addition, to everyone's surprise the town of Woodside had approved the plans for Wally's next big gig, and suddenly he had to hustle to order materials, line up subcontractors, and most of all to get in sync with the prima donna architect. Meanwhile he was maxed out on three of his four credit cards, the lumberyard had laughed in his face when he asked them to extend his account, and most important of all Juke was in jail.

Cell phone to his ear, Wally was sitting in the cab of Old Yeller. The truck was parked in front of OK Lumber in Wally's favorite part of the Peninsula. There's an industrial strip between the railroad tracks and Highway 101 where, as Wally said, the work gets done. In Belmont, San Carlos, and Redwood City hundreds of small shops had been carved out of garages and ramshackle buildings where you could get a metal part fabricated or a print job run or a sofa repaired or a radiator replaced or a hundred other tasks, where craftsmen had set up their own small business so they could be in charge of their own lives and take pride in what they produced while working long hours for little money. It was also the neighborhood where Wally had lived for most of the last twenty years. He didn't feel comfortable in the tonier areas—even if he could have afforded them—and he couldn't imagine shopping at a place like Stanford Shopping Center with its hundreds of classy facades where, as Wally would say in one of his crustier moods, "There's thousands of people carrying out silly plastic bags with a billion dollars of merchandise and not a damn thing anybody really needs—there isn't even a hardware store." And then there was the place on University Avenue that was actually *called* a hardware store—Restoration Hardware—into which Wally had wandered one time hoping to buy some three-quarter-by-seven-inch bolts. What a joke.

On the cell phone Wally was trying to sweet-talk his way through an administrative assistant to the hotshot CEO of an Internet startup, hoping to get an advance on the Woodside job. While talking, Wally was rummaging with one hand through the glove box in search of another pen after the ink had run out of the one he was using, when his fingers latched onto an old thirty-five-millimeter film canister that he had never quite been able to bring himself to throw away, though it didn't contain film and he had been carrying it around in his truck for many years. At just that moment, the assistant put Wally through to the CEO.

"Peter," Wally said, "how are you?" He was trying for the tone of voice of somebody who has absolutely no need of money, calm and comfortable, only wanting an advance payment as an expression of good faith, a trivial matter really, just the customary procedure. Meanwhile, without any attention from his conscious brain, Wally was shaking the film canister between two fingers, hearing the rattle of little tablets.

Peter said he was financing the house through the sale of stock options that would take a few days to clear. Wally tried to suggest a token amount, say perhaps fifteen thousand—

Peter cut him off. Important meeting. Had to run.

Wally flipped the phone shut, looked at his other hand and only then did he realize that he had swallowed three or four little white pills.

Oh well.

He could use a boost. With extreme age, the tablets had probably lost their buzz potential or morphed into some entirely new, unpredictable, hopefully harmless substance.

Ring tone. Wally flipped open the phone. "Peter?"

"Who is Peter?"

"Oh, hi, Opal. What's up?"

"Can I see you? I want to talk about something."

"I'm in the middle of a hundred things right now."

"Okay." Opal sighed. She almost sounded relieved. "I guess it can wait."

"What's the topic?"

"Never mind. I'm already losing my nerve."

Wally tossed the film canister back into the glove box. "Nerve for what?"

"Moving up."

"Up where?"

"Station Four."

"I'll be right over."

"I'm not home. I'm on assignment. I'm a photographer, remember?"

"Where?"

"Half Moon Bay. Kelly Beach."

From the lumberyard to Half Moon Bay was a thirty-minute drive past the peaceful waters of Crystal Springs Reservoir, then over a mountain and down to the ocean. Twenty minutes after departure, Wally pulled into the parking area at Kelly Beach.

Opal was standing by a picnic table with two cameras, a Nikon and a Hasselblad. As Wally leaped out of the truck and bounded toward her, she frowned.

"What's the matter with you?" Opal said by way of greeting.

Wally put his hands in his pockets, removed them and folded his arms across his chest, unfolded and hooked his thumbs in his belt—all in the space of five seconds. "Something wrong?" Wally asked.

"You just drove through the parking lot at forty miles an hour. There's people here. Little kids."

Wally stood with his weight on one leg while the other bent and straightened, bent and straightened at the knee, sort of pumping. He glanced at Opal, at the beach, the ocean, the concrete block restrooms with a flock of seagulls on the flat roof. Tar and gravel and seagull poop. Wally spotted a '68 Impala low-rider parked nearby, baby pink, a thing of beauty. He saw that Opal was still frowning at him. "What were we talking about?"

"My God. You're stoned."

"'Phetamines. Antiques."

"You idiot."

"It was an accident."

"You idiot *asshole*. Get in my car."

As they drove up Kelly Avenue, Opal told Wally that they would buy some burritos and then return and walk along the beach. She wanted to dilute Wally's bloodstream with food and burn off energy with exercise and, just maybe, do her job of finding an outstanding photo opportunity somewhere along the beach. The theme for the newspaper was supposed to be Lazy Daze of Summer.

Tres Amigos, the restaurant, was a melting pot of surfers, tourists driving down Highway One, locals, farm workers, half-naked beachgoers, and a Latino motorcycle gang. Opal bought shrimp burritos and giant cups of fresh carrot juice to go. Wally couldn't possibly sit at a table right then.

It wasn't easy to handle an overflowing burrito, drink carrot juice and walk along the sand at the same time, but Opal wanted to keep Wally moving. They scarcely spoke to each other. Wally wanted to say so much, but he couldn't seem to focus. He hopped up and down or dashed into the sea foam until the water ran over the top of his boots and into his socks. He picked up little broken pieces of sand dollars, shook them in his hands and then tossed them in the air like confetti. He found flat pebbles and skipped them; he picked up long strands of slimy kelp and tried to crack them like a whip. Kids were staring. Opal glanced at Wally sideways with looks of concern and disgust, stopping occasionally to frame a shot of a child building a sandcastle or a dog catching a Frisbee.

The sea air and salt spray slowly seemed to clear Wally's head. His hands stopped their restless random ratcheting motion and settled in his pockets.

Back at the parking lot, Opal sat down at a picnic table. Wally sat beside her, facing the ocean. *Living on this peninsula,* Wally thought, *I take it for granted how gorgeous it all is. Gorgeous, at least, where nobody's built some stupid tacky piece of crap.*

"The best picture," Opal said, "won't happen until sunset."

"Can I wait with you?"

"Didn't you say you were in the middle of a hundred things?"

"Uh, I don't remember."

Frowning, Opal pulled a pen and a little notebook out of her camera bag. Handing them to Wally, she said, "Write a letter to your wife."

Wally held the pen over the notebook page. "What do I say?"

"Say 'Dear Aimee.' Her name is Aimee, right?"

"Uh, right."

"Say 'Dear Aimee. Today I goofed up. I miss you. I need you. Please help.'"

Wally stared hard at the notebook. "Aimee's dead."

"You're still connected. That's why you write to her."

"I stopped."

"Start again. She can guide you."

"I don't think so." Wally closed the notebook. "Opal, will you help me?"

She felt her heart turning liquid and warm and scared. "I'm not sure I know how."

Wally set down the pen. "You're doing okay."

A seagull landed on the edge of the picnic table opposite from the side where Wally and Opal were sitting. For a few seconds the bird studied them—and Opal grasped Wally's arm.

"Wally," Opal whispered, "please make it go away."

"Scram!" Wally shouted, rising slightly from the bench.

The seagull took flight.

Opal still had a firm grip on Wally's arm. "Thank you," she said. She gazed into his face as she rubbed her hand up and down his arm. "Thank you so much."

"Did I just pass some kind of test?"

"I just needed to know if you'll protect me." Her fingers stopped rubbing but stayed on his arm. "Okay. About Station Four. What I wanted to talk about."

"Oh yeah. That."

Opal took a deep breath. Held it. She said nothing.

Wally waited.

Suddenly her words burst out: "Don't step out of a pickup, don't wear cologne, don't have a glazed look in your eyes, don't hit me, don't hurt me down there, don't put your weight on me, don't have a hairy neck, and don't call me *baby*."

Squinting, Wally peered out over the golden sand, little children on boogie boards laughing, shouting, gliding, falling. "I want to kill him," Wally said.

"Too late. He hanged himself. In prison."

"I still want to kill him."

Opal let out the deep breath. "It's taken me a long time to get to— to be able to say—all I just said." She hugged herself, leaning forward, shoulders hunched. She turned her head to look at Wally, and she was smiling. "Wow, I feel so much better."

"Anything you'd like to add?"

"Yes." She straightened herself. "Don't cry afterwards. Don't say you're sorry. Don't make me feel guilty for hating you."

"Okay."

"I didn't mean you, Wally. When I said *you*."

Actually, Wally thought otherwise, but he wasn't going to say so.

Opal said, "I'm more over it than you might think."

"No pressure, Opal. None whatsoever."

"I just don't want to be detached anymore. That's why I said I don't do sex. Because I don't want to be faking it and I don't want to be watching myself from a distance and I don't want—and this is weird—do you know every once in a while you can have an honest-to-God orgasm and not even be there? Actually, of course you know. You're a guy. But I want to be there when I'm doing it, I want to be attached."

"That's fine, Opal."

Opal dug her toe in some sand. "You still want to go to Station Five?"

"What's Station Five?"

"The thing that it's all about. The reason Station Four was invented."

"Do you?"

She wiggled the toe. "I'm still thinking." Now she moved the foot, spreading sand, smoothing it. "There's a basic part of me that wants a baby. Because I want you. But a smarter part of me is saying that's a very bad reason. And I like to be smart. I take pride in being smart. So what now?"

Wally shrugged. "Let's just sit here. Getting used to each other. Getting to know your strength. And my weakness."

Suddenly Wally could see nothing but flowers. Bright flowers on fabric. A large woman in a muumuu was blocking his view, holding a little kid by the hand.

"Is it you?" she said.

Wally stared up at her. She wore sunglasses. Sort of heavyset. A former client? An angry one?

"It *is* you. It must be!"

"Do I know you?"

"You're the one in the picture. The one in the magazine. I know it's you."

"I took that picture," Opal said.

The woman ignored her. "I'm so glad I found you. This is Archie." She nodded toward the boy. His skin was pale. "He's got the leukemia and I thought if you could just touch him, just do something, maybe you could make it go away."

"Lady, I don't—"

"Wally!" Opal said.

"Lady, I'm not—"

"Wally!" Opal said again.

Wally looked from the stern face of Opal to the hopeful, desperate face of the woman to the sad and sallow eyes of Archie.

From his seat on the bench at the picnic table Wally leaned forward. "Hi, there," Wally said to the boy.

Archie met his gaze, and Wally saw a dim spark of life.

"Let's shake," Wally said, holding out his right hand. "I believe in handshakes. Do you believe in handshakes?"

The boy shrugged—wearily, almost imperceptibly—but he held out his hand.

Wally grasped the hand between both of his. The little fingers felt weak and very, very cold.

"Say you believe in handshakes," Wally said.

Archie furrowed his brow.

"Please," Wally said, "say it for me."

"I ...Okay," the boy said softly.

"Okay what?"

"I do."

"You do what?"

Very softly, almost a whisper: "I do believe in handshakes."

For a good ten seconds Wally kept the little hand pressed between both of his. He thought he felt some warmth coming into it.

"Okay," Wally said, letting go. "Come back about ten years from now, and I'll teach you how to build houses."

"Bless you," the woman said. She was crying.

"Good luck," Wally said.

The woman and boy walked away. Solemnly, Archie was looking back over his shoulder.

"You get a picture of that?" Wally asked.

"No."

"Good."

They fell silent.

Opal was the one to break it: "Don't you have work to do?"

"I think so. I don't remember."

"You said you were in the middle of a hundred things."

"Yeah. I'm having a bad day."

"Where's your crew?"

"All over the place."

"Where's Abe?"

"The perfect job."

"With this FrogGirl person?"

"Solo. Using the one tool he has a knack for. A demolition hammer."

"When he was a two-year-old we called him demolition toddler. I guess he was learning a life skill."

"He's ripping out a flagpole and resetting it. Their maintenance guy got it crooked, so they called me. They're on vacation. Nobody there. You can't do demo work when school's in session."

"Whoa."

"What?"

"Which school?"

"Silicon. His alma mater."

"Abe is alone at the high school with a demolition hammer?"

"That's right."

"Didn't I ever tell you about the bat doo-doo?"

A minute later Wally was in the truck and speeding. At the high school he jerked to a stop next to Abe's Honda with open hatchback containing four bags of Quikrete. Rushing onto the campus, the first thing Wally saw was that the flagpole was untouched. He could hear a grinding noise around the side of the main building. Rounding the corner, following an extension cord, he found Abe standing atop a pile of rubble that had previously been the wall of the principal's office. Abe was now demolishing the floor, piece by piece, oblivious of Wally or any other part of the world, ensconced in earmuffs and safety glasses with a red bandanna over nose and mouth as he lifted floor tiles and chipped at structural concrete with a passion that reminded Wally of how he felt himself when entranced in a task in his little woodshop.

Wally unplugged the Hitachi from the extension cord.

Abe stared at the tool, shaking it.

Wally stepped up behind Abe and lifted the earmuffs from his ears.

Abe spun to face him and almost walloped Wally with the hammer.

Wally folded his arms across his chest and said absolutely nothing. Sticking to the hot chisel tip of the tool, little flakes of linoleum tile were smoking with a sulfurous smell.

Abe gaped at Wally. His eyes blinked. He shook his head as if rattling his brain back into order. "'Sup, sir?" he said.

"In all my years of contracting," Wally said, "you are without a doubt the best, the fastest demo man I've ever seen."

"Uh, thank you, sir."

"Even Juke couldn't have destroyed this much wall this fast. Not without a ninety-pound pneumatic hammer and a compressor trailer. You could be an advertisement for the forty-pounder. Give it to me, please."

Abe passed the dusty, cursed tool to Wally's hands.

"I like to see my Alfredos excel," Wally said as he wound the electric cord around the warm body of the hammer. "I've taken some pretty hopeless cases. It's the magic of the job. You see visible results. You're a better person. I've never failed. Until now."

"Uh—" For the first time, Abe looked worried. "You haven't failed, sir."

"Abe," Wally said, "it's only because I'm in love with your mother that I'm not going to kill you."

"Maybe I made a mistake," Abe said, "but—"

"You're forkin' fired."

Thirty-Four

As the summer passed, FrogGirl was discovering she had a domestic streak. Wally saw it as a natural outgrowth of her being, as she said, a neatness freak, but to FrogGirl it seemed to come as a complete surprise. She was learning to cook. She cleaned the entire house and over one weekend carried out enough junk to fill the back of Wally's truck, including four broken bicycles strapped to the lumber rack. With only a few protests—he removed the dog food bowl—Wally hauled the rest of the load to the dump. When he returned, FrogGirl met him in the driveway with debris she'd gathered from the yard including a rusty water heater, thirty-six plastic buckets, half a rowboat, three toilets, the skeleton of a deer, a fiberglass shower unit, the rusted hulk of a player piano, and the rear wheel from a John Deere tractor. Still remaining in Wally's back yard was a stack of scaffolding plus all the construction material they'd removed from the Krainer job.

Wally sighed, shrugged his shoulders, and said, "I could've helped you move that stuff. Especially the water heater."

"You load it," FrogGirl said, and she went into the house to take a bath.

By the end of the day, Wally was on a first-name basis with the toll-taker at the dump.

FrogGirl was an ideal roommate, not just tidy but cheerful, surprisingly quiet, and self-contained. Her most grievous shortcoming was the fact that she was a Dodgers fan, but she tolerated Wally's taping every Giants game to watch later, skipping the ads. It only got ugly when the Giants and Dodgers played each other, and even then the hostility never moved beyond a peanut-throwing episode. She could spend hours in the driveway shooting baskets and more hours sitting on her bed with ear buds, leafing through old *National Geographics* from Wally's moldy stash, pausing sometimes, lifting her eyes, staring into some distant landscape beyond the walls.

At breakfast one day she seemed depressed. Wally asked her, "You okay?"

"It's just scary." She spooned some Grape-Nuts into a bowl of yogurt. "What if I don't like it?"

"As honorary grampa ..." Wally cleared his throat. "I just want you to know that if you ever need to go away—check out—you can leave the kid with Papa Wally. And when you come back, no questions. It's your kid."

"I wouldn't."

"No, you wouldn't. But still. Keep it in mind."

She rarely spoke of her past or of why she'd run away. She did let it slip that her father had died of AIDS when she was eight years old, and her sister was a teen model, and she referred to her mother once as "the psychotic bitch queen."

Wally couldn't put a label on his relationship with FrogGirl. It was partly roommates, partly father/daughter, and partly—in ways that continually surprised him—like husband and wife. Just as Aimee used to do, FrogGirl criticized the sloppy way Wally spent his money. FrogGirl had seen the Notice of Default meaning Bank of America would start foreclosure proceedings in thirty days if he didn't come up with three months of mortgage payments. Here Wally was buying *Popular Mechanics* at the 7-Eleven when everybody knows—if you *must* read the stupid thing—taking out a subscription would cost one-tenth as much. And so Wally pointed out that it was hardly the time to subscribe to anything if he couldn't pay the mortgage. And so FrogGirl said he was missing the *point*, this was a *crisis*, and Wally just didn't *get it*. They got so mad at each other, they couldn't speak for the rest of the evening until finally, in the middle of brushing her teeth, FrogGirl came to Wally and hugged him, and he hugged her in return.

"I just don't want us to lose our house," she said.

Wally pushed her back, held her at arm's length. The toothbrush dangled from her lips.

"I mean," she said, removing the toothbrush, "your house. My home."

And then they went to their separate rooms and separate beds. That was the father/daughter part. Not that she wasn't attractive— face it, all seventeen-year-olds are attractive, that's Mother Nature's plan—but there was a carefully constructed wall in Wally's brain and he'd placed her on the other side where daughters and other children belong. Sometimes the wall had cracked, but never had it crumbled. He occasionally wondered how strong the wall would have proved to be if he had remained a high school teacher for the past thirty years—and the thought scared the shit out of him. It might have been a blessing that he was removed from the temptation. Or, most likely, temptation would have proved to be a nonissue. The fact was that even given ample opportunity with willing adults he'd never been unfaithful to Aimee— not because he believed in fidelity (though he did) but because whenever the moment arrived to go or not, he'd chosen not. You had to watch what a person did with sex, not what he thought, because in Wally's experience there wasn't much correlation between belief and behavior. Aimee, for instance, believed absolutely in fidelity and faithfulness and yet ...And yet. Well, anyway, Wally was aware of FrogGirl's sexuality; he could even admire it, but for him it was like admiring a wildflower in the deep woods, fresh and lovely only if unplucked.

FrogGirl accepted Wally's fatherly protection but rejected most of his fatherly advice. Now in her fourth month, she still wouldn't let Wally reveal to anybody that she was pregnant even though it was becoming physically obvious in spite of her natural stoutness and even though, evidently, she'd told Abe.

"You like Abe?" Wally asked her once.

"He's okay. For a preppie."

"You sorry that I fired him?"

She shrugged. "Never thought about it."

"Have you seen Abe since I fired him?"

"No. Why?"

"Just wondering about your, uh, feelings. Since he's the only person you've told about being pregnant."

"He *knows?*"

"You didn't tell him?"

"Jeezo! I'm glad you fired him."

"He seems to like you."

"Really?" FrogGirl gave the matter a moment's thought. "He knows how to make me laugh." Then she frowned. "If you see him, tell him to shut up about it, okay?"

But Wally didn't see Abe. Whenever Wally went to visit Opal, Abe was gone. He claimed to Opal that he was out looking for a job—and Opal had insisted that he find work so he could repay Wally for the damage to the school—but so far he hadn't seemed to have any luck. Opal wondered how hard he was really trying. She'd heard from a friend, a librarian, that Abe's job-hunting seemed to involve spending long hours at the downtown Palo Alto public library reading back issues of *Scientific American* along with biographies of Galileo, da Vinci, Aristotle, Euclid. At least it wasn't drugs.

Wally limited FrogGirl's tasks. No toxic exposure, for starters, which seemed to eliminate half of construction work. Drywall seemed safe. He tried to restrict her heavy lifting, but she still had to deal with four-by-eight sheets of five-eighths firewall or five-gallon buckets of joint compound. She was quick at cutting, sure at hanging, and creative at texturing—Wally even got two referrals specifically asking for "that girl the artist" and "the young woman with the special touch." She'd wrap a scarf around her hair but end the day with dabs of joint compound on her nose and cheeks and all over her clothes. She never hesitated at getting dirty on the job. Wally would hear her talking and singing to herself all day while working—taping is so mindless—she'd walk out to the truck still talking to herself and then stop short and look around sheepishly.

"I'm turning dotty," she told Wally. "Like a bag lady."

"Yeah," Wally said. "Drywall can do that to you."

One unexpected benefit of having FrogGirl living in the house was that for the first time in a couple years Wally picked up the remodeling projects he'd dropped when Aimee got sick. He completed the kitchen wall, repaired the gutters, and replaced the broken bedroom window. He bought five hand-crafted doors at a garage sale and took them to a stripper to be dipped, planning to replace the cheapo hollow-core flat panel ones in his house. The woman selling the handmade doors said that her father had built them out of construction scraps. He was a craftsman, but with increasing dementia he'd taken to painting all his creations, trying to use up various cans of old paint that were lying around. The man hated to waste anything. Wally could sympathize. The doors were nicely made, but the paint was hideous—different colors in different panels, thick sloppy paint that must have been half-solid with age when the old guy slapped it on. The stripper was backlogged, but Wally could wait.

At dinner one night, lasagna by candlelight with flowers in a vase—FrogGirl wanted every dinner by candlelight—she asked, "How come you never bring your girlfriend over here?"

"You mean Opal?"

"Isn't she your girlfriend?"

Wally had never put a label on it. "I guess so."

"Are you ashamed of me? She didn't know I was living here. Why didn't you tell her?"

"I thought I had."

"Nope. She called here this morning when you were in the shower. She said she didn't want to talk to you."

"Then I wonder why she called."

"She wanted to talk to you when she called. She just didn't want to talk to you after she heard a woman's voice answer the phone—if I may, ahem, call myself a woman—answer the phone and say you were taking a shower."

"Did she know who you were? And yes, you may call yourself a woman."

"She knew who I was. I told her my name."

"And then?"

"She hung up. She hung up mad. It made me feel so—I don't know—so slutty."

"FrogGirl! Don't say that."

"*You* act like I'm slutty. Why didn't you tell your girlfriend about *us?*"

"About us? What about us?"

Her face was suddenly pleading, vulnerable. "Aren't you gonna help me with this baby? Aren't I gonna live here?"

Thirty-Five

Krainer was unraveling like a mini-Enron. In an odd way, Wally found himself viewing Anton with a new respect. The blond bastard had more depth than Wally had ever credited. Over the years, as a matter of self-preservation, a contractor develops a sixth sense about potential clients, but he'd missed the read on Anton. Krainer had moved out of his luxurious Palo Alto rental and was hunkered down in a cheapo townhouse in Sunnyvale. Wally almost felt sorry for him. If you squinted, if you ignored the accounting gimmickry and illegal stock options and rampant dishonesty of their sales projections, you could see Krainer's company as a victim of marauding hedge funds, rumor-mongering short-sellers, and a personal vendetta by one Phineas Pilpont, neighborhood bully.

Krainer's new, unfinished, aesthetically confused though perfectly constructed house was just sitting there on that lovely hillside overlooking Silicon Valley. An appraiser had said whoever bought the land would probably tear everything down and start over, which Wally took as a kick to the gut.

Where had he gone wrong? How had plans for an elegant little house with clean modern lines turned into such a monstrosity of bad taste? There was nothing he could have done to prevent it short of quitting—which would have resulted in going unpaid for a large amount of partially completed work—which, come to think of it, was exactly what happened anyway. Now his name and reputation were associated with this visual disaster.

And the appraiser was wrong, by the way. The basic house was sound. Sprawling, but sound. It could withstand an earthquake that would flatten most of California. Wally had made damn sure of it with strict attention to painstaking details. They nailed shear wall every four inches around the edge. They placed extra rebar and redundant hold-downs. They reinforced all connections with metal ties. They oversized the headers. Wally patrolled the subs with fanatical restrictions on notching or drilling holes in joists.

From a distance the only problem was the tower—the Krainer Erection—breaking the low profile the architect had hoped would blend in harmony with the landscape. That and the seven-car garage. The original plan for three cars looked like a fairly natural extension of the house. Expanded to seven cars it looked like a long, low industrial attachment, as if he'd added a semiconductor manufacturing plant to the house.

Otherwise the problems were in the pimping: the Greek columns on the front porch. The angel fountain. The baroque, hand-carved crown molding of erotic figures in the den. The mirrors on the bedroom ceiling and surrounding the hot tub. The hidden video cameras. The rococo add-ons inspired by an unfortunately timed trip to eastern Europe: fake half-round fluted columns, chair rails with a repeating fruit design, appliqués, and decorative scrolls, none of them ugly in themselves but creating a cumulative effect of unchecked whim, random clutter, and eye-numbing excess like something constructed for a berserk Romanian dictator.

Except the gazebo. It'd come out nice. Krainer hadn't specified any details on that one, so Wally and crew had followed their natural instinct for clean and simple line, a melding of form and function, trusting the wood, tight joints, plain truth.

Gad Berman still said there was a deal to be made if Wally acted quickly and came up with cash to settle the debt. Otherwise, lawyers and creditors would get everything; Wally, nothing. After foreclosure Pilpont could swoop in, buy the land and the uncompleted house from the bankruptcy trustee at a distressed price, and scrape it. Pilpont had already made an offer directly to Krainer, but there was too much bad blood. Anton refused to deal with him. It didn't help that Pilpont would pay for the house with money he'd made by shorting Krainer's stock.

If Wally's business had stock, Pilpont would probably be shorting it, as well. Wally's cash flow crisis already held him dangling at the financial edge with supplies needed for a major new job and equipment to be rented because he couldn't afford to replace what had been stolen while the insurance company was dragging its feet.

Meanwhile, after two weeks the DNA test results had cleared Juke of at least the sex charge, but the D.A. still held him for assault and battery for two more days until Lenora's drug dosage was reduced to the point where she could communicate—by note because her jaw was wired shut—that it was Whitey Benton who had tried to wrench her open with a tennis racket.

Benton, meanwhile, had vanished.

On his first evening out of jail, Juke went to see Lenora in the hospital. At first, she hid under the sheet. A nurse coaxed her out with the news that Juke had brought a handful of pretty daffodils.

Slowly, Lenora lowered the sheet. Bandages covered her nose and one cheek. Her lips were puffy. The area around one eye was not just black but multicolored—brown, red, yellow—swollen, stitched, Frankensteinian. With her jaw wired shut, she wore a Sharpie pen on a cord around her neck. On a thick pad of four-by-six Post-Its, neon orange, she jotted lengthwise and held up for Juke to see:

You???? Flowers????

"Borrowed 'em from a room," Juke said. "Guy in a coma."

On the same Post-It she wrote: *Don't look at me*

"Why not?"

I look awful

"Yeah. Like road kill."

Lenora burst into tears.

The nurse grabbed Juke by the arm and yanked him into the hall. To Juke the nurse seemed Asian-looking, surprisingly tall, flat-assed, and very angry. "Do you know how painful it is to cry when your head's in that condition?"

"Hey, she forkin' asked."

"In two weeks you're her first visitor other than the detective and those are her first flowers. What took you so long?"

"I just got out of jail."

The nurse dropped Juke's arm like a piece of poisoned meat. Juke decided she looked sexy in spite of the flat ass. Great head of hair, thick and black, pinned up. Downy at the back of her neck. But way too bossy. She was talking: "Doesn't that woman have any friends?"

"The way she do, it don't breed much respect."

"Family?"

"They got grudges. She don't talk about it."

"The rumor around here is that some law firm in Boston paid for the private room she's in. And they paid for extra plastic surgery. Normally she'd be discharged by now, but they say she can stay longer. So I hear. But no flowers, no phone call, no contact. What do you make of that?"

"Families is weird."

"So what are you—a friend?"

"We sorta broke up."

"Ex-boyfriend, then."

"She don't do boyfriends. Except as a profession. I'm her ...Aw, forkin' hell. I was her sex toy."

The nurse studied Juke skeptically. "Listen, boy toy, there won't be any messing with her for many weeks. We're talking stitches. And after that, only when *she* wants. *If* she wants. She's been hurt in places a woman should never be hurt. You understand?"

"Uh huh. Gotcha."

"She'll appear different, her body, down below. Scars."

"Goes with the hair."

"What?"

Juke reentered the room, unaccompanied this time. Lenora had placed the daffodils in a plastic pitcher.

"You look forkin' great," Juke said.

On a new Post-It:

Bullshit

"Sorry."

I lost my power

"Huh?"

My face = my power

"You got a good face."

Bullshit.

She peeled off the Post-It and started a new one:

I need to finish school

"Why?"

So I can make

an honest living

"Honest livin' ain't so bad. What kind of work?"

Psychotherapy

"That's honest work?"

Lenora snorted—and smiled—and winced at the pain the smile had caused. On a new Post-It she wrote: *Where's the cat?*

"Nobody seen it."

Benton

"Why would he take your forkin' cat?"

To hurt me

"He already killed you. Almost."

New page:

Meth brain

Insane!!!!

"I hear you lost the condo," Juke said. "Krainer stopped payin'?"

Lenora nodded.

"You still got the Miata?"

Lenora shook her head no. On a new page: *Bastard sold it*

"Where you gonna go?"

New page: *Golden Gate Bridge*

"Can't live there."

I can jump off

"Stay with me. You wanna? Huh?"

Slowly, deliberately, she peeled to a new Post-It and wrote: *???*

I'm thinking

She'd spent one night at Juke's place in East Palo Alto. Juke lived in an unheated garage behind a bungalow that was owned by one of the original Hells Angels and that now functioned as a semiretirement home for a rotating collection of somewhat addled, unpredictable, drooling, hard-drinking motorcycle gangsters. Juke's domicile had one room plus a grubby little closet containing a sink and a toilet. For furnishings Juke had a mattress on the concrete floor, a barber's chair, a drill press, welding torch, lathe, a 1958 Playboy calendar, a stuffed blue heron, and metal shelves piled with greasy machine parts. No kitchen, but Juke did have a coffee-maker, a George Forman Grill, and a refrigerator full of beer. There were bullet marks on the side stucco wall where a cocaine dealer had been executed.

After a minute, on a new page Lenora wrote: *You saved my life*

"Hey. No problem."

Aren't you angry?

"About the tools? Yeah, I'm mad. But that ain't the important thing."

What is?

"I guess ...I oughta say ...I'm still kind of loyal to you, Lenora."

Why?????!!!

"I kind of. Don't laugh. Appreciate. You."

You pissed me off

"The plumb and true stuff? That's who I am."

Lenora held the Sharpie over a new page, wagging it back and forth between her fingers, staring at the pad. Then she wrote: *I respect who you are*

Reaching for the pitcher, Lenora pulled the flowers to her chest. She studied Juke appraisingly and fingered the daffodils one by one.

Juke shifted on his feet. As usual, he found himself under the scrutiny of some woman who understood him better than he understood himself.

Suddenly setting the pitcher on a bedside table, Lenora started writing line after line on the pad of Post-Its. As she finished each page, she peeled it off and stuck it to the sheet over her knees.

I _appreciate_ you
too Juke you are
*straight-ahead _honest_*
about what you want

which is mostly sex
and fixing tools and
getting wasted but
*You should want _more_*

You _are_ plumb and true
*You're so much _better_*
than those bankers
those _no-dick_ lawyers

ass-wipe entrepreneurs
*_fucking suits_*
*You've got _skills_*
You actually _make_ stuff

When you're finished you
*leave something _real_*
Do you know how
SPECIAL that is?

*Do you know how much _better_*
You are than all those
fat sniveling _pricks_?

"Now I'm forkin' embarrassed," Juke said.
Lenora was still scribbling:

*You're _special, Juke_*
You should take some
pride in how you live

Just because you don't
own that place doesn't
mean you couldn't
fix it up a little

It's where you <u>live</u>

Display your <u>talent</u>

Show how <u>good</u> you are

When Juke finished reading, Lenora wrote one more page but didn't peel it from the pad. She held it up for Juke to read:

I need rest

"So you'll move in?"

We'd be weird

"But you'll think about it. Okay?"

Instead of an answer, she closed her eyes. One daffodil had fallen from the pitcher and lay cradled on the sheet between her thighs. The pad of orange Post-Its with the *We'd be weird* still attached was sitting sideways on her chest.

Until this moment, Juke had never seen her looking peaceful—or fragile. It wasn't her nature. He felt an impulse to stand guard at her room and make sure nobody attacked her ever again. But there was work to do.

At the nursing station Juke stopped for a moment and gave an order to the bossy sexy flat-assed nurse: "Tell those snivelin' pricks to send some forkin' *flowers*." Then he strode onward, purposeful, a few orange Post-Its clutched fluttering between his fingers.

Thirty-Six

"I'm not jealous," Opal said first thing when she met Wally at her front door. "Of FrogGirl, I mean. You're not the father, right?"

"Right."

"And you're not doing Station Four with her?"

"For God's sake, Opal. Station Zero. And she says I'm the baby's honorary grandfather."

"Wow. That was brilliant. She neutralized you."

"You *are* jealous."

"Okay. A little bit jealous. She gets to live with you."

"You and me, Opal, you think we're ready to live together?"

"Omigod, no."

"Was that a 'euw'?"

"It was just a no, Wally. I snore."

"Really? Cool!"

"It's not cool. It's embarrassing. I've got veins on my ankles and I giggle when I kiss. I sleep with the light on. You want to live with that?"

"I knew the giggle."

"You don't know anything. I'm scared of boats. Cauliflower gives me migraines."

"You want to hear about my hemorrhoids?"

"No. Euw." Opal rubbed her nose, thinking. "So who's the real father?"

"Nobody."

"Oh. Great."

"Yeah." Wally handed Opal the dozen calla lilies he'd bought on the way over.

"Thank you. I'm touched." Opal's body was blocking the doorway. "Are these flowers about ex-say? About us? Were you thinking tonight?"

"I was thinking maybe. Wondering."

"You said no pressure."

"They're not pressure, Opal. They're just flowers. And it's fine if you snore. Really.'"

"Try this." She made a snore—a sound like a choking chainsaw.

"Euw," Wally said.

"Not tonight. And stop changing the subject."

"What's the subject?"

"FrogGirl."

"Can I come in?"

"Not yet." Opal cradled the lilies in one arm. "Ronny's inside. I want to finish the hard stuff before he sees you."

"Hard stuff," Wally said. "FrogGirl. Okay. Here goes: I'm sorry. Really sorry."

"For what?"

"For ... You know. Whatever."

"Great apology ..."

"Look, I don't do great apologies. You want the fully orchestrated confession with regrets and reparations in three-part harmony complete with waterworks, groveling, and self-flagellation, you better find somebody else. I'm a guy. With all the crap that being a guy implies. Including crappy apologies. But I wasn't hiding anything, Opal. I actually thought I'd told you about FrogGirl living in my house."

"When's she leaving?"

"She kind of assumed."

"Wally."

"She expects to stay. She thought I'd promised."

"Did you?"

"I don't think so."

"Just like you think you told me she was living there?"

"That's the scary part."

"So did you tell her no?"

"I didn't say anything."

"That's the same as saying yes."

"No. I never said—"

"You never said a lot of things, Wally. That's the problem. Is this so you can end up with a baby in your house without having to go through the complication of marrying somebody?"

"No."

"And what about when she starts seeing some guy? What if that guy wants to move in with her? My God, what if it's Abe? Are you going to steal my son away from me too?"

"Opal. Of course not. I never planned that."

"Exactly. You don't plan. You don't even *say* things. Things just *happen*. Like you ended up a contractor when you wanted to be a *schoolteacher*." She put her hand to her mouth.

"Wow." Wally shook his head. "At least I always know what you're thinking."

"Do you? So do you already know that there's an opening for an English teacher at the Star Academy? You already know that my sister is the director there? My sister Charlotte? And she's excited about meeting you and talking about the position?"

Wally pursed his lips as if to begin an answer, then stopped. Once again he shook his head. "Opal. Wowee."

"No pressure. I'll accept your decision, whatever it is. But I just want it to be a decision, not a result of inaction. Is that okay? Will you think about meeting Charlotte?"

"I'll think. But I'm starting a house tomorrow. A big one."

"Fine. Start the house. But will you *meet* with her before you make a decision?"

"I *said* I'll think about it."

"Are you mad at me?"

"Not exactly." Wally shuffled his feet. "Opal, I'm sorry for everything I never said."

She stared at Wally for a moment. "It's frightening," she said.

"What is?"

"How much I'm attracted to you." Rising on tiptoes, she quickly kissed him on the mouth. No giggle. Then just as quickly she backed away before he could get ideas about kissing her back. "That thing you said about not doing good apologies? You have no idea how sexy that was."

"Sexy? You said sexy?"

"Scary too. Sexy and scary. Don't forget I'm the Queen of Mixed Signals. Ronny wants to see you."

"Is Abe here?"

"Of course not. That is, did you see him on the roof?"

"No."

"Then he's not here," Opal said, taking Wally by the hand and leading him inside. "And he doesn't want to talk about it."

Later, with Ronny bathed and bedded, Wally made no move toward Station Four though he watched—keenly—for an opening. He found himself studying the shape and motion of her lips when she spoke, the soft brush-like curve of her eyelashes.

To keep busy, Wally tightened some drawer-pulls on the base cabinets while Opal washed dishes and wiped the stove and explained how she could see that Abe was hurting—not that she blamed Wally for taking the action he had to take, but still she was Abe's mother and she hated to see her son in turmoil. Now Rachel had gone off to college after telling Abe:

1. She still liked him but
2. He exasperated her and
3. She would never ever apologize for her good teeth and
4. She wanted to be free to see whoever she wanted and
5. Maybe things would work out between them and maybe not.

Abe seemed adrift. When he was home he'd sit on the roof for hours. He enrolled in some classes at Foothill, the community college, to get some credits until he could start the winter term at UC Santa Cruz. But Opal never saw him study. Getting dumped by Princeton— and Rachel—and of course being fired by Wally, he was taking hits from all sides.

"He's kind of a magnet for watermelons, isn't he?" Opal said. "This might be the moment when we find out what he's made of."

"At least," Wally said, "he got an education this summer."

"Yes. He learned failure."

"Always a good lesson. But more than that."

"Like what?"

"That's what we're going to find out."

Saying good night, lingering a moment at the door, on an impulse and as an experiment Wally kissed Opal on the mouth. He meant it to be a quick one, over and out before she had a chance to break away—or giggle—but her lips were so warm and her response was so electric that he stayed, and he placed a hand on her hip while she put a hand at the back of his neck, and then both Wally's hands were circling her waist to the small of her back while Opal gripped his shoulder. Their bodies squeezed together. He took in her softness, her heat, the press of her breasts, the clean scent of her cheek. There were no thoughts in Wally's head, no room for them among the wash of sensual delight.

Opal ended it, slowly loosening her hands.

For a moment they studied each other's faces, the dance of their eyes.

"Wow," Opal said.

"Uh huh," Wally said.

"Good night, Wally."

"Good night."

Thirty-Seven

Wally shut off the engine of his truck, and suddenly there was silence except for the crackling of the motor as it cooled. He was scared.

Always, his first day on a new job, he felt the shiver. Which was fine. Fear was good. Working scared, Wally did his best.

Even though it was a cherry of a gig Wally was scared because there are hundreds of ways to goof up a job and only a few ways to do it right. It was like stage fright. Once he started he'd be fine. In fact, he'd be obsessed. His first thought on waking would be the construction. His step would have more spring; his mind would have more clarity. For Wally, starting a new house was like falling in love.

As Wally stood on the muddy lot in a gray mist, the backhoe idling roughly with a belch of diesel exhaust, he tried to visualize the house— Stef and Peter's home—that would rise from an outline of stakes and string. Wally always said that every house tells a story. Building it you leave a record, the first chapter: Pencil marks on rafters, boot prints dried in the mud of the crawlspace, decisions you made and fuckups you don't even realize you made will play out as the story goes on. Then people live in the house and leave behind the next chapters, little parts of themselves: dog-scratches on a door, smoke-smudges from a candle, a child's name etched in new concrete. Wally prayed this day would be the start of a good tale, an epic that would run for centuries.

Today was the groundbreaking. Stef stood beside Wally with Crow Creek Champagne in an ice bucket, snapping into the phone at her husband, Peter, who was supposed to be there too.

"Peter, you're a dick," she said, and she dropped the phone into her purse. Immediately it started ringing. She ignored it. "Champagne?" she asked.

"Thanks, but I can't. Working," Wally said.

"Right." Stef marched to the backhoe, swung the bottle over her head, and brought it down on the engine cover.

Fwop.

The bottle did not break. Instead, it bounced, leaving a bottle-shaped dent behind.

"Hey." Teddy, the operator, leaned out of his seat. "What'd I do to you?"

"Sorry," Stef shouted. "It was supposed to be a christening? Like launching a ship?"

Teddy looked puzzled.

"I'll pay for it."

"Just gimme the bottle," Teddy said. It wasn't like the backhoe was a gleaming new machine.

Tossing the champagne to Teddy, Stef stomped to her Bentley, where a chauffeur was waiting. In stately fashion, albeit with mud on her shoes, she glided away.

Wally always flirted with the idea of going into a partnership with a marriage counselor. If a couple wasn't having trouble already, a construction project would expose all the cracks in their relationship with issues of money and style, power and negotiation, how to disagree, when to compromise and when to stand firm. The strong couples grow stronger. The weak fall apart. And the contractor, like the therapist, has to keep his hands off the clients. As does his crew. For the contractor it's not so much a matter of ethics as it is of getting paid. When that woman in Los Altos Hills asked Juke to take a minute to repair something in her bedroom—every day for three weeks—it turned out she expected a discount. Never mind that she could afford it and never mind that it turned her into the role of high-class whore. She was a woman whose two primary recreational activities were clandestine affairs and shopping for discounts, and here was an opportunity to combine the two hobbies. What saved Wally was the fact that her husband was writing the checks, and Wally subtly threatened to tell the husband exactly why his wife was expecting a price break.

Wally was also thinking that he was getting tired of working for rich people. The money's better but the clients are weirder.

The house, though, would be a builder's dream—something Frank Lloyd Wright might have designed, with a greener approach for this day and age. Sometimes, you luck into a project you can feel good about. Wally's only qualm with the design was that it followed the modern fashion for unbelievably complex roofs, as if there were something shameful about a house with a clean and simple top. Somebody would have to calculate the rafter cuts for broken hips, lopsided polygons, dog-leg bastards—you practically needed a math degree to figure those cuts.

Guiding the backhoe, thumbing through blueprints, out of the corner of his eye Wally became aware of an extra body on the sidelines, not hiding but not stepping forward either. It was Abe.

Wally approached him, saying, "What's up?"—trying to sound not hostile but not overly friendly, either. After all, this was a terminated employee. Potential trouble.

"I'm gonna help," Abe said.

"Abe, I can't—"

"I'm not working for you. You're not paying me. Not one penny. I'm not your Alfredo. I'm your fork-up. I mean if I have your permission to swear, sir. But I'll do every crummy little job you've got. I'll inhale fiberglass. I'll eat dirt and shit concrete. That's a promise. Because I want to show you I really did learn something this summer. In spite of all evidence to the contrary, I got stronger and I got smarter. You know what I learned?"

"No. What?"

"I learned that with a little help I could lift a house. I mean I didn't *do* it, I mostly demolished stuff, but I *could*, and I want to be here when we lift this house. That's all. And you can't stop me unless you call the cops and have them haul my ass out of here."

"Do not touch," Wally said, "do not even *think* about touching any power tool. Unless I say so."

"Then it's okay? Uh, okay, sir?"

"We'll give it a try."

If Abe stuck around long enough, he might be useful figuring rafter cuts. Just the name dog-leg bastard gave Wally a headache—and no, it wasn't a swear word.

More important, though, Wally was glad to offer the chance for redemption. Once before, Wally had hired somebody for no pay. It had worked out pretty well.

Thirty-Eight

With a shovel Abe trimmed out five trenches after the backhoe had made a rough pass. Two of the trenches cut through an old septic drainfield. Abe hauled heavy concrete-embedded plywood forms. He cleaned up stones and mud clods that the drill rig had scattered. He tore out a thicket of thorny blackberry vines that was encroaching on the work area. The shovel gave him blisters; the plywood gave him splinters; the stinking mud permeated his clothes; the vines scratched his arms.

He kept his mouth shut.

Juke and Steamboat were banging forms together. Wally was checking levels and lines with a transit, signaling, calling out to Pancho to make a mark or shift a string or pound a stake. FrogGirl was nowhere to be seen.

Twice Wally went over to his truck to study the blueprints and make some phone calls. Abe noticed that each time Wally stopped, Steamboat hustled over to the transit and seemed to be checking Wally's lines and levels, especially certain spots where Pancho seemed anxious. Abe assumed they were trying to learn the craft, emulating the master. A few times, though, it appeared to Abe that Pancho was moving some of the marks. Nobody said a word to Wally about it, and nobody was ever at the transit when Wally came back.

After work, Juke asked Abe if he'd like a little more labor tonight. "Help me at my home," Juke said. "I'll pay whatever Wally's payin'."

"That'll be fine," Abe said.

He followed Juke to a nasty-looking neighborhood in East Palo Alto and parked the Honda in the driveway beside Juke's El Camino. There were five or six Harleys in the front yard. In the back yard a couple of white-mustache guys in torn black T-shirts were throwing knives at a dart board. Juke waved to them and showed Abe the evening's project at the side of the garage.

With a piece of chalk Juke drew a rectangle on the stucco. "That's the window," he said. "First we gotta make the hole. I hear you're pretty good at makin' holes."

"Yes, sir," Abe said.

Juke handed Abe the Hitachi hammer. "Don't forget to forkin' stop, okay?"

"Okay, sir. Uh. Just one question. What are those other marks on the wall?"

"Bullet holes."

"What happened?"

"If you want to get along in East Paly you gotta stop asking questions."

Juke joined the white-mustache guys for a beer, and the three of them threw knives at the dart board and argued whether a particular Smith and Wesson revolver would fire while held underwater. Abe made short work of the stucco.

While Abe cleaned up the rubble, Juke cut the studs with a chattering red Milwaukee recipro, then measured a couple of two-by-fours for the sill and sides and a four-by-six for the header and cut them with his whining wormgear Skilsaw. The white-mustache guys went into the bungalow to fill up the bathtub.

"Okay, we done the noisy part," Juke said. The sun was just setting.

Juke explained the ground rules: He was working without a permit. Every exterior project would be done nights or weekends so he wouldn't be caught by some random drive-by building inspector. Every project would be completed the same day it was begun, even if it took until dawn. And as much as possible, they would keep the noise down so the neighbors wouldn't complain.

"Stealth mode," Juke explained. "A skill you might need someday."

Juke, Abe observed, was a master of stealth. He drove screws instead of nails. He could work outdoors at night with just the beam of a Petzl headlamp or sometimes no light but the half moon, and he could place lumber without any bang or clatter.

When Juke needed to tap the header into place, he directed Abe to hold a towel against it while he whacked with a mallet. It sounded like the thumping bass speakers of a passing decked-out car. Meanwhile, from the bungalow came the muffled sound of a gunshot followed by loud voices, whoops, and laughter.

Holding a tape measure to the rough opening, Juke asked over his shoulder, "What's center on forty-nine and eleven-sixteenths?"

Abe answered immediately: "Twenty-four and thirteen-sixteenths and a hair."

"Right. I knew that," Juke said. "What kind of a hair?"

"Regular hair."

Juke didn't try to explain anything, but Abe noted how precisely, how patiently and thoughtfully Juke lapped the window flashing into the old black felt paper, how with steady hand, while squinting down his nose, he ran a perfect bead of caulk along the edge of the window and then wove chicken wire into the old stucco netting. When Juke was involved in his work he was no wild man. He was focused: straight, tight, strong. Clear.

Around midnight they mixed up a batch of stucco. Illuminated only by moonlight, Juke showed Abe how to trowel the sandy, sloppy concrete into the netting.

The white-mustache guys came out of the bungalow arguing about who was responsible for repairing the bullet hole in the bathtub. They roared away on their choppers.

Abe washed the tools and the mixing tub with a hose. Finally around one a.m. Juke told him he could go. "I'll get up at dawn and put on the finish coat," Juke said. "Good work, Princeton."

"I'm not Princeton anymore," Abe said.

Juke laughed. "You'll always be Princeton."

What Abe wanted, at least at that moment, was to be a guy in a torn black T-shirt riding off on a motorcycle—with FrogGirl clinging to his back.

The next day at the Woodside job Abe lugged rebar. Without asking questions, he listened and absorbed the meaning and use of a doughboy, waler, pier cage, stirrup. He overheard the problems of working in expansive soil and how to provide for drainage. He discovered—with stunning feeling in his shoulders, fingers, and back—the difference in weight and stiffness between grade 40 #4 rebar and grade 60 #5. He saw the meticulous and muscle-straining preparation for what would become invisible, unbeautiful, mostly buried, and taken for granted. As Steamboat had said—and he seemed to mean it as an essential Law of Life and Human Development—Don't fork up the foundation.

In the evening Abe helped Juke cut a hole in the garage roof and install a skylight while three overweight guys chased each other around the back yard and threw bricks at each other.

As helper Abe fell into the role of manning the tool bucket, trying to anticipate and hand to Juke the proper tool before Juke asked for it. At one point Juke needed to remove a roofing nail. Abe offered him the cat's paw.

Juke looked disgusted. "That," Juke said, "is a *vulgar* tool."

Rummaging in the bucket, Juke pulled out a thin, notched pry bar. Wiggling it by hand, working it under the nailhead, Juke said, "My Pop used to say that. Vulgar tool."

"He was a carpenter?"

"Sorta. Stealth carpenter."

"He taught you?"

"When he was sober." Juke wiggled the nail free—cleanly and silently. "When he weren't locked up or kickin' the crap outa me."

Juke and Abe finished early, 11:00 p.m. The overweight guys had stopped chasing each other and were sitting in lawn chairs watching the work. One of them was chatting on a cell phone.

"Wanna beer?" Juke asked.

"Not tonight," Abe said, and he drove home to find Wally and his mother shouting at each other by the front door. Something about his Aunt Charlotte and how Wally had been rude to her. Stood her up. Not even the courtesy to call.

Wally and Opal stopped speaking, just silently glaring, as Abe walked between them.

Abe went to his room. By the front door the argument resumed in lower voices, gradually rising. Abe could hear every word.

I'm sorry. Very sorry.

Sorry isn't good enough.

Something came up. It happens.

You could've called her.

I've got a business to juggle. I've gotta work for a living.

This isn't about money. It's about respect.

I just forgot to call her.

You're a coward.

Coward? I'm not like you. I'm not independently wealthy, you know.

How dare you?

From the top of the stairs Abe shouted, "How about a little discretion down there?"

A sudden silence.

In a somewhat lower voice Abe said, "I warned you not to hurt her."

Just then Ronny started crying in his bedroom.

Everyone froze for a moment.

Opal, looking stricken, rushed up the stairs. Wally stepped out and gently closed the front door. *He doesn't slam doors,* Abe thought.

From his bedroom upstairs Abe could hear Wally's truck driving away—slowly, almost at a crawl—while the dogs whimpered in the yard.

A few minutes later, with Ronny settled again, his mother slammed a door—stupidly—but Ronny remained quiet. Abe had no doubt that she was in the bathroom. Yep, now he heard water running. Whenever she was upset she'd curl up in the bathtub and cry. Like what used to happen when his stepfather lived here. And before that his real father. *Dickheads, both of them. And now Wally.*

But Abe couldn't maintain the idea of Wally as another dickhead. Aunt Charlotte was a prig. A symphony snob. An icy enforcer of etiquette. She always gave Abe books for Christmas or birthdays, not books that he would want to read but books that he *should* read. Aunt Charlotte *needed* a few stand-ups and rude acts, maybe a desk full of bat guano—anything to bring her out of that school world and into real life.

Removing all his clothes, Abe lay on top of the bedspread. It was a hot night. Even naked, doing nothing, he was sweating. He thought of FrogGirl and his penis stirred. Idly he reached for it, but then the mood passed.

So bummed I don't even want to jerk off. Or is it respect?

Before he and Rachel broke up, he'd never used her as a jerk-off image—it seemed somehow disrespectful. Now maybe he felt the same way about FrogGirl. Maybe he was in love.

It occurred to Abe that he'd been hoping Wally would move in. Just once in his life—even if only for a little while—he could've had a half-decent, normal-acting family. But it always blew up.

Always. Dickheads.

Or.

Maybe ...the problem ...wasn't ...dickheads.

Maybe the problem is Mom.

And what about you, Mr. Mother's-son? What about you and Rachel? See a pattern? Hmm?

Now Abe couldn't sleep.

Climbing out the window, naked to the night, he sat at the chimney. He tried to think of something—anything—he'd done in his life that he could be proud of. Something that proved he wasn't just an overprivileged, underachieving snot. Something that reflected his values. Whatever they were. Abe's father was Jewish; his mother, Presbyterian; but Abe's beliefs were what he had learned on a construction site. And maybe that was enough.

He could smell the embers of a neighbor's barbecue. He could smell cut grass and a rosemary bush. He could hear the dull, distant roar of the freeway. The rough bricks of the chimney felt cool against his back. The sandy shingles dug at his butt. The dogs stopped whining for Wally and lay curled in the yard looking up at Abe until eventually all three—dogs in yard, Abe on roof—closed their eyes and dreamed of running free.

Thirty-Nine

Thumbing through Wally's address book, FrogGirl found the number and called. "Is this Opal?"

"Speaking."

"I'm FrogGirl. You sort of know who I am, right?"

"Yes."

"I'd like to invite you to dinner at our house. Wally's house."

"Is this Wally's idea?"

"My idea."

"Does he know about it?"

"Not yet."

"Don't you think you should ask him?"

"I thought I'd ask you first. So we could meet. It was just kind of an impulse."

"You'd better ask him first."

"Oh. I'm sorry." FrogGirl paused. "Did you guys have a fight or something?"

"Something. I'm sorry I was cold. It was nice of you to—"

"I just wanted to have you over before he lost the house. It seemed right."

"He's *losing* his *house?*"

"He didn't tell you?"

"He doesn't—we don't talk about money. Except when we're angry."

"This whole phone call is a disaster, isn't it?"

"Something like that."

FrogGirl hung up without a goodbye.

Forty

They were pouring concrete. From the cement truck parked downhill on the narrow Woodside country lane, the concrete crackled down a chute into a pumper. A heavy rubber hose snaked up the hillside from the pump trailer bringing a slurry of liquid rock. Juke held the end of the hose, guiding the placement. Abe's job was to stand below Juke, helping to shift the throbbing hose so it didn't snag or drag on anything. Juke communicated with the pumper by hand signal, flapping his arm to indicate start or stop.

It was noisy. The cement truck was growling, the pumper was grinding, the concrete shot out of the hose with a crunchy sound and plopped into the wooden forms. Abe didn't hear a thing to warn him until the last second. With a ripping groan the side of the form gave way. As Abe gaped upward, before he could leap away, a cascade of massive wet concrete dumped over him and pounded him straight to the ground.

Juke flapped his arm. "Man down!"

The pumper stopped.

Everybody ran to where Abe was pulling himself out of a mound of slop. Hands grabbed Abe's arms. In a moment he was out.

"You hurt?" Wally asked.

Abe considered a moment. The concrete had been cold, a pitiless wave, unrelenting, stupid, heavy, implacable. *So that's what death feels like,* he thought with a chill. In the rush of adrenaline never before had he felt so alive. His muscles trembled, his heart pounded, his blood roared. "I'm okay," he said.

"We gotta wash you down," Steamboat said. "That shit burns."

"My fault," Juke said. "Put my weight on that waler. Knocked it loose."

Steamboat hustled Abe away, down the hillside to the cement truck, which had a hose and a water tank. Abe took off his pants, and the driver sprayed him. "You almost did a Jimmy Hoffa," the driver said.

"Who?" Abe asked.

"Guess he was before your time," the driver said.

It was a hot day, but Abe was shivering.

"You want to go home?" Wally asked.

"No, sir," Abe said.

Wally fetched an extra pair of cutoff blue jeans from the back of his truck. The waist was twice Abe's girth. He tightened it using a scrap of Romex as a belt.

The form was fixed; the pour went on.

Abe's job for the rest of the day was to shovel up the same concrete that had nearly buried him. Soon he was sweating. He wheelbarrowed load after load to the parking area where he dumped separate piles limited to a size that could be hauled away later. The hardest part was lifting the spilled concrete out of a trench next to the foundation wall where they would eventually be laying drain rock. By the time Abe got to the bottom, the concrete had hardened enough that he had to stab it apart with a pry bar. A throbbing bruise was growing on Abe's hip where he had fallen to the ground.

All the while, amidst the hard work and the pain and shock of nearly being buried alive, with heightened senses Abe was keenly aware of the smell of curing concrete. It was a wet and yet oddly dusty odor. It was a scent of possibility, of something you could briefly shape with tools, of impending permanence. Abe enjoyed that smell. No, more. He simply loved it: a magic force, so solid and quiet and strong. Concrete, he realized, has dignity. Maybe Abe had a law, his first, his very own: *Honor concrete*. Honor it, at least, until you come at it with a demo hammer.

It wasn't until evening at the garage in East Palo Alto, where for tonight's project Juke was building a sleeping loft, that Abe had a chance to ask, "Why'd you say it was your fault?"

"Cuz it was."

"You never touched that waler. I saw Wally building that section. He messed up. It's his fault."

"I shoulda checked."

"You shouldn't need to check."

"Sometimes you gotta take the fall for somebody."

"Why?"

"Respect."

"Respect for what?"

Juke didn't answer. A woman had appeared at the side door. She was dressed in a conservative brown suit with a bandage across one cheek. In spite of her black eye, Abe knew from one glance that she didn't belong here—or anywhere in East Palo Alto. She had a certain bearing. Good breeding. Resting by one leg was a handsome leather suitcase.

"Lenora!" Juke said. "You're out!"

"I wanted to talk to you," she said.

"You got the forkin' wires out! Come on in!"

She didn't move. "We have to talk. Before I go home."

"This is home. It ain't ready, but it's comin'."

"Will you give me a ride to the airport, Juke? So we can talk?"

"Where you goin'?"

"Boston."

"You said you'd never—"

"I'm going home, Juke. I have to be who I am."

"Who *are* you?"

"The daughter of a Boston Brahmin."

"A what?"

"Money, Juke. We've got money. And I can't live without it."

Juke winced. He stared at his boots, slowly shaking his head.

"I'm sorry, Juke. I have to set some things right. Finish school there. Then in a couple years maybe I'll be back. After I mend some fences."

Juke looked up with a last glimmer of hope: "You need a carpenter for them fences?"

"Not that kind. You're sweet. Has anybody called you sweet before?"

"Don't recall."

"You and me, Juke. We don't do sweet."

"And the snivelin' pricks—they do sweet?"

"Yes, as a matter of fact. They sent flowers! Lovely bouquets—and a nice card. I was so surprised. It broke the ice. Deep ice."

Juke's body was slumping into a slouch.

"Please, Juke. Take me to the airport. I'll send the taxi away."

Juke kicked a metal shelf unit—and a shower of motors and springs and broken tools crashed to the concrete floor. "Can I talk you out of this?"

"No. It's my plumb and true. But let's end it with class."

"Sounds like *you* got the class."

"So do you, Juke. In your own way. And I'm going to miss it."

Suddenly Abe was alone in Juke's garage. Outside he heard the distinctive semimufflered sound of the El Camino backing out of the driveway. He heard voices from the back yard, an argument over who had the louder belch mixed with another discussion of whose girlfriend had the biggest nipples. *Those guys never graduated from fourteen-year-olds,* Abe thought to himself. He hoped he could walk out unnoticed.

Before leaving, he took a look around. In one corner of the garage where previously Juke had hung a girlie calendar, he now had placed a series of orange Post-Its. The top one began: *I respect who you are.* The bottom one ended: *Show how good you are.* Separately to the left was a single Post-It:

Meth brain
Insane!!!!

And to the right was one more:
We'd be weird

Forty-One

Friday at noon, belt sander racing was about to resume after a long and lamented absence. Juke, moping all morning, perked up as he assembled the tracks. Steamboat had ribs on the coals. A festive crowd was gathering. Wally raised spirits even higher as he circulated among the gathering tradesmen and passed out envelopes. Abe, in his usual role of listening, observing, keeping his mouth shut—and not receiving an envelope himself—heard Wally apologizing to various subcontractors for the small payment. Wally was promising he'd eventually find a way to pay in full—plus five percent as "guilt money." The insurance had finally settled for the tools. That money, as well as a progress payment for completing the foundation, was going to pay off the crew—and the subs from the Krainer disaster. The electrician, the plumber, tile setter, carpet installer, cabinet maker, landscaper, the burglar alarm and swimming pool and HVAC guys—some had received step payments but none had received a final. All of them were stiffed when the gig had suddenly vanished. As each phase had completed, Krainer was supposed to pay Wally, who as prime contractor was supposed to pay the subs. From the sound of it, the subs were in a gray area as to whether Wally was actually legally obligated to pay them when Krainer held back. But nobody was suing Wally—at least not yet. The legal fees would be more than the money owed. And besides, they all cut Wally some slack. Some of them had been working with Wally for more than twenty years, long enough to build some trust. *Longer*, it occurred to Abe, *than I've been alive.*

And FrogGirl was there. "Where've you been?" Abe asked.

"Take a guess, Princeton." She was wearing paint-spattered overalls, a scarf over her hair.

"So you're the designated painter, huh?"

"Drywall. Paint. You're a turd."

"Huh?"

"It's nobody's business. How'd you know? Does it show?"

"The time we stopped at a drug store," Abe said. "Inside that bag. You bought prenatal vitamins."

"You snooped!"

"I was worried. I thought you were sick."

"You have no right to worry about me! Don't you ever worry about me."

"Sorry."

"Don't smile!"

"Sorry. And it does show, by the way. If you're looking for it."

"Stop looking!"

Abe turned his head to the side, still smiling, and said, "So since you're healthy and all, would you like to go to the Fillmore with me tomorrow night? David Grisman and Friends? I've got two tickets."

"You're asking me?" FrogGirl stared blankly at Abe. For a moment he was afraid she really was ill. Then she recovered. "I'm flustered. I mean flattered. I mean—"

"That's a yes?"

"Would we cruise through the streets of San Francisco in your automatic Honda?"

"You can insult my car all you want. I'm still asking."

"Yes. I'd like to go. Thank you."

A Grand Marquis, shattered taillight, cock-eyed bumper, one fender primer gray, pulled into the parking area. From the car emerged an emaciated baldheaded man dressed in a suit and tie and carrying a battered briefcase. Not the best-fitted suit and not the neatest necktie, but nevertheless the clothes made it clear that the man was not a tradesman.

"Gad Berman," Wally said. "What are you doing here?"

"Am I interrupting?"

"We were about to start the races. Hey—somebody could loan you a sander. This'll be fun."

"I'm afraid we don't have time."

"We?"

"You. There's a buyer. For Krainer. A gentleman from Thailand. Loves the house. May the good Lord help him. Wants to finish it just the way it is. Except he wants you to put a big old bell in the tower. You can do that, right? Make it a bell tower? How much time would it take to complete the house? Turnkey condition."

"Working fast? Eight weeks," Wally said. "After I finish this place."

"No time," Gad Berman said. "Foreclosure's in twenty days."

"So can't he buy it now and finish it later?"

"No. He'll buy some other monstrosity. Look, this guy owns half of Thailand. He doesn't wait for things. This is your chance. Finish that house in nineteen days and get all the money that's owed plus more, or don't finish and don't get a dime. Your choice."

"Or finish and get screwed. Again."

"Won't happen. This isn't Krainer's money now, it's Mr. Thailand. He just signed an eight-page contract. You sign and he's locked. And with him, a few hundred grand is a rounding error. You're not worth screwing."

"I could put it on a T-shirt," Wally said, holding his hands like parentheses next to his chest. "'Not worth screwing.' But Gad, it would take eight weeks. Working fast."

"Your choice."

"I'm on a big project. I can't walk away."

"Your choice."

"Do I get an advance?"

"Nope. Not a dime unless you complete in nineteen days."

"I can't do it."

"Your choice."

"I'm tapped out, Gad. I just paid my last dollar and still it's only a fraction of what I owe these guys. I can't even pay my mortgage and I can't walk off the job I just started. And you're talking a whole crew working overtime plus all the subs plus I'd have to hire extra help. And the supplies. I hate to sound like I'm whining but nobody's going to credit me for—"

"I will," a nasal voice said.

Wally looked away from Gad Berman to realize that he was encircled by a crowd who had been listening to every word.

The nasal voice was Robert, the cabinet maker, a short, intense man with a reputation—well-deserved—of having a Napoleonic complex.

Strutting up to Wally, Robert handed back his envelope. "It's only noon, right? You're done here for the day, right? I'm booked for the next four weeks, but there's a whole weekend ahead, right? And then there's Monday night, and Tuesday night, and every weeknight and then the whole weekend and so on for nineteen days, right?"

"That's really nice of you, Robert, but I—"

"If we don't finish this house, who gets the money that's owed us? Krainer? The bank? The slickfuck lawyers? Uh, begging your pardon, buddy," Robert said, turning to Gad Berman. "I don't mean—"

"You mean I'm not a slickfuck?" Gad Berman said. "Where did I go wrong? Is it my car?"

"I already built the damn cabinets," Robert said. "Teak and mahogany. Custom fit. Chain-sawed a rainforest just to sit in my shop."

"We all put sweat in that house, Robert, but I can't ask—"

"Same problem," another voice said. "I've got the angel fountain." The voice was Landscaper Lucy, a petite woman who always wore a wide-brimmed straw hat. Because of her short size there were people who claimed they'd never seen her face, just the top of the hat—not true, of course, if they'd ever talked with her. In conversation she would look up at people and pierce them with laser blue eyes. There were others who claimed the hat was to keep people from looking down her shirt as she was often on her knees, bent forward, planting something. Then there were others—Juke, for one—who claimed there was nothing to be seen down there anyway. It was a matter of debate and speculation, and it made Wally wonder how any work would get done if women ever truly integrated the construction field.

"Maybe," Wally said, "you'll have some other client where you could use—"

"Are you kidding?" Lucy, looking up at Wally, pinned him with her eyes. "I had it made custom. You think somebody else will want a totally naked, anatomically detailed, extremely well-endowed, gravity-ignorant Playboy wet-dream angel who stands on one foot and spouts water from her boobs?"

Rudolfo the plumber spoke up. He was stuck with boxes of special-order faucets and even a couple of custom-color bidets for the bachelor. Rudolfo was gay. Everybody knew it and nobody talked about it even though construction is a gay-bashing culture. Even when Rudolfo wasn't around, nobody made fun of him because word might get back to him and he was too good a plumber. You didn't want to be on his bad side.

Kim the electrician had stacks of special-order sconces and a pearl chandelier; the tile-setter, piles of hand-painted tile. Everybody had Krainer inventory—nonreturnable, paid-for, one-of-a-kind items, a huge investment. And if uninstalled, a sad waste.

"What I start, I finish," Kim said, and several heads nodded in agreement.

It was why Wally hired them: Each one had a single-minded focus on overcoming obstacles once a project was begun. Every construction job was basically an endless sequence of weird and unexpected problems. That's what made it interesting—and so satisfying when completed. Leaving a job unfinished was like leaving off the last notes of a song.

Like eating one potato chip. Like interrupted sex. It could make you crazy.

"I'm in," Steamboat said, handing Wally his envelope.

"Got me, Boss," Juke said, also returning his envelope. "Hey, Steamie! Can you loan me a ten?"

Pancho and FrogGirl returned their envelopes without saying a word. Abe wished he had one so he could return it too.

The other subs were closing in, some more enthusiastically than others, but all of them were handing back their envelopes. Each of these people had war stories: the endless punch list, the withheld payment, the shifting standards, the outright fraud. Each had known the client from Hell: the snob, the bully, the young and clueless, the old and treacherous, the dot-com *enfant terrible*, the warring couple in the middle of a split-up. They'd all been hosed—and hosed again. They'd all seen money owed them stick in the pockets of people richer, more powerful than they. They wanted to see a win for the little guy. And it would be nice to make some profit, lemonade from a lemon.

Then there was pride. Bragging rights were at stake. Wally had signed them on with the understanding that the goal was the Perfect House—or at least, the perfect construction of a weirdly idiosyncratic house—which required the perfect electrician, the perfect swimming pool contractor, the perfect locksmith. It was a challenge. A goal once within reach—and then lost—now dangling before them once again.

"I breeng my crew," Alfredo—the original—said. Wally was surprised. Alfredo had no stake in the Krainer job whatsoever.

"This is totally kewl," FrogGirl said.

"I'm in," Larry Ludowski said, and for a moment everybody gaped at him.

"So," Gad Berman said, "are you taking it on?"

Wally studied the faces surrounding him—serious faces, fully aware of the commitment—and risk—to be weighed.

"What kind of bell?" Wally said.

Berman grinned. "Big. Old."

They shook hands. First Wally and Gad Berman. Then Wally and Robert. Then Robert and Gad, and Wally and Alfredo. Soon everybody was shaking hands with sticky, barbecue-sauced fingers.

"Holy forkin' shit," Juke said. "Let's roll!"

Instead of belt sander races, a convoy of vans and pickups rumbled through the horse-and-estate town of Woodside, maintaining a strict speed of twenty-five even on the straight-away and coming to full halt for the stop sign at Mountain Home Road where everybody knew they gave tickets to tradesmen while letting the Mercedes roll through. The caravan picked up speed on Sand Hill Road and then motored down Interstate 280 between the golden-colored pastures that smelled in September of pennyroyal and sage. Exiting at Page Mill Road, they snaked up the mountainside among the oak and madrone to Krainer's incomplete palace, already crumbling like a brand new ghost town in the wind-crinkled wild oats.

Every pane of window glass was broken. On the wall of the tower somebody had spray-painted GIMME DYNAMITE. The boulder at the top of the grotto had been dislodged—how many kids did it take to do that? The rock, forty-six inches in diameter, had rolled down the course of the waterfall and smashed into the bottom of the pool. Now it sat in a crater among radiating cracks and a scattering of beer cans. The front double-door entry—custom-built of hand-carved rosewood— had been tagged BEELZE. Inside the house, holes were punched in the drywall, and somebody had taken a symbolic crap in the alabaster fireplace. Wally tried to imagine Mr. Thailand walking through this place and deciding to buy it. Maybe he worked through agents. Or maybe he had good vision of things not as they are but as they would be—maybe that was how he got so flush.

"Where do we start, Boss?" Juke asked.

"Everywhere," Wally said.

The damage assessment split into teen-age vandalism—like punching walls—mixed with serious professional theft. Fortunately the lighting, plumbing, and kitchen fixtures hadn't been installed. Unfortunately, the heating and air had. The main unit for the geothermal direct-exchange heat pump, the boiler, the high-end water heater, and about five hundred feet of copper piping had vanished.

Destruction was random. A five-dollar temporary light fixture was shattered in a room that held four hundred square feet of lush custom-dyed carpeting, unstained and untouched. Complex inlaid hardwood floors lay unscratched beneath holes in cheapo gypsum drywall.

Since the building plans had grown in such an impromptu pattern even as construction was underway, parts of the house were nearly complete while others were still skeletal. Wally became Captain Clipboard, wandering from room to room assessing what work remained, receiving status reports from each of the subs, jotting it all down. Problems jumped out. The cost of replacing all the window glass would use up every last dollar Wally had. Replacing the heat pump and water heater would have to wait for Wally's next progress payment, at least a week away. While most of the mansion was ready for final trimming-out—plus damage repair—the rear wing, a last-minute addition the size of a normal house, was barely framed. Scheduling a full spectrum of subs in the right sequence so they wouldn't be stumbling over each other—in a nineteen-day deadline—would be mind-boggling. The electric wires, plumbing pipes, sheet-metal ducts, security/data/ cable TV/phone wires, and central vacuum pipes all had to go inside the walls before the gypsum went up, which in turn had to be taped and allowed to dry before painting, and the floors had to be laid and sanded and coated, and the baseboards and crown molding installed, the doors hung, locks installed. Building inspectors had to check off each step of the way—during daylight hours when Wally and almost everybody else would be working elsewhere. And where do you buy a big old bell?

As workers bustled over the job site, Wally noticed a man standing at the edge of the property uphill, hands on hips, surveying the situation. Phineas Pilpont would be none too pleased with this turn of events. His plan for the project involved no complicated scheming and scheduling and coordinating—nothing but a bulldozer.

Another reason to finish this job: *Tough shit, big guy.*

One of Wally's first calls was to a supplier who had been holding a stockpile of vintage mission-style roof tiles for this job. Wally—and before him the long-gone architect—had tried to convince Krainer to use the vintage tiles with their soft terra cotta tones and handmade quality. The roof more than anything else would define the impact of the house. Wally wanted to harmonize with the surrounding land. Krainer wanted bright red tile. Further, Anton disdained used tile or secondhand anything. He wasn't opposed to recycling—in fact, he loved it—he just didn't want anything recycled on his own house. It would be imperfect. He would not believe that something salvaged from a church built in the 1890s—something handmade by *peasants*—could possibly surpass the quality of modern manufacturing. The color was boring. It looked like *dirt*. And those tiles weren't composed of some precious raw material that had to be saved—they were simply *fried mud*. So Wally had waited, hoping for a change of heart, holding off on the roof even though all the prep was in place on every structure except the rear wing. Now Wally would get his way.

Tough shit, Krainer.

Abe and FrogGirl spent the afternoon and evening as a shuttle service in Wally's truck, returning supplies from Wally's back yard to the Krainer site, a thirty-minute trip each way. At 11:30 p.m. they unloaded their final run, fourteen packs of R18 fiberglass insulation batts, and found Wally sitting alone on the front steps under a newly

installed porch light writing on—it looked like stabbing with a pencil—
a clipboard in his lap.

"How much does this guy owe you?" Abe asked.

"Right now? About eight trucks."

"He pays in trucks?"

"My unit of measure. Keeps it real. By the time we're done here,
somebody—Mr. Thailand, I hope—will owe me about twenty-one
trucks."

"You'll be rich."

"I'll owe people about nineteen of those trucks."

"Good trucks?"

"There are no bad trucks."

Wally returned to figuring on the clipboard. Abe and FrogGirl
glanced at each other.

"Okay, you can go home now," FrogGirl said.

"I can't leave," Wally said with a sigh. "Somebody's gotta watch this
place."

"Me," FrogGirl said. "I brought my sleeping bag. And my
Maglite."

"I can't ask you to—"

"You didn't. Hey, this is where you found me, remember?"

"I can't leave you alone here. Now that I've seen what can happen
to this place I'd be too worried about—"

"I'll stay," Abe said. "We can trade shifts and keep guard all night."

Still seated, Wally looked from one face to the other. He had a
feeling that if they were confronted with actual danger, he'd bet on
FrogGirl protecting Abe. "Is this strictly business?" he asked.

"Well,—" Abe began.

"Strictly," FrogGirl said.

Wally arrived home at midnight and found he was wired. The
house seemed empty and cold without FrogGirl around. He could lie
on his bed in the dark and try to will himself to sleep. Or he could do
something useful. The stripper had finally dipped the garage-sale doors
he'd bought from the woman with the demented father. The now de-
painted doors were in the workshop out behind the house. *Might as well
do something.* It would focus his mind, unjangle his body.

In the shed, Wally laid the first door on a table. The surface was
rough from the chemical dip. The grain looked like Douglas fir or
possibly hemlock, dozens of short scraps joined in a random butcher-
block design that was clearly a labor of love by the old guy who built it.

Salvaging two-by-four cutoffs isn't worth the trouble if you're strictly going by cost, but in his dementia the man had rescued them anyway to create something special—and then he'd ruined it with old paint. Now Wally felt as if he were performing a second rescue—salvaging the product of the old guy's skills, discarding the errors of the old guy's judgment.

Wally belt-sanded lightly where he could, but with inset panels most of the door required hand-sanding. With his fingers working the sandpaper into the grooves, Wally felt he was massaging the wood. Likewise, in a feedback loop the wood was massaging his own mind.

His fingers ached. Fire burned in his knuckles and in the wrist where the nail had gone through. Much as he wanted to deny it, arthritis was setting into his body. He was blinking, tears brimming, trying to wash the gritty sawdust from his stinging eyeballs.

Amazing how woodwork could cloud the eyes while it cleared the head.

Abe slept. FrogGirl walked the quiet grounds, eyes alert, ears cocked for sound. The outdoor lights—the few that had been installed—were on, providing a few bright spots and a maze of deep shadows. A smell of sage and dusty dry grass blew from the meadow. She heard the screech of an owl.

She was thinking of her mother and sister back in Pasadena. Why hadn't they come after her? Surely Uncle Anton had told them she was here. What's the point of running away if nobody cares you're gone? Or maybe that's exactly the point. That, and to find a place of her own where she could play at something more important than basketball, make her own decisions and her own mistakes. Which she made big-time. Or was it a mistake, this life inside her?

Beyond the perimeter of light, in the shadows beyond the pool and the grotto, she spotted a pair of eyes.

Two pairs. Three.

Four pairs!

Pointing the Maglite, she saw coyotes. Two adults plus two smaller ones that were larger than pups, not quite full size—gangly, awkward like teenagers.

FrogGirl steadied the flashlight beam. The coyotes pricked their ears, sniffed with slightly upraised noses. They looked like dogs, and FrogGirl liked dogs. Then their lips parted. Fangs bared. A flash of evil.

Would they attack?

She shouldn't be standing there. Could she fight them off with a Maglite? If she screamed, would Abe hear? They saw her as prey. They saw her not as a soul but as scraps of white flesh.

And then it came to her, one thought like a beam of light:

Not my baby!

Gripping the barrel of the flashlight like a billy club, FrogGirl lunged toward the coyotes.

In an instant they were gone. Vanished.

Jeezo. What happened?

Her own heart was pounding. Her lungs sucked air as if she had been running. *Was that me—that sudden strength? That courage?* It felt like something beyond herself, outside her control.

As quickly as it came, like a breath of wind it was over.

Sun-up Saturday morning, Juke arrived at the job site with his Thermos of coffee and saw with a tinge of disappointment that he wasn't the first. Abe's Honda was already there. Inside the house, he found FrogGirl and Abe busily repairing punched-out drywall.

"You work all night?" Juke asked.

"Guard duty. Took some breaks," Abe said, pressing tape into a swath of joint compound.

"He snores," FrogGirl said.

"Runs in the family," Abe said.

"I thought you was lesbo," Juke said.

"We didn't do *that*," FrogGirl said.

"Yeah. Right," Juke said.

Juke, truth be told, had worked most of the night himself. He'd found he couldn't sleep and lacked the usual desire to get wasted. While Wally was sanding doors, while Abe and FrogGirl were guarding and drywalling and not doing lesbo or whatever the hell was going on, Juke had finished framing the loft in his garage. It was coming out nice.

Forty-Two

At the K-Palace, as people were calling the Krainer place, it was a day of fruitful chaos. Wally lost track, but there must have been fifty workers swarming over the place at one point or another. Little Lucy and her crew, all wearing broad-brimmed straw hats, planted butterfly bait and started laying a flagstone path. With the help of five men and a winch, the boulder was hauled out of the swimming pool and placed back on top of the grotto, and then some plasterers started repairing the crater. The fence contractor mounted chainlink to the already-set posts around the tennis court. Kim the electrician and his crew ran rough wiring through the studs of the rear wing while Rudolfo the gay plumber and his crew soldered copper pipes. While soldering, the blowtorch burned a hole through a piece of 10/3 Romex. One of Kim's assistants threw a punch at one of the Rudolfo's, and both had to be escorted from the grounds. All the electrical and plumbing work had to be done while balancing on joists and dodging carpenters from Alfredo's crew who were installing the subfloor under their feet while Steamboat, Juke, and Pancho were laying roof decking over their heads. A box of nails slid off a sheet of plywood on the roof and plunged through a gap, landing within inches of where Robert with difficulty was sliding a cabinet across some joists, causing Robert to strut outside and order everybody off the roof until he and his cabinet were safely out of the way. Abe and FrogGirl continued patching and taping walls. Larry Ludowski brought a truckload of day workers and put them to the task of cleaning up broken glass from the ground and removing shards that remained in the windows. He didn't bother to give them gloves until Wally found out and rounded some up.

The work was hard but the mood was good. Everyone felt a fresh air of freedom. With Krainer out of the picture, some of his annoying excess could be dropped. Wally decided to let each tradesperson choose one *bête noire* and trash it. Robert, for example, removed the rope molding from the cabinets, restoring integrity along with his own peace of mind. Pancho replaced the Greek columns of the front porch with Douglas fir six-by-sixes, rounding the edges with a router but stopping a couple inches short of each end, a simple but pleasing detail. The change was risky—the Greek columns were a prominent item, and Mr. Thailand had already seen them—but it was such an improvement that everybody felt happier with them gone.

"Keep in mind," Wally told everybody, "it's not the money. That's not what we're working for here."

"Yes we are," would always be the answer. Nobody would admit to pride though everybody felt it. With a few changes the house seemed to undergo a remarkable transformation.

Evening came. Quiet gradually returned. Swallows swooped around the eaves of the house. Crickets chirped. Juke and Wally were the last to remain, loading tools into their trucks.

"Where's your watch-guys?" Juke asked.

"They're young," Wally said. "It's Saturday night."

"Skipped out?"

"Abe took FrogGirl to the Fillmore."

"That's still there?" Juke got a dreamy look in his eye. "I used to go to the Fillmore when it was ... Well, never mind."

"Me too. Never mind." The venerable cavern of music held special memories for Wally: He'd met Aimee there. She was wearing a fringed leather jacket, hair down to her butt, glowing face and a shyness in her glance that she later confessed was because she assumed he was much too groovy, out of her reach. Which was the same thing he had assumed about her—in that fleeting speck of time when you could say "groovy" without laughing.

Wally wondered if his younger self and Opal had ever been at the Fillmore on the same night, if their paths might have crossed. She would have been younger, a teenybopper. What if he'd hit on her before he ever met Aimee? Lives would have changed. Children born or not born, souls following different paths. A crack in the universe.

Juke spat a thin stream. "You need one of them rent-a-cops."

"Tried. Shortage. National Guard called them up." Wally didn't mind staying. With the workers gone, it was a nice spot to sit and catch up on paperwork. Quiet. Great view. You could hear coyotes yipping and scuffling, sometimes see them trot down a trail through the grass.

"I know some guys," Juke said. "And nobody would mess with 'em."

"Your landlord? His buddies?" Speaking of coyotes ...

"Look tough, but they're a buncha pussycats. Don't tell 'em I forkin' said that."

"Could I trust them?"

"They got a code. Won't break their word. Make 'em commit."

"Send them over," Wally said. "I'll be here."

A nearly-full moon rose from the East Bay hills and poured its light over the twinkling sprawl of Silicon Valley, outlining silhouettes of cool, dark mountains. Wally was jotting notes on his clipboard when the cell phone rang. "Wally speaking."

"I lost." It was Opal's voice.

"How so?"

"I called first."

"I'm glad you called." Wally leaned back against the front door, sitting on the front steps. 10:45 p.m.

"Did I wake you?"

"Nope."

Wally was aware—and deeply relieved—that some sort of unspoken apology had just taken place, her to him, him to her, about their argument on her doorstep. Or so he thought.

"I haven't seen Abe for two days," Opal said. "I thought you might know something."

"He didn't call you?"

"Who, Abe? Call his mother? Is he all right?"

"Abe's fine. Last night he was helping me. Guard duty. There's a lot to explain."

So much had happened since their disagreement just a few days ago. Wally filled her in about Gad Berman, the man from Thailand, working one full-time project and adding another which was even more than full-time, a tighter deadline, shorter fuse. Hundred-hour workweeks for the next—what was left?—eighteen days.

"So that explains the incommunicado," Opal said. "Not because you were mad at me. But because you were working like mad."

"What about you, Opal? Incommunicado goes two ways. Are you mad at me?"

"No. I'm mad at myself. I shouldn't try to do a make-over on you. On anybody. You'd think I'd know that by now." Opal paused. "I called your home. I got a recording that your phone was disconnected."

"Little mix-up about the bill." Wally shifted his position. His back was hurting. Hard work followed by a hard seat. "I'll take care of it."

Opal was silent.

"You still there?"

"Yes," Opal said. "I'm counting to ten."

"What happens at ten?"

"We talk about money."

"Let's not."

"Eight."

Wally stood up. Something creaked inside his spine. "Let's really not."

"Nine."

Wally started pacing. "Opal. Please."

"Ten. You're losing your house, and you don't want to talk about it?"

"Who told you?"

"Do we have a relationship or don't we? Because if we do, you would certainly want to mention that you're losing your house."

"Mention it? You said you *hated* talking about money."

"My money. Other people, it's fine."

"Well, I'm definitely not asking you for a loan." Wally stopped pacing. "And don't worry about my house. It's just a little mix-up with the bookkeeping. I'll fix it."

"Little mix-up?" She laughed. "Who's your bookkeeper?"

"Nobody." The laugh surprised him. She really wasn't mad. She really seemed forgiving. And immediately he wondered—he couldn't help it, he was programmed that way—was she ready for Station Four? Right now? But what he said was, "I had a bookkeeper. Gone for a while."

"Can't you hire—? Omigod. Aimee. She did your books. Am I right?"

Wally sighed.

"And," Opal continued, "it isn't working so well by correspondence. Right?"

Wally sighed again.

"You know," Opal said, "always the first step is to admit you have a problem."

"Hello, my name is Wally, and I stink at bookkeeping."

"That's good."

Wally was curious: "Who'd you know in twelve-step?"

"My father."

It was a chuckle-stopper. She didn't offer more, and Wally wouldn't ask.

They were quiet for a moment. An owl was hooting in one of the oaks.

Opal spoke: "So Abe's okay? Is he getting any sleep?"

"He's fine. He's a big boy now. Relax. And I'm watching him."

"Sorry. I'm a mom. I can't turn it off. And your problem is not just bookkeeping."

"I know."

"It's a bigger problem."

"I know."

"It's lack of money."

"I *know*."

"Keep calm, Wally. I can do a little accounting. In fact, heck, I used to do back-office work for an insurance company. It's actually sort of interesting if you, you know, find it interesting. Which I do. I can help. Okay? It's not about us, Wally. They're just numbers. Somebody needs to straighten them out."

It began to dawn on Wally what was really her agenda. Instead of head-on tackling the difficult money topics—like who had more, and why, and how it was gained or lost, and the totally taboo topic of power—a woman of comfortable means and a man of, uh, discomfort—instead of those topics they could approach it sideways as a matter of accounting. Bookkeeping. Simple columns of numbers. *Brilliant. Awesome.*

They made a plan for Wally to bring all his papers, bills, checkbooks to Opal's house the following night. It needed to be at her house so she could put Ronny to bed.

With the arrangements made, Wally asked, "When did you do insurance?"

"Just after college. Art history major? So naturally I couldn't find a job. Good old-fashioned nepotism. My father."

"He worked there?"

"He owned it. Until he drank himself into a stupor. Because of me."

"You drove your father to drink?"

"I got raped."

"That's hardly your fault, Opal."

"I never said it was. But it killed my father. He could buy all the insurance in the world, but then ..."

Wally heard loud motors approaching.

"Opal, could you not get any more psychologically complex for a while? I've got a house to build."

"Okay. Sorry. I'll try."

Two single headlights turned off the road and into the parking area. Two men with white mustaches, wearing torn T-shirts, dismounted from two choppers of gleaming chrome in the moonlight.

One of the men shouted: "You Wally?"

"Yes."

"They call me Marmaduke. This is Sir William." They swaggered up to Wally. "You can go now." They smelled of machine oil. Chains hung from their belts. Marmaduke's nose was bent. Sir William was missing two teeth and half an ear.

Wally folded his arms across his chest. "We need to get a few things settled."

"Cash only," Marmaduke said.

"No booze," Wally said. "No drugs."

"You're killin' me." Marmaduke pretended to remove a knife from his heart. Then he smiled. "Beer don't count."

"Don't make a mess," Wally said. "No parties, no damage."

"You're tough."

Wally shook his head. "I thought you were the tough guys."

Marmaduke grinned. He was flattered. "And if somebody comes around?"

"Usher them politely off the property. No weapons, no hurting."

"Gotcha. We'll just hold 'em down—politely—and piss on 'em."

"We got a deal, Mr. Marmaduke?"

"Lemme see if I got this right. All cash. Beer, no booze. No drugs, no parties, no damage, no weapons, no hurting. What about pornicatin'? You got a policy about pornicatin'?"

"Nobody underage."

"Man, you *are* tough. Any more noes?"

"No trespassers. No vandals. And there's a guy uphill, name of Pilpont, kind of worries me. Keep an eye out."

"Deal," Marmaduke said, and they shook hands.

Back home, Wally sanded another garage sale door in the workshop—calming down, a mind massage—and then searched on the Internet for a bell. He'd already phoned a couple of places listed in the Yellow Pages under "Church Supplies," but the salesmen sounded cheesy and were pushing electronic carillon systems. Wally was looking for something special—antique, maybe—with a history and a soul. He wanted, quite simply, the perfect bell.

On eBay he found a gamut ranging in price from a hundred dollars to sixteen thousand, from rusty iron to polished bronze, from cracked to mint, from plain to pretty—school bells, train bells, dinner bells, fire bells. What would Mr. Thailand want? Wally called Gad Berman and tried to get more information, but all Gad knew was that the man said he wanted "a big old bell in the tower." Presumably, that meant one bell. Antique? Gaudy? Simple? Should the tone be deep and soulful, or loud and brassy?

The best that Wally could find was one made by Meneely & Co. of West Troy, New York. It was cast bronze, stamped 1887, no cracks, "original patina." How, Wally wondered, could the seller possibly know it was the original patina? And what could be original about patina, which is only acquired with age? Sometimes Wally had to stifle his teacher gene or he'd start correcting ad copy with a red pen. Anyway, the bell was twenty-seven inches in diameter at the bottom, mounted in A-frame pillars, had a twenty-four-inch clapper and cast-iron yoke, and was turned by a six-spoke wheel. $13,000.

Hmm.

Wally couldn't spare that kind of money—his own money—on spec for a bell that might or might not turn out to be what Mr. Thailand wanted. In fact, Wally simply didn't have any kind of money. Somehow he had blundered into the position of buying gear for a rich man's house on a poor man's pay. Hoping—praying—to be repaid. Or else he was heading for a spectacular bankruptcy dragging all his friends and associates with him, just like Krainer. Wally, the poor man's Enron. *At least,* Wally told himself, *I didn't lie about it.* Still, he knew he'd feel totally responsible if they failed.

Poking around some more, Wally found a Google link that turned out to be a false lead—not a bell for sale but a newspaper article in the Baltimore *Sun* about one Ralph Edmunton in Hoopersville, Maryland, who was arrested for trying to set fire to his neighbor's temple. The neighbor had built the temple for his daughter's wedding to a Thai man. In the temple he'd installed an ornate "Buddha Bell." A photo caption said the bell was four feet tall and weighed 954 pounds.

As soon as Wally saw the photo, he knew what he'd been searching for.

According to Mr. Edmunton, as quoted in the article, the wedding had taken place two years previous, but the neighbor continued "banging the bell" on a daily basis starting around dinner time and sometimes—reading between the lines here—the neighbor would get loaded and keep banging until late into the night. The neighbor insisted that the bell was supposed to be struck a hundred and eight times to atone for the hundred and eight sins of mankind and that each strike of the bell should be allowed to reverberate to its conclusion, each of which might last for several minutes. Not surprisingly, a feud had developed. The bell-ringer's name was Augustus H. Gannymede.

Hmm.

Wally was interrupted at the computer by the sound of his own front door opening and closing and FrogGirl calling, "Wally, there's a motorcycle gang up at the K-Palace and they won't let us in."

"Were they nasty?" Wally asked, finding both Abe and FrogGirl in the kitchen.

FrogGirl considered for a moment. "Actually," she said, "they were perfectly civil."

"They're the new watch-guys." Wally opened a cabinet and pulled out a bag of Oreo cookies. "I'm glad they were civil."

FrogGirl was scowling. "You coulda told us."

"How? Leave a message at the Fillmore?" Wally offered the bag of cookies. Abe and FrogGirl each took two. Wally said, "How many watch-guys were up there?"

"Couple of old farts," FrogGirl said. "Playing with knives."

Abe ate the cookies straight, one bite at a time—Wally's method. FrogGirl peeled the chocolate tops off each cookie with a slight twisting motion as if unscrewing them, which had the effect of leaving all the cream filling attached to one side, none to the other. FrogGirl ate the plain chocolate pieces first. She combined the two chocolate bottoms and their white cream fillings into a double-cream new cookie which she then nibbled, savoring each little piece—Aimee style. An Oreo gourmet.

"So." Wally spread his hands. "You and Abe can have the comfort of your own beds tonight. No guard duty. Get a full night's sleep. Good news, right?"

"Uh, yeah," FrogGirl said.

"How was the concert?"

"Fine."

"What about you, Abe? Was it as good as you expected?"

"Fine," Abe said.

Stonewalled. "All right, sorry," Wally said. He knew the meaning of 'Fine.' "I'll leave you alone now." He stepped toward the hall, then hesitated. "Oh. One thing. Your mother was wondering where you were, Abe."

"Uh, yeah," Abe said.

"She was worried. She'll be glad to see you at home tonight."

Abe shuffled his feet. "Uh, actually ..."

Oh wow. Suddenly it all clicked.

Wally peered from the face of Abe to face of FrogGirl: Both looked ill-at-ease, slightly abashed, but resolute.

"All right," Wally said. "Whatever." He cocked his head, signaling. "Abe, may I speak to you in private for a moment?"

They walked into Wally's messy bedroom—the only room FrogGirl never tidied. FrogGirl remained in the kitchen unscrewing two more Oreos.

In a low voice Wally said, "I just want to explain the house rules."

Matching his low voice—and clearly nervous—Abe said, "This is sort of embarrassing."

"Sorry. But you gotta use a condom."

Abe blushed. "She's already, uh, you know, don't you?"

"Pregnant. Of course I know. What I don't know is your history, or her history, and for this moment a condom is house rules. To protect you both from God knows what. Okay?"

"Uh. Actually. I don't have one. Believe it or not, I wasn't planning on anything like this. And I'm not even sure we're going to need one."

"Be a Boy Scout," Wally said. "Prepared." He rummaged through a drawer removing socks, a pipe wrench, three *National Geographics*, a propane torch and—from the very bottom—a handful of condoms in foil wrappers. "They're ancient. Check 'em first. Okay?" In his fingers he tucked them into a neat pile—three Trojan ribbed, two LifeStyles UltraSensitive—and held them out for Abe.

"This is still embarrassing, sir."

"Yeah. Me too. Take 'em."

"I won't need five."

"Boy Scout."

Abe smiled weakly. "All right, sir."

"And at some point you really should call your mother. She's getting frantic. Maybe she has no right to be, but she is. Just tell her where you are."

"Uh, yeah. So are we done?"

"We're done."

In the morning while Abe and FrogGirl took a long shower—together, singing—Wally called directory assistance and found, sure enough, Augustus H. Gannymede of Hoopersville, Maryland.

"This is just a shot in the dark, Mr. Gannymede, but I was wondering if you might want to sell your bell."

"It's damaged," said a phlegmy-sounding voice.

"How bad?"

"Scorched at the bottom. Fire. We had a little incident. I'm guessing you could buff it out. Other than that it's a beaut if you like this sort of thing. Legend is, if you ring it at a wedding, and then you ring it every night thereafter, the couple will always be happy. But legends, alas, are legends."

"Not happy?"

"Actually, I'd say my daughter's very happy now that the divorce is final."

Mr. Gannymede, once you got him started, turned out to be quite a talker. He'd bought the bell from a woman in Montreal whose husband had just been deported. No idea how old it was. There were three Buddhas, "with eyes and everything," in relief on the sides of the bell along with some calligraphy he couldn't read. At the top was a dragon with an arched back forming a hook so you could suspend the bell by a rope beneath the dragon's belly. There was no clapper. The way you ring a Buddha bell, Mr. Gannymede said, you suspend a short log from a couple of ropes and swing it from the side into the bell. The log should be of cherry wood or something nice—not too hard or you'll get a harsh tone, but not too soft or you'll dampen it. It's a deep sound that lasts for a couple minutes, slowly fading. Sweetest thing you ever heard. Mr. Gannymede conceded that his fondness for the tone was proving to be his undoing. So okay. Ahem. For a fair price, he was willing to sell.

"What's a fair price, Mr. Gannymede?"

"You'd have to move it yourself."

"I'll handle the move. What do you want for it?"

"The woman who sold it was in rather desperate straits. I feel guilty about how little I paid her. I don't want you to have the same torment, so I'll ask for a fair price."

"How much?"

"You won't resent me for making a profit, will you?"

"You're entitled. Please name a price, sir."

"Seven thousand, six hundred and thirty-two dollars."

"May I ask how you came up with that number, sir?"

"Eight dollars a pound."

"Are you an engineer, Mr. Gannymede?"

"Retired. How'd you know?"

"Lucky guess. But I'm disappointed. I don't believe I could go over six dollars a pound."

"I could meet you at seven."

"I'm really stuck at six."

"Six seventy-five?"

"I wish I could go that high. I really do. But I just don't have the—"

"Six sixty-five is my final offer."

Wally sighed. He said nothing.

"Still there?" Gannymede asked.

"I just wish I could go higher. I'm not authorized to pay more than six fifteen."

"I've come down as far as I can go, Mr. Walters. I feel I've made a very generous offer."

"It's a shame, Mr. Gannymede. It really is. I wish I could meet your price."

"Well, if you ever change your mind, give me a call."

"I will. And thank you, sir. Good-bye."

Wally kept the phone to his ear. He heard nothing from the other end. Then:

"Six thirty, dammit."

"Sold," Wally said.

Gannymede broke out laughing. "Okie doke. When can you pick it up?"

"I'll call a trucking company tomorrow."

"Aren't you coming yourself?"

"I'm in California, Mr. Gannymede."

"California? If I'd known, I'd have charged you double."

"Why?"

"Because I hate California."

"Why?"

"Everybody hates California. Don't you know that?"

"Why?"

"I don't know. We just do."

Forty-Three

It was another long day of chaos—and making progress. Steamboat and Pancho stapled Tyvek and built the soffit around the new wing while Juke framed a rear porch. FrogGirl put a second coat of joint compound on the repaired walls. Destructo Princeton, as he was now known, got the job of tearing out the upper wall of the Krainer Erection so they could rebuild, open-style, for the bell. Wally had made a unilateral decision to shorten the height of the tower by ten feet, bringing it in line with the rest of the house, and create a roofed but unwalled space surrounding the bell, hoping it would look like an homage to an old California mission.

But shouldn't it be a temple? Wally asked himself repeatedly. Shouldn't it hang from one of those wooden frames that look like *pi?*

No, Mr. Thailand said a "tower," Wally answered himself repeatedly. But can I get away with mixing a Buddha bell with California mission style? Has my judgment been ruined by working with Krainer?

Alfredo's crew hustled all over the roof chattering in Spanish and laying paper, flashing, and battens. Kim and his crew installed floodlights over the tennis court, shouting to each other as they pulled wires and maneuvered a cherry-picker. The tile-setter and his assistant laid a mortar bed over the cabinets even as Robert, the little Napoleon, grumbling all the way, was below them dodging blobs of spilled mortar as he installed the final details of those same cabinets. Larry Ludowski, keeping to himself as he always preferred, built a small deck that attached to the porch.

And what if Mr. Thailand isn't Buddhist? What if he's Christian? What if he wanted an actual mission bell? Or what if he's not religious at all? What if he wanted a school bell? How do you build to please somebody you know nothing about?

The answer, Wally concluded, was simple: You build to please yourself. And the combination of Buddha bell in mission tower somehow pleased him, a cultural blending that made sense and ought to look pretty darn good.

The glazier, a gruff old guy, walked around measuring the broken windows, then sat down with a calculator and a pile of price books and came up with an estimate that was twice what Wally had expected.

Wally complained: "That's more just for the glass than those entire windows cost new."

The glazier shrugged. "Difference between field work and factory work."

What if instead of *Not worth screwing*, this guy decides on *Not worth bothering to pay*? Gad Berman is a pit bull, but could he hang on against a man who owns half of Thailand?

Little Landscaper Lucy and crew set up the fountain-of-the-spouting-angel-boobs. Wally—and Lucy—would have preferred not to install it at all. Mr. Thailand had never seen it, so chances were good that he wouldn't miss it or even want it. Lucy, though, was desperate to be paid. She'd had to sell her truck and was working out of a leased van. The cost of the statue for her was, quite literally, one truck.

Every worker—male and female—at some point seemed compelled to walk by the newly installed statue. They would pause, thinking nobody was watching, to bend over and stare up at the anatomically detailed space between the angel's parted legs. Then, frowning or smiling or shaking their heads, they moved on.

Maybe, Wally thought, there is a grand plan to all this. Maybe the angel pussy justifies the Krainer Erection.

When not making phone calls or giving directions or solving glitches, Wally kept an eye on Abe and even found a little time to work on the tower stairs. They'd already torn out an earlier staircase because of a dispute with a building inspector. Seems there was a conflict about the size of the landing in relation to the fire code and handicap access regulations and the inspector's own ego—the kind of crap that gave Wally massive headaches and that he tried to avoid by simply agreeing with whatever half-assed solution the inspector wanted. In this case narrower, steeper stairs were somehow the solution for improved handicap access.

Abe, watching Wally work, was surprised to see that Wally had cut one of the stair treads at the wrong angle with a thin wedge of a gap showing at one end. Just what did Wally mean by perfect construction, anyway? How perfect is perfect?

Work continued into the twilight. Wally uncharacteristically left before the rest of the crew to keep a bookkeeping appointment with Opal, driving away slowly like an old man. Lately, Wally had become the slowest driver on the road.

After Wally's departure, Steamboat and Juke examined the new stair treads. Abe said nothing as he cleaned up the last of the debris he had created—scattered nails, splinters of plywood, tufts of fiberglass, pebbles of stucco.

"Hey Destructo," Juke called. "How would you pull this tread?"

Abe examined it closely. There was an odor of nasty chemicals. "Back out the screws."

"Then what?"

"Hope the adhesive hasn't set."

"How do you know there's adhesive?"

"I smell it. Anyway, I saw him working."

"What if it's set?"

"Tap it from under. Try to work a pry bar—a thin one, gently—between the stringer and the tread."

"If that don't work?"

"Go vulgar. Bang it to crap."

"Okay. Do it."

Juke handed Abe his trusty Panasonic cordless with the magnetic screwdriver bit attachment. Don't fuck up, Abe said to himself. What looks simple...He set the controls to reverse, low speed. Carefully he pointed the bit into the screwhead, made sure it was aligned in the Phillips head slots, held the body of the Panasonic with both hands so it wouldn't kick out, and slowly squeezed the trigger. The variable-speed motor started gradually, Abe hardening his grip in sync with the tool. Reluctantly at first, then easily with a sound like rubbing a finger over an inflated balloon, the screw backed out.

Abe caught Juke and Steamboat grinning at one another. "What's so funny?" he demanded.

"Nothing," Steamboat said. "You did good, Princeton."

"No really. What's the joke?"

"No joke," Steamboat said.

"Then why were you smiling?"

"Cuz we're proud," Steamboat said, and he walked down the stairs.

"Proud of *what*?" Abe demanded, and his voice echoed through the tower.

"You," Juke said. "And it's about forkin' time. Now back out the rest of them screws and get the tread out. Then I'll show you how to cut a new one."

"On the table saw?"

"Uh huh. Since you're the math guy, you can count your fingers before and after. See if they match."

"I'll be careful."

"Yep. I think you will."

And he was.

Forty-Four

Opal showered, scrubbed, washed her hair. She dressed with care, hoping to look as if she hadn't. She wanted the effect of a wild bush of lavender blossoms happened upon in a meadow—or some field in Provence— unexpected but natural, unadorned and yet stunning. Ultimately she decided on going barefoot wearing faded flared Levi's with a red patch on one knee. The message was casual, playful. For accent she was wearing turquoise—earrings, bracelet, ring. A message of artful elegance. On top she chose a Bloomingdale's black sweater with blue piping, deep Henley neck, all buttons open. A message of you-know-what. The plunging neckline revealed the work of a painful push-up bra, black lace and satin. She wore it as an offering to Wally. She imagined his big bumbling fingers fumbling with the catch.

Wally arrived at Opal's front door carrying a beer box full of papers. Nonalcoholic beer box, she noticed. Basically, it looked as if he'd swept the top of his desk and emptied a couple of drawers into the St. Pauli Girl carton.

A slip of paper fluttered out of the box and came to rest on the smooth concrete of the front stoop. Squatting, Wally fumbled to pick up the credit receipt. His fingers couldn't seem to get a grip—as if he were wearing invisible gloves.

Quickly Opal knelt and plucked the thin paper from the concrete surface. For some reason she felt embarrassed for Wally. Impulsively she grasped his hand in her own. The flesh was rough and hard. Twists of sawdust were entangled in the hairs on the back of his hands. Brown globs of dried glue clung to his fingers. He smelled of stale sweat. There was a scratch on his forearm, dark drops of hardened blood. On his face, a three-day beard.

She let go of the hand and said, "Wally, you're working too hard."

"Can't help it."

"It's good to see you."

"You too."

She was still kneeling. He was staring down her sweater.

Suddenly embarrassed — *This is not me,* Opal told herself — she stood up, and Wally stood to face her.

"Did Abe call?" Wally asked.

"Abe? No."

"Damn."

"Why?"

"I told him to call."

"He didn't come home, either."

"I know."

"Just what do you know?"

Sighing, Wally set the carton on the landing of the front porch between himself and Opal. "Abe spent last night at my house."

"Your house." Without thinking, Opal fastened the bottom button of the sweater.

"When Abe got back from the Fillmore, he—"

"The what?"

"The Fillmore. He went to a show. You remember the Fillmore, right?"

"I never went there. I never wanted to drop acid."

"Not everybody ...does that. I'm sure Abe isn't dropping acid. I think."

"How reassuring."

"So when they got back from the Fillmore, I didn't need them for guard duty."

"Them."

"Abe. FrogGirl. Abe took FrogGirl to the Fillmore. I tried to send him home. They might stay at my house again tonight. I don't know."

"*They?* They stayed at your *house?*"

"They haven't told me a lot."

Opal fastened the middle button of the sweater. "They haven't told you a lot about what?"

"The—uh—nature of their relationship. This much I know: It involves taking showers together."

"Oh good. At least they're clean." Deliberately, Opal fastened the top button.

"Opal, what was I supposed to do?"

"Tell me, for openers."

"I just did."

"Sooner."

"It was Abe's move. He's at the point where I shouldn't go around tattling on him."

"You just tattled."

"You asked."

"I'm angry." Opal studied her fingers. "I had bigger dreams for Abe. I wanted Princeton. I wanted Rachel. I never dreamed he'd end up a construction worker. There. I said it."

"You came to me, remember? Hinting around about a summer job?"

"Not a career. Not a pregnant, dropout, low-rent girlfriend with bad teeth."

Wally went silent.

"Wally?"

He remained silent.

"Wally, I'm sorry. I shouldn't have said that."

Wally sighed. "I don't get it with you women. You have this chemical thing. You take an instant dislike and it's all over. You've never even met her."

"I spoke with her on the phone. She seemed nice. I was the bitch."

"She's volatile. But yes, she's nice. You might want to give her a chance."

"She messing with my son."

"Actually, I think it's the other way around, who's messing who. And—hey—those dovetails you love? On the toy chest? You said they were naively brilliant? FrogGirl made them."

With the fingers of one hand she clutched the top button of her sweater, as if she could close it tighter. "I wish, sometimes. I wear the turtleneck and the hoop earrings and people think. Bohemian. Arty. Photography. Or tonight I wear this ...this tart costume. But I am who I am, Wally. I had a Volkswagen covered with flower stickers but it was a brand new car. I grew up thirty miles from San Francisco and I never tried marijuana. And the whole sexual freedom thing never, I guess you know, worked for me. Maybe I'm just projecting, but now I'm fearful for Abe. For getting hurt. For bad judgment. For consequences."

Opal picked up the St. Pauli Girl carton. The weight surprised her. Numbers shouldn't weigh anything. Neither should love. Or family ties. A son separating from his mother, growing up, moving on. But the weight was almost overwhelming.

She spoke as flatly as possible: "Leave all the paperwork. I'll look it over."

"I thought we were—"

"Leave it. And go."

Instead of leaving, Wally planted his feet, thumbs jammed in belt loops. "And what is the nature of *our* relationship, Opal? We really should keep money out of it."

"And just take showers together?" She shook her head. "We can't."

For a moment Wally stood there. He seemed to be searching for an opening. Finding none, he turned to go.

In the box in her arms Opal knew she held all his check stubs, bank statements, bills due, as if he was leaving papers to be graded. Almost as if his whole personality was to be judged. Somehow in the numbers she expected to find answers to Wally, to herself, the future. Abe wasn't the only one who trusted in math.

Halfway to the street, Wally stopped, pivoted back to face Opal. She was still at the door, carton of papers held snug against her chest.

"I just want to put out one thing," Wally said. His thumbs remained in his belt loops.

Opal glanced from side to side. Next door, elderly Mrs. Gluberman was clipping roses. Watching.

Wally glanced at the neighbor too, but he didn't try to lower his voice as he said, "I want to say that I love Ronny, and I love Abe. I don't want to see harm come to them and I will do everything in my power to prevent it. Abe took a few hits this summer. He'll come through. You've put good values in him and he'll find them sooner or later. And he's a good boy."

From the doorway Opal said, "He's at your house. Not mine."

"I told him to call you. I swear—"

"It *hurts*."

"Opal, you're so tense. You need—you know what you need? You need a massage."

Opal stared at her bare feet. After a moment, she looked up, met Wally's eyes which seemed suddenly out of focus, unsure, distressed. She said, "Hello, my name is Opal, and I'm much too bourgeoise. Now go home. Tell Abe I say hi. Good day."

Inside the house, with the carton in her arms she leaned her back against the door as if to block Wally from bursting through.

Stupid, stupid, *stupid*.

Her first impulse was to run to the bathroom, fill up the tub, and cry like the scared little girl she was. Once was. *Used* to be. Her second impulse, and the one that she acted on, was to carry the St. Pauli carton to the kitchen table, sit down like an adult, and pore over numbers. Dollars and cents. Accounts payable, receivable. Payroll, depreciation, operating margin, taxes, interest rates, bad debts. Like reading tea leaves, she might divine the future.

Slowly driving home, some asshole behind him honking to pass, it occurred to Wally that never once had Opal said she loved him. He wondered how many times he had told her. Had he just said it again? Or did he just say he loved Ronny and Abe? And wasn't that the same thing? After some consideration, Wally decided he'd declared his love at least twice. Would he go for three?

Three strikes and you're out.

In the kitchen well beyond midnight, Opal was still sorting numbers. She had a calculator and a pad of yellow paper. A pattern was emerging. Wally had included everything, his contract with Krainer, filled-out standardized client questionnaires that rather nosily included make of car and policy number of homeowner's insurance, his receipts, rough cryptic jottings about small jobs performed by his crew that appeared to be off-the-books, even his notes for the estimates on fixing up the Krainer place, replacing glass, the heat pump, and something about a bell. She had names, phone contacts, account numbers on the invoices: the lumberyard, Gad Berman, the insurance (which, she saw at a glance, was a mess), taxes (omigod!), Visa, Bank of America, Wells Fargo.

It was only money.

Tomorrow she'd make some calls.

In the workshop Wally sanded another garage-sale door. Oddly, the way to relax after a day of tough carpentry was ...more carpentry. The sawdust from these doors was pleasant to the nose with a sweet smell like powdered candy—though irritating to the eyes.

Maybe Opal was right. Maybe he should quit contracting. Maybe he should teach, and with all those school vacations he could make wooden toys in his workshop and sell them at flea markets. Or set up a web site.

But what about Juke? Where would Juke go without Wally? And what would Wally be without Juke? They'd been a team for so long, yin and yang, they could finish each other's sentences.

What would life be without Juke, Steamboat, Pancho, Alfredo, even Larry forkin' Ludowski? What about the belt sander races? It was a separate society, a culture of the trades with its own laws and structure and competitive camaraderie. Wally lived in that society and yet sometimes felt like a tourist observing from the outside. Opal had recognized that ambivalence in him right away. Some day maybe instead of teaching he should write a book about construction. From the male point of view. Carpenter Culture: The Tools They Love, The Wood They Respect, The Women They Nail. Or mix 'n' match.

Before going to sleep, against his better judgment Wally checked phone messages. Gad Berman had called. He said he'd gotten word to Mr. Thailand, sent him a description, and he *loved* the idea of a big old Buddha bell. Great work, Wally.

Occasionally, against all odds, he could still do something right.

Forty-Five

Framing goes fast. In just one week Abe witnessed the transformation of the Woodside house from an ugly jumble of concrete piers and grade beams to a recognizable structure of "sticks," as Abe was learning to call framing lumber. The carpenters called their work stick-building, and Abe couldn't discern whether it was a term of pride or self-mockery. Analyzing the subtle implications of words wasn't something you could discuss with the other carpenters — even FrogGirl seemed puzzled when Abe tried to engage her in wondering whether calling a two-by-four a *stick* was an act of modesty and self-deprecation, as in "It's only a stick" and "I'm just playing with sticks," instead of acknowledging the skill, the strength, the exacting standards required to fashion those sticks into a house. Rachel would've enjoyed talking about it. Used to be, with Rachel, he could talk about anything. Right now FrogGirl's concerns were less intellectual, more basic — and very pleasantly so. Abe needed more condoms after only two nights.

Monday morning without any comment Juke handed an old Hitachi NR 83A pneumatic nailer to Abe and told him to "bang the blocking."

"Wally said I couldn't—"

"This is a forkin' order," Juke said.

Later, Wally walked by Abe and never uttered a word. Steamboat and Juke kept a watchful eye. At first Abe was allowed to nail the joist blocking, the squash blocks, and the cripples. By the end of the week he was allowed to bang studs, plates, joists, and rafters when he wasn't fetching and carrying one staggering load after another.

Whenever Abe finished a task, he checked in with Wally to see what he could do next. As a result he saw fragments of the working life of a contractor, which seemed mostly to involve talking on the phone and jabbing a pencil at a clipboard when he wasn't giving assignments to the crew or solving the problem du jour — right now, what to do when the plan specifies installing a four-inch pipe inside a three-and-a-half-inch wall cavity. Abe also knew from overhearing that Wally had worked out a schedule for all the work to be completed by day seventeen of the nineteen-day deadline, which meant Wally actually believed the work might be completed by day 18.7 when you add the mandatory ten-percent fuckup factor—reduced from the more customary and realistic fifty-percent factor—and that was assuming all the workers and subs were willing to stay on the job through the evening and sometimes through the night and definitely through the weekend when it was their turn to complete a task, and assuming that all the fancy hardware was delivered on time without a scratch in good operating condition, that the building inspectors showed up when they were supposed to, and that the San Andreas didn't crack the Big One, since the K-Palace was sitting just a few miles from the fault line.

Abe was waiting his turn as Wally was taking a call from somebody named Diefendorf. Juke was there, also, waiting to show Wally that the lumberyard had sent the wrong kind of hold-down for the second floor corners.

Wally, flipping the phone shut, told Juke the news: Whitey Benton had turned up in Fresno at a pawn shop where he'd tried to sell a six-foot aluminum level, four chisels, a leather jacket, a heat pump, boiler, water heater, and a three-legged cat. The pawnbroker had said he couldn't take the heating equipment and laughed at the cat; Benton flew off the handle; the pawnbroker called the cops; Benton ran away leaving all the items behind. The pawnbroker said Benton was punching a glass display case and literally drooling from the mouth.

It was Wally's aluminum level. He'd etched his driver's license number on it years and years ago. On a stub in the leather jacket's pocket Benton had written a phone number, unlisted, and an address that led to the back room of a "Tool, Farm Supply and Fine Meats" shop operated out of an old canning company warehouse in Watsonville where Benton had actually managed to unload the huge pile of copper piping plus two shovels, a shop vac, and a Delta ten-inch table saw, the latter etched with Wally's license number.

Juke asked, "Can we get our stuff back?"

"I'll send Pancho," Wally said. "He's got family in Fresno."

"Get the cat for me too, will ya?" Juke said, and then he frowned. "Never see them other tools again, will we?"

"Got the insurance," Wally said. "Half the value."

"I miss my Debbie Doofus," Juke said with an ache in his voice. "Nobody understands her like I do."

Meanwhile in the evenings and going well beyond sunset, they worked at the K-Palace. Between the two houses, Abe was seeing every phase of construction and every type of trade. He was coming to the opinion that cabinet makers had authority issues, electricians were obsessive by-the-book rule geeks, plumbers were smarter than people gave credit, painters were flat-out nuts, and drywallers were all Jesus freaks—except FrogGirl, of course, who incidentally wouldn't reveal her real name. It was starting to bug him. And she was driving to work with Wally, not Abe. She hated that Honda. She dug trucks, even one as funky and unsexy as Old Yeller. Wally let her take the wheel.

Friday there was no belt sander race. Nobody could take the time. There would be another week and a half of this madness—and then, the following Friday, there'd be a party like no other. Or else they'd all be at each other's throats. Perfect construction was still a goal, but now in addition they needed perfect timing and execution among tradespeople who weren't famous for their punctuality or predictability. One weak link and they'd all break.

Abe once again was next to Wally—waiting to ask what he was supposed to do next—while Wally was talking on his cell phone to somebody named Gannymede, something about a Teamsters strike, freight backed up, Wally looking stressed and ten years older than when Abe had first met him. The phone call had interrupted a discussion Wally was having with the glazier, a notoriously short-tempered old fart, who got tired of waiting and stuffed a piece of paper into Wally's free hand before walking away.

With the phone call ended, Wally stared at the thin sheet in his hand. Abe waited patiently, well aware of his place in the pecking order. Behind Wally Abe could see the hazy expanse of the valley with golden-colored mountains rising on the other side. Dark low clouds brought the smell of a change in the weather.

Wally pulled off his wire-rim spectacles, rubbing his eyes with the back of his hand. Without the spectacles, he squinted at the piece of paper. Then he turned to Abe.

"What's it say, Abe?"

"Need new glasses, sir?"

"New eyes," Wally said. "It goes wavy."

"What goes?"

"Comes and goes." Wally blinked. "Pretend I never said that."

"Yes, sir."

"And don't tell."

"They're already pretending they don't know, sir."

"Crap." Wally sighed.

Abe was a little worried about how tired and sad Wally looked. There were bags under Wally's eyes, about a week's growth of beard, smears of dirt and grease on his face and arms. One boot was untied. Both shoulders slumped forward and one was higher than the other. One hand was absent-mindedly rubbing the high shoulder as if he were in pain. His left knee was trembling slightly. There was a hole in the front of his shorts, and one pocket hung through like a herniated intestine.

Abe studied the piece of paper. "It's an insurance form. State Farm."

"State Farm? Really? I thought I had Allstate."

"It's not yours. Under policyholder it says Anton Krainer."

"What the hell."

"It's a transmittal form. There was a check at the bottom. The glazier guy tore it off. For the glass."

"How much?"

"About a truck and a half, sir. And four cents."

"Am I losing my mind? I don't remember making a claim."

"Krainer."

"Doubt it. Not his money now." Wally stared at Abe in a way that made him squirm. "I believe I've got a job for you, Abe. You and FrogGirl. You think you guys can stay friendly in close quarters for about a week?"

They would drive Wally's truck to Hoopersville, Maryland. They would hand a cashier's check to Augustus H. Gannymede, load up the 954-pound bell, swaddle it in blankets, and drive it back to California. With luck, they could make the round trip in six days.

Abe had to confess: He'd never driven a clutch.

"You'll learn fast," Wally said, and he explained how to get there: "Take Interstate 80. Then something else. Cross the Chesapeake Bay, turn right, look for Hoopersville. It's on Hooper Island. Might involve a ferry ride, I'm not sure. Get the bell, eat some oysters, turn around, come back. Did I just feel a raindrop?"

"Yes, sir. It's starting to rain."

"We better clean up. Let's move."

Within minutes, it was pouring. In typical California fashion, there had been no rain to speak of since April. All week long in the after-hours Alfredo and his crew had been carefully laying vintage mission-style tiles, inspecting each one for cracks, tossing a few, mixing the variations in terra cotta tones for a pleasing blend of color. This would be the roof's first test. As workers brought tools inside and spread sheets of plastic over unfinished portions, Wally wandered through the palace looking for leaks. Only a third of the window glass had been replaced, so Juke and Pancho were outside in the downpour tacking up plastic and sheets of plywood. Wally climbed into the attic, shining his flashlight along the rafters. Tight.

His cell was ringing.

"Wally speaking."

"There's a river running down my stairs!" It was Opal.

"Your roof is leaking?"

"Duh."

"Okay, I'll send somebody."

"Can't you come? I haven't seen you in a week."

"Busy. Anyway, scrambling over a roof in the rain. In the dark. I'm too old for that shit."

"Really? So you admit it?"

"That much, I admit. And thanks for the insurance check. I assume that was you."

"Check? Singular? There should be three insurance checks. Glass, heating, interior damage. Try reading your mail sometime. And send Abe over for the roof. He's the one who wrecked it. I haven't seen *him* for a week, either, not that I'm going to bore you with that."

"Abe has another assignment. If it's all right with you. It's got seat belts. It may look kind of beat up, but it's safe."

"What is?"

"My truck. Promise you won't scream at me. Okay?"

"I'll try not to scream."

And she didn't. Instead, she became very quiet. She tried to persuade herself that Wally was a good judge of character, that Abe would be cautious and act wisely driving a pickup truck across America in the company of this pregnant girl with whom he took showers. Persuasion proved difficult. Putting "caution" and "Abe" together in the same thought was like trying to push the wrong ends of two magnets together.

Instead of Chunky Chip ice cream, her usual tonic for unsettling situations, Opal decided to have a glass of wine. Maybe two glasses. With wine, persuasion might be easier, or at least the barriers would be lower.

She had just poured a third glass of Chablis when Juke arrived. He was already soaking wet. He brought no ladder but Wally had told him he could go out Abe's dormer window. "That is, if it's okay with you, ma'am."

"Just stop the water from running down my stairs. Whatever it takes. Would you like a glass of wine?"

"Got to work, ma'am. Maybe later."

"Can you be kind of quiet? My little boy is in bed."

"Yes, ma'am."

She tried not to let it bother her that Juke was tracking water and mud into the house and up the stairs dragging giant sheets of blue tarp. Then he hauled an armful of dirty dripping two-by-fours through the house.

"Are you building a new roof?"

"Naw. The sticks hold down the tarp."

"So you'll be hammering?"

"Naw. Got screws."

She could hear his boots on the roof. She stood in the hallway outside Ronny's bedroom on the second floor, listening, but Ronny didn't stir.

Suddenly there was a thump from above and a curse and she heard a body slide scraping and scratching over the shingles. She raced to the window. She expected to see Juke's last desperate living moment and braced herself for the sickening thud of a body hitting the ground. Instead, she heard his boots again, and a few seconds later Juke climbed through Abe's bedroom window and then trotted to the stairs, running down and then returning with a coil of rope.

"You okay?"

"Yes, ma'am."

"Did you fall?"

"Caught a vent."

"You scared me."

"Sorry, ma'am."

"Please be careful."

"Yes, ma'am."

She could hear the rustle of tarp, the soft whir of screws being driven, the clomp of the boots. Then she heard the tap-tap-tap of raindrops striking the plastic. And the water—thank Heaven!—stopped running down her stairs.

When Juke reappeared, she was ready with towels. "Are you done?"

"Yes, ma'am." He toweled his hair. The rest of him was dripping a puddle onto the floor. "It's temporary."

"I'm so grateful. That must have been horrible."

"It's okay."

She offered a bundle of clothing. "Take this shirt. These pants might be short, and the waist will be too big, but try it. They were my husband's. You can change in the bathroom."

"It's okay, ma'am. I'll just go home."

"You're shivering. Please. You'll catch cold."

"Thank you, ma'am."

When Juke emerged from the bathroom, she had to suppress a laugh. Her second ex—Ex Two as she called him—had been something of a dandy. On Juke the white fancy shirt was so small that his arms shot a good three inches beyond the cuffs and the front couldn't be buttoned higher than the navel. The khaki pants fit like knickerbockers. If Ex Two were buffed, on steroids, he still couldn't match this chiseled and weathered face, the clear eyes that knew sun and rain and hard work. Juke was not a pretty man and not brilliant by any means. Or at least, not the same way. What was brilliant about Juke at that moment were the wet tattoos rippling over the muscles of his chest and thick wrists. Juke moved with a manner that spoke of lessons hard earned, expressed not in words but in the language of the body.

"Appreciate this, ma'am."

"Warm enough? I could find a sweater."

"Don't need it." Juke shook his head. "It's you, ma'am. You been shakin' all night."

"I'm not cold. I thought the wine would stop it." At some point she'd misplaced the stem glass and started drinking straight from the bottle, which was still in her hand.

"I been tightened up like you." Juke glanced at the Chablis. "Never tried wine for it."

"Want some?"

"No, ma'am. I ain't tightened."

"What do you use? To untighten."

"Other stuff, ma'am."

"You don't drink for it—is that what you're saying? I don't drink much, either. My father was an alcoholic."

"Sorry to hear that, ma'am. My father was a drunk."

"That must have been hard for you."

"Was some, yes, ma'am."

"But if you don't drink, what's your—"

"Oh, I do drink, ma'am. Yes, ma'am."

"But for the tightening. What do you do?"

"Smoke a jay. Get a massage. Get lai—uh—like that."

"What's a jay?"

"Uh, nothing, ma'am."

"You mean marijuana?"

"Yes, ma'am."

"And it helps?"

"Yes, ma'am."

"I've never done that."

"Yes, ma'am. That's probably good, ma'am."

"You happen to have some?"

Juke frowned. "Maybe you better not. No more wine, neither."

"Do I sound drunk?"

"Not too bad."

"Where do you go for a massage?"

Juke squirmed. "Not a good place for you, ma'am." He studied her a moment, thoughtfully. "You might want to find one."

"You're the second person who's told me I need a massage."

"Reckon you do, ma'am."

"You think you're some kind of an expert?"

"No, ma'am."

"I'm sorry, I didn't mean to sound hostile."

"Yes, ma'am."

"You want that glass of wine now? There's just a little left in this bottle, but I could open—"

"I better go. Thank you anyways."

"No. Wait. I didn't mean to insult you."

"No, ma'am."

"About the massage, I mean."

"No, ma'am. I ain't insulted."

"I want a massage. Where do you go?"

"You ain't in no condition, ma'am. And it ain't no kind of place. For you. For what you need."

"What do I need?"

"You need a *real* massage. Like this." He put his hands on his own shoulders and demonstrated.

"You know something about massage, don't you?"

"Yes, ma'am. No school or nothin'. It's your neck. Shoulders. Mostly. Ribs too."

"Can you show me?"

Juke was silent a moment, studying her. "You sure?"

"Please."

They were standing in the hallway between Ronny's room and Abe's. Juke touched her shoulders with his fingertips, lightly, then ran them up the side of her neck. "Mostly here, ma'am."

"Where else?"

"Here." He ran his hands down her back and then up along her sides.

Opal twisted, giggling, surprised. "That tickled."

"Sorry, ma'am."

"I laughed, didn't I?"

"Yes, ma'am."

"Will you do it again?"

Again Juke was silent a moment. "Uh, yes, ma'am." He ran his fingers up the side of her cotton T-top.

She laughed again and curled her body away from his fingers. "Stop!" she said.

Juke stopped.

"I laughed again, didn't I?"

"Yes, ma'am."

"I'll be damned."

"Beg pardon, ma'am."

"Will you do it again? This time, don't stop."

"Uh, yes, ma'am." He tickled again.

She laughed. "Stop, stop!"

Juke stopped.

"Why'd you stop?"

"You said 'stop,' ma'am."

"I said don't stop."

"Then you said stop."

"And you stopped."

"Yes, ma'am."

"Do you always stop?"

"It's my peelosophy."

"What is?"

"Don't do what a lady don't want. Do what she do want."

"I like your peelosophy. But you can't always know what a woman wants."

"Touchin', I do."

"And the rest of the time?"

"I ain't so good at that, no, ma'am."

"How do you know what she wants?"

"Like a piece of wood. You got to respect it. Find the knots. Find the soft spots."

"And you can fix them?"

"I can work with them, yes, ma'am."

"Would you try? Please? Just a little?"

"Uh, yes, ma'am."

She closed her eyes. "That feels so good." He was kneading her shoulders, lightly. "You found a knot."

"Yes, ma'am."

"Don't stop."

"Yes, ma'am. You got nice hair, ma'am."

"Stop."

Juke stopped.

"Just testing," Opal said. "Can you go a little lower?"

"Yes, ma'am."

"You ever play Red Light, Green Light?"

"Huh. Not for thirty, forty years."

"Green light."

"Yes, ma'am."

Forty-Six

FrogGirl drove first. She was careful in the rain. Traffic was heavy and slow, nothing but taillights and windshield wipers on the skyway through San Francisco and over the Bay Bridge. After Berkeley they picked up speed. It took three hours to reach Sacramento. FrogGirl saw a shopping mall and took the exit. Midnight. The lot was empty.

"First lesson, Princeton."

They switched places.

Wally was right. Abe learned fast. In a quarter hour he had the hang of it enough to drive Old Yeller to a Union 76 station. Using Wally's credit card they filled up on gas, coffee for Abe, and chewing gum.

With only a few lurches—witheringly critiqued by FrogGirl—Abe drove back to the Interstate, up the ramp, got to fifth gear and cruised. Climbing into the Sierra, night traffic was mostly trucks—even with the Teamsters on strike there was a river of freight. Radio sucked. FrogGirl tilted her seat back and dozed. Passing lights washed across her face, and Abe couldn't stop admiring her. She was calm in sleep, soft, a natural smile on her lips. Abe had never seen anybody who smiled in sleep before, not that he'd seen a lot of sleeping people. Once when he was with Rachel she'd fallen asleep, and he'd been struck by how serious, how severe her features had been—and how lovely. He'd felt a new and deeper bond with Rachel that night. Sleeping together was more than sex. Now he'd had a week of sleeping with FrogGirl but he couldn't recall seeing her face at rest. Time in bed with her was either vigorously active or the profound sleep of the truly exhausted. They never seemed to simply relax together, until now. She swore she'd only had sex one time before being with him, and it wasn't even fun, and looking back on it she sometimes wondered if it ever really happened at all. Now at least she didn't have to worry about getting pregnant and it was definitely something she'd have to be careful about in the future, given that she had a conception rate of one hundred per cent. Maybe it was the lack of that worry or maybe it was just her nature, but she tackled sex with a gusto Abe had never experienced or even imagined possible with

Rachel, who had always been somewhat reserved. Rachel had been shy about her body, self-conscious though she had the features of a model. FrogGirl with her solid belly and big freckled thighs was exuberant in nudity, lights on, top-mounting, athletic—and it was a blast.

"Whatcha thinking, Princeton?"

"Nothing."

She pulled the seat back upright. "I don't believe I'm gonna sleep much in this thing."

"You want to stop?"

"Not tonight."

Abe drove another mile. The grade was getting steeper. He successfully managed a downshift to fourth gear.

"Bravo!" FrogGirl applauded.

"I was thinking about sex. How good it is with you."

"Hey, you too." FrogGirl smiled. "Not that I have much to compare. Maybe it's really awful sex and we just don't know it. You think, Princeton?"

"No. Who was the other guy?"

"Nobody." Her face turned serious.

"Why'd you get pregnant?"

FrogGirl snorted. "Jeezo, Princeton."

"You used protection?"

"No."

Abe said nothing.

"Don't be so superior," FrogGirl said. "Don't tell me you've never been an idiot because I know you have. Mr. *Princeton*. So I did something idiotic but I only did it once and I was only a teenager."

"Was?"

"Yeah. Was. And your problem is that you still are."

Abe stayed in the left lane, pedal to the floor, holding fifty in fourth gear, passing an endless string of trucks that were laboring toward the top of the Sierra Nevada.

"I don't love you," FrogGirl said. "Just so you know."

"Why'd you say that?"

"So you'd know."

"Okay. Now I know."

"Hey. Don't be mad."

Abe stared straight ahead out the windshield. "I'm not mad."

"You think I should get an abortion, don't you?"

"No."

"Liar."

Abe glanced at her, saw that she was watching him closely. "Okay. Yes," he said. "Not for me. For your own good. Like you said, you're only a teenager."

"Was, Princeton. *Was.*"

"No. You're FrogGirl. Not FrogWoman."

She became quiet. She reached for the radio, tried scanning the entire dial, switched it off, and flopped dramatically against her seatback. "Miranda," she said.

"Really?"

"Miranda Krainer."

"That's right!" Abe thumped his hand on the steering wheel. "He's your uncle!"

"Black sheep."

"Him? Or you?"

"Both." Her voice was detached, distant. "We're from Romania. Our grandparents."

"Being Romanian makes you black sheep?"

"Part. Me and Uncle Anton, we got the Romanian blood. Made him a turd, made me a frog." She shrugged. "Weird, huh? But it's true."

"Wait. You're not saying you're vampires, are you?"

"Nope. Jeezo. That's all crap." She tapped her lip with her finger, thinking. "You like Wally?"

"Yes. I've learned so much."

"Me too. What has he taught you?"

"Everything."

"Like what? Name one thing."

Abe thought a moment. "Wood. How to read it. The grain. The heart."

"Okay. What else?"

Abe thought again. "Drywall."

"You suck at drywall. What else?"

Abe thought some more. "I don't know."

FrogGirl leaned forward in her seat, toward Abe. "The thing is, I never see you working with him. At the job. You're always with Juke or Steamie or Pancho. Seems like they do most of the teaching."

"Yes, but it comes from Wally."

"How?"

"I don't know. It just does."

"I was just asking." FrogGirl settled back again. "Because I don't exactly get it either. He taught you wood grain, then you taught me. Remember when we were moving the barn wood? You gave me this whole lecture, and it was him. He was talking. 'The real gold.' It's a little creepy. Like he plays the drums, background, lays down a beat and everything depends on it, but mostly what you hear is the guitars."

Donner Pass.

FrogGirl punched Abe on the arm. "Gotta pee," she said.

"Me too." Abe took the exit. "Then you wanna try it?"

FrogGirl looked skeptical. "Think we can do it in the truck?"

"One way to find out."

"We can try." FrogGirl frowned. "Where are you going, Abe? What do you want to do with your life?"

Abe threw his head back against the top of the seat. "Holy crap."

She reached across the seat for him, touched his upper arm, rubbing it with the back of her fingers. "Don't worry. We'll do it. There's no right or wrong answer. We're gonna fuck, okay? I just want to know."

"I want to work for Wally. I want to learn what he knows. I want to be as good as Juke."

"You want to *be* Juke, don't you?"

"I dunno. Maybe."

FrogGirl shook her head. "Really, Princeton. You're dumber than batshit."

They tried it in a far dark corner of the rainy parking lot behind steamy windows, FrogGirl on top, seat tilted back. It was clumsy, splathering, uncomfortable for both of them. FrogGirl wondered if somebody outside could see Old Yeller rocking. She was feeling less than enthusiastic and the whole thing was going nowhere and might never have ended except, teasing playfully, like a vampire she nibbled at Abe's neck. Abe laughed and came so hard he nearly passed out.

FrogGirl disentangled herself and crossed awkwardly to the driver's seat. She felt wet, smelly, disappointed—and the cab was seeming much too small.

She didn't want to see but couldn't help being aware as Abe unpeeled the condom, cranked the truck window open a crack and dropped it with a splat.

Litterbug. Disgusting.

At least he didn't drop it inside. There were paper coffee cups and gum wrappers on the floor, maps on the dashboard, dirt in all the cracks. It was no place for a neatness freak. A mother named Miranda. Pushing a stroller? Buying a pacifier? Caring about who wins the school board election? Abe was oblivious, satisfied, sleepy. And five thousand miles to go.

Forty-Seven

Wally woke at dawn. Sunshine. How had Opal's house fared in the rain? That was a bitch of a job he'd given Juke, scrabbling at night in a downpour on a six-in-twelve slope. Nice to have someone he could rely on.

It was Saturday morning. Sunrise was much too early for telephones. He might as well swing by Opal's before heading to the K-Palace, just a drive-by so he could take a look.

He was driving Abe's Honda. The rear was jammed with tool boxes, tool buckets, tool belt, and free-floating tools that clanked against each other as he rounded each corner. He'd instructed Abe and FrogGirl to check in with him twice a day so he could follow their progress. They hadn't called yet.

When Wally arrived at Opal's house the first thing he noted was the big blue tarp on the roof reflecting the early-morning sunshine. The second was Juke's El Camino in the driveway. The third was Juke himself wearing clothes that were too small and too dressy. He looked ridiculous. He was standing casually next to his El Camino with one elbow on the roof of the cab, talking to a woman who was wearing a blue terrycloth bathrobe. Opal. She finished what she was saying. She placed her hands on Juke's shoulders. She leaned forward and gave him a hug.

Wally shut off the engine. He twisted his body to reach in the back, shoving tools and extension cords aside until his fingers found the twenty-four-inch steel pipe wrench. He stepped out of the car.

Juke was walking toward Wally. He'd started with a wary look on his face—and then he saw the pipe wrench in Wally's hand. "Shit, Boss!" He held his hands out in front of him.

Wally said nothing, raising the pipe wrench to shoulder height.

Juke turned and ran.

Wally ran after him.

"Wally!" Opal screamed. "*No!*"

Juke ran straight through the rose bushes next door. Streaks of blood appeared on his arms. Wally swung the heavy wrench like a machete and blasted through the roses behind Juke. Mrs. Gluberman gaped out her front window.

With Wally in hot pursuit, Juke bounded into a rainbow spray of sprinklers and through a wooden gate into a quiet back yard. Skirting the pool Juke hurdled a couple of lounge chairs and jumped against the wooden fence. Juke hoisted himself to the top and dropped out of sight on the other side.

Moments later, Wally reached the fence. Unable to hoist himself, he swung the pipe wrench like a three-iron and blasted a loosely nailed one-by-six. The board sailed. Wally blasted a second board, a third, and then squeezed himself through the fence and ran down a garden slope on the other side, boots sinking in the soft soil. Juke was nowhere to be seen.

Wally's chest was heaving. The smell of crushed nasturtiums rose from the ground. Below him, in the back yard of somebody's McMansion, a mow-and-blow crew were just bringing in their equipment.

"*Donde va?*" Wally shouted.

"*No se.*"

"*De veras! Donde va?*"

"*No se, Señor.*"

For a minute Wally stood there, catching his breath. He was certain that the gardeners knew where Juke had gone. They were gaping at Wally like he was a crazy man.

Sweat fogged his glasses. His T-shirt and shorts were wet from the sprinklers.

A siren wailed.

One of the workers looked fearfully toward the siren, shrugged off his blower and started running away.

The last thing Wally wanted was to bring heat on those guys.

Slowly, Wally walked back the way he had come. In the street in front of Opal's house a small crowd was gathering. A deputy car idled with blinking lights. The dogs were barking in the yard.

"Hiya, Dief," Wally said.

"Put down the weapon."

For a moment Wally was puzzled. Then he dropped the pipe wrench.

"Come here," Diefendorf said. "Let's talk."

There was a vibration in Wally's cutoffs. He pointed to his pocket. "My phone's ringing. Can I answer it?"

"No."

Wally stood before the sheriff's deputy. Opal stepped up beside him. "I have a terrible headache," she said. "Let's not shout. Okay?"

"You all right?" Wally asked.

"Nothing happened. And it was my fault."

"What was your fault?"

"That something could have happened." She spoke in a soft, level voice. "It didn't happen because I tried—" she glanced at the sheriff's deputy "—tried smoking something—against Juke's advice—and then I had to talk to Ralph on the big white phone. Juke stayed to make sure I'd be all right. Which I am—except for the humiliation factor. I've got to check on Ronny. Excuse me."

Opal hurried into the house, clutching the bathrobe tightly closed over her chest.

"I'm a fool," Wally said.

"Aren't we all," Diefendorf said.

Juke came walking down the street. Dribbles of blood ran down his arms where the roses had clawed.

"Juke." Wally held out his hand. "Sorry 'bout that."

Juke hesitated, squinting, sizing things up.

Suddenly it hit Wally: Juke might submit his forkin' resignation— and really mean it. A cold shot of fear wiggled down Wally's spine and settled in his colon. He could face losing his business, his house, and all his money, but he couldn't bear the thought of losing Juke.

Still holding out his hand, Wally said, "Juke, I had no call to do that. I'm really sorry."

Juke frowned. "You had call. But forkin' shit, Boss. I mean, you know, forkin' shit."

"Yeah," Wally said, still extending his hand. "I'm forkin' shit sorry."

Juke nodded. He stepped forward and shook Wally's hand. "Happens." He went to the El Camino and settled inside.

Wally turned back to Diefendorf. "We okay here?"

"You better clean up your mess."

Wally faced the crowd of neighbors. "I'll make good on any damage I caused."

"He means it," Dief said.

Juke was driving away.

A few minutes later, Wally knocked on Opal's front door.

She was still in the blue bathrobe. "At least I'm not the only dolt," she said. "You want to come in?"

"Ronny okay?"

"He's watching Rugrats."

Wally remained outside the door. "One thing, I'm sorry, I have to ask. If nothing happened, why are you in a bathrobe?"

"I took some things off. Don't shout. I was getting a massage and then I talked Juke into letting me try some marijuana and then I puked all over. Then Ronny woke up and I still haven't had a shower. Don't you smell it?"

"A little." Wally stepped inside. "So did the, um—" he looked around to see if Ronny was present. He could hear the sound of Rugrats from another room. "Did you like the marijuana? I mean, before you hurled?"

"It didn't do anything."

"If it was Juke's," Wally said, "it was powerful shit."

Opal winced at the swear word.

"Shit is a technical term," Wally explained. "For *sinsemilla*. How much did you smoke?"

"One."

"One hit?"

"One cigarette. It's because of you. I'm trying to reinvent myself. Or at least get back to who I could have been, would have been. For your sake. And mine. I can't say it's working yet."

"It's in you, the sinsemilla," Wally said. "You don't recognize how it's affecting you."

"I don't feel any of that woo-woo stuff."

"It's not always woo-woo stuff. People react different ways. Now. About Juke."

"Juke did nothing."

"Nothing? A joint? A massage?" Wally bonked the side of his head with his hand. "What was I thinking, sending him here? I never send Juke to a house where there's a woman situation."

"I'm a situation?"

"You were a sitting duck situation."

"Don't blame Juke."

"Juke presses. Juke is Juke."

"No, Wally. Amazing. You've known him all these years, and you don't know that. He doesn't press."

"He did it once."

"Only—" Opal hesitated, watching Wally closely. "Only if she wanted."

"*Don't say that!*"

Opal grimaced, holding fingertips to her temples, eyes shut.

"Sorry," Wally said.

"Please be quiet."

Wally waited.

After a long silence, Opal opened her eyes, lowered her hands, and at last she spoke: "I'm sorry. But, Wally. He didn't force anybody. He wouldn't. Ever. He finds the soft spots. Then he waits. He's patient. You always know he's there. Available. Not forcing. But a force. An attraction. A temptation. He won't take charge until you let him."

Wally felt the tears welling in his eyes, the tracks down his cheeks.

"Oh, Wally. You have to forgive."

"I do. Every day."

Wally took off his spectacles and wiped his eyes with the back of his hand.

"I'm sure she loved you, Wally, just as much as you loved her. I bet she's looking down on you right now, still loving you."

"I don't know if I believe in that," Wally said. "The looking down part."

"But you still love her."

"Yes." Wally sighed. "I love her and I'll always love her. She was the love of my life. She *taught* me love. She's gone. And I still have that love. Now I love my children and I love …your children. And you. I don't know how it happened. Your puppy eyes. The warmth of your voice. The way you challenge me. Your blurt. Your backpedal. Your mixed signals. Maybe I met you thirty years too late. Maybe it isn't a wild passion and it isn't fueled by hormones. But it's real. It's a middle-age kind of love."

"Omigod."

They became silent again, studying each other's faces.

"I've got to shower," Opal said.

Wally wagged a finger. "Don't ever smoke that stuff again."

"Don't worry." Opal grimaced.

Wally felt tired and melancholy. He stepped toward the door. "I'll go now. Three swings, three misses. I've struck out. I've got a house to build."

"Please stay."

Wally stopped, looked back at Opal. "Why do you want me to stay?"

"Just please. I feel safe with you, Wally. Safer than I ever felt with my husbands. Which is kind of a sad thing to admit."

"They *hit* you?"

"Not physical. I just didn't feel safe. Emotionally. Sexually. Personally. You make me feel safe. Would you please stay?"

"If it's not too long." Wally sighed. He'd just been called sexually harmless. It didn't seem like the kind of attribute you want to brag about with other carpenters. "I could watch Ronny. Until you're dressed."

"Ronny will be fine. For twenty minutes. More. He'll go right into SpongeBob if I don't stop him. I want to see what it's like."

"What?"

"To be a teenager. Maybe it's all a fantasy and it isn't like that, ever. I mean it can be awful being that age but at least you should get the wonder. To discover. So will you join me?"

"What?"

"In the shower. No funny stuff. Just shower. You want?"

Wally was speechless.

"This," Opal said, "will be a big blow to my self-esteem. If you say no."

"I'm just surprised."

"I want to discover you. Do you want to discover me?"

"Yes. Opal. Yes."

"Then let's take a shower. I never had that chance. The wonder. The fresh wonder. You think we're too old for this? Too old and ugly? You think it's too late?"

"I think it's just the right time."

Opal told Ronny that Mommy was going to take a shower and if he needed anything, he should come to the bathroom and knock. Ronny, glued to the TV, didn't answer.

In the bathroom Opal closed the door and—Wally noted—she locked it. For a moment she leaned with her back against the door, eyes closed.

Will she actually do it? Wally was already in awe of her courage.

She dropped her robe. Beneath, she wore nothing but underpants, white, large. "Sorry, these are awful," she said, and she pulled them off. "Now don't laugh."

Wally was sitting on the toilet seat, still unlacing his boots. He saw the twice-mother belly, poodle-hair muff, heavyish breasts, erect nipples pointing slightly downward. "You're lovely," he said. "Simply lovely."

"You're kind."

"You really are lovely, Opal. All soft with curves."

"That's a benign way to put it." Opal stepped into the shower. From behind the curtain she said, "When are you going to fix this bathroom?"

"I haven't got a work order." Wally pulled off the boots.

"Now you do. I'm worried the tub will crash through the floor."

"Me too." Wally pulled off his shirt. "It won't happen today. Probably." Quickly he removed his cutoffs and then stood just a moment outside the shower curtain wishing his dick would behave. Same thing used to happen with Aimee. He wondered what to say about it. Then he joined Opal behind the curtain.

"Nice tan lines," Opal said.

"Sorry about the erection," Wally said.

"I've seen little boys before."

Wally sighed.

"I mean," Opal said, "I've seen men before. It's not little, Wally. There, there. At least we know it works."

"Not scary?"

"That thing? No way." She was standing in front of the single showerhead, blocking the water. "How do we do this?"

"We take turns in the water," Wally said.

"You've done this before?"

"With Aimee. Yes."

"No comparisons. Okay?"

"Opal, you're the only person on my mind right now."

"Likewise." Opal smiled nervously. "I hope she isn't looking down right now."

"She'd approve," Wally said. His flesh was getting misty from the steam. "And I'm not thinking about her."

They fell silent.

Opal stood slightly off-center in the tub so some of the water would reach Wally.

"You need a hand-held shower thing," Wally said. "I could add it to the work order."

"That would be nice."

An awkward silence was developing. Wally sensed an untouchability, a certain dignity in Opal's bearing as she stood naked, just one arm's length away. *Poise is poise*, Wally thought. *With or without clothes*.

"I wanted wonder," Opal said. "But this is weird."

"Should I get out?"

"Where do you hurt?"

"You mean my body?"

"I want to touch you where you hurt, Wally. I need to keep busy or I'll get embarrassed."

"I'm beginning to believe you could never be embarrassed."

"Not true." Opal shook her head. "And I scare real easy."

"We could just wash."

"Not yet. Where are your knots?"

"My shoulder. Right shoulder."

Opal reached for him, arm's length, and touched with fingertips. "What if I massage it a little?"

"That would be great."

She squeezed different places around the shoulder, rolling her fingers over muscle and tendon. "Am I doing it right?"

"Yes."

"You wouldn't think, looking at you, you had such big muscles."

"Is that some kind of backhanded compliment?"

"Just a fact." She stepped closer. "Am I doing okay?"

"You have a good touch."

"Really? You hurt anywhere else?"

"Elbows. Wrists. Fingers."

"Okay."

"Neck. Upper back. Lower back."

"Uh huh."

"Hamstrings. Knees. Ankles. Feet. Toes."

Opal frowned. "You hurt *everywhere?*"

"Below the waist, above the hamstrings, nothing hurts."

Opal nodded with approval. "Excellent plumbing."

"Heart's fine too. Right now it's thumping."

"Mine too. Turn around."

Wally turned. Opal began massaging his upper back.

"Still doing okay?" Opal asked.

"Still good."

She worked her way down the spine to his lower back, then skipped the butt and worked down his legs until she was kneading his feet. Her touch was more exploratory than healing, actually, but Wally wasn't complaining. He had turned around again to face her. She was kneeling, water streaming from her hair. Wally rubbed her shoulders. She rose to face him. They were standing so close, the tip of Wally's penis touched her lower belly. Their eyes locked.

"Now soap," Opal said.

Opal soaped Wally. First his back, his butt, the back of his legs. Then turning him around she soaped his chest, his belly, moving lower.

"May I?" Opal asked.

"You bet."

She soaped between his legs. Gently she soaped his scrotum. "This okay?"

"Very okay."

She started to soap his penis.

"Maybe you better not," Wally said.

"I don't mind," she said. "Really."

With an expression of curiosity on her face, she placed her hand around the penis and soaped twice, thoughtfully, slowly, up and down. Wally ejaculated.

"Omigod," she said. "That was quick."

"Sorry."

"Don't be sorry. It was ...interesting."

"Icky?"

"No. Kind of ...amazingly ...simple."

"You never saw that before?"

"Sleep with the light on, sex with the light out." She still had her hand on his penis. "Is it over?"

"Yes."

She soaped the front of his legs and worked her way down to his feet. As she knelt, Wally began soaping her back.

Opal stood up. "I'll wash your hair if you'll wash mine."

"Deal."

"Can I wash the beard too?"

"I'm not growing a beard."

"Then what do you call it?"

"Not shaving."

Opal washed his hair and the not-beard. Then she turned her back, and Wally squeezed shampoo onto his hands and rubbed it into her hair. To his surprise he still had a semi-erection. The tip brushed against Opal's butt.

"Good grief, Wally. Does that thing ever go away?"

"I guess you woke it up."

She placed her head under the shower nozzle and rinsed out her hair. Wally began soaping her lower back, then continued working his way down.

"Sorry about my big butt," Opal said.

"I like your big butt," Wally said. "Matches mine. Now turn around."

He soaped her neck, upper chest. When he first touched her breasts, she drew in her breath.

"Okay?" Wally asked.

Her eyes were closed. "Very okay," she said.

Wally soaped the breasts thoroughly, enjoying the warmth and heft, the smooth underside, the thrust of the nipple against the palm of his hand, not lingering, moving on down the belly. He stopped just above the crotch.

"Okay?" he asked.

"Yes. Unless I say no."

"Keep me informed."

"I will." Her eyes were closed. Water rippled from her shoulders between and around her breasts, carrying soap bubbles down to Wally's fingers. Lavender soap.

Wally washed her muff and then cautiously, gently moved his fingers between her legs. Her belly stiffened. Wally lingered there just a moment trying to deny the sensation of water that was getting cooler by the second. He placed one finger between the lips of vulva. Opal jumped.

"Wally it's freezing!"

She shut off the water and stepped out of the tub.

"Guess that's it," she said.

"Guess so," Wally said, opening the curtain all the way. "Unless we continue without water."

"I think that's all the wonder I can handle for today."

"For that work order, can we put in a bigger water heater?"

"Yes, Wally. When you're ready."

"Ready for what?"

"To stay." She handed Wally a big blue towel.

"Is that an invitation to move in?" Wally began drying himself.

"Sort of not." Opal was wrapping her hair in a pink towel. "But sort of. I've never had men fighting over me before."

Wally was wiping his arms. "We weren't exactly fighting. Juke was running."

"What were you planning to do with that wrench?"

"Smash his brain."

"Wally!"

Wally said nothing. He was drying his chest.

Opal had finished wrapping her hair and was pulling another towel, this one burgundy, from a shelf. "Well, it was horrible, but it made me feel special."

"You *are* special."

"We still need to have a chat about money."

"Oh shit."

"It won't be so bad. Maybe." Opal was drying her back. The motion of the burgundy towel made her breasts jiggle and sway from side to side.

Wally stared in fascination. His erection, which had nearly wilted, suddenly returned.

Opal glanced at him, then looked away. "Did you take a pill?"

"No."

"I guess I should take it as a compliment."

"It is." Wally was drying his legs. "Opal ...why don't you ever say you love me?"

"Because I'm practical. We have issues."

"So you're withholding love? There are always issues."

"I'm not withholding anything, Wally. My God, we're standing here naked. I mean, what do you want?"

"To hear that you love me."

"What if you started living here? Where does Abe go? Does he bring that FrogGirl here?"

"She's not 'that' FrogGirl. It's her name."

"I know nothing about her. Her background. Anything. I hope he's using a condom."

"He is."

"You know for sure?"

"I gave him five condoms. He promised to use them."

Opal stood absolutely still. She'd finished drying herself but held the towel in her hands. Her eyes were closed. "You give my son a construction job and five condoms and a girlfriend and a house to live in and then you expect to move into *mine*?" She opened her eyes, glaring. "Will you give him your house to *keep*? Who needs Princeton, anyway?"

Wally glared back. "I didn't lose Princeton. Abe lost it all on his own. And he can't have the house. Bank of America gets the house."

"Is that why you want to move into mine?"

"No." Wally softened his voice. "I want to be with you."

Opal softened her voice to match Wally's. "You're not losing the house," she said. "I made you current."

"I had money? You found something?"

"No. I paid."

Wally, like Opal, had finished drying. He was holding the towel wrapped around one hand like a boxing glove. "I can't let you pay my mortgage."

"It's a loan. You'll pay me back."

"You had no right. You should have asked."

"Wally, I haven't seen you for a week. You're working eighteen hours a day. Your bookkeeping is moronic. Do you even know what depreciation is? You had an emergency. A money emergency. You'd be living out of your truck if I hadn't paid. And the amazing thing is, you don't even know it."

"Is this our money chat?"

"Not the way I'd planned. But at least it's started, and there hasn't been a homicide yet, and we just need one more chat about one other topic which we can schedule for a later time. About marriage. Don't panic. Not that I'm necessarily for it. But we ought to put our cards on the table."

"Wow. Opal. Wowee."

"Sometimes I surprise myself too. Maybe after I take a nap, I'll wonder what the heck happened." Opal's eyes dropped, checking Wally's midsection. "Looks like I found a way to kill that thing after all."

Wally sighed. "I'm not sure I need the play-by-play commentary."

"Sorry, but to me it's rather interesting. My husbands were never so naked for so long, at least when I could see them. It's like your body sending out semaphore signals. It's so honest." She thought a moment. "You should meet my mother some time."

"Didn't you say she has Alzheimer's?"

"Yes. You can try to make a good first impression—over and over, until you get it right."

"I'll do that," Wally said, and he dropped his towel on the floor.

Opal stared pointedly at the towel.

Catching the stare, without comment Wally picked up the towel and hung it on the shower curtain rod. Then he began dressing, pulling on his underpants in a standing position lifting one leg at a time.

Opal wrapped her body in the big fluffy towel. Wally noted that the burgundy body towel coordinated nicely with the pink hair-wrapping towel. It never would have occurred to him to use color-harmonizing towels on his body. It was one of those reasons women are so wonderful and strange.

They found Ronny in front of the television, riveted to SpongeBob. He glanced at Opal who was dressed in towels, then turned back to the screen and said, "See? Aren't baffs funner? Wiff Wally in da room?"

Opal blushed.

Hey, she *can* get embarrassed.

Opal glanced at Wally. Then she giggled. "Yes, funner, wonderful," she said. "Full of wonder. And I feel clean. What a bonus."

Forty-Eight

As usual, Juke was first to arrive at the job site—first of the day crew.
He found Marmaduke and Sir William sitting in plastic chairs by the
grotto and the empty pool, shirtless, flabby in their white body hair,
facing the rising sun and the view of the Silicon Valley. They had a thing
about sitting all night in shorts without a shirt. Sometimes they used to
sit in the upper deck at Candlestick Park before the Giants got the new
baseball stadium, and they'd be in shorts and no shirt for night games
with the cold Candlestick wind whipping through while everybody else
was bundled in winter jackets. They claimed alcohol in the blood worked
as antifreeze. Juke thought it was bullshit but he kind of admired them
anyway.

There was an Igloo cooler between Marmaduke and Sir William
on the deck. Each had a can of Miller in one hand and a cell phone in
the other.

"Just beer," Marmaduke said, dropping the phone in his pocket.
"See? And no mess."

"I ain't the forkin' boss," Juke said.

Sir William pocketed his phone and pulled out a KA-BAR survival
knife. It looked like genuine US Marine Corps issue. Casually he tossed
it in the air, watched the seven-inch blade flip three complete circles,
and then caught the knife by the handle.

Another thing about these guys, Juke knew, was that in spite of
their weight and their age they were surprisingly quick and nimble.

"Any action?" Juke asked the question every time he saw them.

"A little."

The answer had always been *No* before. "What happened?"

"Guy came around." Marmaduke was pulling a black T-shirt over
his head. All his shirts were the same: black, ripped. Juke assumed he
had an entire closet full of them. Marmaduke continued: "Guy said he
worked here. Said he was supposed to remove the pool pump. Said it
was defective."

"You let him?"

"Fuck no. He's a meth-head piece of garbage, got a meth mouth. Used to be a biker. Hangs out in Fremont."

"Blue Dodge?"

"You know him?" Marmaduke stood up and stacked the two chairs together.

"Name's Whitey Benton," Juke said. "He ripped up a lady-friend of mine. Ripped her bad."

"Huh." Marmaduke shrugged, indifferent.

"He stole my nailgun."

"Your *nailgun*?" Marmaduke was outraged. "Now that was *evil*."

"Custom. Did it myself."

Marmaduke was impressed. "You chopped a nailgun?"

"Yeah, you could say that. No chrome or nothin'."

"We'll ask around." Marmaduke stashed the plastic chairs behind the pump house. Lowering his voice, he asked, "You want him dead?"

"Not yet."

"Okay." Marmaduke picked up the Igloo, handed it to Sir William.

"Maybe later," Juke said.

Wally listened to his messages as he was driving to work. FrogGirl had called from a pay phone in Elko, Nevada. She and Abe had added four quarts of oil in Winnemucca. Just thought he should know. They'd driven all night and were planning to drive all day, then stop for a motel if they were making good time. She said Nevada was awesome. She hoped they made it across the Great Salt Lake Desert before it got too hot. Why didn't he have air conditioning in this little old rattletrap? Abe snored like a chainsaw. It was getting on her nerves. They were having some disagreements about the radio and a couple other things. She might have a bladder infection. Don't worry, she wasn't letting Abe touch the credit card. Bye-bye.

Wally had given FrogGirl the credit card but he hadn't said anything about keeping it away from Abe. Was it one of their disagreements? Was either of them mature enough to hold a card that had a fifteen-thousand-dollar credit limit?

Wally realized as he listened to FrogGirl's voice that his own children hadn't called in a long time. Somehow he hadn't noticed. He'd been feeling very much the active father lately.

As it turned out, that Saturday morning message was the last phone call from FrogGirl for a week. Abe, on the other hand, called on Sunday evening from the San Francisco airport: "Could somebody please pick me up?"

"What?!" Wally shouted into the phone.

"We sort of fell apart," Abe said.

"Where's FrogGirl?"

"Somewhere east of Omaha."

Wally pictured his little yellow truck rolling through the deep green night of Iowa, FrogGirl with one arm out the window, one hand on the steering wheel, hair ruffling in the wind, scent of harvesting corn, a pregnant runaway angel humming to herself across the vast bounty of America. He envied her. And he prayed she'd come back with the bell before the remaining ten days of deadline passed, in spite of an infected bladder, a truck burning oil, a heavy load, and nobody to spell her at the wheel. Or else Wally would lose everything. A flop at fifty-five. A lemon, loser, washout. His fate rested in so many hands, so many tradespeople, so many quirks and personal motivations and weird obsessions—and one pregnant young woman.

"Abe—why don't you call your mother for a ride?"

"Because I'm not going back to that house."

"What's wrong with that house?"

"She's tough on failure. You may find that out yourself sometime. And anyway, I'm too old to be living with my mother."

"Since when, Abe?"

"Since I got too old for that."

Abe had spent six nights in Wally's house and then two nights on the road with FrogGirl. Somewhere in that extended week Abe seemed—at least in his own mind—to have crossed a line.

"So where do you figure on sleeping, Abe?"

"Could I stay at your house? Please, sir?"

It was nine p.m. Sunday. Wally was at the K-Palace cleaning up a few details in the trimwork, removing the erotic crown molding and filling in holes before the painters arrived on Monday. He'd be there another hour even without having to deal with the home life of an unmoored teenager. "Staying at my house, Abe, would make things a little sticky between your mother and me."

"I'm sorry, sir."

"Stop calling me *sir*, Abe. It's gone too far. You're not a failure. You're turning into a good worker. And she's not nearly as tough on you as you are on yourself." Wally had already made a note to put Abe back on the payroll—assuming he ever found a way to pay it. Matter of fact, Wally had written and mailed a letter of recommendation about Abe— but he wasn't going to mention it at this point.

"Maybe I could stay with Juke," Abe said.

Now that, Wally thought, *would be Opal's worst nightmare. And maybe mine too.*

Who could he send to the airport? At that moment Pancho was driving back from Fresno with the heat pump, boiler, water heater, the six-foot aluminum level, and—at Juke's insistence—the three-legged cat. Steamboat would need a couple more hours to finish up in the tower—now the belfry—where he was trimming out the wall opening. Juke, though, was available. Juke had just completed the porch railing and was talking secretively with Marmaduke and Sir William, who had arrived for the night's watching. They were whispering, glancing over their shoulders, whispering some more.

"Juke!"

"Yeah, Boss?" Juke ambled over to where Wally was standing on the front steps.

"What was all that whispering about?"

"Found Benton."

"Who found?"

"Them guys. A little search-and-destroy operation. You don't want to be associated."

Wally examined Juke closely. "Are *you,* Juke? Associated?"

"Only the search."

"And they destroyed?"

"Benton mighta come through. They didn't stick around to find out." In a low voice Juke explained that Marmaduke and Sir William had tried to engage Benton in a conversation as he was walking out of a laundromat in Fremont but that Whitey wasn't much of a conversationalist these days. To find out what they wanted to know they'd had to be, well, sorta persuasive. Benton was probably finishing up his dry cycle just about now. "Tools are gone, Boss. He don't have no more."

"Just as well, Juke. Now we can drop it."

"Can't, Boss. Not Deb. That's what they was askin' about. Found out who got her."

"Who?"

"Don't concern you, Boss."

"Stay out of trouble, Juke. It's only a nailer."

"Not only. My sweat. Your blood." Juke quickly shook his head. "Had her so long, my fingers wore a groove in the handle. Fits like a forkin' glove."

Wally was taking note of Juke's nervous energy, higher than usual, a shuffling of feet and rapid movement of hand as he ran his fingers through his hair and rubbed the back of his neck and picked at his ear while his eyes darted about—he was like a race car on rapid idle. And Wally realized: "Krainer, right? He's got the Doofus."

"You knew?" Juke was incredulous.

"Just figured it out."

Juke ground a heel of his boot in the dirt. "Back at the races, he even asked me which tool was worth most. And I *told* him. I'm a forkin' turdbrain. I'm gonna make that—"

"Don't do it, Juke. Nothing stupid. And don't send your biker buddies to do it for you."

"Pissbag!"

"You just got out of jail, Juke. Think about it. Please. Maybe you can negotiate. Buy it back."

"Forkin' shit!"

"Juke, promise me you won't—"

"I already promised."

"You did?"

"I said I wouldn't."

"You said *pissbag forkin' shit*."

"See? I *told* you." Juke was still grinding dirt with the heel of his boot. He'd already excavated a small hole.

Wally became silent, letting Juke cool down for half a minute before he said, "Somebody needs to pick up Abe at the airport. And don't get him wasted."

"Yessir, Boss." Juke lit up. "I'll take care of Abe like my own forkin' son."

"That's what scares me." Wally tried to imagine Juke raising a kid. Any kid. "He wants to stay at your place."

"Oh yeah?" Juke smiled. He seemed honored.

"Come on, Juke. A few months ago this was a nice kid who was valedictorian of his class. A real nice mother in a real nice neighborhood. Which you saw. Now he wants to live in a garage and work as a carpenter."

"In my forkin' neighborhood."

"Yes. In your stinking neighborhood. No offense, Juke, but ..."

"You sayin' this is all my fault?"

"Not exactly. But he worships you. Maybe you could help."

"Maybe you just dissed my neighborhood."

"Juke, it's a terrible neighborhood."

"Yeah, but it's mine. Look, Boss. He gotta choose. Everybody gotta choose their own neighborhood."

"I'm sorry, Juke, I didn't mean—"

"I know what you mean." Juke lifted and adjusted the set of his tool belt around his waist. "We was on the roof Friday, he was figurin' hip cuts, valley rafter cuts in his head. His forkin' head."

"Did he get them right?"

"Forkin' perfecto, man. *That's* his neighborhood. Then he cut 'em not so great. But figurin'. Oh, man. He was my kid, I'd kick his ass to college."

Juke returned to Marmaduke and exchanged a few more words which involved more whispering and furtive glances over their shoulders.

Sir William pulled a plastic chair from behind the pump house and settled down in the grotto next to the pool, whittling a scrap of wood with a long nasty-looking knife.

Marmaduke hopped on his chopper and roared away into the night.

Juke, in his El Camino, drove off to the airport.

Wally called Opal and told her that Abe was at the airport. He wasn't sure where Abe expected to spend the night except that he explicitly didn't want to go home. But at least she should know that Abe was back and was all right.

"Depends on what you mean by 'all right'," Opal said.

"Well, yeah," Wally said. "He's still got some decisions to make."

"You want to come over?"

"Another money chat?"

"No, Wally. Not tonight. Later. Sometime. It's just. You know. We need to talk about that roof estimate. Seems like it's been through a lot of stages."

Wally heard the smile in her voice. He said, "Oh, absolutely. Yes."

"So you'll come over?"

"You bet. Give me an hour to finish up here."

"And then you'll take it slow, right? Because a Stage Four roof estimate might need to be gentle, you know, and maybe have no ultimate goal in mind except to be careful about all the assumptions, you know, make sure we touched on everything, you know, just to make sure we don't freak out."

"Actually, I'll be there in ten minutes."

"Don't speed."

"I can't speed," Wally said. He blinked. Blinked again. "Especially at night."

"Is it Abe's car? Is something wrong with the car?"

"No, it's the eyes." Still blinking. "Opal, I can't see shit."

"Wally!"

"Comes and goes. Don't make a big deal."

Opal took on a professional tone that would brook no nonsense like the voice that answers a 911 call: "Who could give you a ride?"

Wally agreed to wait until Steamboat was finished in the belfry, then hitch a ride with him to Opal's house.

"We'll have to talk about this," said the 911 voice.

"I'd rather do the roof estimate."

"Wally, this could be serious."

"All the more reason," Wally said.

Juke found Abe waiting by the curb at Frontier Airlines.

"'Sup?" Juke said as Abe swung himself into the passenger seat.

"Nothing much," Abe said.

"She okay?"

"FrogGirl? Yeah, she's good."

They didn't say another word as Juke drove out of the airport and south on 101. Abe was imagining what he would say to Wally, how he could explain what went wrong between himself and FrogGirl. They'd argued over a particular fiddle player in a particular band, a guy Abe liked but she hated with a passion Abe couldn't fathom. She wouldn't let Abe touch the credit card. She had an irritating need to stop and pee every fifteen minutes. Most important, he was coming to realize, was the stunning change it made to be sharing a ride with a young woman named Miranda instead of a wild thing named FrogGirl. You could imagine a FrogGirl being possibly a vampire. Miranda you might imagine burping a baby over her shoulder, little globs of burped-up milk running down.

Abe was picturing Wally's response, the easy smile, the skepticism and practicality, and he could hear Wally's voice speaking as if he were there in the cab: Abe, maybe you need to go easy with the demo hammer ...

And that was the problem, Abe decided. He was too quick with the destruction. Nothing FrogGirl said had justified total demolition. She hadn't changed, not that much. It was how he saw her that seemed so different.

And it had happened before. How he saw Rachel had seemed so different after he met FrogGirl, as if FrogGirl had framed her: cute, privileged, repressed. Now Miranda had framed FrogGirl: wild, unformed, rebel.

But what do I do, Wally? Seems like I start out like a shining light, absolute bliss, and then it all blows up. How do I stop the flameout?

Abe could see Wally furrowing his eyebrows, removing his glasses and rubbing his knuckles over his eyelids, then replacing the glasses — and Wally seemed to be asking if Abe wanted to build a lasting relationship or was he just looking for endless bliss.

So Abe thought it over for a few minutes and decided what he wanted was to build a relationship just like you'd build a house, piece by piece, break it into tasks, solve the problems, fix the fuckups, lots of heavy lifting and ...hey. Exactly that. Slow down and do right. Except that now he wanted to do it with Rachel. None of this baby-growing stuff. Girl gets pregnant, she turns into something weird. Worse than a vampire. A mother.

Still on 101, it was only as Juke passed the giant blimp hangars of Moffett Field that Abe realized they weren't going to the K-Palace. They'd already passed the Redwood City exit for Wally's house, the East Palo Alto exit for Juke's, the Oregon Expressway exit that would lead to Abe's house in the foothills or beyond, higher, to the K-Palace.

"Why are we in Sunnyvale?" Abe asked.

"Stealth job," Juke said, pulling to the curb. "You want to help?"

"I'm here," Abe said. "Wherever you're going, I'm going."

Juke studied Abe for a moment. "You want to drive?"

"Why?"

"Thought you might want. See what it's like. If you was me."

"Yes," Abe said. "I'd like that."

"Clutch rides kinda low," Juke said, stepping out.

Abe didn't really know what Juke meant about the clutch, but he found out when he first started. The El Camino lurched forward before he was ready — and with a power that astounded him.

"Holy crap!" Abe shouted. "What kind of motor have you got?"

"I mighta modified it some."

Juke guided Abe past strings of cookie-cutter townhouses and condos built to the sidewalk without front yards. Everything looked brand new. "Forkin' shame," Juke said softly, shaking his head.

"What?" Abe asked.

"I was a kid, useta pick cherries here. Twelve years old, I made three bucks a day. Livin' in a broke-down Packard."

"With your father?"

"Naw, this was after I run away."

"You were *twelve*?"

"Shoulda run sooner. Cherries, plums, 'cots. Best forkin' summer of my life."

Juke told Abe to park the El Camino on a corner next to a six-foot concrete wall. Behind the wall was an older-looking townhouse complex, old enough that the palm trees had grown tall and raggedy. Street lamps on long curved poles arched over the road casting an orange light.

"You got a darker shirt?" Juke asked.

"No."

Juke rummaged under the seat and pulled out a black T-shirt. "Put this on."

They walked side-by-side along the concrete wall. Low-flying jets roared overhead on their approach to the San Jose airport. There were no pedestrians other than Abe and Juke. A few cars and a motorcycle rumbled by. It was not a people-friendly road in spite of the sidewalk. Both sides of the street were lined by concrete walls, one for the townhouse development and the other for a condo complex. *A street without soul,* Abe thought. Aloud he said, "No cherry orchards now."

"Nope." Juke was walking briskly. "Nothin' left but the termites. Lotta these happy homeowners, they're findin' that out."

Abe had to hurry to keep up. "You're right," Abe said. "Forkin' shame."

Juke smiled wistfully. "Had my first lady somewhere near here. Irrigation ditch. Under the stars. Older woman."

"How old?"

"Thirteen."

Abe laughed.

Juke was gazing up at the heavens where no stars could be seen through the glow of lights and haze of smog. "Name was Tina," Juke continued. "Showed me how. I didn't know shit. Touchin' her was like strokin' a peach. Aw, man. What ever happened?"

Half way down the concrete canyon they came to a break in the wall where a private road entered the townhouse development. Like the street outside, the townhouse loop was not designed for pedestrian access. Carports lined the road with storage lockers at the rear of each parking space. Numbers on the carports told you where you were; the living units were half hidden from view. What you saw was people's clutter, the kind of overflow that is stored in a carport: camping gear, surfboards, garbage cans, cardboard boxes, motor oil. There was a run-down feel to it all. A dry breeze rustled the palm branches. In spite of the wall around the compound, the noise of the road—especially one loud motorcycle—never faded.

Juke turned and walked through an empty carport, Abe following. They passed between two storage lockers and entered the small front yard of a two-story unit that shared one wall with another unit. Juke rang the doorbell and using a bandanna to protect his fingers casually unscrewed the bulb in the porch light.

Nobody came to the front door. No lights were on inside the unit.

Abe watched Juke. With cool glances, the man's eyes flicked over the deadbolt lock on the front door, the casement windows, the exposed concrete rim wall below the siding.

Without a word, Juke stepped to the unattached side of the townhouse and entered the narrow passage that separated it from its neighbor. They were walking on a gravel path, crunchy under Abe's feet, but Juke seemed to move effortlessly, quiet as a puma.

Suddenly Juke stopped. Lifting his shirt, he revealed the tools wedged between his body and his belt—a thin pry bar, a multipoint screwdriver, a Channellock wrench, a mini-Maglite. Kneeling, he swung open a small piece of plywood that was hanging from a hinge and aimed the flashlight into the crawlspace under the house. Lying on his belly, he wriggled inside.

Abe wriggled after him.

About eighteen inches separated the hard dirt surface from the bottom of the floor joists, less when there was a drain pipe or heat duct to squeeze under. Most of the dirt was dry except for one corner where there was a slow drip from a pipe. As they slithered past the wet area, Juke shone his light on a scrap of old wood half-embedded in the mud. On top of the scrap sat a spider.

"Black widow," Juke said. "Just leave her be, and she'll leave you be."

Abe gave the spider as much of a berth as he could while scrabbling forward, crab-walking, his face at Juke's heels.

"You do this often?" Abe asked.

"Naw. I quit."

"Something happen?"

"Got my forkin' brains beat out."

"By the police?"

"By Wally. Then he gimme a job."

"You've still got a job. Right? So why are we here?"

"Just comin' for what's mine."

Juke swept the flashlight beam along each bay between joists, pausing to examine, then scrabbling on.

Abe was starting to feel claustrophobic. He heard a groaning, creaking noise, and hoped it was just the sound of the house settling, timbers cooling after a hot day. *What if there's an earthquake while I'm down here? We'd be crushed under the weight of the house. Buried alive.*

"You ever been to jail?" Abe asked.

"Couple times." Juke had stopped, examining a return air duct where it rose into a wall cavity.

"So you've got two strikes?"

"Sorta." Juke started crawling again.

"If you don't mind my saying so," Abe said, crawling along, "you really shouldn't be here."

"Yep."

Juke stopped beneath the exposed bottom of a bathtub. Lying on his back, shining the light upwards, he pointed.

"Perfecto," he said.

It was a panel built into the wall allowing access from inside the living unit to reach the plumbing for the tub. Juke banged on the panel with his fist, and it dropped back. Using the Channellock, Juke loosened the nuts and removed the P-trap from below the tub. Smelly, greasy water with a ball of hair spilled from the trap onto the dirt. Now there was just enough space to squeeze a body between tub and two-by-four if you were flexible.

Juke nodded. "You first, Princeton."

Arms in front, pushing some skis and ski poles out of the way, followed by head, body, legs, feet, Abe twisted and climbed into the bedroom closet of Anton Krainer's townhouse. Juke came right behind him.

"What are we looking for?" Abe asked.

"Nailgun."

"That's *all?*"

"She got worth to me."

"Why would Krainer want a nailgun?"

"Payback." Juke shone the little flashlight around the bedroom. He kneeled, peering under the bed. "There was a lady involved." Juke remained on his knees, shining the light into corners. "She played me, she played Krainer, she played the dipshit stole it. She got bad taste in men. Not that I hold it against her. Women didn't have bad taste, you and me, we'd never get any action."

You and me? We're the same? And then Abe realized: *We're both here.*

Abe considered how a woman with good taste—already in college at this moment and safely on track for an interesting and productive life as an adult—say, a young woman like Rachel—how she would judge what he was doing right now. Probably the same way FrogGirl would judge it: dumber than batshit.

Juke opened dresser drawers, lifted clothing, then neatly set everything back, refolding if necessary, and closed each drawer. "Anyway, dipshit, he tried to sell a whole mess of tools, but all the K-guy wanted was Debbie the Duo-Fast."

Abe hadn't given any thought to what he was expecting, but nevertheless he was surprised that the bedroom was so tidy. The bed was made, pillows fluffed, covers unrumpled. The dresser top was bare of any clutter—no coins, no cufflinks, no ticket stubs. The giant mirror over the head of the bed was so clean, it startled Abe at first to see two other men in the room. The floor was carpeted, soft, with no clothes or shoes waiting to be put away.

"What about Tina?" Abe asked. "She had bad taste?"

"Her mama thought so. Said if I followed, she'd cut my dick off. Took her to Mexico to have the baby."

"You have a child in Mexico?"

"More'n likely. Growed-up now. You woulda done different? I was twelve. Whole forkin' world was kickin' the shit outa me."

The rest of the townhouse was equally tidy. No dirty dishes in the sink, no newspapers, and only two magazines, which lay neatly stacked on the tank at the back of the toilet: *Wired* and *Penthouse*.

And no nailgun.

"If you had a pneumatic nailer," Juke said, "where would you keep it?"

"Me?" Abe thought a moment. "If I was spick-and-span like this, I'd keep it in the garage."

"Pissbag! Forkin' shit!" Juke slapped his head. "I been outa business too long."

They'd walked right past the storage locker in the carport.

"Can we just go out the front door?" Abe asked. He was suddenly anxious to leave.

"Alarm," Juke said. "Doors and windows."

"You think he has motion detectors?"

"Didn't see none."

Abe went first, lowering himself through the access panel into the crawlspace. Going down was actually more difficult than going up because, feet first, he couldn't see where he was going. In the process Abe scraped his back against a protruding nail, ripping his T-shirt, drawing blood.

Abe had crawled all the way to the exit before he realized that he was alone. Looking back, he saw Juke lying on his back under the bathtub, reaching up, pulling the wall panel back in place.

"Do you have to do that?" Abe said in a loud whisper. "Does it really matter?"

"Pro-forkin-fessional courtesy," Juke said, and he continued adjusting for a better fit. "Gotta put the trap back too. Tight so it don't leak. Pro-forkin-fessional pride. Go ahead, I'll be right out."

When Abe emerged from the crawlspace, he stood and brushed himself off. He heard a vehicle pull into the carport, engine idling. *Oh, shit, Krainer's back.*

A light was shining on the front of the townhouse. A radio sputtered. Abe peeked around the corner.

Not Krainer. Worse. It was a police car with a spotlight. One driver, no partner. Silent alarm. Somehow they'd tripped it.

He could run to the rear, vault over the concrete wall and be gone. Safe and sound. And Juke, coming out, would be dead meat.

Without further thought Abe sprang from the shadow into the beam of the police car. *Sometimes you gotta take the fall for somebody.*

Abe ran straight toward the carport and right past the police car.

"Hey you! Stop!"

Abe ran fast as he could directly down the center of the road, keeping in plain sight. Without looking he could tell by the growl of motor and squawk of tire that the cruiser had jerked backwards out of the carport and was coming at him. Now he was caught in the headlights, distance closing fast.

Abe sprinted past the entrance and continued on the loop road. Blue lights were flashing as a loudspeaker from the police car blared "Don't make this hard on yourself!"

Would he shoot?

Abe made a quick right turn and ran into a carport, squeezing by a Chevy Suburban where—dammit!—there was a gate with a lock on it. He heard a door slam on the police car and the slap of cop footsteps running, getting closer. Abe rattled the gate. No give. There'd be a booking, mug shot, fingerprints. A cell. A court appearance. This probably wouldn't look so good on a college application.

Abe ran to the left into another carport darting around a Mazda sedan and over a postage-stamp lawn in front of somebody's home-sweet-termite-home, veering into the side path and through a—thank God!—unlocked gate into the back yard where an old German shepherd was startled out of a sound sleep. The dog raised himself shakily on arthritic legs and started to run stiffly toward Abe who, meanwhile, with a leap and a heave and a painful scraping of body, was over the concrete wall, landing on the sidewalk of the street-without-soul.

Where now?

No place to hide. Juke's El Camino was at the far end of the block, but Abe had no key and didn't want to call attention to the vehicle because Juke might still get away free. He heard the police car making a W-turn and then gunning for the entrance.

Better go somewhere, Abe decided, and he started running with all his strength, lungs heaving, quadriceps pinging pain, feet pounding, racing down the sidewalk of the concrete canyon in the opposite direction from Juke's truck. He felt speared in the headlights of oncoming traffic and knew the police car would be coming up on him in a matter of seconds with blue lights flashing; reinforcements were probably already on their way. In a couple minutes the road would be swimming with cop cars and meanwhile, right now, from behind, Abe heard the deep bellow of a motorcycle.

A gleaming chrome chopper passed Abe on the sidewalk and skidded to a swerving stop—skillfully executed by the driver. Abe recognized the face, white mustache.

"Git on."

Abe swung a leg over the seat, grabbed onto the ample belly and felt his own body thrown backwards by the force of acceleration. He held on as the Harley bounded from the sidewalk onto the road, made a U-turn toward the oncoming police car, ran a red light, cut through the parking lot of a funeral parlor to another road, bounced airborne over a speed bump that nearly threw Abe out of his seat, and crossed a freeway on an overpass. The motorcycle turned left through a red light and went weaving among low buildings with signs announcing Finisar, Accuray, Medarex, AirMagnet, QuickLogic, Ion America, Molecular Devices, TAKEX, OmniVision, Cepheid. Abe looked back, and nobody was following. A sign on an office tower said *Yahoo!* They blasted through a quiet old neighborhood of bungalows and across some railroad tracks and entered a mall and exited again and they were melting into a stream of traffic on Stevens Creek Boulevard, an eight-lane commercial strip.

"Where to, Big Boy?" the driver shouted.

"We've got to get Juke," Abe shouted.

"Juke'll be long gone." Steering with one hand, the driver reached his other hand over his shoulder. "I'm Marmaduke."

Abe grasped the extended hand and squeezed it in a handshake. "My name's Abe." Abe's T-shirt, thoroughly ripped, was flapping in the wind.

Marmaduke withdrew his hand.

Abe was happy to see both hands on the handlebar.

Marmaduke shouted, "Nice decoy action, son. You got promise."

"*I never want to do that again.*"

Marmaduke's ribs started shaking under Abe's grip. He's laughing, Abe realized.

Marmaduke goosed the gas, and the big metal machine surged forward as he changed lanes. "Okay, Abe. Now where you want to go?"

Good question. Abe's heart was still racing, lungs, still gasping for breath. Blood and sweat were oozing down his back. A few hours ago, he'd been seat-belted in an airplane looking down on the sleepy fields of Nebraska. The stewardess had given him a little bag of pretzels and a can of Campbell's tomato juice. Passengers watched the Disney movie, worked crossword puzzles, studied spreadsheets on their laptops. Everything was predictable, under control, you just sat in your seat and behaved. *Aw, man. What ever happened?*

Abe leaned toward Marmaduke's ear, shouting to be heard: "Take me home. *Please.*"

Forty-Nine

Opal dug her elbow into Wally's side. "You hear that?"

"Uh huh." Wally sat up. They were on Opal's bed, naked. He'd fallen asleep. She'd left the light on and had been lying on her side, head on hand, watching him, considering her future.

The dogs were barking in the yard. There was the rumble of a loud motor. Voices—more than one—at the front of the house. It was 1:25 a.m.

Wally searched the floor, found his briefs, slid them on. Next to the dresser, leaning against the wall for some reason was a bicycle pump. Grabbing it, Wally stepped into the hall dressed in blue cotton Jockey underpants.

Opal pulled the sheet to her chin. She was happy to have Wally investigate the noise, happy they'd had sex, happy they'd gotten it over with. The entire roof estimate had proceeded at a far faster pace than either of them had planned. The outcome for Opal was not unpleasant, like sunshine after long rain. No rainbow, but at least a freshening, and thankfully no thunder. She'd felt attached. The details were private, not to be discussed nor would she even think about them. What she was just beginning to consider, meanwhile, was that she had never mentioned Wally to any of her friends, particularly not to Sylvia, her best friend and choir-mate. The sharing was long overdue. It was time to admit that at some level she was ashamed of her attraction to Wally and that she had better start working on it and had better fully appreciate this man who at this moment was protecting her house and her sleeping Ronny—this man who was defending her bedroom, armed with a bicycle pump.

Wally stood in the hall, listening. The dogs were simultaneously whimpering and snarling, ambivalent behavior. The motor growled and departed. There was a scuffling noise at the front door.

Wally went to the stairs. Halfway down, he saw the front door open.

Stepping inside, Abe closed the door and paused a moment in the entry, kicking off his shoes, never glancing up.

"Hello, Abe."

Abe gaped. "You're *here*."

"Your mother wanted to check my eyes. She was concerned."

Abe stared at the hairy-bellied man in blue underpants who was standing with one hand on the stair banister and the other holding a bicycle pump.

"Also," Wally said, "your mother and I, we needed to talk about a roof estimate."

"Just shut up."

"I admit this is a little awkward," Wally said, shifting his feet.

"You sound ridiculous."

"Sorry."

"Where's my car?" Abe was frowning. "I didn't see it outside."

"At the K-Palace. Steamie dropped me here. The eye thing."

"Good. I want you to stop driving."

"You ordering me around?"

"Somebody's got to." Abe shook his head. "My God, Wally." Then he grinned.

Questioningly, tentatively, Wally grinned back. "It's true, Abe. She really was worried about my eyes."

"Would you please shut up about that?"

"Sorry."

"Are you moving in?"

"We haven't exactly finalized anything."

"I've already been through one stepfather," Abe said seriously, "so if you stick around I'll try to skip all the Freudian crap." He paused. "But I'm not handing out condoms, either." He paused. "Sorry, that was the Freudian crap breaking through. Inappropriate. Discretion is advised. Ahem." He cleared his throat. "You're right, this is awkward." He paused, scratching his head, then looked up at Wally and said, "You met Rachel, right? What did you think of her?"

"She seemed tough. And really nice."

"Tough. Good word. Yes. Well, she's also brilliant."

"I'm sure she is, Abe. Tough, brilliant, and very beautiful."

"I think it's the brilliance that attracts me."

"Hmm." Wally frowned. "Be careful."

"I will." Abe thought a moment, scratching his head again. "Maybe I could do the roof repair. Since I wrecked it. Save my mom some money."

"I could tell you what to do."

"Maybe I could build a catwalk from the window to the chimney."

Abe scratched his head. "We charged the plane ticket—FrogGirl charged—on your credit card. I'll pay you back." He paused again, scratched again. "I saw antelope this morning, sunrise outside Cheyenne. They were leaping around in the sagebrush. Now ..." He shook his head. "I guess that's all. If you'll suck in that belly so I can pass by on the stairs, I'd like to go to my room."

"Hey. This is muscle." Wally slapped, and to his dismay the belly jiggled slightly under his hand. He tried sucking it up but saw little effect.

"Whatever," Abe said. "Please. My room."

"Yes, sir," Wally said, stepping aside.

Fifty

In a Motel 6 in Moline, Illinois, Miranda awoke for the third time and padded to the bathroom. She felt hot. Lately, it seemed, she was always hot. She'd already showered twice this night but still felt prickly. Returning to bed, unclothed on top of the sheets but perspiring yet again, she couldn't drop back to sleep. The red letters on the bedside radio said 4:43 a.m. Faintly she could hear a television in the next room, which struck her as pathetically sad. She heard the drone of a small airplane landing at the Quad Cities Airport nearby. She wondered what the other three cities were and why anybody would fly here at 4:43 a.m. According to some pamphlets on the nightstand, she was near the headquarters of John Deere, Inc., which they seemed to think was something she should know, and only eight miles from the Snowstar Ski Area, which was either a joke or else she was losing her mind.

She thought she needed to pee yet again, started to roll out of bed in the dark, and then stopped. She lay perfectly still.

It was a flutter, something new.

The flutter of tiny frog legs.

Inside her.

A life! Connected, a part of her. *Sweet Jesus,* she thought, and that is exactly what she saw: Outside her second-story window, curtains blowing inward from a breeze, a glowing, bearded man was reaching toward her, cupping his hands as if offering a drink of water. She rose from the bed unashamed of her nakedness and approached the cupped hands, which receded as she walked toward them.

A beam of headlights crossed the window; the vision disappeared, never to return.

Miranda stood by the curtains, a cool, moist breeze washing her flesh, the low, steady throb of trucks, the hum of nighttime machinery, the cones of light, the wind-borne scent of farms and fields from the invisible distance of interstate industrial America, the first hint of dawn in the still-black sky. Now, even on her feet, she could feel the tiny flutter.

She wanted to sing. To dance. To laugh out loud. But all she did— and it was quite enough—was stand and smile.

Fifty-One

Monday morning, in the Subaru, Opal brought Wally and Abe to the Woodside job. Juke as usual was already there. He'd set up the compressor and was happily installing knee walls with a familiar nailgun.

"I'll be danged," Wally said.

"Yep." Juke smiled. "This is my tearful reunion."

"How much did it cost you to get that thing back?"

"Almost more'n I could afford."

Juke winked. Abe was looking jumpy. Wally chose not to ask.

As soon as Wally was satisfied that a day's work could be done without him, he and Abe returned to the Subaru for what Opal called "the car shuffle boogie." She dropped Abe at the K-Palace where his Honda sat waiting, still packed with Wally's tools. While Abe drove back to Woodside, Opal drove Wally (with Ronny in the back seat) to the Palo Alto Medical Clinic where, as it turned out, he spent an entire day being tested and waiting for results and being tested again. They drew blood and asked picky questions and, to Wally's amusement, wanted a sample of his pubic hair, which they explained was slow-growing and thus contained the longest record of his toxic exposure. Wally plucked the longest hair he could find down there. Finally, after what seemed like hours in the examination chair aided by eyedrops that expanded his irises to the size of nickels while he became familiar with every pore on Dr. Stephanie Liu's face in addition to a comma-shaped mole near her nose, Wally lay on a table as a needle was inserted into his eyeball, and he didn't feel a thing. "You're an interesting case," Dr. Liu told him. "You're the youngest I've ever seen."

"I should be older?"

"You should have one foot in the grave." She smiled.

"Will I go blind?"

"Probably not."

After remaining under observation for another half hour, Wally, wearing an eyepatch and dark green plastic sunglasses, reported to Opal. She had returned an hour ago expecting to pick Wally up. She was looking frazzled from trying to entertain Ronny in the waiting room. Wally told her, "Dr. Liu said I have one foot in the grave and I might go blind but it's okay to go back to work right away."

"She did not." Opal grimaced. "I already talked to her. The regular work day is already over and you're not going to that idiotic palace this evening. That painkiller has addled your brain."

"Oh." Wally started to lift a knuckle toward rubbing his eyes, caught himself, lowered his hand. "Somehow I didn't hear that." He thrust his hands deep into his pockets. "What else did she say?"

"She said you've got arsenic and lead floating around in your eyes. What the heck have you been doing?"

The doors. The hand-crafted doors. Wally wore glasses, not goggles, and the sawdust found its way around the lenses and into his eyes. The old guy, Mr. Demented Carpenter, using up old cans of paint, must have used lead-based primer, which soaked into the wood beneath the surface. Stripping hadn't removed the lead. Sanding had. The arsenic would be from pressure-treated lumber that the old guy had mixed with other wood scraps in building the doors. Fresh in Wally's mind was the history he'd just given of thirty years of exposure to copper chromium arsenate, pentachloraphenol, toluene, chlordane, PCBs, benzene, asbestos, and a long, sorry stew of chemicals used in some phase of construction. Even the ones that were outlawed were still lurking in old crawlspaces and attics, embedded in the dust and the lumber itself. You try to protect yourself, but also you try to get the job done. Respirators, goggles, earmuffs, body suits are all hot, bulky, and uncomfortable. You weigh risks against comfort and speed. Sometimes you make the wrong choice. Even at your best there are accidents. After thirty years of weakening his body's defenses, Wally had allowed sawdust containing lead and arsenic to float directly onto his eyeballs.

And FrogGirl! Had she been in the workshop? Wally racked his memory. In no way did he want that fetus exposed to his folly.

As far as he knew, she hadn't set foot in there since building the toy chests. If one of them had to be poisoned, Wally wanted it to be him. Further proof, Wally realized, that FrogGirl was like a daughter to him. He'd take a bullet for her. And for his honorary grandchild.

"I was sanding some doors," Wally said. "I let my guard down. It was new work containing old lead paint. I just didn't expect it."

"But you'll stop now?" Opal asked.

"Of course."

"Good. Now listen," Opal said. "You're not a textbook case, Wally. Dr. Liu said it's difficult to predict." Opal recited what the doctor had told her: There was a very good chance that the shots could reverse the degeneration, at least to some degree. One of Wally's eyes was worse— the one the doctor injected. Because that eye was so bad, Wally had been compensating by using mostly the other eye, which wasn't in such great shape either. The better eye sometimes got tired, which was why Wally felt that his vision came and went. Also, for some functions one eye would be enough, but for others—such as depth perception—he needed two. So when he needed two eyes he thought he was going blind, whereas when he only needed one eye he felt all right.

"And," Opal continued, "even though you look like some shabby guy who should be standing on a street corner with a white cane and a beggar's cup, your feet are nowhere near a grave, though one of mine is dangerously close to kicking your butt."

"Why would you kick my butt?"

"Because you lied about being allowed to work today and you're starting to feel sorry for yourself."

"Well *somebody* ought to feel sorry for me. Abe said you're tough on failure."

"He's right. I suppose I am. You're not failing. You're just having eye trouble. I'm sorry you have to go through this, Wally, and I can't imagine having a needle stuck in my eye, and of course it's scary that you could go blind, but most likely you're not, so let's try to look on the bright side of your life."

"Which is?"

"That's for you to figure out."

"Hm. Bright side." Wally glanced at the other faces in the waiting room, which hastily turned away from him. "I thought we had a pretty good roof estimate."

"That's so mechanical, Wally. Can't men ever talk about feelings?"

"When I talk about feelings, Opal, I end up saying I love you, and you don't say it back. So no, I don't want to talk about feelings."

"I love you. Jeesh, Wally. With all my heart and soul. And I'm mostly happy about the roof estimate, but I think it needs a little work. Now let's get out of this room. People are staring."

Wally was smiling, but his feet were planted. "Shabby? You called me shabby?"

"It's the not-beard. It makes you look like a bum and at least for me it detracts from the roof estimate."

Wally ran a hand over his jaw and down his fuzzy neck. He remembered her words: Don't wear cologne, don't hit me, don't put your weight on me, don't have a hairy neck ...And also, afterwards: Don't say you're sorry. "All right, I'll shave."

"How about a haircut?"

"You don't like my hair?"

Opal made scissor motions with her fingers. "The pony tail."

Wally grimaced. "It's who I am, Opal."

"Who you are is a heck of a nice guy who works too hard and doesn't take care of himself or his own house, though he takes care of other people and their houses very well indeed, and he manages his business badly but seems to inspire loyalty in his workers and can talk to children and even teenagers and carpenters and other odd forms of life. Who you are is not your hair."

"I'll make a deal. I'll cut my hair if you'll marry me and have my baby."

Opal frowned. "Wally, please. Are you serious?"

"Yes."

"Could we talk about this somewhere else?"

"I'd like an answer."

From the chairs in the waiting room four sets of eyes were watching them—that is, assuming the eyes could see anything since they were, after all, in the office of an ophthalmologist.

Opal sighed. "No. On the baby part. I'm sorry, Wally. Though I suppose there's still room for discussion. I do love being a mother. I do sometimes wish—never mind. But soon with any luck you'll have grandchildren. And we've got Ronny. Now could we please leave?"

Wally didn't budge. "And the other part?"

"I'd like to. Jeesh again. That is, I think so. Mostly. Probably. Yes."

Wally broke into a broad grin.

Ronny was clinging with one hand around Opal's leg, one around Wally's. He looked deeply worried, on the verge of tears.

Wally kneeled down and pulled Ronny into his arms. "Sorry, man," Wally said. "We weren't arguing. Not really. Matter of fact, I think that was just the mixed-signal acceptance of a proposal of marriage." Standing, he held Ronny to his chest. To Opal Wally said, "I guess under the terms of our agreement I'm supposed to cut half my pony tail. Are you compatible with that? Or should we hire a professional arbitrator?"

Now Opal looked on the verge of tears, though she was also smiling. "I'm compatible."

From a chair a silver-haired woman with coal-black skin and big thick eyeglasses broke in: "Cut it all off. It looks stupid."

Her companion, a baldheaded man, spoke up: "Keep it while you've still got it."

"Anybody else?" Wally asked, looking around.

A slim woman with strawberry blonde tresses said, "No comment."

A girl beside her, about twelve years old, also strawberry blonde said, "It doesn't matter."

Wally addressed the girl: "You mean nothing will help? I'll look dorky no matter what I do with my hair?"

"I didn't say that," the girl said, blushing.

Her mother said, "She means you'll look distinguished, debonair, and accomplished regardless of what style you choose."

"She's trying to be nice," said the silver-haired woman, "but we all know the truth about ponytails on men."

"What," asked Wally, "is the truth about ponytails on men?"

"The truth," the woman said, leaning forward, "is that a ponytail is attached to a horse's ass."

"Thank you, everybody." Wally turned back to Opal. "Am I your new rehab project?"

Opal furrowed her eyebrows thoughtfully. "You don't need rehab, Wally. Just good maintenance."

"I think I need some luck too. I've got nine and a half days to finish that house."

"Stop worrying, Wally. You won't fail. You might go bankrupt, but you won't fail. You can always teach."

Wally groaned.

Opal playfully kicked his butt.

Ronny giggled with delight. He was still nestled in Wally's arms, a pleasure for Wally to hold but an increasing pain to his lower back.

"She'd kick a blind man," Wally said. "Watch out, Ronny. Now let's go home."

The silver-haired woman called from her chair: "You're supposed to kiss her."

"I will," Wally said.

"Now," the woman said.

"Oh all right," Wally said. "If it's okay with her."

"It's quite all right," Opal said, stepping close.

But before they could act, Ronny kissed them both, one after the other, on the cheek. Then the boy immediately—and clearly to his own surprise and puzzlement—belched.

"Euw," Opal said.

"Home," Wally said.
And they moved on.

Fifty-Two

Juke, Steamboat, and Pancho spent the morning framing dormers on the Woodside job. Abe had a separate assignment: He was to lay out the arc of three second-story decks. The radius was to be twenty feet, too far to stretch a string when there were walls in the way. The deck would have a downward slope of one-quarter inch per foot. Any point on the arc would be offset from the center by radius times sine of the angle—$r \times \sin\theta$—and offset from the maximum depth by $r - (r \times \cos\theta)$, and the drop would be length in inches divided by twelve times one-fourth. That is, $1/4(L/12) = L/48$. Piece of cake.

There were three dormers to frame. With Wally absent, Abe was curious how the hierarchy would shape up. Each man—Juke, Steamboat, Pancho—could have worked alone on each separate dormer. Instead, all three men worked together, one dormer at a time. Steamboat was the measurer, marker, and decision-maker; Juke was the cutter and rough banger; Pancho was the detail man who got the edges lined up and tight. Each of them wordlessly, though sometimes grudgingly, recognized the strengths of the others. If you talked to them off the job site, each of them would claim to be best at all tasks. On the job, they conceded to the priorities of teamwork—and that was exactly how this day began. To Abe it was satisfying, crisp, like in baseball watching a cleanly executed double play.

Abe remembered moments, other days, when he was struggling to hold a heavy board in place so he could nail it, and an extra hand arrived—unasked, unexpected—and took the weight while Abe banged. And then the hand would move on, no thanks given or awaited. No big deal. And yet, to Abe, it was a very big deal. It thrilled him, actually sent shivers down his spine. Every time.

Juke and Steamboat were rivals; Pancho was the friendly outsider. Wally united them, maintaining a quiet discipline and authority. But Wally was missing.

It erupted suddenly. All three men were straddled over different pieces of the roof frame. Below them, Kim the electrician was running

Romex on the second floor and Rudolfo the plumber was roughing in a bathroom.

Pancho tossed a jack rafter back to Juke, who had cut it. "Too short, mon."

The board unfortunately bounced against another rafter, sending it into a flip before reaching Juke with a slap on the elbow. Juke winced. "Too *forkin'* short, mon," he said and then hurled the two-by-four like a spear at Steamboat, who had measured and marked it. Steamboat looked up just in time to raise an arm and deflect the piece of wood from his face, but it caught his ear.

With a scowl Steamboat rose to his feet, balanced on two joists, and deliberately unbuckled his tool belt. Juke, saddled on a rafter, unbuckled his. There was mayhem in their eyes. Pancho, athwart the header, said, "Sorry, mon. Eet was only a leetle short."

Abe, from the other side of the roof, scrambled on hands and feet across rafters like a spider scuttling over a web. Without a clear plan, he dropped through an opening while swinging from a rafter by his hands, feeling like Tarzan on a vine. He swung directly into the rising mass of Steamboat, who absorbed the blow with a stagger and a step backward, his heel just catching the top edge of the two-by-ten behind him. Abe, still without plan, placed his arms around Steamboat as if embracing a life-size teddy bear with bad body odor. Steamboat, struggling for balance, made a couple of stutter steps on the undecked ribs of the attic floor, which were spaced sixteen inches on center and which he could not see with Abe blocking his view. Abe instantly began calculating that if Steamboat's boots were, say, twelve inches long and there was a fourteen-and-a-half-inch gap between each two-by-ten (actually fourteen and seven-sixteenths since the wood was still green) the odds of his placing a foot firmly on the one-and-seventeen-thirty-secondths-inch edge of a board were, assuming only the center six inches of the foot would be firm, and assuming the foot was at a ninety-degree angle to the joist, which was actually unlikely, uh...For a moment, math failed him. And for a moment it appeared that both Steamboat and Abe in their embrace would crash bruisingly and painfully to the joists with the strong possibility of falling through the gaps to the floor nine feet below.

Juke's face had turned in quick sequence from anger to worry to outright fright. Swinging his leg from the saddle, he ducked beneath the rafter and was starting to reach toward the pair just as the tottering Steamboat planted both feet and steadied himself with Abe still attached.

Juke froze, arm outstretched.

Steamboat stared at Juke's extended hand.

After a moment Juke broke into a grin. "May I have the next waltz?" he asked.

Steamboat snorted.

Abe unwrapped himself and stepped gingerly onto the joists.

For a few seconds nobody said anything.

"I—uh—I've got two of the decks figured out," Abe said.

"Let's build 'em," Juke said, and it was settled. Abe and Juke worked on the decks, Steamboat and Pancho finished the dormers. Never a word was spoken about what had happened.

That evening at the K-Palace, paint-spattered Cathy and her young assistant Patricia, known to the male workers as Pink Patty, were coating the exterior while Chuck the carpet installer was working the hallway and growling at anybody who came near. Johnson, who nobody ever addressed by any name other than Johnson, whose family name was not in fact Johnson but who was known for one outstanding body part, was setting up to reinstall the HVAC equipment.

It kept surprising Abe to see so many workers showing up for voluntary overtime at what had to be difficult hours on a gamble that at best would pay them only standard wages. Abe knew they didn't want to lose the time and materials they'd already put in, and they had their pride invested, but Abe had the sense that the main reason they kept working was that they wanted to feel like they won one over the suits. Problem was, the suits would leave them nothing but a mouth full of shit if they couldn't finish perfectly and on time.

Abe avoided talking to the subs. They were testy, kibitzing, critical of everything. One screw-up and the whole job would go up in smoke. Everybody watched everybody else, which kept the pressure on and kept anybody from slacking off. But it created a crabby atmosphere.

Once they'd carried the heat pump and boiler inside, there was little that Wally's crew could do without getting in the way. Steamboat and Pancho took off. The painters Cathy and Patty quit as it became too dark to work. Chuck closed up his carpet van and said he'd return tomorrow and nobody better walk on what he'd done. Johnson, a man of few words, and those few were generally obscene, left without saying anything, which was probably for the best. Marmaduke and Sir William arrived, nodded casually at Abe and Juke, and set up plastic chairs by the pool.

Juke started walking, and Abe, out of curiosity, followed him back beyond the pool and grotto, beyond the rear of the house, beyond the gazebo to the far side of the tennis court where they'd built a small, elegant observation platform out of ipê—Brazilian walnut—one of Krainer's final whims that, like the gazebo, had come out nicely because Wally's crew had chosen the details. Juke switched on the tennis court lights and began gathering wood scraps. Abe, without being asked, joined him.

"Just the ipê," Juke said, carrying an armload of cutoff ends toward the house.

Abe followed with an armload of his own. "What for?"

Juke didn't answer until he'd walked all the way to his truck and dropped the wood into the rear bed. "Him," Juke said with a nod toward the cab. "Or her. I forkin' forget."

Perched on the top of the driver's seat sat an old, gray, three-legged cat.

"Name's Peanut," Juke said. "Belongs to a lady I useta know."

"The one with bad taste?"

"Maybe it weren't so bad."

Juke and Abe walked back to the observation platform, which felt like a remote corner of the estate.

"If I lived here," Abe said, "I'd shut off the lights and erect a telescope here. Great platform for stargazing."

"And daytime," Juke said, "you could check the downhill neighbors. Some lady of leisure. Watch 'em sunbathe nude and rub up with coconut oil."

"They do that?"

"I know for a fact. All them rich ladies."

Abe looked down the mountainside toward the lights of the valley. Other than the K-Palace and a few truly ostentatious estates, many of the houses in view looked no fancier than the ones in Abe's own neighborhood—in fact, parts of Abe's street were visible far below.

Juke had a dreamy look in his eyes. "They all got perfect tits," he said. "Buy 'em at the body store."

"If you say so," Abe said, shrugging. "They're also mothers, you know. They have children and laundry and stuff."

"Or their windows at night," Juke said, still dreamy-eyed. "You could watch how a lady balls a millionaire." He flashed a quick smile. "Not that I'm into that."

Abe for the first time found himself feeling sorry for Juke. To change the subject, he said, "What's the cat going to do with all these scraps?"

"Gonna make a hangout for the Peanut. A house. A cat house. You know what they need? I never seen a cat house outside Nevada."

"Usually, people just let them roam around," Abe said, gathering more scraps.

"I'm thinkin' I'll build it a cat palace, a nice one, lots of carpet scraps if Chuck don't mind, a safe place so it don't—"

He was interrupted by the sound of shattering glass.

Juke and Abe dropped their wood scraps and ran toward the house—ran around the perimeter of the tennis court, ran past the gazebo, skirted the grotto and raced over the pool deck and around the house from the rear—and found Sir William, who weighed an easy three hundred pounds, seated on the chest of a skinny and very angry young man. In spite of wiggling and thrashing, the captive was not likely to go anywhere. Sir William began calmly, deliberately cleaning his own fingernails with a survival knife. "Don't shake me," he said to body beneath him, "or I might acci-dont-ally cut something."

Marmaduke, meanwhile, was on his motorcycle below the house in the moonlight, bouncing across the meadow in pursuit of a body outlined by the headlight. A body sprinting as if life depended on it— and possibly it did.

Sir William paused in his nail-cleaning and looked up at Juke. "What do we do with him?" he asked.

"I think we're supposed to kill him," Juke said.

"Somebody call Wally," Abe said.

"We could break his legs," Sir William said, returning to nail care. "Then he couldn't run away while we par-sue this dish-cussion."

Abe crouched over the teenager. The kid had greasy black hair, a hawk nose, and terror in his eyes. It appeared he was having trouble breathing with three hundred pounds of butt planted on his chest. "What's your name?" Abe asked.

"B-uhhhh," the boy said with a soft sigh.

"Uh, Sir William?" Abe said. "Could you maybe slide down a little so this guy can breathe?"

"If I slide lower," Sir William said, "you're gonna see a reincarneration of his lunch." Sir William shifted his weight slightly, rearranging the placement of his feet.

The boy took a deep breath.

"Now," Abe said, "what was your name again?"

"Ethan."

"Not Beelze, by any chance?"

"Other guy."

Marmaduke returned on his chopper, alone.

"Catch him?" Sir William asked. "Catch the Beelze bubba?"

"Sorta. Sorta not." Marmaduke walked over to where Ethan was lying crushed beneath Sir William, one hand wiggling listlessly like a squashed beetle. Sizing up the situation, Marmaduke said, "I woulda preferred to bring him back alive."

The hand stopped wiggling.

Abe settled himself cross-legged next to Ethan's head. He saw only soft defiance in the boy's demeanor, not a hard-core punk by any means.

"We could just drill a hole in each knee," Juke said. "I mean, we got the forkin' tools."

"Something we've all been wondering," Abe said. "How'd you move that giant boulder? The one you rolled into the pool? How many guys did it take?"

"Two."

"How?"

Ethan sneered. "Give me the place to stand, and I shall move the earth."

"Hey!" Abe said. "Force one times distance one equals force two times distance two."

"Don't," Ethan said, "disturb my circles."

"*Noli turbare circulos meos*," Abe said.

"What the fork," Juke said.

"Colonel Tilton, AP physics teacher, Silicon High," Abe said. "He was an Archimedes freak. This guy Ethan was telling us he used leverage to move the rock. Archimedes practically invented leverage. Archimedes was one awesome dude. A pissed-off Roman soldier came up on him as he was writing equations for some circles he'd drawn in the dirt. Archimedes told the soldier not to disturb the circles. *Noli turbare circulos meos*. Those were his last words. And apparently Ethan goes to my high school." Returning his attention to Ethan, Abe said, "I just graduated from there."

"I'm aware of that."

"You know me?"

"You're the dude who was boning Rachel Rappaport."

Abe stood up. "Let's drill his balls out," Abe said.

"Hey, I like that," Sir William said.

"I'll get the extension cord," Juke said.

Abe was standing over the teen. "That was crude," Abe said.

"Sorry."

"It was disrespectful."

"*Sorry*," Ethan said. "I'm sure she's a fine human being."

"Yes, she is," Abe said. "You a senior this year?"

"So far. If I survive."

"You live around here, right?"

"Maybe. Maybe not."

Sir William reached under his own thigh, fished around a moment, and extracted a wallet from Ethan's pants. "Ethan Crandall. Moody Road. Rich bitch."

"Not," Ethan said.

"You live on Moody Road," Sir William said. "You in disputeration with that?"

"Not rich. Not even close."

Sir William leaned over, face to face with the boy. "What kind of car you drive, Ethan?"

"No car."

"What kind of car your pop drive?"

"No father."

"Okay, your mom."

"No mother. No car. I live with my grandmother."

"What kind of car does grandma drive?"

"A wheelchair."

Sir William hesitated. Then he tried one more time: "Lessee— uh—how many bath-a-rooms in that house?"

"Half."

"Half?"

"We live in a trailer."

Sir William slapped his own knee. "Hey boy, you don't fit in around here."

"No shit."

"Who's Beelze? Another misfit?"

There was a pause. Ethan seemed to be thinking, perhaps reprioritizing his options and alliances. After consideration, Ethan said, "He could fit if he wanted."

"Rich?"

"His father owns an optical multiplexor company."

"A what?"

"He's rich."

Idly, Sir William flipped the KA-BAR into the air and caught it by the handle. If he had missed, it would have plunged into Ethan's mouth. "You ain't the leader," Sir William said. "I don't see 'Ethan' tagged on the walls." Sir William flipped the knife again, frowning. Ethan's eyes followed every turn of the knife blade. "You think your bud woulda stuck around and fought for you? You fell in with the wrongerono rich bitch, Ethan."

Juke returned, unrolling an extension cord. Under his arm was tucked a Makita drill with a big blue one-and-five-eighths-inch Lenox hole-saw bit sticking out from the chuck. "This orta do," Juke said.

"We've been chatting," Abe said.

"That so?" Juke plugged the Makita into the extension cord. "What about?"

"I think Ethan might be wanting to apologize," Abe said.

"That so?" Juke goosed the trigger on the drill. *Mrrrrr. Mrrrrr.*

"Yes," Ethan said.

"That would be 'Yes, sir,' " Juke said.

Ethan said nothing.

Juke leaned down face to face with Ethan, whose eyes were wide. Juke held the jagged teeth of the hole saw just under Ethan's nose. *Mrrrrr.* "I said, 'That would be 'Yes, sir.' "

"Yes, sir," Ethan said.

"Also," Abe said, "I think Ethan might be in need of an after-school job. To help pay for those windows he broke."

"That so?" Again Juke goosed the trigger. *Mrrrrr.*

"Yes, sir," Ethan said.

"What's that? I can't hear you." Juke's ear was six inches from Ethan's mouth.

"*Yes, sir!*" Ethan shouted.

Slowly, Juke rose to his feet. He gave a nod to Sir William, who also stood up.

Ethan raised himself on his elbows. He seemed to be catching his breath.

"Here's the question, Ethan," Juke said, absent-mindedly fondling the body of the drill. "Can you lift a house?"

Fifty-Three

Abe was at the wheel of the Honda heading up 280 toward Woodside.
The foothills behind Stanford were an odd mix of bucolic ranchland and high-tech gadgetry where the Silicon Valley met the San Francisco Peninsula. Wally rode shotgun, one arm propped in the open window. Cool morning air ruffled his as-yet uncut hair. Behind Stanford University they rolled by the fields that were speckled with cattle and wooden watering troughs. They passed below the big dish antennas that listen to satellites deep in space. They cruised past a horse barn, a vegetable farm, and then directly over the two-mile-long, shotgun-straight linear accelerator where physicists were busily smashing atoms and studying quarks.

Wally wore a black eyepatch but no sunglasses. He was freshly shaven. He said, "I hear you broke up what could've been a bad situation."

"Who told you?"

"I know everything, Abe. It's my job."

Abe took the Sand Hill Road exit and headed away from the investment bankers and their vats of money. The Honda sped up and down the hill between a horse park and the remnants of a Christmas tree farm.

"I had to do something," Abe said. "They were ready to kill each other."

"Not killed. Not likely. Maiming, maybe."

"So I should've stayed out of it?"

"No. You did just the right thing."

Abe turned onto Portola Road, where multimillion dollar estates sat directly on top of the San Andreas Fault. "Then when I had them apart," Abe said, "I didn't know what to say."

"You said the perfect thing. Namely, nothing. What're you gonna do? Sit them down and talk about their feelings?"

Abe smiled at the thought. He veered onto a narrow lane where among vine-covered fences you might catch a glimpse of a massive stone castle with a nine-car garage or a whimsical ultramodern house of glass and steel with horses in the front yard nuzzling at bales of hay.

"And you hired an Alfredo," Wally said.

"If he shows up after school," Abe said, turning up a driveway and parking at the job site. "If you approve."

"He'll show."

And he did. Wally felt like he knew Ethan already. He'd met him hundreds of times: the outsider, unable and unwilling to fit in to a high school culture that both attracted and repulsed him. Living in a trailer with his handicapped grandmother, walking a mile and a half to a school where every other guy seemed to have the best clothes, the fastest car, the blondest girl, the privileged life. A wary and yet malleable personality, eager for a friend—the kind of kid you hoped would fall into the right crowd but who could just as easily fall prey to the wrong one.

Ethan's work day began. When Juke casually tossed him a bag of concrete, Ethan fell over sideways. The resulting expletive led to a lesson on the need to ask permission to swear and, incidentally, on the concept of fork. Steamboat started Ethan on a concrete stair landing that just happened to be waiting—which is when Abe realized that there was always a small concrete project set aside in case an Alfredo showed up, something to make the point that carpentry isn't just about wood and to impart lessons about caution and planning, attention to detail, the need to get dirty, and a full dozen of Wally's Laws. What had seemed random to Abe was now all falling into a larger pattern, and he felt a sense of pride in what he'd learned and how far he'd come. He said so, recapping his thoughts to Wally at a late dinner, ten p.m., chicken *à l'orange* that Opal had baked after Ronny had gone to bed.

"Yes," Wally said. "You've come a long way, Abe. Though you've still got a few things to learn."

"No shit," Abe said.

"*Excuse* me." Opal stiffened. "You will not bring that language into this house."

"Yes, ma'am," Abe said.

"Don't smirk when you say 'Yes, ma'am.' And that goes for you too, Wally."

Wally sat up straight. "Yes, ma'am."

"Sorry," Opal said. "But it matters. All this talk about what Abe has learned is fascinating, by the way. Fascinating and revealing."

"Your son," Wally said, "and I bet you're not ready to hear this, Opal, but your son is showing real signs of leadership. He could conceivably someday take over this business."

"Really?" Abe said.

"You're right," Opal said, pushing away her plate which was still full of food. "I'm not ready."

"What about the other guys?" Abe asked. "Wouldn't they take it over?"

Wally waved his fork. "Steamie and Juke are great carpenters, but they shouldn't run a business. And they know it. They're at the peak of their game right where they are—and that's a darn high peak. They're happy with it. As for Pancho, he'll run his own business soon, but the way things go, he'll start his own company. He broke in as an Alfredo with me, and just like the original he'll go off. If I have it I'll probably loan him the money to get started. All he needs is the language, so he can speak to the clients. He's getting there. Then he can hire guys I can't even talk to. And those guys will make better money than they ever dreamed of, and their kids will have a head start and be the bosses of the next generation. That's the future. You can't hardly find an Anglo kid who wants to do this anymore. About the only time I can grab one is when he gets into trouble, like Ethan."

Opal was pushing her plate in circles, studying intensely. She raised her eyes to Wally and said, "I think I owe you an apology."

"What for?"

"You *are* a teacher. You've been one all these years, haven't you? A darned good one, hands on, one on one. And you love it. I should respect that."

"Thank you," Wally said.

"And Charlotte still wants to talk to you about maybe teaching one little English class, just an hour a day."

"Crap."

"Ahem."

"Sorry."

"By the way, Abe, you have a letter," Opal said, reaching to the sideboard and tossing an envelope to her son.

Abe slit the envelope and started reading. Opal whispered to Wally, "On guard, everybody. It's from Princeton."

Abe slapped the letter on the edge of the table. He seemed annoyed. "They're reconsidering my admission again."

"Why?" Opal asked.

"A strong and persuasive letter of recommendation."

"That was me," Wally said. "Sorry for butting into your affairs, but I wanted to let them know what they were missing when they turned you down."

"What in the world did you say?" Opal asked.

"I told them about his valedictory speech. The first half, anyway. I said he'd taken all those lessons to heart and it had given a solid foundation to an already brilliant mind."

Opal looked skeptical. "Abe? Brilliant?"

"Don't be so critical of your own children," Wally said. "You're raising two wonderful boys."

"Thank you," Abe said, "but I've already moved on. Princeton is history. You said I had a future with your business."

"*Aaaaaaagh!*" Opal screamed.

From under the table, the dogs whimpered.

Abe looked taken aback.

"Abe," Wally said, "first you go to college. Then you might want this kind of business or, just as likely, you'll find something you don't yet even know about that would be the perfect fit for you. You might be the next Einstein. We have to find out."

"I'm not Einstein," Abe said. "Unless he started as a total screw-up."

"Actually, he did," Wally said.

Ronny appeared, padding to the table in footie purple pajamas. "Somebody screamed," he said, climbing into Opal's lap.

"Sorry," Opal said. "I got frustrated."

"Why?"

"Your brother."

"Abie?"

"Yes, me," Abe said. "All right, if you're gonna gang up on me, I'll think about it. I'm not making any promises. But even after college—*if* I go—I reserve the right, every once in a while especially when there's a female involved—and I beg your pardon, Mom—I reserve the right to do something dumber than batshit."

"Yes, you probably will," Opal said. "And we'll probably love you anyway."

Fifty-Four

A rumor started circulating that Juke had nailed Wally's eyeball. Wally heard it first from a yardman at Pine Cone Lumber, which Wally dismissed because this same yardman would jokingly say things like "You want Douglas fir? That's one more than Douglas three, right?" and "It says here you ordered S&B — split and bent." But then Wally heard it from a cement truck driver and finally from Larry Ludowski, who was finishing up some details on the little porch deck he'd built at the K-Palace.

Larry was the last straw. Wally ripped off the eye patch and shouted, *"Look at it! See? There's no hole in my eyeball!"*

Larry leaned in, bald and unsmiling, studying closely. On Wally's eyeball there were spots of red floating among the white. "So it wasn't Juke?"

"It was a doctor!"

"They shouldn't let doctors have nailguns."

Wally heaved the eye patch as far as he could, which was only slightly more effective than throwing a feather. Later the patch reappeared on the statue, tied looping around one hip and down between the buttocks like a G-string, not quite covering the crotch of the angel-with-spouting-boobs. Without asking, everybody assumed it was the work of Little Landscaper Lucy. Nobody would blame her.

Wally could already detect an improvement in his vision, especially when he was looking at a woman, so on Saturday morning at the K-Palace he could appreciate the features of the lady who stepped out of a black Ford Explorer and walked toward him with brisk self-confidence, fully aware that each man on the construction site was following her every move. Wally instantly hated her. She had southern California glam — the sweeping sunglasses, strapless tan, perfect lip gloss, toned blonde hair, botoxed face and, one could assume, major enhancement of body parts. Plus a dazzling smile. She had the aura of control that a gorgeous woman could instantly command — at least until she opened her mouth.

"Mr. Walters, I presume?"

Oh wow. She had a Joisey accent.

Wally was walking around with a clipboard and a frown, clearly the guy in charge, with Juke and Abe standing nearby waiting for assignments. "How can I help you?"

"I'm looking for Miranda."

"Me too," Wally said. "And you are ...?"

"Miranda's mother. My name is Ellen Krainer. How do you do."

"I'm Wally."

"I know who you are. And I believe that you know where Miranda is, and since she is not yet eighteen and you have been keeping her as a virtual slave in your house, you could find yourself in a difficult legal situation. A lawsuit situation. Not to mention the sexual predator situation."

"Oh please." Wally rolled his eyes.

"I know the law. My boyfriend is a lawyer. Are you a lawyer?"

And do you know, Ms. Krainer, that your daughter refers to you as the psychotic bitch goddess? The cell phone was vibrating in Wally's pocket. Irritated, he fished it out and tossed it to Juke. Turning back to Ellen Krainer, Wally said, "Your daughter is somewhere in America. Free as a dove. She's driving my truck, and if she doesn't show up soon you and I can both of us call the troopers."

"Boss!" Juke was waving the phone.

Ellen Krainer was talking: "The fact that she escaped does not absolve you."

Wally walked toward Juke while saying, "Your daughter is running an errand for me. Hopefully back in Nevada by now. She's driving a yellow pickup with a 954-pound Buddha bell in the back. She was supposed to call me twice a day, and she hasn't since she left a message exactly one week ago. It would be nice if she had her own cell phone but apparently you never saw fit to let her have one, though she told me her sister has had one for years. Not that I want to get in the middle of *that*."

"Don't you dare criticize how I raise my children."

"All I'm saying is, she's not a slave. I'm employing her. I'm a contractor. Are *you* a contractor?" Wally reached for the phone.

"Don't you dare belittle me."

"It's her," Juke said.

Wally took the phone from Juke and placed it in the hand of Miranda's mother. "You might as well take the call," Wally said. "It's FrogGirl."

The woman looked puzzled. "Who?"

"It's your daughter. Miranda. We call her FrogGirl."

"That's insulting."

"Maybe you should ask her about that. When you're finished, I need to talk to her."

Ellen Krainer snatched the phone and jammed it to her ear. "Miranda? Is that you?"

Battling the noise of a construction site, Wally always kept his phone set at high volume, so in the silence of the moment he could hear the reply: "Hey, Mom. How are ya?"

Ellen Krainer moved the phone six inches out from her ear. "Where are you?"

FrogGirl's voice sounded tinny: "I'm in the lobby. Pay phone. They said I could leave today."

"Who said?"

"Johns Hopkins."

"John who?"

"The hospital. I had a kidney infection. I'm in Baltimore."

"*Baltimore!*" Wally shouted. "Give me that phone!"

Ellen Krainer stepped away from Wally and spoke into the cell: "How about if you just tell me all about it."

Wally was quickly calculating: From the present time on Saturday morning until the final inspection of the K-Palace at four o'clock Wednesday afternoon, FrogGirl had four days and four nights to drive an overloaded, underpowered, oil-burning pickup truck from Baltimore to California if she were to arrive by Wednesday morning. Then they would have a few hours to lift and install a 954-pound bell in a tower twenty feet above the ground, hoisting it by a crane that Wally would have to hire and keep on standby, costing hundreds of dollars an hour. And then—in, like, three hours—they'd have to build the world's fastest roof over the top of it—a round roof, no less, requiring special skill and careful details. No! Wait! They could build it on the ground ahead of time and have the crane lift the entire roof in one piece after they'd installed the bell. But could FrogGirl, driving alone and just out of the hospital, cross the continent in four days and four nights?

Ellen Krainer was sitting on the steps of the front porch with the phone held six inches from her ear. She was weeping. "I just wanted to help you, Miranda. That's all I ever wanted to do."

Juke edged up to Wally. "Are we screwed?" he asked.

"Not worth screwing," Wally said. "But we might be dead."

Wally turned his back to the porch and gave instructions to Juke and Abe. Drama was interesting, but he had a house to build. Rudolfo and crew were installing gold-plated faucets while Kim and crew were trimming gold-plated switches and outlets. So far no dings, no defects.

When Wally checked back, Ellen Krainer was hunched forward in a crouch, speaking angrily into the phone: "Who did this to you? Was it that awful man?"

A stucco crew was coating the rear wing. The top coat was tinted the color of dry oat grass in late summer, selected by the architect to blend structure and landscape.

Ellen Krainer was leaning against the post of the front porch, patient and weary: "You can be as stubborn as you want, Miranda, but we can get a blood test."

Cathy and Pink Patty were trying to paint the exterior trim, working around the edges of the stucco crew. The wood trim was to be a rusty brown, accenting the outlines of the structure while evoking earth and redwood-bark. Anton at one point had changed the color plan to bright yellow with accents of red, but now Wally could overrule.

Ellen Krainer was pacing back and forth, speaking with a weary tone: "This isn't really about you, is it, Miranda? It's about me."

Landscaper Lucy was, as she called it, "ferning out" the grotto. Bits of lichen had already attached themselves to the boulders. Sorrel and delicate violets were starting to flourish.

Ellen Krainer was snapping into the phone: "That is so not true. Don't you dare say that."

The swimming pool contractor was fine-tuning the filter system. The pool was in the shape of a teardrop with the waterfall entering midway through the neck so one could swim under and behind.

Ellen Krainer was pleading: "Please don't do this, honey. You're heading for a life of regret."

Chuck was installing carpet and growling at anybody who came near. At the entry, woven into the fabric was the monogram AK. Wally wondered what Mr. Thailand would make of it.

Ellen Krainer seemed bored: "Basketball was never the answer, honey."

Johnson was doing something in the utility room—nobody knew what and nobody understood HVAC anyway, but they knew Johnson would get it right.

Ellen Krainer was in a debate: "You know absolutely nothing about how to raise a child. No, I—That's an *unkind* thing to say. I was doing my best."

Alfredo and crew were assembling bottle and keg racks in the wine cellar. Pancho was building oak shelves in the library. Wally told them to keep it simple and functional. Let the beauty of the wood make its own statement.

Ellen Krainer was looking in a hand mirror, dabbing at her hair, and saying "Your sister has nothing to do with this. No, your sister would never do anything that stupid."

Juke, Steamboat, and Abe were laying out the round roof for the bell tower. All the rafters would meet at a central point. Abe was calculating the angles.

Ellen Krainer was sitting once again on the steps of the front porch, contemplating a fingernail as she said, "That would be ludicrous. Why would I apologize? You were defective, honey. It wasn't my fault."

Larry Ludowski and some day laborers were setting posts for a garden fence. Wally at the end of each day would pay the day laborers directly in cash, the only people not working on spec. Larry picked them up on a street corner, and you never knew from day to day who might show up.

Ellen Krainer sounded exasperated: "Because he's a *fisherman*, that's why."

The glazier replaced the window glass that Ethan had broken, and Ethan was given the job of assisting him—and listening to the glazier's opinion of vandals who break windows—and, incidentally, learning something about setting glass.

Ellen Krainer was standing up, brushing some dirt from the back of her pants as she held out the phone toward Wally. "You wanted to talk?"

As Wally reached, Ellen Krainer kept the phone slightly out of his grasp and said, "I just want to say one thing. In spite of whatever she told you, I never treated her like a frog."

"I'm glad to hear it." Wally tried to take the phone.

Ellen Krainer placed the phone behind her back. "Are you a parent, Mr. Walters?"

"Three children, yes."

"Then you understand sibling rivalry. There was never any favoritism. Comparing wardrobes or allowances is simply not fair. Miranda's sister is exceptionally graced with beauty and as a result has exceptional needs. The Alfa Romeo was practically a job requirement for a model of her stature. The collision was an unfortunate accident. The alcohol reading was a malfunction. Everybody knows those instruments don't work half the time. The cocaine didn't belong to her and she had no idea the boy had planted it. The shoplifting incident was a misunderstanding that was blown all out of proportion. My behavior with the store manager was above reproach. Nobody assaulted the security guard, it was completely the opposite. I simply will not tolerate anyone spreading rumors that I would—"

"Yes, Ms. Krainer, I have no doubt."

"Just so we understand. Let me remind you. There are penalties for defamation of character."

"I understand."

"Don't you try to follow me. My exhusband is a police detective." She dropped the phone into Wally's hand.

"FrogGirl? It's Wally."

"Hey, Wally." She sounded morose.

"What should I call you? Miranda?"

"No." Sighing. "Not yet, anyway."

Ellen Krainer had climbed into the black Ford Explorer. Shaking a pill out of a plastic bottle, she popped it into her mouth and began punching numbers into her own cell phone.

"Are you okay?" Wally asked.

"She did too treat me like a frog."

The black Explorer was driving away. Ellen Krainer was talking— jabbing words—into the phone as she steered.

"I believe you," Wally said. "I've seen her with my own eyes."

"I thought I could talk to her. I thought maybe this once I'd have her attention. She's gonna be my kid's grandmother. We need to get the hang of this somehow. I mean, I shouldn't have to run away from home. It's not right. When she told me my sister's in detox, I thought maybe I could even go home. My sister's the poison. She's like a clone of my mom. I'm like my dad. And he got out of there a long time ago."

"The police detective?"

"She told you that one? And who did she say her boyfriend is—the governor? She's so amazing. My dad was a hair stylist. He left her when I was four and died of AIDS when I was eight. She's in total denial. The wrong one died. Wait! I didn't say that! I swear ..."

Wally could hear her crying. *Good*, he thought. *Clear it out of your system.*

After a minute, Wally said gently, "Miranda, I have to say it's touching—"

"FrogGirl. Call me FrogGirl."

"It seems like an insult."

"Hey. I'm proud of who I am. I am *not* my mother's daughter. It's just the ...the baby thing. When that happens. Then I think I'll have to be Miranda. I mean, if you were a kid, would you want a mother named FrogGirl?"

"I might. I'd definitely want a mother who was proud of who she was. Anyway, it's really touching that you had such hope. It's admirable that you wanted to work things out with your mother. I imagine you'll always have that hope, no matter how many times you fail. I guess this wasn't the right moment."

"It's never the right moment. For seventeen *years* it wasn't the right moment. Do you know how hard it always is to—" there was a gasp, a sound like sobbing "—to have someone like her—"

Wally waited a minute for FrogGirl to compose herself. In every gig, it seemed, there was a soap opera moment when somebody's emotional life would go to the brink. Usually it was the client. It was almost a Law.

There was a gulping sound. "Sorry," FrogGirl said.

"You okay?" Wally asked.

"Fine."

She'll need a role model for motherhood, Wally thought. *Opal, maybe, if I can bring her around.* There was no time to think about this. Of course Opal will come around. Wally had deadlines to meet. He plunged ahead: "There's too little time and too much distance. I'll fly somebody out to meet you along the way. You can—"

"I've got Eric."

"Eric." Wally had a sinking feeling.

"He's a waterman. His father's a waterman. His grandfather. On the island? I was shooting some hoops, waiting for the hoist—to move the bell, you know—and Eric came along. He's pretty good for a waterman. Almost beat me but he missed a lay-up. He's building a sailboat. He likes frogs." She paused. "Actually, he catches frogs." Pause. "He cooks them."

She stopped talking.

"And?" Wally said.

"And he's standing right here. You want to talk to him?"

There was static, rustling, the sound of a phone changing hands.

"Hello," Wally said. "Is this Eric?"

"Yup."

"My name's Wally."

"Yup."

"You want to drive to California?"

"Yup."

"Why?"

More rustling.

FrogGirl's voice: "Eric doesn't talk much. He's never been past Baltimore. He wants to see the Pacific Ocean."

"You understand what's at stake here?"

"Absolutely," FrogGirl said. "Billions of dollars, right?"

"Not billions. Though it feels like."

"And speaking of billions, we had to hire a guy with a hoist—like I said—to move that bell into the back of the truck. It sorta swang? Broke the rear window and put a big old dent in the back of the cab. Mr. Gannymede said it: You work with what you've got when you're on Hooper Island. Oh—and the hospital, they needed a deposit, so I put it on the credit card. Okay?"

Wally mopped his brow. "Anything else you want to tell me?"

"No oysters," FrogGirl said. "Chesapeake got so polluted, they all died. What? Okay."

Wally heard rustling, the phone changing hands.

Eric's voice: "They're tearing down all the oyster houses and putting up condos."

"That's a shame," Wally said. It was one of those moments he hated as a contractor, when somehow he became guilty for all the rampant development of the world. "I'm sorry."

Rustling. FrogGirl's voice: "Augustus H. Gannymede is a sweet old man. His wife is salt of the earth type. Great people. They know Eric, they know his family. Eric brought me to Johns Hopkins because he said it's the best hospital in Maryland. He stayed here all three days. It was so awful painful. You know I could've died?"

"FrogGirl, if you died, that would really mess up the work schedule."

"Jeezo, Wally."

"I'm kidding."

"Don't worry," FrogGirl said. "I'll be there in time. If the good Lord's willing."

"If He's good."

"Oh, He is, Wally. Don't you know?"

Fifty-Five

For a week now Wally had been sleeping at Opal's house. To Opal, in many ways it felt like an invasion. But also an adventure.

He left hairs in the sink. He wore boots indoors and dropped pellets of dirt everywhere. He emptied pennies from his pocket that for some reason Ronny deposited in the toaster. He took out the garbage, came back with claw marks on his arms and face, and said he'd messed with a raccoon. He brewed tea and carried it off and forgot about it until, days later, in a kitchen cabinet next to his box of beloved Grape-Nuts she found a mug of black scum with bugs floating on top. He woke up at three in the morning, padded off to the bathroom, and repaired a leaking faucet before returning to bed.

He said he "forgot" to stop at the store to pick up the ham and paper towels. When she probed, he finally admitted that he'd skipped the store because he had no money and his credit was maxed and he sure as heck wasn't going to ask her for cash. She went to the ATM, handed Wally two hundred dollars in twenties, and they both felt humiliated and neither of them could find the words to make it right and yet somehow it didn't really matter. Because somehow, in spite of different qualities, they meshed.

She liked Mozart, he liked Jerry Garcia; she liked French pastry, he preferred a hot dog with sauerkraut. Socially she was bolder. In private, however, she dithered over nuances and endless possibilities, and she dreaded decisions. He got things done.

More and more she was coming to appreciate the meshing, the finding ways to work out differences and get along. He didn't *want* to wear wretched socks; he just didn't have time to replace them. She bought some new ones; he seemed pleased. Even his hands, rough and hard like a dry sponge, could be softened with conditioner—unscented, of course, as he didn't want any girly smells.

In trepidation, Opal called Sylvia. With a law degree and three children in grade school, Sylvia was a part-time public defender. She was a realist at best, a cynic at worst. Opal sang soprano in the choir;

Sylvia sang alto. They'd been roommates at UC Berkeley and good friends ever since.

Opal confessed that she was living with a carpenter.

"Is he smart?"

"Yes."

"Because you need that, Opal, you want that. You know you do."

"He's not brilliant. Especially with finances. I—it isn't what it seems but—well."

"You give him *money*?"

"It's temporary. The financial thing."

"Right." A pause. Opal could picture Sylvia shaking her head. "It always is."

"It's not what you think."

"I think that you're right—he *is* smart. And I think that you, Opal, one of the most sensible people I know in every way but one, have found a new way to be an idiot about a man. And I vowed never to let you do this again. How are his tools?"

"His—are you saying—?"

"People will assume. I guess what I'm asking is, what's the attraction?"

"He's down to earth. He's kind. He likes my children. I feel safe with him. And yes, it's even sort of physical and after all the—you know—what's so bad about that?"

"Does he drink?"

"Not anymore."

"Oh. Wonderful."

"I don't think he ever had a drinking problem. It was ...drugs."

"Oh. Even better."

"He's not a con man, Sylvie. You're making this whole situation sound like a—a bad translation of a good poem. A poem of everyday life. And what's different is, he would never try to make me feel inferior."

Not that she felt superior to Wally in any way. Well, except in the area of bookkeeping and financial planning. And maintaining good clothing. And cleanliness. And having goals. She worried about him. Wally was developing a nervous tic at one corner of his mouth. His back was always sore and his feet grew worse through the course of each day so that he'd taken to steeping them in warm water each evening, soaking the pain away.

"Did you drop something on them?" Opal asked.

"It's just arthritis," Wally said. He pulled a chair up to the bathtub, rolled up his pants and dangled his legs over the side while Ronny bathed. Ronny thought Wally's feet in the tub were hilarious.

On this Saturday night Wally tossed and turned in bed. He said he had a tension headache. Opal stroked his brow, lay her head on his chest and felt it rise and fall with each breath. She heard the lub-dub of his heart and the gurgling of his belly—or was it her own belly? Somewhere in the distance, a siren wailed. She ran her fingers through the gray chest-hairs. They were both naked. Wally insisted—he said it was a Law—they would both sleep naked together every night regardless of the cold, regardless of whether they wanted to have sex, that sleeping naked was what couples should do. She sensed the ghost of Aimee in this Law, which was slightly creepy, or perhaps it was simply an echo of the 1960s, which seemed quaint and yet deeply touching—in all senses of the word. She was willing to try, though not sure what she would do if Ronny wanted to snuggle in with them in the middle of the night.

In return she told Wally she had to sleep with the light on. Wally couldn't stand the glare of a lamp, so he installed nightlights in six outlets around the room.

It was the key to how couples survive: You compromise, you comfort. For every take there is a give.

Still brushing her fingers through Wally's hair, she heard a new sound—a soft snore. It equalized them, the fact that they both snored. Naked and noisy, entwined, softly lit, they would make it through the night.

Fifty-Six

Sunday, like Saturday, workers swarmed over the K-Palace. It was pretty much a continuation of the previous day except that Rudolfo was installing the bidets and warning everybody not to mistake them for something else, and Kim was debugging the remote-controlled curtains, which for some reason would spontaneously close themselves whenever the air compressor went on. The super-expensive garbage disposer in the kitchen was making a weird, scratchy noise—they'd have to replace it—and the jets in the hot tub were squirting water into the fireplace. The Sub-Zero refrigerator hadn't been delivered yet, was two weeks late, and the Wolf gourmet stove was three-fourths of an inch wider than the space between the cabinets. Wally—Captain Clipboard—was getting frazzled. The security alarm installer—a substitute, the regular guy was sick—drilled through two plumbing vents and a central vacuum pipe and was sent home. A hummingbird got trapped in the dining room and was beating itself against the skylight, trying to escape. Juke brought in a stepladder, climbed to the top with a towel in his hand, lunged for the hummingbird and fell, grasping the chain to the chandelier, which held for a moment and then detached from the ceiling and crashed shattering to the floor. Juke landed on his feet. He said his ankles hurt bad but he didn't think they were broke. The ladder as it fell punched a hole in the drywall. Abe opened a window, and the hummingbird flew out.

The more they pressed, the more accidents would happen. Wally knew the syndrome but couldn't stop it. Deadline pressure was making everybody nuts. *Slow down and do right.*

Wally noticed a visitor, a young man wearing sandals, plaid shorts, a knit shirt, and a small backpack, standing in front of the house looking like a well-groomed day-hiker.

Wally approached him. "Can I help you?"

"Mr. Walters?"

"Yes."

"I live up the hill."

"Mr. Pilpont, I presume?"

"We should talk."

Aren't rich people supposed to be old? Wally wondered. *In Silicon Valley they're all younger than me.*

"Okay." Wally set down the clipboard. He offered his hand. "Nice to meet you."

Pilpont seemed surprised at the greeting and offer of a handshake — and pleased. His face lit up with a boyish grin as he shook Wally's hand.

Watch it, Wally told himself. *Krainer had that same boyish grin. Fooled me once.* "What's up?" Wally asked.

"This is a lovely spot," Pilpont said.

"Yes," Wally agreed.

"I'd like to make it lovelier."

"So I've heard."

"I won't try to be coy, Mr. Walters."

"Wally."

"Okay, Wally. Call me Phin. Your goals, I presume, are the same as mine. We want to maintain a green planet. And we want to make money. We are environmentalists, you and I, and we are businessmen. I speak as an equal. We want this place to be beautiful. I will pay you more money to stop working and walk away from this place than your client will pay you to finish."

"We can't stop, Phin. We have a contract to fulfill."

"I know about your contract and I know that for the right price you'd be better off breaking it." Shrugging off the backpack, reaching inside, he pulled out a small leather bag. Loosening the drawstring, he held the sack out for Wally to see. "Gold," he said. "A natural element. A gift from Mother Nature. Why shouldn't money be beautiful?" Again, the boyish grin. "These are American Eagles. Thirty of them. One ounce each. Do you happen to know how much an ounce of gold is worth?"

"No."

"Today, six hundred and forty-four dollars. Tomorrow, slightly more or slightly less. You can sell them anywhere. No forms to fill out, no reporting to the IRS. Take them as a deposit. You could enjoy a very nice vacation with that money—how about an eco-tour of Costa Rica? Or buy yourself a very fine truck—how about one that runs on vegetable oil? There's more where this came from. Much more. It's yours if you walk away and never come back."

"I'm into this for more than one truck," Wally said. "A lot more."

"I'm aware how much you're into this. I'm offering you a way out. No risk. High reward. You want to haggle?"

Wally was beginning to suspect that there was something personal between Pilpont and Krainer. Pilpont had already destroyed Krainer's business and bankrupted him personally. Now he seemed bent on obliterating every last physical trace of Anton's existence.

"No. I have a responsibility to all these workers. Good day."

Pilpont didn't move. "I have a checkbook," he said. "It doesn't have to be gold. How much would it take to make all these workers—and you—go away?"

"And then what would happen?"

Pilpont grinned. Like a Boy Scout. "It wouldn't concern you."

Wally considered. An early payday. Go home and be happy. No more risk, no more long hours into the night, no more worrying whether they could finish on time, no more wondering how Mr. Thailand might screw them. It was money. No, it was better than money—it was gold.

And it was awful.

It *would* concern him. Wally would break a contract with somebody he'd never met and whom he had no reason to dislike. The unfinished house would become part of Krainer's bankrupt estate, from which Pilpont would buy it for less—much less—than the market rate that Mr. Thailand was already willing to pay. All their craft—the beauty and the excess—a year of hard labor—would be destroyed.

"You're the one who has to stop, Phin. We caught two of your boys."

"I had nothing to do with that."

Interesting, Wally thought. He'd just thrown it out, fishing, bluffing as if he knew something, and Pilpont if he were innocent—or a good liar—should have said, What boys? What are you talking about?

From the unease that flashed momentarily across Pilpont's face, he seemed to realize he'd made a mistake.

"One of the boys is working for me now," Wally said. "He's given me information that would be of some interest to the police."

"Then you should inform them," Pilpont said, his composure regained.

"I believe I will." Wally pulled his phone from his pocket, flipped it open, and began thumbing numbers.

"Put down that phone," Pilpont said. "It was entirely their own idea."

"What was their own idea?"

"Whatever they did."

Wally flipped the phone closed. "Good day, Mr. Pilpont."

Pilpont's eyes were hard. "Here," he said, thrusting the sack of gold coins into Wally's hand. "I want you to have this. No obligations."

"I can't take this."

"No obligations. It's a gift."

Gift? It was hush money. Wally held the leather bag toward Pilpont, who refused to take it back. After a few seconds, Wally dropped it. The sack landed with a *chink* on the asphalt of the driveway.

Pilpont turned and walked away.

Wally watched Pilpont leave the grounds. Striding with a youthful bounce, he never looked back. Wally went into the house.

As the door closed behind him Wally thought he'd better do something with those coins. Spinning around, he opened the door and returned to the driveway. He could put the sack someplace for safekeeping until he could return it—mail it, ship it, somehow deliver it—to Pilpont.

But the bag was gone.

Wally looked around. There were workers everywhere.

"*Who took it?*" Wally shouted.

Heads turned.

"Took what?" Lucy asked from the garden.

"A small leather sack. It was right here."

Silence. Uneasy glances.

"Nobody took nothing," Alfredo called from the roof.

"*I want that bag returned to this spot!*" Wally shouted. "*No questions asked.*"

It wasn't the money, exactly. It was that somebody must have *known* it was money, not just some random little bag, to have moved so quickly to race out and grab it in the few moments before Wally returned. And if that person knew it was money, did that person know Pilpont was coming?

The sack of coins, now secretly in somebody's possession, was toxic. It was as if Pilpont had poisoned the well. Suspicion would seep into everything. And Wally had to wonder: *Could Pilpont have a mole among the workers here?*

Wally found Ethan in the dining room where he and Abe were discussing Fermat's Last Theorem while at the same time Abe was showing him how to patch the hole made by the falling ladder. Ethan was holding a scrap of two-by-four inside the wall cavity. The ends of the wood scrap on the inside overlapped the edges of the torn drywall. Abe was driving screws through the good drywall into the scrap of wood.

Abe was explaining every move, step by step. A few months ago, Wally had explained the same procedure to Abe.

"Ethan," Wally said, "I'm sorry to interrupt. How's it going?"

"Good enough, sir." Ethan held the piece of torn drywall in place over the block of wood. He had long thin fingers, sure hands. He wore a baseball hat turned backwards. You could see in a glance that Ethan and Abe worked well together. Ethan, in fact, had latched onto Abe the way Abe at one had time latched onto Juke.

Abe drove three screws through the patch and into the scrap of wood that was backing it, and the patch was in place.

"Now we tape and mud," Abe said.

"Yes, sir," Ethan said.

"Let's talk about Pilpont," Wally said.

Ethan froze. He had big brown eyes, moist, startled—the mole in the headlights.

"I just had a chat with the man," Wally said. "Pilpont says it was entirely your own idea."

Cautiously, Ethan said, "Just exactly what did he say was my idea?"

"It."

"It?"

"Exactly."

"I—uh—I couldn't say," Ethan said. "Sir."

"I need to know whose side you're on."

"Yours, sir. I couldn't say if Pilpont knew about it. Mario brought it."

"Brought what?"

"It. Sir."

"If you're on my side, Ethan, now's the time to tell me what 'it' is."

"Gasoline."

Abe took a step away from Ethan.

Ethan, seeing Abe distance himself, looked stricken.

"Who's Mario?" Wally asked.

"Beelze. Mario's tag is Beelze."

"Is Mario connected to Pilpont?"

"Mario's dad runs an optical multiplexor company. Pilpont invested in it. That's all I know. I don't follow that crap."

Wally had a vision of another bag of gold, this one in the form of a financial instrument—stocks, bonds, something—dropped into the multiplexor company, whatever that was. Another poisoned well.

"What was the plan for the gasoline?"

"I told him it was stupid."

"Why was it stupid?"

Ethan looked chagrined. "Nothing noble or anything. It was stupid because if you toss a can of gas, if you mess up, some of it can splash out on you. Then you spark the lighter, and you're a torch."

"Safety first. I like that. If you work for me, Ethan, that's a good quality."

"Uh, yes, sir."

"But doesn't anybody know how to make a molotov cocktail these days?"

"What, sir?"

"Nothing. Joke. So you knew exactly what the plan was."

"I'm sorry. What can I say? I thought he was cool. Mario. He came on like my friend. He's got a Porsche, a 914. He can get tickets to *anything*. He set me up with somebody."

"A girl?"

"Yes, sir. Somebody I thought I wanted to know."

"How'd it work out? The girl."

"Not so great."

"And now? What do you think of Mario now?"

"He's a—request permission to swear, sir."

"He's a shit. So what happened to the gasoline?"

"You didn't find it?"

"I didn't know we were supposed to look for it."

"He dropped it when he ran. Somewhere out in the meadow."

"You and Abe. Go find it. Now. And don't light any matches."

"Yes, sir." Ethan headed for the door.

Wally grabbed Abe by the arm. Nodding toward Ethan, Wally asked, "Can I trust him?"

"I think so," Abe said. "I really do. You can always trust an Archimedes freak."

Less than five minutes later, they returned with an empty red can.

Wally found Juke in front of the bell tower. The round roof was framed and sheathed as a single unit. Now Juke and Steamboat were applying felt paper and battens for the tile.

"Juke," Wally said, "I want you to tell Marmaduke we need extra help. For the next few nights. I want this place *crawling* with guards."

"Okay, Boss."

Wally knew he'd probably neutralized the arson threat by means of his bluff with Pilpont. The man couldn't risk it now, not knowing how much Wally knew or how much could be testified against him. Or could he? When you have that much money—and that much personal animosity—do the rules of normal risk-taking apply?

"Do you know where that sack of coins went?"

"No, Boss."

Wally looked Juke in the eye, searching for any sign he was lying. And it chilled him. *Three more days to finish this house, and I'm wondering who might betray me.*

Thirty coins, and everything changes.

Fifty-Seven

FrogGirl called on Sunday evening.

"Okay, we're moving," she said.

"Where are you?"

"Hagerstown."

Wally was at Opal's house, in her kitchen. He sat down hard on a stool. Something was flittering in his chest. Was this how it felt to have a heart attack? "Isn't Hagerstown somewhere in Maryland?"

"About seventy-five miles west of Baltimore. You want the short version or the long version?"

Two days and one night after leaving the hospital, they were still in Maryland. Wally felt another flitter in his chest. "What time is it there?"

"Twenty after midnight."

"You're sitting in the passenger side, and Eric is driving. Have I got that right?"

"Correct."

"Okay, let's try the long version."

Wally's truck had thrown a rod. Eric had hitched back to Hoopers Island and returned driving his grandfather's old Chevy pickup. They'd parked it tail-to-tail with Wally's Toyota and talked a tow truck driver into lifting Wally's front end. The bell slid halfway into the back of the Chevy. Eric then backed the Chevy against a bridge abutment until the bell was pushed snug inside.

"Hurt the bell?" Wally asked.

"Not much."

Old Yeller was now in a garage in Hagerstown. The shop said they'd be willing to accept the body, such as it was, in return for the cost of the tow. Eric advised it was a fair trade. In any case, Wally would have to deal with it. In addition to his grandfather's Chevy, Eric had borrowed his sister's cell phone and brought his own cash box. Wally's credit card was declined when they tried to buy gas — the hospital had maxed it out.

Now they were spending Eric's sailboat money. FrogGirl had promised that Wally would pay him back. "You will, right?"

"Of course I will," Wally said, wondering if he was lying, if Eric would be yet another victim of this looming catastrophe. "Why didn't you call sooner?"

"Eric says, 'Don't snivel, fix it.' Family thing. It's kind of a code."

"I like that code." In fact he liked Eric, sight unseen. Wally was thinking the flitter in his chest must be some kind of gas thing. Or a nerve thing. Heart attacks were painful, right? He was feeling discomfort, not pain. "You can't stop driving. Ever."

"Pit stops."

"That's all." Wally told them they'd have to drive all night, every night, no motels, and arrive within sixty hours at the latest. Sooner would be better. In the background, over the phone Wally could hear music. "Is that a polka?"

"Eric's grampa has a pile of CDs."

"You like polka?"

"Well, Eric does."

In Wally's opinion two days and three nights confined in a truck cab with polka music would violate the Geneva Conventions. Would sharing a drive with Eric end up like sharing with Abe? Out loud Wally asked, "You sure you can make it? How old's that Chevy?"

"It's a fifty-six."

"How many miles?"

"Odometer's broke."

"With a CD player?"

"Eric put that in. So his grampa could play polkas when he was hauling crabs. Oh, Wally, this is incredible! What a gorgeous night! Milky Way! Isn't it cool? My kid's going all over America. And he isn't even born yet."

"It's a he?"

"Feels like a boy. I dunno, I could be wrong. But I've got a fifty-fifty chance."

And, Wally thought, at best so do I.

FrogGirl called again at 6:10 Monday morning. Wally staggered out of bed. He'd left the phone on Opal's dresser.

"Where are you?"

"Gas station. We had to replace the rear tires."

"Money holding out?"

"Hope so. This thing eats gas."

"Where did you say you are?"

"East Galesburg, Illinois. Lost a couple hours on the tires. At least we got a sit-down breakfast."

Another call came as Wally was just arriving at the Woodside job. It was Marmaduke.

"Some dude here in a white limo. Says he wants a walkthrough."

That would be Mr. Thailand. Gad Berman had notified Wally in advance, but he hadn't known the time of the visit. "Let him in," Wally said. "I'll be right over."

By the time Wally arrived in the Honda, Abe driving, the limo was gone from the K-Palace.

"Speedy guy," Marmaduke said. "And oh so polite. Lotsa questions."

Wally's heart flittered. "About the construction?"

"About the hogs. He spent more time looking at our metal than going over the house."

Besides Marmaduke and Sir William, there were three other men and two women lounging about. Several of them were sipping an early-morning beer. None looked younger than sixty. There were six motorcycles in the driveway. Wally tried—and failed—to imagine a conversation among this group with a man who owned half of Thailand. "What did he say?"

"He thanked me for allowing him the pleasure of a tour. Here." Marmaduke handed Wally a note. "He wrote this for you."

Wally's eyes were having a good day but still he couldn't read for shit. He passed the note to Abe. "What's it say?"

"Wow, calligraphic pen," Abe said. "Nice script. Three lines. It says, 'Please remove bedroom mirrors. Please remove statue. Where is the bell?'"

East Galesburg, Illinois. In the bed of a polka-playing '56 Chevy pickup driven by a nonsniveling boy from an island in the Chesapeake Bay, accompanied by a pregnant young woman who could be as tough as a nailgun or as vulnerable as a frog. *And I trust them. God help me. I have to.*

"Any trouble?" Wally asked. "See anybody?"

"Just coyotes," Marmaduke said. "They act like they own the place."

Fifty-Eight

Already the days seemed too short. By sunset the air was chilling rapidly.
Over the K-Palace hung pink wisps of cloud. A vee of birds headed
south.

The crisis du jour: The top plate of the bell tower was imperfect.
The plate was a circle cut from lengths of plywood, doubled in
thickness, with staggered joints in a handmade custom gluelam, a lot
of time and effort and material, and the radius was an eighth of an inch
too short—the width of a saw cut, which Abe had failed to allow in the
calculation—a rookie error. It was usable. It would be covered by fascia
anyway, so what did it matter?

On any other gig an eighth of an inch in rough framing didn't matter.
Happened all the time. Did they still have to be perfect? Krainer was
out of the game now; did his obsession have to become their obsession?
They were racing an insane deadline; structurally it was totally sound.
Visually—and only to an expert—it was imperfect. No builder in his
right mind would even question it.

They tore it out.

They owed it to the house, the concept, everything they'd tried so
hard to accomplish on this impossible and frustrating gig. They owed
it to their pride. Or maybe, Wally thought, just maybe, we're all going
nuts.

"Remember, everybody," Wally kept saying, "it's not the money.
That's not what we're working for."

"Yes, we are," would be the constant answer.

Now Abe wanted to show Ethan how to use a nailgun.

Wally said, "You think he's ready?"

"I do."

Did Abe resent how long they'd kept him from using a nailer?
Possibly Abe was anxious to help Ethan avoid the humiliation Abe had
felt. And it was touching that Abe cared so much to protect Ethan—
they were hitting it off nicely. A pneumatic nailer isn't that complicated.
Probably more injuries are caused by hammers, though they tended to

be less serious. In Abe's case they'd been extra cautious—partly because Wally's injury was fresh in everyone's mind, partly because Abe was, well, Abe. But Ethan had the moves of a natural carpenter and had already mastered the use of a regular old-fashioned hammer, which requires more skill than a nailgun.

"Get the Hitachi," Wally said. It was their easiest nailer, a good old NR 83A, light in weight and yet so well-built that it was basically bombproof.

"Pancho's using the Hitachi," Abe said.

Which reminded Wally: Pancho was complaining that the air compressor wasn't shutting off when it should. It was building up too much pressure, causing the nails to overshoot, and it was likely to blow out a hose. Nobody had time to deal with it. Just two more days. "How about the Senco?" Wally said.

"Senco's jammed," Steamboat said.

So unjam it, Wally thought, but he held his tongue. The politics of nailguns could drive him crazy. Steamboat considered the Senco to be his own personal nailer even though Wally had bought it and Juke had rebuilt it and theoretically it was for the whole crew. If Steamie wanted his own, he should buy one. But a good carpenter is hard to find, and if treating the Senco as Steamboat's private tool was the price of keeping him happy, then Wally would go along. Wally could buy another Hitachi. He would too, as soon as he got paid for this giant fiasco of a gig. If he got paid. Paid enough to break even.

Abe said, "Let me use Deb."

Juke scowled. "Nobody uses Deb."

"Why?" Abe asked.

"Cuz you *don't*." Juke marched up the stairs of the bell tower, Debbie Doofus in hand, trailing a black air hose.

Wally watched him go. That Duo-Fast had been a great tool, but at some point a body stops being old and starts being frail. Was that a crack in the head of the cylinder casing? Or were the cracks in Wally's eyeballs?

Unspoken to Abe but also on Wally's mind: He wanted Juke to nail the new top plate, not Abe or Ethan. This time, it had to be perfect. Had to.

Phap phap. The air compressor started buzzing. *Phap.*

Wally turned to Abe. "You and Ethan need to clean up all those wood scraps on the floor of the tower." They were a hazard, nail-embedded.

Abe hesitated. "Why's Juke so touchy about that Duo-Fast?"

Compressor still pumping. Shouldn't it shut down now?

"Because he pretty much built it," Wally said. "And also it's—"

Odd sound. Not a *phap*.

A crash.

Clunk. Not any old clunk but the distinct sound—somehow your ears are tuned for this—of a human body striking the floor.

Juke's voice from above: *"Forkin' shit!"*

There are certain moments when your life is stunningly lucid. What seems important, isn't. Deadlines, money, nuances of perfection, politics of tool possession, overdue phone calls—it's all crap.

Your mind clears.

You race up the stairs to the bell tower and find blood running like somebody opened a faucet. Juke is sitting against the half wall with one knee in the air, one leg out at a funny angle that can only happen if it's broken. You know he fell eight feet from the top plate onto nail-embedded wood scraps and it isn't even the main problem, though you're glad he fell forward to the interior instead of backward to the ground, which would have been a twenty-foot drop. You suspect that in a desperate instant he made a choice between a bad outcome or a horrible outcome and somehow forced himself to fall this way. Shrapnel from the exploded nailer is lodged in the floor, the wall, and most importantly in Juke's body.

"I'm forkin' castrated," Juke says calmly as he pulls a piece of metal, round and jagged like the top of a tin can, from between his legs. Blood spurts from the rip in the crotch of his pants. Meanwhile more blood is running from nail punctures in his cheek, his left arm, and a stain is spreading below his chest.

You tear off your shirt and put pressure on the groin and Juke says, "Don't tell nobody you touched me there." You are crouching in a spreading puddle of red. You shout orders and maintain pressure on the crotch while Steamboat and Abe pick up Juke's body like a floppy bag of sticks, vaguely thinking about the damage you must be doing to the broken leg but knowing the bones won't matter if you can't stop him from bleeding to death. All of you try to fit down the stairwell at the same time. Juke says, "I thought I knew pain but this is forkin' *turdballs*," and his eyes roll up inside his head as the lids close down. You place him in the bed of Pancho's F150 because you know Pancho drives like a rocket pilot, and you try to hold your shirt against the wound and keep Juke's body from sliding all over the bed as Pancho screeches down the twisty road. Abe and Steamboat, who are riding with you in the bed of the pickup, tear off Juke's shirt, where you see a ragged wound below his right nipple. Abe puts pressure on it while Steamboat finds some gauze in the first aid kit he grabbed on the way to the truck. Abe starts making bandages for the smaller wounds while Steamie unties Juke's boots and pulls them off, and then you pull off Juke's pants, being careful now of the broken leg. You even remove his socks to see the extent of the damage and you discover a hole in his calf about the size of a dime, but it doesn't bleed much, probably because it's all coming out of his thigh—he isn't castrated but was hit right at the inside top of the thigh, a deep wound where an artery is gushing, and you reapply the pressure and you're more effective now but there's already a sticky pool of crimson around your knees.

Steamie tries to fashion something like a blanket out of spare bits of clothing.

You talk to Juke though you don't think he hears you. You tell him he's not castrated and you'll take care of him and everything's gonna be all right and would he please stop bleeding dammit? You place a hand on Juke's chest and can feel the heart beating extra hard and his breath is panting like a runner who can't get enough air. The nonbleeding leg is the broken one, and you force yourself to look at it though it makes you gag to see a leg changing direction sideways at the knee like some wooden puppet dancing on a string. You note that Juke's face is totally pale like the skin is transparent and there's no blood underneath.

The color has drained from his lips.

His toes are turning blue.

Suddenly Juke opens his eyes and looks startled to see you and to find himself in the bed of a pickup and to feel the pain and the ebbing of blood and his heart working so hard to pump whatever still remains in his veins. He fixes you with a steady gaze and says, gasping, "She never loved me ...Boss ...you should know that ...she only loved you," and then he closes the eyes again.

The ride seems like it will never end, the raw air is cold and merciless, and Pancho is gunning up 280 and then down Sand Hill Road with his horn blazing, right through the red lights. From their Mercedes the venture capitalists and investment bankers and dot-com zillionaires are staring at you like you're from another planet. You've tossed Steamboat the phone to call 911 and they must have forewarned Stanford Hospital because when Pancho pulls up to the emergency entrance a team is waiting with a gurney. There's a fast pass down a corridor and suddenly he's gone—you can't follow.

You wait.

You wonder what to do.

For the first time you notice that you're bathed in blood from your knees to your shoes. Your socks are squishy from soaking up blood. Your knees hurt from kneeling over Juke in the hard metal bed of the truck as Pancho banged over potholes and skidded around corners. Your back hurts from bending over his draining body as you were pressing with all your might on that open hose of an artery. You feel selfish for thinking about your own pain.

You smell fear, your own fear.

The scent of fear seems to you like the scent of drying blood, which is like the scent of redwood heart, a scent you love in the deepest reaches of your soul like the scent of the ocean and the scent of a woman and the scent of dirt after rain. Many scents, one world, and it will keep going, uncaring, whether Juke lives or dies.

Who do you call? Juke has no wife, nobody who loves him. Nobody waits for him to come home.

You wish you had shut down the compressor. You wish you'd said something about the cracks in the nailer. You replay the moment over and over trying for a different outcome but you can't make it happen. You could have prevented this. You were distracted. And a long time ago you never should have allowed Juke to modify a nailgun because nobody should do that. Ever. It's your fault.

People have to pass through a metal detector before they're allowed into the Stanford emergency waiting room, and you imagine what must have happened to make the hospital want to install it. You glance uneasily around the waiting area, wondering if any gang members are lurking here, planning revenge. Then you see Ethan passing through the detector followed by Lucy, who must have brought him, and you wonder for just a flash whether Lucy and Juke ever got it on. Ethan looks scared, and you wish you hadn't left him behind or at least had given him a thought, but you did what you had to do in the time you had to do it. You're pleased to see that Ethan cares so much, and you know you've found a good one. Lucy lays a hand on the kid's shoulder like the mother he doesn't have. And now here comes Kim the Korean electrician and Rudolfo the gay plumber and Alfredo the success story and Robert the Napoleonic cabinet maker and even Larry Ludowski, who Juke always gave a hard time, all of them filthy from a day's work. Some of them get stopped at the metal detector because in their pockets they're carrying screwdrivers or a Stanley knife or needlenose pliers, and Rudolfo has a miniwrench that he carries on his keychain and Larry has a pocketful of self-tapping screws. And now here comes paint-spattered Cathy and Pink Patty along with silent Johnson the HVAC guy and grouchy Chuck the carpet installer, and then comes Marmaduke, looking pissed and arguing with the security guard at the metal detector because he doesn't want to leave his big old KA-BAR knife on the table. You know Sir William and a bunch of their geriatric Hells Angel buddies in torn black T-shirts would be here too if they didn't have to guard the Palace right now and you hope they're guarding it well.

You call Opal, and you find you can't say much of anything, but the catch in your voice tells her everything and she says she'll be there as fast as she can but she'll have to bring Ronny, and you say "Is he sleeping?" and she says "Yes," and you say you don't want her to wake him and she says "But I want to be there," and you say "I'll be okay," and you suspect she'll come anyway but meanwhile you sit there among a row of chairs with Steamie on one side and Pancho on the other, Ethan and Lucy sitting across from you while Abe paces up and down smacking his fist in his palm. You reach out and grab Steamboat's giant mitt, and on the other side you find Pancho's artisan fingers, and you hold hands without shame there in the emergency waiting area wondering how much life a body can lose.

Fifty-Nine

When Juke opened his eyes his brain was floating. He had no idea where he was. There were tubes stuck in his arm and a nurse standing by the bed adjusting bags on an IV stand, while some asshole machine was going *blp ...blp ...blp ...*

"What the donkeyshit happened?"

The nurse took his wrist between her fingers and studied her watch. "How do you feel?"

"Can't move my forkin' leg."

"You shouldn't. It's in a cast. Is it hurting?"

"Little bit." Actually, it felt like somebody had stabbed an ice pick through his knee and was wrenching it back and forth, sending jolts of agony through his body. Juke had a habit—carried from childhood— of never admitting to pain. Almost never. "Beg pardon, ma'am. The language."

"*De nada.*"

"So what happened?"

"Your heart was running on fumes. It must be a strong one, or you would have died."

Juke remembered squatting over Debbie Doofus, squeezing the trigger, and then just like he always knew it would happen, it happened. Only it turned out a little worse than he expected.

"Didn't know she was gonna castrate me," Juke said.

"She?" The nurse raised her eyebrows. "She didn't. She severed your femoral artery."

"I got a female artery?"

"Femoral. Everybody has one. Two, actually. One in each leg."

The nurse was younger than Juke by maybe a dozen years, pretty, a dark complexion, a slight Spanish accent and Spanish rhythm to her words.

Juke's fingers explored the outline of the bandage over his groin. Sure enough, he still had the equipment. "It was a machine. Not a lady. Cut me."

"I know. I have your chart."

"What day is it?"

"Tuesday. It's one thirty in the morning."

Juke's head was clearing. He was with a pretty woman. Certain things are automatic. Ingratiatingly, smiling through pain he said, "So you got stuck on graveyard shift."

"We don't call it graveyard. Not in a hospital." The nurse was jotting a note on a clipboard. "There's a big motley crew out there wanting to see you."

"Yeah? I'll go now."

The nurse laughed. She had a deep laugh, a manlike laugh that struck an old memory in Juke, like somebody he once knew. She said, "You're not ambulatory."

"Huh?"

"You can't walk yet. You stay here. We have to wait a couple days."

"For what?"

"To see if your toes recover. Parts of you got too little blood."

Juke yanked the sheet to the side and stared down at his feet. The toes on his right leg were deep blue, almost black, as if frost-bitten. "What if they don't?"

"The surgeon will remove them."

Juke whipped the sheet up and over his head, hiding his body from the nurse as he slid the gown away and saw, yes, it was okay.

Coulda been worse, he told himself, lowering the sheet again. *At least the dick ain't blue.*

The nurse was studying his face, and Juke studied her right back. She had fine wispy eyebrows that turned up on the outside like a smile. And the eyes. Whew. There was something about those eyes. Soft. Deeply set, big and brown, with a spark of fire. Eyes that seemed to challenge him. Eyes that, if he dared, would welcome him inside. He'd been partial to those eyes—and those wispy smiling eyebrows—since he was a kid, almost like he'd been searching for them in every woman he'd known.

"You have an unusual name," the nurse said. "Juke. It made you easy to find."

"Who's lookin'?"

She was still holding the clipboard. For a few seconds she tapped the pen against her chin and stared thoughtfully down at Juke. "I found you a long time ago. I saw where you live, Mr. Juke Jacobs. It's a bad neighborhood."

"Not so bad. Usta be the shits. Do I know you?"

"No. You never met me. My mother told me not—" The nurse stopped herself. She tapped the pen against her chin. "My mother is Tina Uribe Gonzales. Does that name ring a bell?"

"Tina Uribe?"

"Yes." The nurse was watching him closely. "I always thought you might show up here some day. Most carpenters do. I just didn't expect it would be on my floor."

"Tina's *here?*"

"San Jose."

"*You shittin' me?*"

The nurse frowned.

"Sorry," Juke said. "I'm not too good at ...So you're my forkin' daughter?"

Wincing. "If that's how you want to put it, yes."

"Crap I'm sorry. I mean—not crap. I mean. You know. I got a bad mouth. Wait a sec." Juke closed his eyes and shook his head rapidly from side to side. He could feel his brain scrambling, sloshing, reshaping, settling down. Opening his eyes, he smiled. "Nice to meet you. What's your name?"

"Juanita Gonzales Alicabo."

Juke squinted. "Name tag says 'June.'"

"That's what she always called me. Junie. June."

She looked like Tina. It was more than the eyes. There was a hint of wildness in her. A spirited woman. Like Tina. *I teach you something,* Tina said, *and then you never be same again. De veras.*

"How long—?" Juke began. "I mean—when did she—about me—I mean—"

"You were in prison. She found your name. She sent you fudge."

"That was *her?*"

"She was always scared to see you."

"She talked about me?"

"She didn't want to. I bugged her. I had to know. She tries to forget you."

"She's mad?"

"No. Not angry."

"I always wondered. Did she say it was my fault?"

"No."

"Well it wasn't her fault."

"Are you saying I'm somebody's fault?"

"Shit no. Uh, sorry. You're wonderful. You're a miracle. You're like—you know what you're like? You're like a perfect plum."

Juanita—Junie—seemed skeptical. "You mean that as good, right? Looking like a plum?"

"I mean me and Tina, we were picking plums. What happened—we just grew up kinda fast. So she married some guy Gonzales?"

Juanita frowned. "For a while."

"Divorced?"

"No. Disappeared. And nobody is looking for him. Are you married?"

"Never come close."

Juanita narrowed her eyes. "She raised me. We had nothing. She put me through nursing school. She cleans houses. You went to jail. You live in a bad place. She doesn't know what kind of person you are anymore."

"I got a cat."

"A cat?"

"Old gray cat with three legs. Somebody left it at a pawn shop. I rescued it. Okay?"

"Okay, what?"

"I ain't the same guy who went to prison."

"Because you have a cat?" Juanita folded her arms across her chest. "She had a hard time. She's a good person. She doesn't look the same. You might not like her." Juanita leaned over the bed, over Juke, face to face. "If you see her—if you want to see her—"

"I want to see her."

"If you hurt her, I will kill you."

"If I hurt her," Juke said, "I'll kill *myself*."

Sixty

Just as Wally had suspected she would, Opal woke Ronny and brought him to the hospital, where the little man earnestly shook everybody's hand before having a meltdown and eventually falling asleep in Opal's lap. A nurse finally allowed them to see Juke—a few at a time. Everybody tweaked Juke's toes for good luck. Juke seemed distracted and clearly in pain, though he wouldn't admit it, and he couldn't seem to keep his eyes off the nurse who in turn seemed to show special concern for him, which everybody said was typical Juke. Wally stayed at the hospital until three a.m. He told the crew to forget the Woodside job, shine it on, get some rest, and they'd meet late in the afternoon at the K-Palace.

The next morning, Tuesday, when Wally finally checked his messages, he had two from FrogGirl. The first came Monday evening while Wally was at the hospital. FrogGirl and Eric were in Des Moines. It had taken all afternoon to cross half of Iowa. Vapor lock. It was a warm day and the engine was already running hot from the heavy load and anyway it wasn't geared for high-speed travel. Eric eventually came up with a solution, sort of, involving cutting a grapefruit in half and sticking it over the fuel pump, held on by baling wire, to cool the fuel, but even then they had to stop every fifty miles and change the grapefruit.

Wally had actually done something similar with an old Indian motorcycle he'd had in college. The difference was that Wally had used tomatoes.

The second message was from Tuesday morning while Wally was sleeping in. They were in Omaha. It had taken all night to cross the other half of Iowa. The headlights had died, taillights too. A fuse kept blowing and they couldn't find the short by flashlight, so finally Eric ran new wire to each light with the help of a bakery truck driver who'd stopped at an all-night gasomat and was admiring the old Chevy.

According to Wally's road atlas, the distance from Omaha to San Francisco was 1,691 miles. He needed that bell Wednesday morning in order to lift it and install the roof and be ready for final inspection at four o'clock Wednesday afternoon. A three-speed fifty-year-old truck built before there were Interstate highways, a truck built for farm roads and short hauls, a truck prone to vapor lock and blown fuses, a truck playing polka music, for Pete's sake, would have to lug a 954-pound bell at an average speed of seventy miles per hour without stopping or breaking down for the next twenty-four hours.

Maybe there was a shortcut between Omaha and San Fran, some secret highway only the locals knew about ...

Face it, Wally told himself. You're just about forked.

But still he hoped for something. Divine intervention, if necessary. He made a quick search of the Internet. No bells nearby, and no bells nearly as nice. The best Wally could find was in Michigan, and the bell had a crack in it, wasn't as pretty, and the man was asking three times what Wally had paid. FrogGirl was already closer than Michigan. According to Gad Berman, Mr. Thailand loved the idea of the big old Buddha bell. He was expecting it. Nothing less would do.

"I'm praying for you," Opal said.

"You do that? You actually pray?"

"Yes."

"It's not about the money, you know. What I'm after. With the job. That's not the goal here."

"Is there a goal somewhere to be self-supporting at some point?"

"Aw crap."

"I'm even buying your socks, Wally."

"Of course I plan to be self-supporting. Couple-supporting, actually. Couple-with-step-kid-supporting. With maybe even a little left over to buy my own socks."

"I believe you, Wally. But I'm taking it on faith here. And what exactly is the goal of that job?"

"I wish I could say. I just don't want to focus on the money. Maybe I really believe I can build the perfect house. Maybe I believe in miracles."

"Me too. The miracles." Opal wrinkled her brow. "And next Sunday when the job is finished and you won't have to work, will you come with me to church?"

"I don't do church, Opal. That's so ...I don't know. Middle class."

"Is that a half-joke? Or no joke?" The wrinkled brow turned into a pout. "Have I been sleeping with the enemy? I don't know if this can go on."

There it is, Wally thought. *No church, no nookie.* Was that a half-joke? She looked half serious. How well did he really know this woman?

"I'll go," Wally said. *Whatever it takes.* He truthfully wanted to hear her sing in the choir.

Opal broke into a broad smile. "I've met your crew. Now at church you can meet my friends."

"So they can approve of me?"

"They already don't approve of you."

"Why? What do they know?"

"Just the outline. They need the colors."

"What's the outline?"

"Carpenter. Had a drug problem. Borrows money."

"You could have drawn a better outline."

"I did, but they hear what they want to hear. They don't understand you, Wally. They don't understand me, either. Not anymore. Suddenly I'm a rebel. A late bloomer. I might lose my friends."

"Jeez, I'm sorry. Am I worth it?"

"They don't know what I know."

"What do you know?"

"You're not as bad as you look."

At the K-Palace there was a frenzy of finishing details. And late Tuesday evening there was a call from FrogGirl. The phone was dying, so she kept it short: "We just left Salt Lake City."

She didn't know how fast they were going because the speedometer didn't work, but Wally calculated that they'd just covered nine hundred miles in thirteen hours. Eight hundred to go. There might be hope after all.

Wally was in bed when the next call came. It was 2:20 a.m. He found the phone on the dresser and sat on the edge of the bed. Opal raised herself on one elbow, breasts hanging softly, lit by nightlights, while she rubbed the fingers of one hand over Wally's lower back.

FrogGirl's voice: "We hit a cow."

"You all right?"

"We're fine. Totaled the cow. Eric saw it at the side of the road as soon as the headlights picked it up, and he started to slow down, but the brakes aren't so great and we were going flat out. It stepped right in front of us. Eric cut to the side but it clipped the fender."

"How's the truck?"

"The fender's pushed against the tire. Headlight's history. Tire's blown. Radiator's leaking. It's a mess. The bell smashed into one corner of the bed. Eric says it bent the frame."

"Bent the bell?"

"No, bent the truck frame."

"Where are you?"

"Nevada. Somewhere. Actually, nowhere. There is absolutely *nothing* out here. No wonder this cow committed suicide. It was lonely."

"You sure you're okay?"

"Wally, I'm so sorry. I promised we'd get this bell to you. There's a light but it's miles away. Eric's got a chain and—" Snap crackle pop.

The phone went dead.

Sixty-One

Wednesday, like Tuesday, Wally canceled work at the Woodside job with a promise that it would have his undivided attention starting the next day. Undivided, that is, if he wasn't tarred and feathered first.

Instead of a crane Wally had hired a guy with an extended forklift who was standing by, charging a hundred dollars an hour, in case the bell showed up.

Which it didn't.

They'd mopped up the blood except for what had seeped into the cracks. For better or worse, Juke was now a permanent part of that tower.

Everybody was waiting for the building inspector to arrive—every tradesperson who had worked on the place. Marmaduke and company were there. The locksmith, the fence crew, the security alarm installer, the driveway paver, the swimming pool contractor, the septic tank digger, the floor installer, the tile setter, the stucco crew, Cathy and Pink Patty and Alfredo and Robert and Rudolfo and Kim and Lucy and Johnson and Chuck and all their helpers were there. A cement truck driver and a lumber delivery guy were there even though Wally didn't owe them any money—they'd made drops, watched the progress, and they were curious. Ethan had skipped school to be there. The architect, fired by Krainer, was there and seemed gratified by how it had turned out. Wally could understand everybody's keen interest—not to mention financial stake—in the situation, but he was a little concerned that somebody in the crowd of onlookers might accidentally jostle something. The problem with a perfect house: It had nowhere to go but imperfect.

On the hillside above, Phineas Pilpont was watching through binoculars. For one fleeting moment Wally worried that Pilpont might have bought the building inspector.

Even Juke was there. He arrived in a taxi and pushed himself out with one leg in a cast, his feet in socks but no shoes, a shirt on top with a hospital gown hanging down below it, no pants, no crutch.

"They discharged you like *that*?" Wally said.

"Nobody de-charged me. I borrowed some wheels and made a break."

The driver was removing a wheelchair from the trunk. The back of the chair was painted *Property of Stanford Hospital*.

"You all right?" Wally asked.

"Still got balls," Juke said.

The inspector arrived a half hour early, something that had never happened before in Wally's thirty years of construction.

"We've still got one detail," Wally told him.

The inspector wore a hearing aid and had thick eyeglass lenses that made his eyeballs appear to swim. "I can't wait around," he said. "You know the rules."

"What rules?" Marmaduke interjected.

Wally explained that inspectors weren't allowed to wait for work to be completed. In fact, they could be disciplined for it. In the past there had been too many abuses of the practice.

"Don't you wait around for them to show up?" Marmaduke asked. "That ain't fair." He was chewing on the tips of his white mustache.

The last thing Wally needed right now was a confrontation between an elderly, somewhat cantankerous inspector and an elderly, possibly belligerent Hells Angel. "Let's go inside," Wally said.

As Wally ushered the inspector into the Palace, he caught Steamboat's eye and pointed—first to the forklift, then to the roof assembly lying on the ground, and lastly to the top of the tower. "No nails," Wally mouthed silently.

The inspector was named Marsh. He was decent enough, though he came with certain pet peeves that everybody had learned to anticipate. Marsh would check every ground fault circuit interrupter and measure the gaps in every deck rail. He was a stickler on framing details but would never poke his head in an attic or leave the ground floor—rumor had it that he'd once fallen off a ladder. The common joke was that you had to create a perfect handrail at the bottom of the stairs but could do whatever you wanted at the top end. Marsh was respected, though, as decent and fair. He walked with a limp. On the slightest provocation he'd whip out photos of his grandchildren. Another story about Marsh was that he became oddly flummoxed in the presence of mothers with young children and had once signed off on a flagrantly substandard remodel done by a fly-by-night carpenter when the homeowner showed Marsh around while carrying a newborn baby—a remodel for which Wally had been called in later to clean up the botches. Marsh was known to be particularly tough on large corporate builders, which (again according to rumor) made him take heat from the bigwigs in the building department but also definitely made him popular with smaller, more quality-oriented contractors such as Wally—not that Marsh had ever cut Wally any slack. Code was code. The large corporate builders got mad at Marsh for enforcing the code in tracts and condos. The smaller contractors, doing custom homes, took enforcement for granted.

Marsh checked the weather-stripping on the exterior doors. He made sure there were fluorescent fixtures in the kitchen and baths even though everyone knew—and Marsh knew too—that as soon as the house was signed off most of the fluorescent lights would be replaced by something with friendlier color—as happened in every high-end house in the state unless the owner was hard-ass green. Such was the dance of the building code. Wally made no judgment. He just built what people wanted to buy and hoped to nudge them toward green if he could.

In every room, Wally tried to position himself so that his body was blocking any window that might have a view of the forklift raising the roof to the tower. No need to call attention to it.

Marsh admired the inlays in the hardwood floor. He complimented Chuck on the apparently seamless carpeting. He even had a kind word for Rudolfo about the fit and finish of the plumbing fixtures: "Man, they really sparkle, don't they?" As expected, he tested each GFCI and tried to pass a four-inch ball through the gaps between deck rails. Not expected, though not especially worrisome, Marsh kneeled (wincingly, painfully) next to the porch of the rear addition and shone a flashlight under the deck.

When he straightened up, he looked grim. With a somewhat strained formality he adjusted the eyeglasses on his nose and said, "Could I see the approved job copy of the plans, please?"

Wally had been carrying them in a roll under his arm. There were dozens of sheets.

Marsh leafed through page after curly page until he came to the detailed drawing of the porch. He peered closely, tilting his glasses down his nose. Frowning, placing a finger on one corner of the sheet, he said, "Just as I thought. Half-inch bolts."

"What's the problem?" Wally asked.

"You attached the ledger to the side of the house using quarter-inch bolts."

Twenty bodies threw themselves to the ground and peered under the deck while thirty more stood over them asking "Is it true?" Sure enough, those were quarter-inch bolts.

"*Who did that?*" Wally shouted.

"Larry butt-fuck Ludowski," Juke said grimly from his wheelchair.

Larry had built the whole minideck. And it was vintage Ludowski: Undersize something that nobody would normally see and that wouldn't be discovered until years later when the structure finally failed.

Or was he bought?

Wally looked up the hill. Pilpont was no longer in view.

And—it just occurred to everybody—Larry Ludowski wasn't among the crowd. The one person missing.

"I'm sorry," Marsh said. "I can't pass that."

To Wally's mind it was starting to seem like a remarkable coincidence that the one unusual place that Marsh had inspected was the one code violation in the entire project.

Would Mr. Marsh mind waiting a few minutes? Please? Does anybody happen to have a few extra bolts lying around? The nearest hardware store would be a thirty-minute drive each way. How about a threaded rod? Anybody got one? How about if we shoot it with a bazillion nails? Couldn't you just sign off the house with an asterisk and a promise?

"I'm sorry," Marsh said, shaking his head, looking genuinely upset. "I can't."

Could he just wait a few minutes?

"No."

Wally stayed glued to Marsh's side, pleading his case. From the corner of his eye, such as it was, he saw workers huddling. Marmaduke, Sir William, and friends hustled toward the front of the house. Ethan and Abe sprinted off across the meadow. Steamboat began unrolling an extension cord while Pancho inserted a half-inch bit into a drill chuck. Alfredo was crawling under the deck.

Marsh was walking slowly toward the parking area. Wally was in front of him—in his face—slowing him down and begging for a break as strenuously as he dared without threatening. One thing you never do, ever, is threaten a building inspector. They had the power. No church, no nookie.

"I'm sorry," Marsh kept repeating. "It's a shame. A real shame."

"Can't you at least wait a few minutes? Give us a chance?"

Wearily, Marsh explained—as Wally knew—that they check the time logs. He couldn't risk it. "I'm too close to retirement. I wish I could help you. I'm sincerely sorry."

Wally ceased walking entirely, blocking Marsh as he said, "I hate to ask, but did somebody suggest that you look under that minideck?"

Marsh's face grew troubled.

"Put it this way," Wally continued. "I'm wondering if you might be the innocent dupe of somebody's larger plan."

"Well." Marsh's swimming eyeballs were looking everywhere possible to avoid meeting Wally's unblinking gaze. "I really can't discuss what goes on inside the building department. People are watching me. Especially on—well—never mind. As I say, I'm too close to retirement."

"People are getting screwed here, Mr. Marsh. Little people. The ones who do the good work. The ones who put in the seamless carpet and the inlaid flooring and the sparkling faucets."

"And you."

"Yes. And me." It occurred to Wally that Marsh was one of the little people too. Trapped, just like them.

Marsh seemed genuinely distressed. "Regardless of why I looked there, the fact remains that the bolts are substandard. I'm aware of them. I can't pass them. And I can't wait an hour and a half for you to run out to a hardware store and run back and install them. I'd be overtime, and I'd have dead hours on my time log. As I say, people are watching me. *I'd* get stiffed."

Wally had run out of arguments. He stopped blocking Marsh. His stomach felt hollow. He wanted to rage, to hit something, to scream. He wanted to lay his head on Opal's breast and cry like a baby.

Coming around the side of the house, Marsh stepped down the flagstone path to the parking area.

Eyes swimming, he looked to the left.

He looked to the right.

"Where's my car?"

Ethan knew the territory. Abe followed. At the grapestake fence Ethan pulled out four loose pieces of wood. Crouching, the two boys scooted through some shrubs and then dived under a trellis, cracking a few pieces of lath and scraping their backs as they wiggled through. Now they were in semidarkness among a labyrinth of piers and beams and joists, with slits of light shining between slats of decking above them. There was a steady hum that seemed to vibrate each bit of lumber—the hum of a hot tub pumping water through its jets. The tub was sitting on a part of the deck that had a reinforced substructure to bear the extra weight—reinforced by, among other things, half-inch bolts joining doubled beams.

Ethan and Abe set to work loosening nuts with a wrench and pulling out bolts with a pry bar, glancing nervously above, fairly certain but not positive that the whole hot tub wouldn't suddenly collapse on top of them. The bolts weren't bearing weight. They were simply holding beams together. And the beams wouldn't go anywhere anyway as long as they were pressed in place by the dead weight of the hot tub. The beams would be stable as long as nothing shook them.

Ethan and Abe found and removed five bolts.

They needed six.

They heard footsteps above them, the pad of bare feet. Following Ethan, Abe crab-walked to the underside of some stairs where there were a couple of knotholes in a riser. Putting their eyes to the knotholes they saw a naked, flawless, superb female body slipping into the hot tub, followed by Phineas Pilpont.

"Bought those tits at the body store," Abe whispered.

"Money well spent," Ethan whispered back.

"You come here often?"

"Used to."

Exploring further in the labyrinth, they found another bolt holding some sort of joist-type board to a beam. They weren't sure what it was for, actually. They knew one thing: They needed that bolt.

As quietly as possible, they unscrewed the nut. Then slowly, cautiously, Abe used the pry bar to work the bolt free, the wood groaning as the bolt withdrew. Vulgar but efficient. The wood continued to creak.

"Let's get outa here."

At the trellis they hesitated.

"He might see us," Abe whispered.

"I think he's busy," Ethan whispered back, and he made an obscene gesture involving his hips and the circle of his hand. The deck was creaking with a steady rhythm.

They scooted beneath the trellis and shot into the shrubs. Quickly they made their way through the fence. Down the hill. Across the meadow.

Suddenly Abe flew head over heels in a somersault and found himself flat on his back.

Ethan doubled back. "You okay?"

"Tripped."

"Coyote den. You stepped in the hole. Hey." Ethan pointed at the ground. "Look at that."

Abe studied the dirt around the coyote hole. There was a scattering of gold-colored coins and a well-chewed leather pouch. "Later," Abe said.

"Yeah," Ethan said.

Bolts in hand, they raced to the house.

With a folding metal clipboard in one hand and a blue Universal Building Code book in the other, Marsh paced back and forth in front of the house waiting for the police to arrive. Wally paced beside the inspector, commiserating, telling him that there'd been a lot of crime for such an idyllic-looking neighborhood, that all Wally's tools had been stolen, that windows had been broken and somebody had even tried to set fire to the house. Further, it was quite likely that the police would encounter the car on their way up here. There was only one road into and out of this place. To leave, the car had to take it. A white Ford Bronco with an official Building Inspector insignia on the door would be hard to miss.

Wally's words may have had some effect as Marsh didn't seem particularly upset. In any case, it wasn't Marsh's car. He'd called the police; the missing vehicle was duly noted and reported; he couldn't be blamed. Wally said he'd be happy—in fact, he'd be honored—to give Marsh a ride back to the office.

Wally was interrupted by Abe, who had something to tell him.

When Wally rejoined Marsh at his pacing, he suggested that maybe they could take another look at those bolts while he was waiting for the police.

Marsh scowled. "Don't think I don't know what you're doing. And don't tell me you have nothing to do with that missing car."

Wally raised his hand as if taking a vow and placed his other hand on Marsh's blue book: "I solemnly swear on the Universal Building Code that I know absolutely nothing about that missing car."

"All right then." Marsh seemed satisfied. There was almost the hint of a smile on his face.

He came early, Wally remembered. The one time in his career that he ever showed up early at a building site. It was as if Marsh had wanted to give Wally a chance.

At that moment another vehicle pulled into the parking area—not the police but a green Subaru with two golden retrievers in the back, wagging tails and pressing noses against the rear window. Opal stepped out and began unbuckling Ronny from his car seat. She had a camera strapped over her shoulder.

Wally called out to her: Did she happen to see a car coming down the hill as she came up, a white Bronco with an official Building Inspection insignia on the door panel?

Holding Ronny by the hand, Opal walked up to Wally and Marsh. "No," she said. "I don't think so. Sorry to barge in, but the suspense was killing me. And I thought a picture today might be a good follow-up to the last one."

"Right," Wally said. "You can call it *Nailed again.*" He squatted. "Hi, Ronny."

As always, Ronny and Wally shook hands.

"Mr. Marsh," Wally said, rising, "I want you to meet my most junior carpenter. This is Ronny."

Ronny offered his hand.

Marsh, bending forward with a big silly grin, shook Ronny's hand.

"Here, Ron," Wally said, placing something in Ronny's fingers. "I want you to hold this for me." It was the inspection card.

Marsh pulled his wallet out of his back pocket. "Let me show you some pictures," he said.

"Before we see your grandkids," Wally said, "could you please take another look at those bolts?"

They walked to the rear of the house. All eyes were on Marsh. The inspector bent down on his knees, shone his flashlight under the deck, and then straightened.

"Okay," he said.

There was a sharp collective intake of breath.

Wally nudged Ronny. "Ron, will you please give that card to Mr. Marsh?"

Ronny held it out with both hands.

Marmaduke, Sir William, and friends slipped away. Marsh placed the inspection card on his clipboard and studied it thoughtfully. Wally glanced over the top of the house to the tower. Roof in place. Not nailed, but Marsh would never check.

"Nice job," Marsh said, and he signed the card. Final Approval.

There was a cheer.

"It's not over," Wally said.

There was a happy babble of voices. Nobody seemed to want to hear Wally's caution, just as nobody heard a distant cracking, groaning noise; and nobody noticed the sudden burst of water briefly washing down the hillside or the two naked, muddy bodies scrambling back up. Rudolfo, Kim, Alfredo, and everybody else shook Marsh's hand. Tossing off her wide-brim hat, Little Landscaper Lucy ran up to Marsh, threw her arms around him, and hugged him. The top of her head barely reached the bottom of his chest.

Flustered, he gently pushed her away. "Well," he said. "It's nice to make somebody happy for a change. Too often I feel like a meter maid." A crowd had surrounded him.

It took a few minutes for Marsh to make his way back to the front of the house.

In the parking area, undamaged and in fact slightly cleaner than he'd left it, was the white Ford Bronco. Sir William with the tail of his torn T-shirt was buffing a spot on the hood.

Coming up the road were three more vehicles: a police car, a battered old Grand Marquis, and a white limousine. Dan Diefendorf, Gad Berman, and Mr. Thailand himself.

In his pocket, Wally still carried the folded, battered note that Mr. Thailand had written in tidy calligraphic script:

Please remove bedroom mirrors.
Please remove statue.
Where is the bell?

Well, Wally told himself, two out of three isn't so bad.

Sixty-Two

Diefendorf said there wasn't much he could do if somebody had taken a joy ride and then brought the car back. He'd file a report, and that would be the end of it.

Gad Berman, wearing an ill-fitting suit and a crooked necktie, introduced Wally to Mr. Thailand, who was conservatively—and exquisitely—clothed in a silk suit. As with every other billionaire, he was younger than Wally. His name sounded something like Tongdee. Close enough. Mr. Tongdee greeted Wally with a prayer-like gesture that Wally tried awkwardly to imitate. In sweatshirt and blue jeans, Wally felt slightly uneasy, disadvantaged in the presence of this small but dapper man. Tailoring is power.

Wally gave Tongdee a tour of the house and grounds. Gad, who was carrying a battered briefcase, pulled Wally aside and whispered, "Don't touch his head."

"I wasn't planning to," Wally said.

"It's taboo in Thailand to touch someone's head or point with your feet."

"Wasn't planning to do that either," Wally said.

"The foot is considered the dirtiest part of the body. The head is the most sacred. And books. They respect books so highly that you should never slide one across a table or set one on the floor. Also never step over somebody or step over food. It's an insult."

"Wasn't planning to step over him, Gad. I promise I won't kick him, either, or beat him on the head with a book. And I won't drop-kick any pumpkins while he's here. Where'd you learn all this?"

"I read it on the Internet."

"A little nervous, Gad?"

By now Berman knew all about Wally's finances and realized that if this deal fell through, he wouldn't get paid. He needed the money just as desperately as Wally. In Gad's case, he had a habit to feed.

Wally's crew had removed the master bedroom mirrors as requested. The paint was still wet on the bedroom walls. Tongdee was pleased. They'd removed the statue as requested, and Little Landscaper Lucy had crafted the fountain to bubble out of the top of the rocks like a natural spring into the grotto. Tongdee was very pleased.

The kitchen had been designed by Anton Krainer, a noncooking bachelor who believed bigger would always be better. There was an oven large enough to roast an entire pig, a six-burner commercial range, a built-in widescreen flat-panel television, a walk-in, glass-door Sub-Zero refrigerator, a microwave that could vaporize a brick, and a trash compactor that could crush a small Volkswagen.

"We will need a rice cooker," Tongdee said quietly.

Wally conducted Tongdee through the butterfly garden, past the gazebo and tennis court. They stood on the elegant observation platform built of ipê wood. The viewpoint was intended for watching tennis, but Tongdee turned his back to the court and took in the meadow, the folds of hills, the valley far below. "This will be wonderful for flying kites," he said softly.

Wally was coming to like this guy.

Tongdee turned to Wally and said, "We will need to build a spirit house."

"What's that?" Wally asked.

"A house for spirits," Tongdee explained as if the meaning was obvious. "I hope you weren't planning a vacation. There will be a lot of work for you."

"Yes, sir," Wally said. He ran a hand over his hair and down the ponytail behind his neck. There hadn't been time yet to trim it.

The tour ended in the empty seven-car garage, where their echoing voices gave the feeling of standing in an airplane hangar.

"Can we make this smaller?" Tongdee asked.

"Gladly," Wally said.

"Then everything is satisfactory," Tongdee said gently. "I am comfortable at heart."

Gad Berman flipped open the catches on his beat-up briefcase. "Shall we sign the papers?"

"First, please, let me see the bell."

Frantically, Wally glanced around. His eyes lit on Marmaduke and Sir William. "Would you like to look at some motorcycles?"

"The bell. If you please."

"Show him the bell," said Gad Berman.

Wally felt himself breaking into a sweat. "I'll show you where it goes," he said. "Everything's ready for it."

Tongdee folded his hands in front of his waist. Standing perfectly poised and perfectly still, he said, "There is no bell?"

"It's a beautiful bell," Wally said. "It just isn't here yet."

Tongdee's face was a blank as he said, "There is no bell."

"There *is* a bell." Wally tried to convey calm. "It's just—the truck that was bringing it hit a—had a delay." It occurred to Wally that hitting a cow might not add value to the bell in the mind of a Buddhist.

"I'm very disappointed," Tongdee said quietly.

"Let's proceed," said Gad Berman, hurriedly laying papers on top of his briefcase.

"No," Tongdee said in his gentle voice.

"Uh—what?" said Gad.

"Without the bell there is no deal."

"We have final approval," Gad Berman said. "The house is officially complete and can legally be occupied."

"Good," Tongdee said. "Then someone can buy it."

"At midnight," Gad Berman said, his voice rising, "this house will belong to a trusteeship controlled by a court. There's a class action lawsuit against Krainer's business and creditors for his failed winery. They'll try to lay claims against this house. It will be in limbo for years. Gigantic legal fees will be generated. At the end the house will be sold at auction, and if any money trickles through to these men it will be *pennies* for all their hard work and by that time they'll already be *ruined*."

"I'm sorry." Tongdee's face showed not one speck of emotion.

"We could adjust the price," Gad Berman said in desperation. "In consideration of the missing bell. We're ready to deal here."

Tongdee was walking out the open door of the garage. He headed toward his white limousine where the driver was standing by the door while a distant banging noise grew gradually louder and nearer. The sound came from an old faded-red Chevy pickup missing half a front fender, with rags tied to the radiator and smoke billowing out from under the hood. In the rear, held by ropes, was a mass covered by blankets. The driver of the truck, a young man with curly blond hair, was almost cute. Beside him sat FrogGirl. Through the open windows came the oompa-oompa of polka music.

The truck lurched to a stop behind the limousine.

FrogGirl, with a big grin, burst out the door and shouted, "Hello, everybody! I thought we'd never make it up this mountain."

Eric, with a rag over his hand, lifted the hood. A combination of white steam and blue smoke wafted into the air. Moving to the rear, he began unraveling ropes while FrogGirl peeled off the blankets to reveal a massive bell covered with designs of Buddha and dragons and birds mixed with a thicket of oriental characters that no one could read. No one, perhaps, but Mr. Tongdee. The bronze in its recesses had a grayish-green patina, which served to highlight the golden glow of the protruding designs, burnished by blankets during three thousand miles of travel.

With hands folded behind his back Mr. Tongdee, at the side of the truck, quietly studied the bell. Gad Berman stood beside him. From a distance Wally was watching Tongdee intently. Not entirely trusting his eyes, Wally glanced at Juke, who had been scrutinizing Tongdee from his wheelchair. Juke met Wally's glance. And Wally made up his mind.

Tongdee turned to Gad Berman. "Yes," he said. In low voices they conferred briefly.

Berman, beaming, hustled over to Wally. "We have a deal."

The forklift maneuvered itself to the rear of the truck.

"No," Wally said.

"What?"

"Stop the forklift," Wally said.

Everybody stared.

A benign calm had come over Wally. He reached for Opal's hand. Ronny stood behind Opal with his arms wrapped around her right leg. "There's no deal," Wally said.

Berman was mystified. "What are you talking about?"

"No deal."

"Why?"

"The vibe."

"The *what*?"

"It's bad."

Total silence had fallen over the group.

Now Berman was incredulous. "You're gonna let this *collapse*?"

"He was going to stiff us," Wally said. "With no feeling whatsoever. It's like I just stared into the face of death."

"It was just a matter of business," Berman said.

"Exactly," Wally said.

"It was nothing personal," Berman said.

"Exactly." Wally looked at the crowd of tradespeople who had gathered around him. Now he was staring into the face of puzzlement and growing fear. "All our work meant nothing," Wally explained. "That's what death is. It doesn't care. It doesn't matter what you did or what you believe or what you love. It's death. It comes. It's over."

"Wally, this is a bad time to be having a nervous breakdown."

"I'm not. I'm seeing life clearly. Maybe for the first time."

"Not *now*." Berman waved his arm at the crowd of worried, angry, fearful workers. "You owe it to these people."

"I'm fed up," Wally said. "I have an offer to teach school. Listen, everybody, I'll pay you all back. It may take a while, but I'll make good. I'll sell my house. I won't earn much on a teacher's salary, but sooner or later I'll pay you all back."

Robert the cabinetmaker spoke up: "Are you *nuts*? Finish the deal, *then* you can teach school."

"I put my heart into this house," Wally said. "We all did. We should be proud. We did a magnificent job. Then, on a mere technicality, he was willing to let the whole thing fall through."

"So are you," Robert said.

"It was an insult," Wally said.

"I'll take the insult," Robert said. "If it comes with the money."

"I have to take a stand," Wally said.

"This is a betrayal," Robert said. "You're worse than Larry Ludowski."

Opal squeezed Wally's hand. "Are you sure about this?"

"Never been surer," Wally said, though he was feeling more doubt every second.

"He's right," Juke said from the wheelchair.

It was just what Wally needed to hear.

"What's so right about it?" Robert demanded.

"He said he looked death in the face. I know something about that. You gotta do what's right. You only got one life."

"But how is this *right*?" Robert shouted. "*Take the money*. Don't be a stupid *hippie*."

Responding to a slight flick of Tongdee's head, Berman had gone to consult with him. They were speaking earnestly in low voices while standing at the tailgate of the Chevy. The wide, heavy mouth of the bell yawned next to them.

"Don't do this for me," Opal said. "I don't want to be responsible."

"I'm doing it for myself," Wally said.

"He's got a point," Little Lucy said. She'd retrieved her hat. "We make so many compromises in this business, sometimes it feels like we let our integrity slide away. You wake up one morning and realize you've lost all the values you were working for. This was supposed to be the perfect house. It should have a perfect sale."

"An imperfect sale is better than *no* sale," Robert said. "You want to be perfect? Or do you want to be solvent?"

"Solvent," Lucy said, "though I do understand what he's saying. Wally, sweetie, I sympathize. But you're choosing the wrong moment."

Abe stepped up to stand beside Ronny, who was still clinging to Opal's leg. Abe placed a hand on Ronny's head and studied Wally, searching for the meaning of all this. Was this another lesson Wally was trying to impart? Like the virtue of mucking in concrete? Was this all part of his education, his apprenticeship? Abe had been a little worried about Wally ever since the encounter on the staircase with Wally in his underwear babbling about a roof estimate. Was he losing it?

Berman returned. "Mr. Tongdee is very sorry you feel insulted," Berman said. "He wishes to convey to you that he meant no offense."

"But still," Wally said.

"Still what?" Berman said.

"No forklift," Wally said. "No bell."

Wearily, Gad Berman shuffled back to Tongdee, shaking his head.

"I feel like this is all my fault," FrogGirl said.

"No," Wally said. "You did what you could."

"It's all because I had an infection," she said. "If I was smart, I would've treated it before it got to my kidneys. I was *stupid*."

"It wasn't you," Wally said. "So many things happened."

"But that's something I could've prevented. I could've been here three days ago."

"I don't want you to feel bad," Wally said. "This is my decision. You could say it's all my fault."

"I already say that," Robert said.

Berman returned. "He's really very, very sorry."

"I believe that," Wally said.

"He doesn't wish the house to have bad karma."

"Exactly," Wally said.

"He urges you to reconsider."

"Is that some kind of a threat?"

"The only threat is that he's about to get in his limo and drive away. He's authorized me to give you this one last chance."

Tongdee, standing by the bell, gazed at Wally impassively. It was clear to Wally that at this moment Gad Berman was speaking directly on behalf of Tongdee conveying exactly what Tongdee had told him to convey. In other words, Wally knew, his own lawyer had given up on him—abandoned him—and was working for the other side. *Is Juke the only one who understands?*

"Let me be clear," Berman said. "Mr. Tongdee respects your feelings. He honors your labor. He humbly apologizes for any misunderstanding."

Wally looked to the sky. A red-tailed hawk was soaring in an updraft. Wally looked to the meadow. Four coyotes trotted single file through the grass. Wally looked at the roof of vintage, handmade earthtone tile, the warm coloring of the stucco, the meticulously painted trim, the natural grotto of stone and fern and falling water, the garden where at this moment brilliant blue butterflies were fluttering over blooming aster, the gazebo standing quiet and apart like a small temple of craftsmanship, the bell tower, now shortened and opened, complementing the solid flow of the original house design—all of it bound by their sweat, their blood, the work of their hands. Wally looked at the faces of the men and women who had brought this miracle to life.

"No," Wally said.

Robert was making fists. Lucy looked like she was going to cry.

"Sorry," Wally said.

"In that case," Gad Berman said, "Mr. Tongdee has authorized me to offer on top of the already agreed settlement price, to be paid directly to you and to be distributed as you see fit, subject to your acceptance of this offer, an additional one hundred and fifty thousand dollars."

Wally closed his eyes. He took a deep breath and slowly blew it out. His lips began curling into a smile.

"Sold," Wally said.

He walked toward Tongdee, extending his hand.

Sixty-Three

"You coulda got lynched," Juke said.

"Yeah," Wally said. "But you saw it too, right? How he was looking at that bell?"

"Yeah. You done good."

Wally was sitting on the front steps, with Juke beside him in the wheelchair. Opal and Ronny were wandering in the butterfly garden. Everyone else had departed. The sun was receding behind the mountain, leaving them in cool shadow beneath tufty orange clouds. Below them the valley was a soft lavender bowl beginning to sparkle with lights.

"I have to admit," Wally said, "I never imagined he'd offer so much."

"Yeah." Juke shook his head. "People is weird."

"I was about to give it up. Then you backed me. We're a one-two combo, Juke. We're a team."

"Maybe. Sorta." Juke looked away. "Thought you was quittin' to go teach."

"I exaggerated a wee bit. I'll teach one class, starting next semester. See how it goes. We have to finish Woodside and already Tongdee wants changes. He wants a spirit house. That should be fun. We've got a lot of work to do, you and me."

Juke kept his hands on the wheels of his chair, rocking back and forth. He was never one to sit still. "Hard to quit, ain't it, Boss?"

Wally nodded, leaning back against the step. "When can you come back to work, Juke? I need you. Any idea?"

Juke steadied the chair. "I got some business to do. A lady in San Jose. Had an appreciation. Long time ago. More 'n I ever appreciated in my life. And I just met her daughter. I gotta be loyal. Me and this lady and her daughter, we're sorta related."

"Related? How?"

"Her daughter, sorta, is my daughter."

"My God, Juke."

"I got some work to do. Gotta take some pride in myself. Things is different. Fences to mend. Gotta see how it goes." Fixing Wally in his gaze, Juke said, "I ain't comin' back, Boss."

Wally sat up with a start. " You're disabled? It's *permanent?*"

"Naw. I'm quittin'."

Wally stared, speechless.

"Me and Opal," Juke explained. "There's a spark. I ain't goin' through that again."

"Juke, that's crazy. She won't. You won't. We're getting married."

"'Zactly." Juke squinted, looking out across the valley to the last ray of sunlight glinting off the top of Mt. Hamilton. "Some stuff, you always been blind."

"Aimee was different. We were younger. I was popping pills."

Juke shook his head. Wally looked down at his own hand and saw that it was trembling. He could stare down Tongdee, but this was scarier. A weight was crushing Wally's chest. He felt the press of time, of all the years, all the houses they had built together. "You planning to work for somebody else?"

"Naw. For myself."

"Juke, you're breaking my heart."

"Naw." Juke smiled. "Won't break. You got a strong one."

Sixty-Four

Friday morning in a chilly light rain, Wally and Abe drove to Woodside.
Parking in mud, they met Steamboat and Pancho and started setting up
tools. Their breath made clouds. Tiny droplets of rain perched like jewels
on their sweatshirts and the hair on their heads, gradually soaking in.

Steamie poured fresh charcoal in the grill. He'd brought a cooler
full of ribs.

First task today would be the framing of an arched ceiling. Wally
had outlined the procedure to Abe. Steamie and Pancho would teach
Abe the details.

On Wally's mind was an early-morning call Opal had received from
her editor at the newspaper. Her assignment was to photograph an old
bell. A revered, ancient Buddha bell had been missing from a temple
deep in the rainforests of Thailand for over a century. The bell, along
with the secretive society of monks who had created it, had disappeared
during intertribal warfare. Crafted with exquisite designs on its face,
composed of a mysterious bronze alloy, the bell reverberated with a
deep and complex timbre and had once been considered the pinnacle
of bell-making art. The sonorous peal could carry for miles. Already
there had been a complaint from a neighbor who lived just uphill,
claiming that the noise would reduce his property value. A man named
Tongdee rediscovered the bell and immediately made a purchase from
the unsuspecting owner. Major museums were expressing interest. Dr.
Milton S. Chung, an appraiser of international antiquities, said that
most experts had assumed that the lost bell long ago had been melted
down for its metal. Until now the most recent sighting of the bell had
been a black and white photograph in the June 1904 edition of *National
Geographic*. Dr. Chung estimated that upon confirmation of authenticity
the bell could be worth two and a half million dollars.

Wally was gaining a new appreciation of the word *chagrin*.

By noon, Wally's jeans and sweatshirt were smudged with sticky
clay. In spite of the weather, a festive crowd was gathering for the belt

sander races and Steamie's ribs and, oh, by the way, their checks for completing the K-Palace. Checks that would include a nice bonus.

Handing an envelope to Abe, Wally said, "Don't spend it all at once. Unless it's for college."

"Actually," Abe said, examining the check, "I'm buying a motorcycle."

"Opal know about this?"

"She might be okay when she finds out I'm riding it to Princeton. With a side trip to Massachusetts. There's a girl I need to visit."

"Rachel?"

"I'm bringing her a watermelon. See what happens."

Wally gazed with some regret at the hard muscles that had developed on Abe's shoulders and arms. Over the summer his skin had gone from pale and soft to tan and tough; his hands were callused, fingers hard. Most important, he had developed some judgment. Now just as he was getting useful, he was leaving. And Juke was gone. Was everybody moving on?

As if reading Wally's mind, Abe said, "I'll stick around a couple more weeks. I'm just giving you notice. Maybe you can help soften the news to my mom. Be on my team for a change."

"Abe, I was always on your team. Even when I fired you."

Larry Ludowski, showing more courage than Wally would have credited, showed up for his check. A hostile crowd immediately gathered around him.

"Sorry about the bolts," Larry said nervously. "Bad habit."

Wally had an envelope with a check for Ludowski in his pocket, but he wasn't ready to hand it over. "How much did Pilpont pay you?"

"Who?"

"Don't play dumb, Larry."

"Nobody paid me." In one hand was a belt sander, gripped knuckle-white tight.

Robert called out, "Let's belt-sand *him*."

Ludowski started edging away.

The crowd immediately blocked his exit.

"Why'd you undersize those bolts?" Wally asked.

"Bad habit. I told you." Ludowski was glancing around, sizing his chances of escape.

"Why'd the inspector look under that deck, Larry? How'd he know?"

"Coincidence." Ludowski shrugged. "Bad luck. I swear."

Robert called out, "Buttfuck bullshit!"

"I'm here," Ludowski said. "I got my belt sander. You think I'd come here today if I was bought?"

"Yes," Robert said, "if you thought you'd get paid."

"This would be easier," Wally said, "if you admitted what you did. Then maybe I could forgive you."

"I didn't do anything except use the wrong bolts. Maybe you could forgive me for that. And pay me for the work I did."

"You're making this hard, Larry."

"Nobody bought me."

"The inspector, Larry. How'd he know?"

"I told you. Bad luck."

"Nobody believes you, Larry. But I tell you what. I think I could forgive you. And not pay you."

"How about you pay me? And not forgive me?"

"That's what you want?"

"Of course that's what I want."

Wally removed an envelope from his pocket. "If you take this check," Wally said, "you take your belt sander and go. We don't want you here ever again."

Ludowski stared hard at his own boots. "That's what I want."

Nobody said a word as Ludowski walked away, envelope in one hand, belt sander in the other. He climbed into his truck and spun away, tires spitting gravel.

"He'll be back," Steamboat said. "Couple weeks. Asking you to forgive him."

"But you won't, right?" Robert said.

"Actually," Wally said, "if he'll just own up to it, I will."

"Why?" Robert demanded.

"I'm kind of a sucker," Wally said. "And I'm okay with that."

The races commenced. Alfredo's old Porter-Cable was chewing up the competition. Without Juke, there was no serious challenger.

Wally didn't notice when the old faded-red Chevy pickup came banging onto the site, but suddenly FrogGirl and Eric were standing there and Eric was saying, in what Wally already realized was a long speech for him, "You hiring?"

"Might," Wally said. He could match brevity for brevity. "You staying?"

"While," Eric said.

"While, *sir*," Steamboat corrected, standing behind Wally.

"Yes, sir," Eric said.

Wally turned to FrogGirl. "Where've you guys been?"

"Eric wanted to see California."

"And you're done already?"

"He saw redwood trees. He saw the Pacific. Golden Gate Bridge. And he said—tell him what you said, Eric."

Eric frowned. "I said, 'That's that.' Sir."

"We've got a lot of work to do," Wally said. "You think you can—"

Eric cut him off: "Yes, sir, I can lift a house."

Wally turned to FrogGirl. "You coaching him?"

"Not everything," FrogGirl said, glancing over Wally's shoulder and backing away, poker-faced.

Steamboat also backed away. The races had paused. Everyone watched with blank expressions.

Nonchalant, light on his feet, whistling a tune, Abe was walking toward Eric carrying two bags of concrete, one under each arm.

Abe--Opal's son--An immature high school grad who was accepted into Princeton until he pulls a trick on the wrong man.

Amanda (Frog Girl)--A pregnant, 17-year old runaway.

13. You buy a good tool and you take care of it.

14. Get wasted after work.

Wally's Rules:

1. Work safe.

2. Work smarter, not harder.

3. What looks simple; ain't.

4. Measure twice, cut once.

5. Honor thy tools.

6. Respect the tree.

7. You have to get dirty.

8. Don't leave a mess.

9. Help your crew.

10. Slow and do it right.

11. Build it tight.

Clear Heart by Joe Cottonwood

Wally--A building contractor who is just existing, each day a struggle to overcome the death of his wife as well as the betrayal of his wife. His highest hope is to create a house that is as close to perfect as possible for an impossible client.

Juke--Wally's best friend is a misfit with no responsibilities and seemingly no cares except to do his best work for his boss, Wally.

Opal--The photographer/writer who is the force that causes a healing and growing that takes place for Wally, her, and her children.